# GREYWOLF'S HEART

Other books by C.M. Banschbach

The Dragon Keep Chronicles
*Oath of the Outcast*
*Blood of the Seer*

The Drifter Duology
*Then Comes a Drifter*

· SPIRITS' VALLEY ·

# GREYWOLF'S HEART

## C.M. BANSCHBACH

To Paul, Holly, and the kids.

Paul. We might not have always gotten along
growing up, but you've turned into a pretty awesome
older brother, and dad to some amazing kids.

# ONE

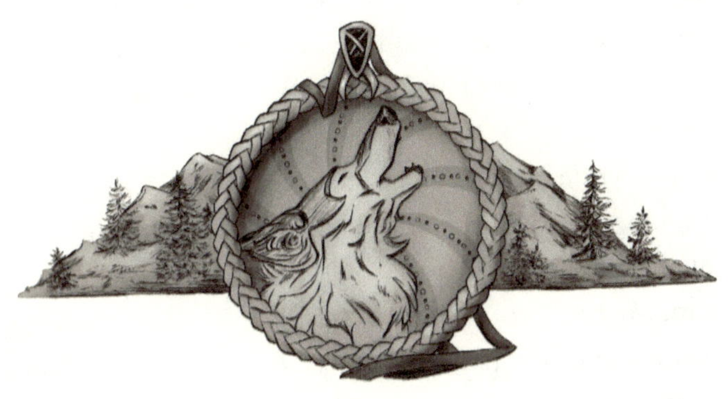

## COMRAN

The promise of more snow hung in the air. A chill wind whipped across the open valley floor, skittering over the sheen of ice to tease at my fur-lined cloak. My gloved hand curled around my spear as Eska, my greywolf, shifted beneath me, grumbling low in his throat, impatient at standing still.

This stretch of border was empty. For now.

Wolfriders had reported seeing Saber tribe prints along the border stones since early summer. A healing scar marked my left forearm above the leather bracer from one of their swords after a short fight with their tribe several countings ago.

Other riders milled around, letting our wolves scent the air for sablecats lurking across the border, watching with sharp yellow eyes and waiting to pounce. They'd tried to take some of the east-re, but I would send myself to the dark woods be-take any of our lands.

"Nothing, Comran." A rider reined in his greywolf at my side. Eska's growl pitched higher in greeting to the wolf.

"Let's keep riding." I nudged Eska and gave a sharp whistle. The seven other warriors who rode with the pack fell into a line behind me as we kept riding east across the valley towards the frozen river.

An hour's ride brought sight of another pack loping our direction in a long line. Recognition of the pack leader sent my hand tightening over the reins.

Etran. My half-brother.

Bastard son of my father, who had seen fit to raise us up side-by-side, melding us in the ways of the chief of the Greywolf tribe.

And two nights from now, he would choose one of us to take his place.

"Anything?" I raised my chin.

We'd been sent out together, each with a pack, a ritual of sorts to prove either of us could be worthy to carry the staff and wear the wolf cloak.

"Three-day-old tracks on their side of the stones." Etran reined in his female greywolf. She settled into the same stillness so characteristic of her rider. Always so solemn and aloof. Even then keeping a slight distance between himself and the rest of the pack.

"Maybe not enough to leave a patrol," I said.

He glanced over the border, tall and rigid in the saddle. It took a moment before he agreed. Annoyance flickered through me. I was always quicker to answer, quicker to action, but he weighed every thought, every outcome.

And it earned him more with Father.

"Comran, you think it will be safe to leave the border?" One of the warriors in Etran's pack nudged his wolf a little closer almost joining the close-knit pack standing with me.

A faint quiver to Etran's jaw barely betrayed him, but he looked at me evenly. Challenging, almost. I sank a gloved hand into the thick fur at Eska's shoulder, mostly to hide the tension in my fist.

"There's been no sign of them along the miles we rode today."

But our border with the Sabers ran the many miles across the open mouth of the valley and around the western side, where they had taken land from the Blackpaw tribe eight years ago.

"It could not hurt." Etran's even voice came over a fresh gust of wind.

Eska shifted his front paws, picking up on my surging irritation. Etran always had something to say, some point to try to make.

But it gave me more satisfaction to see the members of his pack looking to me instead. The way many in the tribe had looked to me over our whole lives, expecting me to take our father's place.

Etran didn't shift his focus, still daring me to contradict or agree. Waiting for me to make the wrong decision and be told so by Father. But maybe in a few days it wouldn't matter. I would be free to make my own decisions.

"We'll leave a small pack to rove for the next day," I said. "Just to make sure."

Even with the distance between us, a small bit of me had never wanted to argue with him. Besides, it was the mark of a good pack leader to work with others.

Etran dipped his head. "Half from each?"

I nodded and turned to my pack. Most didn't look happy with the decision, hoping, like me, to be racing for the lodge houses and warmth until the next patrol went out. But they didn't complain and took my picks.

The remnants of our packs fell in together, and I edged Eska away from Etran, keeping the distance again.

Long hours of loping through the snow, loosening reins and letting the greywolves pick their own way, passed before we made short camp in the darkness, pitching small hide tents in the open valley with the wolves clustered around.

When dawn teased its timid light over the fresh powder, we packed camp and began to ride again. Refreshed by a night's rest, the wolves bounded eagerly, scenting home. Skinny tendrils of smoke appeared on the horizon and Eska yipped, tossing his head back at me to make sure I'd seen.

I raised my spear and gave the order. Shouts and laughs answered as we urged wolves to a run, racing each other across the open valley toward the village.

Warriors on the training field paused and shouted to us. Many riders raised spears and whooped back, drawing a laugh from me. The figure waiting for us at the village's entrance killed the lightness brought by racing the valley with Eska, sword on my hip and spear in my hand.

*Father.* Waiting to judge.

I reined in. Etran had already slowed, coming to a more sedate pace. I kept the spear in my hand as my boots thumped to the ground.

"Comran!" A rider jogged to greet me. "How was it?"

"I'll tell you later." I cast a glance over to Father's imposing frame, already sensing the frown on his face.

Amund gave a wry grin. We'd been at each other's sides nearly our whole lives. He knew my hesitation. I reluctantly surrendered Eska's reins to him. Father would not want to be kept waiting.

A few other wolfriders gave me nods as I made my way toward the lodgehouses. It had been a more familiar sight over the last few days after Father had announced he would be making the choosing.

The pronouncement had not been a surprise. We had all expected it since the summer when he had suffered an illness the healer blamed on his heart and brain. He hadn't physically been the same since, and he and the council of elders had decided it was time.

Many had thought he would just name me instead of putting both of us through the trials. It did not make many happy. It had left me with some confusion and anger when he had told us.

I made my way over to Father, Etran coming up behind me. Father waited, arms crossed to hide the way the fingers of his left hand stayed curled no matter what he did. He regarded us impassively, then turned and made for the head lodge, the slight hitch to his step more noticeable across the uneven patches of snow.

Anger flashed at his lack of greeting, though after this long I had become accustomed to it. My father is a cold man. He always has been. Affection would only get in the way of guiding the tribe the way he should, at least in his mind.

I don't know why I always expected something different from him. Some sign that he might care for me.

I am his first-born son. By right, the place of chieftain should have been mine. But he had never favored me the way a father should. I had to earn every scarce word of praise. Fight for my place at the warrior's table. Brace my heart against the cold words he spoke so matter-of-factly.

He'd always favored Etran more. Something which had always stung.

We stepped into the lodge reserved for councils or small gatherings. The elders were there, waiting to hear his decision. They would give Father their opinion on who should be chosen. But he would do what he wanted. He always did.

"How was the patrol?" Father finally spoke, his voice deep and even.

Etran stood a few paces off to my left. He stayed silent, letting me speak first as he always did.

"The border was clear on the route my pack rode."

I kept my gaze fixed on the wall hanging in front of me to avoid seeing the way Father's stern features would soften slightly as he looked at Etran.

"We found tracks, three days old on their side of the border. Nothing else," Etran said.

"You both rode in short of riders." A bit of accusation edged his tone as he turned to me.

"We each left a half pack at the border to ride once more to make sure." I hooked a hand into the collar of my breastplate, this time meeting his gaze.

"And who made that decision?" Father swept cool grey eyes between us.

My jaw clenched automatically. *He thinks it a poor decision.*

"We both did." Etran surprised me.

I glanced at him, but he didn't deign to look. Easier to keep his distance from the blame that might befall me.

"We agreed it might be prudent to leave someone for another day at least."

While he was not wrong, it still soured in my gut the way Father now nodded, agreeing with Etran.

*Did he just claim the praise for it even if I made the suggestion first?*

My thumb ran along the shallow decorative tracings etched along my breastplate's collar. Maybe, but he'd never rubbed my nose in any of his many victories with Father. He just stayed irritatingly distant.

"Good. Any other trouble?" Father seemed to look a little

longer at Etran, but we both shook our heads.

"Birgir is setting up the next trial now that you have returned," he said abruptly. "The choosing will be tonight. You are awaited on the training grounds."

Taking this as the dismissal, I pivoted and stepped back out into the bright mid-morning.

"Comran."

Surprised, I turned to face Etran. His jaw worked slightly.

"Good luck," he finally said, and it seemed like it was not quite what he wanted to say.

I wasn't sure what I wanted to say either, so I just nodded, and we went our separate ways.

Hours later, we stood beside each other in the lodgecircle, both stained with dirt and sweat, our leather armor molded to our bodies after fighting through the final tests held in high tradition by our people to prove the worth of the next chieftain.

Father looked at us both, his face impassive. My heart thudded, with excitement or fear, I couldn't quite tell in the shocking stillness of the gathering. He raised his staff. My hand tightened around the leather-bound hilt of my sword.

And he pointed to the man beside me.

Murmurs rippled through the crowd, the echoes falling dull on my shocked ears, my mind telling me only one thing. I was not the only one surprised at his choice. I blinked, and blinked again.

It was not a mistake. I had not been chosen.

I forced my head to turn, my neck sticking like a frozen wheel. My half-brother's face conveyed the same confusion. He met my gaze and betrayed the faint triumph lurking in his eyes. I could have bent the knee then and there, but there would be time enough at the ceremony later. Instead, I gripped his arm, murmured something, I knew not what, and turned to walk from the arena in silence.

Warriors and tribesfolk melted away before me, some faces rejoicing in the decision, others making it clear they thought my father had chosen poorly. I cared not. I did not stop walking until I reached the river, frozen still beneath the grip of winter.

My breath exploded in a puff of white, but my body still held the heat of the trials. I stared at nothing. Ice creaked somewhere upriver, and a slight breeze sent frozen pine needles tinkling together.

Heavy boots crunched the snow behind me. I knew who stood there, but I had not the heart to turn. I could not bear to look him in the eyes and hear him list my deficiencies in a practical manner.

"I had a dream."

*A dream.* My faint scoff burst forth in a quick plume.

"You led the tribe to battle as chieftain. We fell to the enemy." His next words came so soft, I thought I might have imagined them. "You died."

"And if it was just a dream?"

"The *talånd* said it might have been a warning sent from the spirits."

"Then it would have been a good death." The words burst quick and hot from me.

"Comran." His voice came sharp. "It was not. And if you are not chieftain, then it will not come to pass. You will not die."

I finally turned to face my father. "And you care so much for me then?"

His hand reached out to snag my arm before I could brush past. "I do."

I wanted to ask him why he had never shown it, to scream that whatever *this* was, it came too late. But my tongue was bound, and I could only stare at him through the steely grey eyes he had given me.

"I held you in my arms first, knowing I could not protect you from every cold thing in this world. You have learned much over the years, but the place of chieftain would destroy you. You have the quicker sword, but he the quicker mind. You will bend the knee to him."

It was a simple statement of fact. I knew I had no choice.

"Then I should go prepare. Is there anything else—Father?"

I thought his gaze softened slightly, but it might have been my heart wishing for a sign from him. He released my arm and let me pass.

Hot water awaited me in the back rooms of the lodge. I rinsed the trials from my skin and dressed in new clothes. A belt of soft leather fastened over my blue tunic, crusted in painted porcupine quills that lay in sharp-edged designs along its front. I sat on the low bench, folding a fur-lined cloak in my fists, staring into the fire.

*How am I to say the words to him?*

"Comran." My mother's voice whispered soft behind me, and she rested a hand on my shoulder.

The flames mesmerized me with their dance. I didn't know what to ask her first.

"I knew he would not choose you."

Her admission sent another knife into my heart. She sat beside me on the bench.

"You would have been our third born. But the All-Father saw fit to take your brothers before they could enter this world."

I finally turned my head to look at her. In my twenty-three years, I had not heard this. Tears trembled in the corners of her eyes.

"Before I knew I carried you, your father and I agreed. He needed an heir. And if I could not give him one, he should find someone who could."

"You let him?" Anger boiled inside me. Somehow it was worse, knowing she had allowed it, rather than thinking my father had simply betrayed her and the marriage bond.

"I told him to. He chose Etran's mother. You will never know how I wept the three times he went to her. I knew I was with child before she did, but I did not think you would make it." She reached to smooth damp hair from my forehead. "But you proved me wrong. You had a strong heart to make it into my arms. You still do."

"Do I? Then why didn't he choose me?" Spirits, it stung *so* much.

She sighed. "He wanted to raise both of you as his sons. I agreed. He couldn't show one more preference than the other. He believed the All-Father gave him security for the tribe in both of you. But it meant choosing one."

"Why did you think he would choose Etran?"

Her hand slipped to my wrist, squeezing it tight with her deceptive strength. "You are my son, Comran, and I love you with the heart of a mother. You lead with your heart. Etran leads with his mind. And sometimes the mind must rule."

I jerked my hand from her grip. *Am I the only one who thought he would choose me?*

A floorboard creaked and Etran stood in the shadows at the edge of flickering light. Gone was the confusion, and I could see no triumph in his eyes. Instead, doubt played across his features. Mother pushed to her feet, resting a hand upon my shoulder.

"I will let you speak."

I caught her glance between us, the way it lingered on Etran with sadness, but no hate. Instead, a bit of wistfulness, as if she wished he could have been hers. I had never seen it before, and a bit of jealousy stirred before I quenched it.

Then she was gone, and we were alone.

Etran took a hesitant step into the light. He dressed much like me in the finery of the chieftain's family, deep blues and blacks, edged with painted porcupine quills.

It seemed he didn't know what to say any more than I did. We never spoke much to the other, keeping in different circles our whole lives.

"Neither of us thought this day would come," he finally said, caution directing his look towards me.

"But it did."

"Comran, I—I don't know why he chose *me*. I know what I am. There have been plenty to remind me of it all my life."

I cast him a startled glance. He had turned his gaze to the fire, his jaw tense.

"My mother told me why I had been born when I was six years old. Then I understood why I called him father, you brother, but a different woman mother. I understood the distaste part of this tribe has for me, but that you never did. At least, that I never saw. And I learned to see much."

I still said nothing, something like shame filling me that *I* had never seen.

"I know I am not the brother you wanted, but fate threw us together. I don't pretend to understand her plans. I do not even know if I can lead this tribe. But I know you. And even if there is no love between us, I think I can trust you."

Etran met my stare. "I want you as my Battlewolf."

"Me?"

In our tribe, the Battlewolf commands the packs and ranks

almost as high as the chieftain. It is not a position to be given lightly by a chief.

"Yes. You and I both know that different people supported us. I will not see this tribe divided over this decision. We stand together, or not at all."

I accepted his reasoning with a forced nod. *He is quicker with his mind.*

"Even with this, some will not be happy," I warned.

"I will hold your back, if you hold mine." His shoulders squared as he faced me, green eyes boring into me.

I finally stood, narrowing the space between us with a step. "Was that the point of all those drills?"

One eyebrow raised in shock, and he appeared taken aback by my question. A slow smile flickered over his face. Thirteen years in the ring together. We might not love one another as brothers, but we knew how the other fought, how to uphold a fellow Grey-wolf in danger.

"Perhaps." He inclined his head. "Will you stand with me?"

I hesitated yet, torn between the desire to accept, or to refuse and take the place I had believed was mine all my life. But a small voice had begun to nudge my heart.

*You've never wanted it.*

I tried to ignore the thought. My mind told me what my heart had trouble accepting. I had not been chosen. But I had been offered a strong place at the new chieftain's side. I would be a fool not to take it.

"I will stand by you."

Relief caught in the relaxed set of his shoulders, and a faint smile brushed his face again.

"Thank you. You should finish preparing. It is almost time."

He left with a faint creak of the floorboards. I sat on the bench once again, rubbing a hand through my short hair, now almost dry. Exhaustion from the day crept over me. I wished to sleep, but waking would only bring the changes that the day had wrought.

When the first horn rang out, summoning the tribe to the center of the circled lodgehouses, I stood and draped my cloak around my shoulders. I stepped out into the dying light of the day, boots crunching under the fresh crust of snow brought by the falling temperature. A shadow moved alongside the lodgehouse and Eska rose to meet me.

My hand sank into his thick fur, and he rested his heavy head on my shoulder. He grumbled low in his chest.

"We'll run tomorrow," I promised.

His tail lashed back and forth, his mouth parting in a fanged smile. He understood well enough the words I said. A smile found its way to my own face. With my boots on the ground, we stood even for height and I rested my forehead against his.

"And by the moon's rise, you will have earned new paint to wear to battle."

His ears perked and his deep amber eyes bored deep into mine, as if asking why I didn't sound so happy about it.

"I'll tell you tomorrow when we race the mountainside."

His cold nose pressed my forehead and he nearly knocked me over with his heavy body before following me into the wide circle spanning the area between lodges.

Fires blazed bright in the circle's center, the snowy earth around them already filling with men and women. Children lurked on the fringes, those old enough daring to stand with their parents, the rest darting to find the best vantage point, waiting for the feast and dancing to come.

Other greywolves settled on the edges, or sat beside their

warriors, their shaggy bulks catching an almost blue tint in the fading light of the sun.

Father took his place at the top of the circle where the tribe's *tâkn* towered above the lodges, a mighty oak trunk etched in painted greywolves, the history of the tribe and the valley, and legends of the spirits, all capped by a howling greywolf's head. Smaller trunks stood behind it, myriad carvings showing the more recent histories in a sacred grove.

The murmurs silenced as he raised one hand. Mother ghosted forward to join him on his left side as our *dronni*. Etran's mother emerged on his other hand, casting a haughty look at my mother.

"Today I have chosen the new chieftain from between my sons," Father began without preamble. "There have been those that questioned me, but he bears my blood, and will lead this tribe to prosperity and victory."

*Unlike me.* The bitter thought escaped.

*It was but a dream,* I strove to remind myself.

My father called Etran forward, and together with the *talånd*, draped the wolf cloak about his shoulders. The *talånd* dipped fingers into dark green warpaint, and drew a crooked line across Etran's forehead, followed by a curving line along his left cheekbone, thicker bands across his right cheek, and a solid line down his chin. His sword was touched to the *tâkn* as the *talånd* began to sing.

He sang power and strength, wisdom and healing over Etran. And then it was done.

Etran sheathed his sword and turned to receive the adulation of the tribe and the howling of the greywolves. Eska joined his deep bay to those of his kin, but I could barely add my shout to the rest.

A hush fell as Etran raised a hand. My father's battlewolf stood beside the former chief. Tradition held that a new chieftain chose a new battlewolf the same night. Several of the wolfriders who Etran called friends leaned forward in anticipation, hoping to hear their names called.

I pitied them, knowing well the disappointment waiting. For a brief moment, I entertained the fear that he would not hold his promise, and for the second time that day, my name would not be called.

But his gaze found me across the lodge circle.

"Comran."

I forced my feet to action, Eska rising and padding alongside me. The crowd melted away before me again, some faces appeased by the decision, others still declaring that I should have been the one choosing a new battlewolf.

I halted two steps from Etran, and he spared me a brief nod. He dipped his fingers into the paint the *talånd* proffered, and traced a double line down my right cheek, and a single horizontal line below my left eye. He wiped his hand as a new spear of hardened ash was pressed into my hand, its surface etched in runes and wolves.

Finally, he took the iron medallion and placed it over my bowed neck. The howling wolf's head rested upon my chest. I unsheathed my sword, twisting it to rest along my forearm and offering the hilt to the *talånd*. He pressed it to the *tåkn* as I knelt and pledged my life, honor, and obedience to the new chief.

I'd done it once for my father when entering the ranks of the wolfriders, never imagining I would do it again. But the words still came steady, ringing with a sense of finality over the gathered tribe. We were now duty bound to each other and no one could question it.

The *talånd's* lilting voice called down another blessing upon me before he returned the hilt to my palm and it was done. A glance up caught a look of almost desperate relief in Etran's eyes as I finished, as if he thought I might not have done it after all. It was odd seeing something other than confidence in him.

I took my new place to the left of Etran as the warriors began to gather to swear their new allegiance. Our father was the first to kneel and as he rose, I caught a look of something that might be pride flicker between the two of us.

From the twitch of Etran's hand I knew he had seen it, and, like me, did not know what to do with it. I felt a brief flash of kinship towards him, something that had been rare enough over the years.

Over an hour later, the oathtaking was done, new torches were lit around the circle, and the great fires re-stoked to keep lending their heat to the gathering. Children darted about, now free to run and clamber among the wolves, who tolerated them like energetic pups. Men and women moved to bring the tables into the circle— the greater lodge at the head of the circle not big enough to hold the entire tribe together. Within minutes, food had been brought out from where lodgefires had kept it warm, and the feasting began.

Winter's chill grew as the moon began its path across the sky, but the bonfires leapt high and greywolves offered extra warmth. I sat beside Etran by right. We did not speak to one another, in part, I think, because we were both starved from the day's trials.

I crumbled a crust of flatbread between my fingers, gazing around the gathering. It seemed there was a division in the tribe, clear in the way men and women had chosen their seats. Those I felt closer friendship with, sat on my right hand. Those I knew favored Etran, sat to his left.

"You see it too?" Etran murmured, leaning to re-fill his cup with foaming spruce ale.

"Lines have been drawn, with or without our consent." I nudged my cup closer to him as he indicated the pitcher with a nod. He filled it without pause.

"So it seems."

"And how do you plan to bring them together?" I did not mean to sound accusatory. I simply wanted to know.

But he bristled slightly before his shoulders lifted. "How would you?"

*So, he doesn't know. Well, neither do I.* But I did not voice my thought.

"Perhaps time will make things easier for everyone."

He'd spoken of trust in the lodge, and I had something of that. Trust that he would do the honorable thing, that he could watch my flank in battle, even that he could do well as chieftain. But there was no kinship, no bonds of brotherhood, no knowledge that I would sacrifice myself for him, or he for me.

"Perhaps," he agreed, but I caught a glimpse of regret in his face. Not regret that he had chosen me. Regret that we could not have what other brothers did.

Something of the same stirred deep within my heart. Maybe time would tell.

# TWO

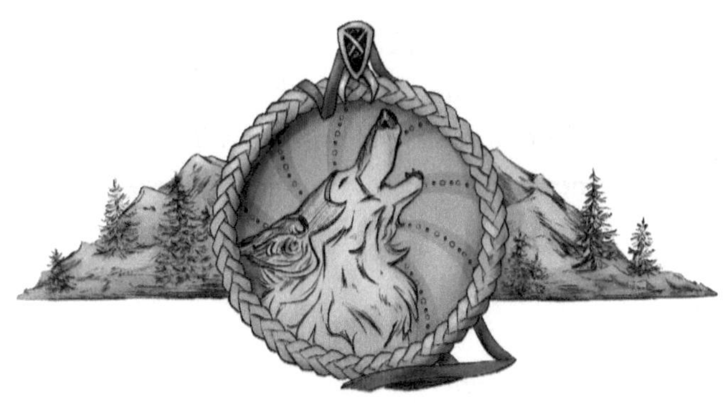

## COMRAN

My first order of business as battlewolf the following day was to find Birgir, the old commander, and learn what I could from him. We spoke for several hours, him passing the knowledge of almost twenty years as battlewolf to me.

*Someday I will do this for the battlewolf of my nephew.* But I shoved the thought away. I had barely held the position for a day and Etran had shown no interest in marriage yet.

We lingered over our spruce ale, the remains of the noon meal scattered before us on the table.

"Are you not upset you were also replaced?" I asked.

Birgir shrugged. "I have more than one grey hair. My joints ache and creak with the weather's turning. Maybe it is time for me to live an easier life. Perhaps I'll take up woodcarving."

A smirk teased and I settled my cup down. It faded at the

thought that I must now step into his boots and lead, perhaps be stronger than him because of who had given me the medallion.

"It's a hard position for you, Comran." Birgir twisted his mug, mentioning the unlikely choosing for the first time. "A chief rules the entire tribe, but for many warriors, the battlewolf is their chief. You have a delicate power. Not all warriors will respect you. There are a few who never accepted my naming, but they never challenged me."

He leaned forward on the table closer to me, voice dropping in warning.

"But if you do not appear in support of your chieftain, there will be such strife as this tribe has not known in many long years. You will disagree with Etran, sure enough. Your father and I did many times. But always in private. To the warriors, to the tribe, you present a strong union. Remember, the chief's word is the final law. When he orders, you obey."

"And if I cannot?"

I remembered a time when unrest had threatened the valley. Birgir and my father had argued about riding to battle. I knew, because I hid in the lodgehouse and listened. My heart was with Birgir. But he and the wolfriders had stayed in the village as my father ordered.

"Then your place will be given to another, and the orders will be obeyed. Though perhaps Etran might be more forgiving than your father." Birgir's craggy face softened as he looked to me.

I swallowed the last bits of my ale and thumped it down on the table harder than I intended. In some ways Birgir had been more of a father to me than my own. He had overseen my training since I had first stepped into the ring thirteen years ago, quicker with a word of praise or encouragement than Father.

He rested a hand on my tensed forearm. "You're a fine warrior,

Comran. You will do well as battlewolf. Many others besides my-self were pleased with the choice."

His words were meant as comfort, but my heart still stung. The tension inside was broken as a warrior stepped in to join us.

"Battlewolf?"

It took a moment, and Birgir's nudge, before I remembered he addressed me.

"Yes?"

"The chief has asked for you."

A quick pang of anxiety struck, and then passed, as I remembered I would be joining Etran and not my father. I jerked a nod.

I tapped fist to chest at Birgir in customary address. Habit would be hard to break.

He smiled and returned the gesture. "Battlewolf."

A smile touched my lips before I followed the warrior outside. Eska greeted me just outside the door, his low grumble reminding me of my promise to him.

"Later," I reassured, pausing a few moments to rub along the band of dark fur streaking the left side of his muzzle.

He dabbed at my cheek with a quick tongue in forgiveness and wandered off to scuffle with an energetic greywolf a summer younger than him. Would that I could forgive and forget that easily.

*Perhaps time will tell.* I turned my feet toward the lodgehouse across the wide circle. The remains of the bonfires from the night before still smoldered in their pits, the snow melted away enough to reveal the brown of dormant earth just waiting for spring's first touch. But the cold air burned at my lungs. Spring was still several months away. Plenty of time to stay close to the village and learn my new place in its life.

A young trainee greeted me by name before hastily correcting himself with my title. I reassured him with a quick smile. It would take time before I was used to it myself.

I reached the other side of the circle, pausing for a moment, unsure of which lodgehouse to go to. Etran and his mother had not shared our lodgehouse, preferring to keep him as a child in the lodge where she had grown up. He had spent plenty of time in the chief's house growing up, but always with one of us keeping distance from the other.

Was that our decision or influenced by the way our elders treated our situation?

"Battlewolf." The warrior who had given me the message flicked a hand in the direction of Etran's family lodge.

I nodded my thanks. Normally, the new chieftain would be in the lodge of the old chief as his son, but as had been obvious all my life, this was not the normal way of things.

The heavy door rested open as two young girls carried benches back into the hall.

"You should have named someone else!" A sharp voice echoed from the dimness inside. Elin, his mother.

"I made the choice I thought was best." Etran's voice had a terseness to it suggesting the argument had been made before.

"You elevated him too high. He could challenge you."

"And what would you have me do? Cast him out?"

"How do you know he wouldn't have done it to you, had your places been switched?"

"Mother…"

"He has never respected you!" Elin hissed. "How do you know he won't overthrow you the first chance he gets? You gave him the warriors!"

The thought had not yet occurred to me, and I almost laughed to think that the woman who hated and feared my new status had given it to me. I strained to hear what Etran might say in return.

"We both survived this long together. He's had plenty of chances if he thought to do anything. I was named chief. You got what you wanted, so why argue about this again?"

"It's not enough, Etran! There should never have been a choice. Your father wanted me to give him an heir and I did, but then he nearly threw you away once he got his son. He barely gave you anything."

"He never gave Comran anything either." Something more than irritation came through Etran's words, and I recognized the same pain I felt when wishing for some sign of affection from our father.

"I still don't trust him."

"You don't have to. But I do."

A faint warmth nudged my heart at Etran's firm declaration. Perhaps I could find it in me to trust him. I decided I'd heard enough of their conversation and pounded my fist against the doorframe before entering.

Elin drew herself up, hands clenching at her sides as she directed her coldest look at me. There had been plenty of those from her over the years, but maybe I was just now seeing the threads of hate in her eyes. She cast a glare at her son and swept from the lodge. I tracked her progress and turned back to see a wry smile on Etran's face.

"How much did you hear?"

I shrugged, holding a short debate within myself. "Enough to know that she still has no fondness for me."

He huffed a laugh. "I'm sorry. I just—" He lifted one hand in a halfhearted gesture. "You met with Birgir?"

I nodded. "I think there is still too much for me to learn."

"Aye, and I've met with Father, the council—my mother…" He flashed another rueful smile. "I'm not exactly sure where to start."

The admission took me by surprise. Etran always radiated confidence, assurance. I, on the other hand, had a harder time hiding my emotions.

"I briefly thought to take Eska for a run and forget about all of this until tomorrow," I said instead.

"That might be the best idea I've heard all day."

I flashed a quick smile, but I wasn't sure I wanted to let him intrude on the quiet I needed. "She was wrong."

Confusion cut a furrow in his brow.

"I swore my oath to you. I have the warriors, but you have my sword. Like you said, we stand together or not at all."

He tilted a small nod, not quite deep enough to hide the relief flickering in his eyes. "Together."

# THREE

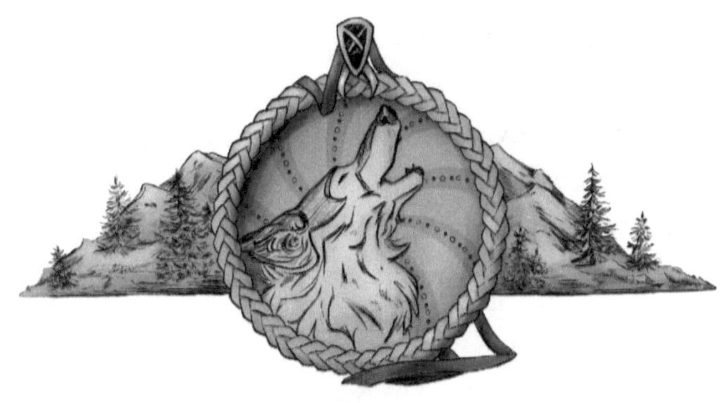

## COMRAN

Eska's paws whispered over the snow as we darted between the trees, the chill air stinging my cheeks in our speed. He surged forward, his pent-up energy slowly fading in his long lopes as we settled into an easy rhythm. Paws swiveled effortlessly in response to the reins, and I reached to steady the sword at my side.

We turned uphill, bounding around snow drifts and over fallen trees, finally slowing to a halt by a rocky overhang. I slid from his back, leaving the reins loose about his neck. He shook himself with a mighty huff, the saddle leathers slapping together. I stepped out onto the ledge, taking a seat and letting my feet dangle over. Eska showed more caution, sinking to his haunches a few feet from the edge, a low growl rumbling in his throat at my apparent stupidity.

I ignored him. He complained every time we came out here. But here, surrounded by the whispering of slender aspens, the deeper chuckles of pine and blue spruce, and the rush of the air as it swept off the mountain peak behind me, I found only calm.

Our territory spread out before me. A wide valley, broken by a plateau of low, forested hills and the bare glint of lakes to the west, spread as far as the eye could see. The mountain range swept from east to west, curving around the northern edge of the valley where waterfalls roared from the jagged yellow cliffs. On a perfectly still day, their distant thunder rumbled across the valley.

A river, fed by many tributaries from the waterfalls and the western lakes, wound through the valley in an ice-crusted thread. Chunks of trees scattered along its curves, rebellious outgrowths from the forest coating the mountains and hills. Herds of great-elk and bison roamed across the valley, their dark shapes nearly indistinguishable from my vantage point. Larger shadows darted across the white fields—wolfriders hunting to fill our larders.

Eska shifted behind me, relaxing onto his stomach.

"You think I could have ruled over all this?"

We held the eastern mountains and the valley all the way to where the river roared into frothing rapids before falling into the lowlands thirty leagues to the south. The Blackpaw tribe used to hold the low western mountains and hills and the lakes that nestled in their forests, but their lynxes were rarely to be seen. And even if they were, they would hold no love for us, the ones who had not come to their aid against the Saber tribe eight years ago.

I glanced over my shoulder when there was no answer. Eska looked back at me with amber eyes, declaring that I, at least, was the center of his world. I shook my head with a wry smile. I didn't know why I had expected honesty from him.

My gaze fell down to the village, nestled in the sheltered curve of the mountain roots. The lodges were dark rectangles arranged in a circle, three deep, joined at the top by the *tâkn*. Nearly forty in total, they each sheltered upwards of ten families. Generations of families sometimes resided under the heavy rafters. Family was everything to the Greywolf tribe.

*Why is it I feel I have never had what everyone else does?*

I brushed rogue snowflakes from my trousers. Grey clouds had begun to gather again, scudding across the sky to obscure the brief glance of sunlight the day had given us. I tipped my head back to feel the air. The breeze swirled gently, absent of the heavy threat of another blizzard. Just a light snowfall, then.

But still. Darkness would come early, and the mountain would lose its friendliness. I swung my legs back over the edge and stood. Eska rose with me. I checked the girth again, knocked loose by our brief stay. He grumbled in annoyance as the leather tightened, but I had no sympathy. I didn't want to take a tumble on our run back.

I settled into the saddle, pulling my fur-lined cloak about me against the new chill. Eska padded away from the cliff and followed our trail back down the mountain. He picked up his pace to an easy lope, occasionally indulging in a pounce into an unsuspecting snowdrift, showering me with the remains.

"Eska!" I chided with a chuckle, brushing snow from my hair.

He barked in return and headed for a larger drift. I kicked free of the stirrups, knowing what came next. We plunged into the powder and he rolled. I slid off, retaliating by wrapping my arms around his bulky neck and dragging him further in. He yipped and shoved me with a paw, knocking me loose enough to make my face an easy target for his sloppy tongue.

I wasn't quick enough to evade and laughed as I tossed snow into his muzzle. He sneezed and leapt over me, kicking up snow with front paws to shower me in a miniature blizzard. I scrambled to my feet and slammed into his side, taking us both down. He managed to get a paw around me, trying to hold me in place long enough to nibble at my hair. I wriggled free and he twisted to pounce again.

The snowdrift lay destroyed by the time we straggled free. Eska panted, his tongue lolling from a mouth wide in a canine smile. So he thought he won that round. I scratched his ear and readjusted the saddle.

He still had enough energy to lope back to the village. We passed across the wide field outside the village, emptier in winter, but come spring it would be full of warriors training and games of stickball. I left Eska's saddle and bridle in the stables beside the training field. He rubbed against the wooden wall, scratching the damp fur that marked the saddle.

"Who won?" Amund's amused voice sounded behind me.

Eska yipped and moved to nudge at the warrior's shoulder before circling back to me. I laughed and brushed away more snow hidden in the hood of my cloak.

"He seems to think he did."

Amund chuckled. "If I had not seen the two of you in battle, I'd never believe you to be as ferocious as people claim."

I gave a slight roll of my eyes. It's not as though I had seen much battle, but stories tended to be exaggerated with time. Amund's smile faded, and he beckoned me farther behind the shelter of the stables. He glanced around before speaking.

"Comran, you know many weren't happy with what happened. Some are talking of making it right. Are you going to fight the decision?" He hesitated over the question, his brown eyes flickering to meet mine.

"No," I replied, even though a stubborn part of my heart warmed at the thought that part of the tribe had believed in me.

His eyes widened in surprise, and he stepped closer. "Why? You're the chieftain's first son. Some think his only son. It should have been yours."

"Perhaps. But what is done, is done. I won't do anything to change it. It would destroy the tribe, and then what?"

"You would do well as chief," he mumbled. "And I don't just say that as your friend."

"Maybe I could. But to take the power at the expense of the lives of men and women you grew up with? Trained with? It's not worth it. We were both good choices." I lifted my shoulders in a shrug. "But the prize went to Etran."

The words did not taste as bitter in my mouth as they might have.

Amund tipped his head in a small nod, some relief softening his features. "I won't deny I'm glad to hear that. I know men on both sides."

"Who else, Amund?" I sensed his hesitation. *There is something else.*

"There are a handful of others who won't see reason so readily. They are prepared to act in your name and ask forgiveness later."

An icy calm settled over my heart. *This cannot happen.* "Who?"

He paused a moment more.

"Amund," I warned.

He finally jerked his head in a nod. "Hakkon is the most vocal. He's advocating the change soon."

I cursed. If I thought with my heart, then Hakkon did not think at all. My cousin from my mother's side was prone to fits of rashness, a trait that had lost its charm long ago when he endangered five good wolfriders in a border spat with the Saber tribe.

"When?"

Amund raised his eyebrows and tossed one hand. "I said soon, didn't I? Loke and I have been trying to find you."

I cursed again, and whirled, not caring to find Etran first. I needed to find Hakkon and most likely beat sense into him. I stalked through the lodge circles and across the open space. The spirits must have been looking down, for Hakkon opened the door to my family's lodge.

He met my stare and stood waiting, a slight smirk on his face. It took all my strength not to sprint the rest of the way and throttle him. He didn't move as I halted at the single step up.

"Have a moment?" He leaned against the door frame.

I placed a hand on his chest and shoved him inside. "What have you done?" I snarled.

His brow wrinkled in confusion. "What do you mean?"

"Amund told me what you're planning. What have you done?" I drew out the words. And what was he doing inside my lodge when he hailed from my mother's old lodge?

His confusion melted back into his typical self-satisfied smirk.

"Nothing. Yet. The next chieftain should have come from this lodge. Etran will fall and then you will take his place. That bastard doesn't deserve the honor."

An anger sparked in me at the word. An anger I never knew I had. I gripped his tunic and slammed him against the wall.

"Listen to me carefully, Hakkon. Etran is the chief. Etran will stay the chief. I have pledged to him. He has my sword. There will be no challenges."

He gripped my wrist, but couldn't shake me away. "You would defend him, knowing what he is?" His lip curled in disgust. "Your father dishonored this tribe, dishonored your mother by taking up with *her!* I know you feel that."

I refused to let the truth show on my face. I knew that feeling, but perhaps not as well as he thought.

"There has been no objection to Father raising Etran as his son these years. His choice was valid."

"Valid!" Hakkon scoffed, finally succeeding in shoving my hand away. "His existence is an affront to the spirits. This tribe will live to see misfortune if he continues as chief."

"Only if you insist on bringing this misfortune," I hissed.

"You are a fine warrior, Comran. A good leader who commands loyalty from many in this tribe. Does that mean nothing to you?"

"It means a great deal to me. I stand as battlewolf. There's no reason to cast any of that away."

He tried to push me backwards, but I refused to move. "You will continue to let him overshadow you?"

My jaw tensed. So the tribe knew as well as I that Etran was the more favored one between us. The knowing glint in his eye infuriated me even more. I didn't trust my voice to reply.

"Amund thought you might disagree. So we planned to move with or without you." Hakkon sneered. "It seems it will be without you."

"If you move against him, you will have to go through me." I shoved him back into the wall. "You are family, Hakkon, which is the only reason I won't kill you for treachery right now. Treachery against your battlewolf and your chief."

His eyes slit in anger. "You wouldn't."

I wrenched a knife from my belt and pressed it against his chest, angry enough to try. "You let anyone else stupid enough to listen to you know that I stand with Etran. I will not see this tribe divided. This talk dies right now or I go to Etran, and I will stand by him as he casts you all out."

This time Hakkon dislodged my hand.

"Don't be stupid, *cousin*," he spat. "Unless you think he's family. Don't tell me you actually consider him a brother?"

My irritation bubbled further at the fact I had to tilt my chin up to meet his gaze. "I consider him my chief. And you would do well to do the same."

He shoved at my chest, but I had planted my feet and couldn't be moved.

"Well then, perhaps we need new blood. Your father already proved he did not deserve the title with his actions. And you stand here and defend his offense. Perhaps you are not as deserving as I've thought all these years..."

"Is that a threat, Hakkon? You want to try your luck with me?" I shifted the grip on my knife.

"If he's the side you're choosing, then you better pray that bastard gives you enough thought to watch your back." Hakkon leaned close, tempting my knife, before stalking away.

I waited until he left the lodge, sending the door swinging on its leather hinges, before I sheathed the knife. I closed my eyes for a moment. No matter what he told his followers, there were ears everywhere in the lodgehouse. The tribe would know of our meeting by sunset. There might even be a small chance it would not ignite the war I'd hoped to stop. Either way, Etran deserved to hear it from me first.

I stepped out of the lodge, watching Hakkon's path across the circle to where he murmured with two other wolfriders. He looked up to see me, his features twisting into a dark scowl. The older warrior darted a glance between us, uncertainty creasing his features. The other, younger than me, flashed an eager look to Hakkon, ready to take on whatever the idiot commanded.

Another warrior joined Hakkon's group and he sneered a smile at me. It faded as a familiar shadow stood to my left. Amund rested a hand on his knife. I allowed my own smirk as a taller figure joined my right. Loke—a swordbrother since we could toddle around with sticks. Stian lounged from the lodge step behind me, his lanky figure almost stick-like against the bulk of Loke's.

Amund would know others from Hakkon's group. Loke would watch my back. And Stian, a cousin on my father's side, and friend of both Etran and I, would make sure the tribe knew my stance.

Hakkon whirled and disappeared among the lodgehouses, followed by his conspirators.

"Would you like the true account of what happened, or can I give my own spin?" Stian smirked.

I gave a slight toss of my head. "You always told your own version anyway."

"True," Stian allowed with a shrug. "Still, there are some details that are too delicate to be retold."

I nodded. There would be war if the angry words were repeated.

"Loke, this is where you stand?"

Loke nodded. "You know I follow you, Comran. I thought it would be as chief, but I am not opposed to Etran holding the staff." He cast an almost apologetic look at me.

I gave a half-smile in reassurance. "It seems neither am I."

Both Loke and Amund chuckled.

"Thank you for the warning, Amund." I turned to him.

He dipped a nod. "You know I'll stand with you, Comran. I'd hoped for it to be as chieftain, but the word of the battlewolf always meant more to me anyway. I follow you, and if that is following Etran, then I have your back."

I clapped his shoulder before turning to my cousin. "And you, Stian? Do you care which way the wind blows?"

He tilted his head back with a quick grin. "Not if I can keep my balance and stay afloat."

I flashed a wry smile. "Where's Etran?"

Stian jerked his chin towards the head lodge that rested to the left of the *tâkn*.

"Make sure they know where I stand," I said, and turned away.

I entered the lodge without knocking, ignoring the startled glances of the elders who sat in a half circle around Etran. He glanced up at me with something almost like relief in his eyes at the interruption. But my angry mood had returned at the thought of what I had to say.

"We need to talk," I growled more forcefully than I intended.

He stepped out of the circle and led me into a small adjacent chamber.

I settled my arms across my chest, not sure how to begin. He waited, adopting the same guarded posture. My heart clenched for a brief moment as I realized how much he looked like Father.

*He's not Father*, I forcibly reminded myself.

"It seems there are a few idiots who have decided to try to take matters into their hands," I said. "There was talk of killing you and putting me in your place."

He stiffened, an emotionless mask falling over his features. I had always been jealous of the way he could hide his feelings from the world.

"And?"

"And I've let it be known that you have my sword and my loyalty. They might want to see me in your place, but they will have to go through me to get to you."

He rubbed at his chin. "Why do I get the feeling that it's not going to settle as easy as that?"

I snorted a mirthless laugh. "Hakkon is the leader. I'm about ready to disown him as family. I told him as much if he didn't give up this foolishness. But thinking was never his strong suit."

Etran offered a half smile. "What course do you suggest?"

"We wait. I have men I can trust watching my back. It's my duty to protect you as chief."

He tilted his head slightly. "This sounds like you're using me as bait."

A smirk teased the corner of my mouth. I hadn't yet thought of it like that, but he'd said it.

He shook his head. "And what if this group decides to go through with their plans?"

"Hakkon made me angry enough to threaten his life. Family or not, I am prepared to see him cast out for his words."

My anger at Hakkon's threats still surprised me. I'd not expected to ever jump to Etran's defense that quickly.

"Just be careful, Comran. I do not want to tear a further divide in this tribe once family gets involved."

Too late for that. "Name someone you can trust. I think it will be best if both sides work together."

"Jens." He did not hesitate to name a warrior who had been at his side for years.

"What are you planning?" Etran relaxed the tightness of his crossed arms.

"To start, I need *rokrs*. I want Loke and Jens." The warrior and I were on good terms. He was a sturdy fighter and one that any wolfrider would want by his side.

Etran tipped his head down in a nod, clearly pleased by the choice.

I hesitated, debating on letting him see my uncertainty. "As for the rest of the plan, I'll let you know when I have it."

A slight smile creased his face. "Any chance it might get me away from this lodge?"

My faint smirk answered his. For some reason, I was pleased to see him as uncertain as me.

"You have only been chief for one day."

"Aye, any chance we will get better at this?"

My amusement faded for a moment at the thought of the future.

"The next days might tell us if we will."

I was prepared to bring in Hakkon and the conspirators I had seen immediately, but they had made no direct move against Etran, or me, yet. It was just words.

"I look forward to hearing how you're going to deal with this, then."

I dipped a nod. "Yes, Chief."

Relief at the title shone bright in his eyes for a moment before he masked it. I followed him from the room and watched with no envy as he returned to the council, and I left for the freedom of the crisp afternoon.

Perhaps I did not regret Father's choice after all.

# FOUR

## ETRAN

"What does one need to do to get a word with the chief?" A voice stopped me as I finally stepped out of the council lodge. My tension melted away at the sight of Maren leaning against the lodge. Finally, a friendly face and a chance to maybe forget my troubles for a moment.

"Put in a formal request and wait for hours." I tipped my chin up in something vaguely aloof.

She grinned and shoved away from the wall. "All that just to congratulate you?"

I shrugged. "I suppose I could make an allowance for a friend."

Her clear laugh sent my heart jumping an extra beat, as it had taken to doing recently around her. Maren's long hair had been bound back in warrior braids, resting over her shoulder. She was just as comfortable on the training grounds as she was at the table splicing plants and drying for weaving later.

"And are you too busy for a celebratory drink? I've hardly seen you since the choosing." She reached to tap my shoulder.

"It's been busier than I thought."

And with more threats against me than I had expected. But

perhaps even more confusing was Comran coming to my side. Or appearing to be. We had exchanged more words in the last few days than I remembered us doing in the last year.

"Are we celebrating finally?" Jens jogged up. His slender male greywolf followed close behind.

"Yes," Maren said. "I managed to catch him."

Jens slung an arm around my shoulders and steered me towards his lodge, ignoring my protests as we went. The day was not over yet and there were still things to attend to. Though the way many of the tribe had been looking at me, perhaps avoiding them for a few minutes with a drink wouldn't be a terrible idea.

It seemed the only thing worse than my existence, was me existing as chief. The flame of triumph which had filled me for a short time when Father had chosen me had since died to ash that weighed heavier in my stomach with each passing day.

Maren and Jens were two of the very few who had dared to reach out as friends over the years. I hated to bring the looks to them as we walked together, Jens with his arm still over my shoulders and Maren striding alongside with arms swinging freely, but at least they'd never hear the hated word.

"Jens!" The call stopped us in our tracks. Amund slowed to a halt, and tapped a—somewhat hesitant to my eyes—fist to his chest. "Chief."

I offered a nod, the same unsurety that Comran and I had of each other apparently extending to his circle of friends as well.

"Comran wanted to see you, Jens."

Jens drew back a little in surprise. "Me?"

But a bit of relief stirred. He'd listened to me and had decided to honor my choice. Maybe.

"Nothing to worry about." Amund grinned, the action smothered a little by the patches of pale skin spreading across his tanned left cheek and under his jaw. He'd been in danger of being shunned as a child when it had appeared, until Comran punched a tormentor so hard he drew blood.

But he'd never stepped to my defense like that. No one ever had.

I nudged Jens away. "No, it should be something I already spoke to him about."

That did not appear to reassure Jens, but he left with Amund, casting a suspicious glance over his shoulder.

"What is that about?" Maren came to stand beside me.

"Comran asked who I might trust as a second, and I told him Jens." Anything else stuck on my tongue. She knew plenty of what I'd encountered over the years in the tribe, but for some reason I did not want her to worry about Hakkon and the others who were plotting against me.

She gave me a considering look. "You two truly are trying to work together?"

"Surprised?" I forced some lightness into my voice.

A gentle shove to my shoulder accompanied her eye roll. "How many times have I watched the two of you keep your distance?"

It brought a slight wince to my face. Was it so obvious to others? No wonder so many thought Comran might side with them against me.

"He's a good man," Maren said, leaning a little closer to me. "I think you did right choosing him as battlewolf. He'll stand by you."

"Will he?" It slipped from me before I could stop it.

A faint huff escaped. "If you would spend some time outside that head of yours, you might see some things more clearly."

My fingers fiddled over the engraved knife hilt in my belt. Her eyes never left mine and it seemed she tried to say something else underneath the words. It wasn't the first time I wondered if she'd also started to feel as I did. But same as before, I couldn't bring myself to ask. I could not risk her friendship if she didn't, and if she did, I would not bring her down beside me in the eyes of the tribe.

"Perhaps a drink might help." I shrugged back into motion. Maren's smile softened, but the something seemed to linger in her eyes a moment more before she shifted to go with me, this time to her lodge. Jens could catch up later, and I would get his report on what Comran intended. But my hand stayed close to my knife and I watched every shadow and warrior a little closer. And wondered if I could ever rest easy in this new position.

# FIVE

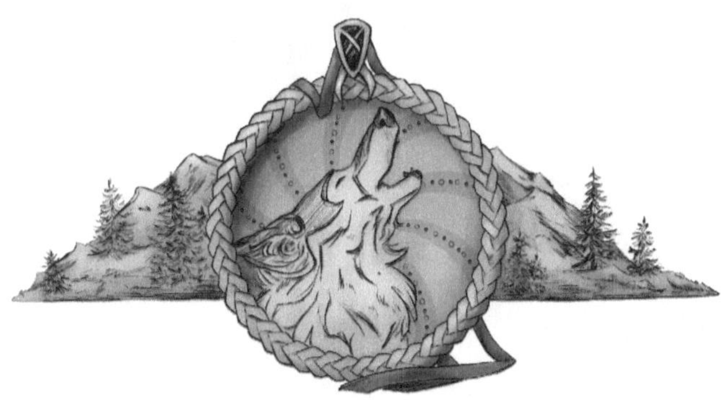

## COMRAN

"What *is* your plan?" Amund leaned on the table.

"Aye, I'd like to know the same." Jens crossed his arms and stared down at me.

I gestured for him to sit, and he took a chair across from Loke. The warrior had accepted my offer of *rokr* readily enough, but caution still showed in his gaze, still not sure of the way things were between me and Etran.

"We protect Etran," I said, and the tension eased in Jens's shoulders. "Hakkon won't wait. I think he has enough fools on his side to do something soon. The question is, how many men can I trust to help protect Etran and not let Hakkon do the job? Or help watch my back if Hakkon decides to come for me as well."

"Men who would support both of you?" Loke eased back against his chair. "Unfortunately, the list likely won't be long."

I tilted him a glance and he shrugged.

"He's right." Jens offered a rueful smile. "No offense, Comran, but I am a little surprised you included me in this number."

"Etran and I have agreed that it's better we stand together. He named you among those he trusts. I agreed with him."

He nodded and pressed his clenched fist against his chest in salute.

"I still haven't heard a plan," Amund interrupted after a pause.

I shook my head and smiled. Always impulsive.

"We've no war right now to arrange for the chief to conveniently fall. He wouldn't dare attack in the midst of the crowded lodge."

"Poison?" Loke guessed.

"This has become personal for Hakkon. I'd bet he wants to do it himself. Besides, poison is subtle."

Amund snorted in derision of my cousin's intellect.

Jens smiled. "Midwinter falls tomorrow night. Etran will enter the lodge for the sacred ceremony."

"Attacking the chief there?" Loke raised his eyebrows. "He'd risk the spirits?"

I tapped my knuckles against the table. "Etran dies in the lodge. It looks like the spirits and the All-Father don't favor the decision."

Loke rubbed his chin, frowning in thought. "And how do *we* go there? No one enters besides the chief and the *talånd*."

"I'll discuss it with the *talånd*."

"Best do it soon," Loke said. "He'll enter by next moonrise."

I nodded and stood. Time wasn't on our side.

"Find some warriors we can trust. We'll meet again tonight."

I stepped from Loke's lodge. His family was loyal to me and we had no fear of betrayal within the walls. All the same, our wolves lounged about the building. They all sat or reclined against the ground, tails gently swishing through the muddy snow. But their ears pricked, and they kept watchful gazes in all directions, a tenseness in their shoulders belying their relaxed posture.

I paused to ruffle Eska's ears. He rumbled a reply, his amber eyes meeting mine for a moment before he returned his attention to the open circle in front of him.

My footsteps turned to the *tåkn* grove at the head of the lodge circles. The *talånd's* lodge nestled against the broader bulk of the longhouse that acted as the bridge to the All-Father and his spirits.

Low chanting led me around the back of the houses. The *talånd* sat before a shallow fire pit, wrapped tight in his colorful robe. He rocked back and forth as he chanted, occasionally reaching out to cast a handful of dried herbs into the flames. The sweet scent of their burning twined through the air to dampen the bitter scent of smoke.

I waited respectfully, offering my own quick prayer to the Greywolf spirit for guidance, hoping he might care enough to carry the request to the All-Father. The tangled matter before me might require more than man's power to lay straight.

The *talånd* turned his wrinkled face up to follow the last of the scented smoke and sighed deeply.

"Battlewolf, what brings you here?" He stood and stepped away from the fire.

I cast a glance around us, but nothing stirred in the whispering pines standing guard thirty paces from the lodges.

"A matter of some delicacy," I said.

He nodded and touched my arm to invite me into his lodge. A young man glanced up from his workbench as we entered. Bundles of dried herbs hung around him and ground dust filled the mortar and pestle in his hands. A faint bitterness lingered in the air and my nose rebelled at the scent. A bundle of scarlet flowers lay on the table beside another bowl filled with red scattered grounds.

"Mikkel, give us a moment," the *talånd* instructed his apprentice.

Mikkel nodded, open curiosity in his gaze as he gathered his plain grey cloak and left the lodge. The quick swish of the door was not enough to dispel the aroma.

"If he listens at that loophole, will I have cause to worry?" I raised one eyebrow at the open knot beside the fireplace.

The *talånd's* weathered face creased into a smile and he shook his head. "We pledge our allegiance to the spirits and the All-Father. We do not carry tales to men."

I nodded. "Then you know why I've come?"

"There is much unrest in this tribe. It's no great mystery why you might be here." He eased onto a stool beside the hearth and added a log to the snapping pile. I took the stool opposite him at his invitation and leaned on my knees.

"You know I stand with the chief."

He folded his hands within his cloak despite the warmth of the hearth and gave a nod, although a quick flash I couldn't quite discern passed across his eyes.

"I think some of this tribe will try to kill him soon, possibly at midwinter."

The *talånd* raised greying eyebrows. "In the sacred lodge?"

I shrugged. "It seems a mad idea."

He straightened with a deep breath. "Some consider it an offense to the All-Father Himself for any man besides the chief or *talånd* to step inside that lodge on the sacred day. You are sure they will risk such a thing?"

"Murder, or see the chief struck down by the spirits?"

He pursed his lips in a frown. "Maybe they are smarter than I thought moments ago."

A smile cracked my face and I waited for an answer to my unspoken question.

"It is tradition for the chief to enter alone on midwinter's night. No man, other than the *talånd*, has stepped inside with him in many, many years."

"So there is no law against it if I should enter?"

The *talånd* slowly shook his head. "Do you know why only the chief and *talånd* are allowed into the lodge on the sacred nights?"

His voice took the tone of teacher that every member of the tribe had heard as a youngster when learning our history.

"It is not the first time men have tried to force the spirits' hands?" I guessed.

"You did pay attention after all." He smiled. "It has become tradition, and that is nearly as powerful to the spirits as sacred law. Men would be just as foolish to try to violate it."

"Perhaps there will be no need for me to enter at all."

"Would you do what is best for the tribe?" the *talånd* asked, that strange look passing across his eyes again.

A faint quiver of misgiving touched my stomach, sowing doubt in my mind. "Yes. He is our chief." The words came stern and the *talånd* nodded.

"He is. I only sought to make sure you would do what you think is right. I do not want you to risk the spirits' wrath. It is terrible to behold."

*His existence is an affront to the spirits.* Hakkon's words came back to me and a reticence to share anything else locked my tongue.

I stood, dipping my head in a bow. "Thank you, *talånd*. You will not speak of this?"

The *talånd* stood and clasped my arm. "As I said, Battlewolf, we do not carry tales to men."

My smile barely covered the doubt growing inside. He released me and I stepped outside, the fresh chill driving away the heady scent of herbs clinging to the heavy wooden beams of the house. I paused to consider the sacred lodge. Mighty oaken beams had been laced together long ago, interspersed with pine and spruce, the ceiling made from carved aspen logs—the wealth of the valley come together to house the spirits.

One more day, and Etran would enter.

*Do I dare step inside it? Even to protect him?*

The whisper of cold iron against my neck startled me, and a hand dragged me back into the shelter of a longhouse. I cursed my distraction that had allowed my unseen enemy to strike.

"What business did you have with the *talånd?*" Hakkon hissed in my ear.

I stiffened, jabbing an elbow back into his stomach and twisting. He cursed and drove his knee up into my groin, catching me as I stumbled back, and shoving me into the wall. The knife pressed against my neck.

"What are you doing, *cousin?*" he snarled close to my face.

"I could ask you the same," I growled.

"Don't." He pressed harder as he caught the movement of my hand towards my own knife. I slowly raised my hands.

"Answer the question." He prodded and a dribble of warmth edged down my throat.

*Bastard.*

"A man can't consult with the *talånd* when he wants? Perhaps I had a request of the spirits."

Hakkon huffed a laugh. "And what was your request?"

"I wanted to make an offering to the Greywolf spirit to guide me as battlewolf. How am I supposed to lead if I do not have his guidance?" I curled my lip in a sneer. *I should make an offering once this fool gets off me.*

Hakkon relaxed a fraction, a bit of understanding coming over his face. "I don't trust you anymore."

"Give up your foolish cause and we can talk like men again."

The anger filled his eyes. "You know I can't do that. I'm sure the spirits are more than offended to have that imposter hold the staff. You could still join us. We would still accept you as chief." His voice softened, a bit of pleading edging through.

I brought my forearm crashing down on his elbow, breaking his hold, and shoved the knife away. He recoiled with a curse.

"I already gave you my answer. Make a move, Hakkon, and I will see every last one of you punished. Or I'll kill you myself."

We glared at one another, chests heaving in suppressed anger, the promise of future death staining the air between us.

"Not if I kill you first." He backed away, sheathing the knife, and disappeared around the corner.

I sagged against the wall and dragged a hand through my hair. *It is done. I will see this family sundered. Is the half-blood I share with him worth it?*

A wolf's howl jerked my head up, my heart racing. It had come from the forests behind the spirits' lodge. *Surely just a wolfrider out on the hunt...*

But my heart wasn't so sure. I cast a glance up at the *tâkn* where the wolf's head howled at the sky. When night fell, the nose would point to the northern star which marked the entrance to the All-Father's lodge.

*I have made my vow. I will protect him.*

Perhaps the spirits would look favorably upon what I would have to do. I pressed a shaking hand to my throat, wiping away the traces of blood beading the nick in my skin—enough evidence to bring before Etran now if I wanted. Blood had just been spilled in the struggle.

*But I would just bring in one man, out of who knows how many. And Hakkon would never tell.* Best to wait until they made their move.

I stalked towards Loke's lodge. We'd need to pair up to prevent another attack from happening. And someone would need to stay with Etran until midwinter.

"Comran."

Father's voice brought my attention across the circle. He stood in the doorway of our lodge, his rigid posture commanding my presence without a word. I fought the childish urge to keep walking. As battlewolf, I did not have to obey him. But I turned and joined him within the house.

"Stian brought me a tale of you and Hakkon."

"Thought we were too old for that anymore." I wasn't ready for him to hear what had happened. It would just be another reason for him to doubt my worth.

"Comran. He threatened you. He threatened Etran."

My heart clenched at the difference in the way he said our names. *He will always care less for me.*

"And I'm handling it," I growled.

"How?" He crossed his arms, and I stiffened defensively.

"I think they will strike at midwinter."

My father raised his eyebrows in the closest to surprise I'd ever seen. "I had never taken him for that much of a fool."

I almost smiled. Clearly, he didn't know his nephew. "I just spoke to the *talånd*. There is a way for me to protect Etran if I need to."

His gaze softened a fraction. "You will support him?"

I stared at him. *Did he not think I would?*

"I swore my oath, didn't I? Don't worry. The chief you chose won't die." The hurt bubbled out and I tried to push past him, but he grabbed my arm to halt me.

"Comran," he said as gently as his gruff voice would allow. "What happened here?" His thumb brushed the stinging cut on my neck.

I jerked my chin away. "Nothing."

He didn't release my arm for a long moment. "Hakkon?"

I finally tipped a nod.

"Then he has marked himself as a traitor. Bring him in."

"I don't know who else plots with him. If I accuse him now, another attack may yet come."

Reluctant understanding came to Father's face. "You place Etran in danger."

*But no care for me.* "He knows the risk. I have already spoken with him."

He stepped back to allow me to pass. "Is there anything I can do, Battlewolf?"

"I've appointed seconds. They are finding men who support both of us, however few those might be."

"There might be more than you think," he said.

"Make sure Uncle knows of his son's treachery. I have already threatened this family. I don't want to see it sundered completely."

He nodded and I left him.

# SIX

## ETRAN

"I can't say I like this." I leaned on the table, glancing up at Comran. Light flickered from the clay oil lamp between us, its light barely touching the walls of the training lodge, now his domain.

"Me neither." Comran shoved his arms across his chest.

This time tomorrow night I would enter the spirits' lodge and hopefully come out alive.

*Of course, he could be wrong, and they could be waiting for us as soon as we step out of here.* I banished the foolish thought. Six wolfriders and eight wolves stood guard around the lodge. We would have warning. The uneasy thought struck next that maybe he'd been lying to me and I would get a knife in my back as soon as I turned.

"If the laws were different," Comran said, "I would walk in as you tomorrow night."

And just like that, the thought vanished. For all that we didn't get along, or truly know each other, Comran had never been able to lie. Honesty lurked about him, along with constant energy and a ready smile. He seemed truly serious.

But I shook my head. We shared enough similarities in our

build and the dark color of our hair, but I was a little taller and my features were a shade lighter than his tanned skin. He had our father's grey eyes, but I'd inherited my mother's green.

It might be enough in the dim twilight to trick an enemy's sight, but I had to perform the chieftain's duty within the lodge.

"Comran—thank you. You're risking much."

"So are you."

I offered a wan smile. "I'm just ready for this to be over. This position seems a foolish thing to wish for now."

He half-laughed. "I am not jealous anymore."

It felt strange to hear he might be jealous of me. I twisted to sit on the table, taking a moment to look up at him, weighing my words.

"I trust you." It came almost a surprise to taste the truth of the words. I truly did trust him. "I know you'll have my back tomorrow night. Know that I will have yours should anything happen."

This time, he stared at me, like it was so hard to believe *I* might be sincere.

"Thank you." He cleared his throat, turning back to business. "Jens and Amund will stay with you tonight."

"And you? Your lodge is right next to that traitor's."

"Stian and Loke will watch with me."

I nodded and shoved to my feet. "Here's to a long night and day ahead of us."

He clapped me on the shoulder, both of us a little surprised at the friendly gesture. "I'll see you to your lodge."

"Just as long as I don't get an offer of courtship after." I smirked.

Comran laughed as he stepped to the door and cracked it open. The warrior outside nodded the all-clear. He went first, still watchful in the failing light.

We walked side by side to my lodge, Eska and my female grey-wolf, Frea, trailing behind. There were still men and women outside, finishing their tasks for the day before heading to their lodges for the evening meal. They cast us glances as we passed.

*What stories have circulated today already?* I forced my hands away from my weapons, trying not to see enemies in every face. There was no sign of Hakkon or the three men we knew to stand with him.

"Eat at my table tonight," I said.

"You think that will be enough?" His footsteps didn't pause.

"The more we are seen together, the better. Whatever happens tomorrow, at least they will know we broke bread together tonight."

Comran nodded and followed me into the lodge. A frown soured Mother's face at his presence, but she ordered a chair be pulled up for him at the head table. She was not the only one to look strangely on Comran taking a seat beside me. It was not so odd for me to be seen in Father's lodge. But for Comran to come into mine?

It was nearly like seeing a trout walk on the riverbank.

Mother sat in frozen silence on my left side, not deigning to even glance his way. A sudden smirk crossed his face. He rubbed his chin to likely smother a laugh. My own laugh bubbled in my chest, sudden and near frantic. Here he was, trying to save her son, and she would most likely still hate him until her dying day.

I pressed my lips together, a tell-tale twitch betraying me. A snort of laughter broke from him, and his grin spread. I turned my face away and tried to block the laughter with my fist, to no avail. He leaned forward onto his hand, shoulders shaking.

*We're both mad!*

I cleared my throat, determined to regain control of myself.

Until a dish was offered to Comran by one of the girls on serving duty. Smoked river eel with ground hash. A dish I knew he hated after sharing a table with him before.

I raised my eyes to the ceiling, lips pressed together, praying for strength to keep it in this time. Mother leveled a smug glare at him, and the girl darted an uncertain glance between us. Comran waved the girl away with barely controlled dignity.

A strangled noise broke from Comran as he shook his head, still trying to maintain a straight face. My body shook with a newly-suppressed laugh and I leaned forward, pressing my hand over my eyes as I gave in to the urge.

His laugh joined mine. The buzz of conversation halted for a moment as the rest of the long tables paused to take in the sight of us. But I didn't care. The strain of the day vanished for a moment.

I took in a breath, gulping down my last chuckle. He wiped at his eyes and shook his head.

"And what's so funny?" a grizzled old warrior, my mother's brother, rumbled from down the table.

Comran glanced at me and we both smirked again.

"Nothing, really," he replied.

The wolfrider chuckled. "Well then, I don't know that I've raised my cup to you two as chieftain and battlewolf. You boys will both do us proud." He thumped his mug on the table and lifted it high, rivulets of ale sloshing over the sides. More than a few beakers were raised with him along with shouts that echoed his words.

We acknowledged them with our own beakers and drank.

*Maybe we have more support than we thought.*

Comran's shoulders relaxed under the same thought. I refilled his beaker with dark oak ale, and he tapped his mug against mine.

"Here's to good hunting tomorrow," I said.

He saluted and drank. We would need every bit of luck we could get.

And with that, we fell back to silence, not quite knowing what to say to each other unless discussing tribe matters. I wished it were different. That the laughter we'd just shared would be easier to come by.

I had looked up to him throughout my life, though him barely two months my elder. Wishing, sometimes desperately, to be part of the circle around him. But there were reasons why I wasn't, and I was a big part of those reasons.

Strange that now I was chief and he was second to me. I ripped a bit of flatbread apart almost savagely. Mother hadn't married, hadn't had more children. No one would dare place an iron wedding band around her wrist after she gave a son to the chief, even if it was outside a marriage bond.

He was my only chance at a brother, and he hadn't ever given a sign he wanted the same. And Comran was as easy to read as the stars on clear nights.

Though maybe past tomorrow it wouldn't matter. A sense of fatality had settled over me. It had been clear all my life there were plenty within the tribe who would not be sad to see me die, to vanish and never come back to sully the tribe's honor. And only now, when elevated to the highest position besides *talånd*, were they ready to make a move at me.

Perhaps they were like me and thought I would never have made it so far as to wear the chieftain's mantle.

The sound of benches scraping away from tables and wooden trenchers clattering brought me back to the present. Comran sat back from the table, dusting his hands. Jens met his look and started making his way up to the head table.

"Amund should be here soon," Comran said.

I shifted in my chair. Again, we seemed stuck on what to say to each other, worse than two shy youths thinking to court each other.

"I'll see you tomorrow, then." He pushed back from the table, glancing over my head. I caught the moment Mother glared at him as his jaw tightened. But he still tipped a slight nod.

He headed to the lodge door, replying to a few warriors who called to him, wishing him a good night. My joints unfroze and I followed.

"Comran." I halted in the doorway.

He turned as he tugged his cloak tighter about him against the cold.

"Be careful."

He tilted his head, then nodded. "You too."

Spinning on his heel, he strode in the direction of his own home, three lodges down. A figure appeared and I relaxed once I recognized Loke. The bigger warrior nudged Comran's shoulder, and a brief laugh filled the empty night.

I glanced up at the stars, finding the north star guarding the entrance to the All-Father's lodge. We weren't brothers, but I'd never wanted harm to come to him.

*Spirits, keep him safe.*

# SEVEN

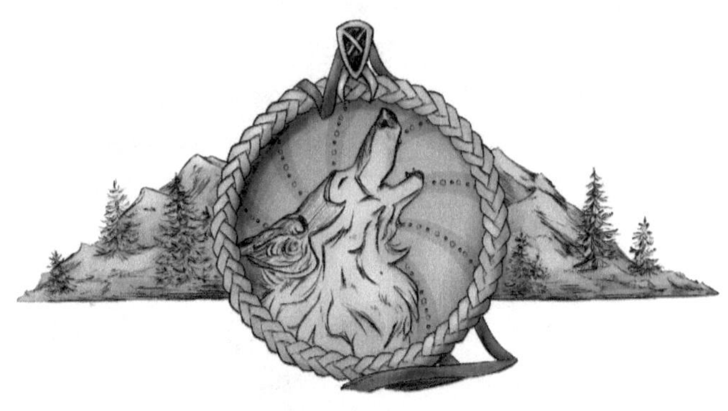

## COMRAN

I squinted my eyes against the faint light sneaking around the animal skins covering the window slits and pulled my furs closer around me. The benches lining the hall were still full of sleeping men and women and I resisted the urge to rejoin them. The night had been a long one, broken only by brief snatches of slumber.

But there was no knife stuck between my ribs, so the day was off to a decent enough start.

Loke's foot nudged my shoulder. I half sat up, scowling at him through sleep-filled eyes.

"I think that one slept all night." He frowned at Stian, who snored comfortably in his nest of furs.

"Why do you think I wanted you along?" I pushed my blankets away and pulled my tunic over the thin undershirt.

Loke did the same and we rolled our blankets up to shove

against the wall, taking cloaks to wrap around our shoulders before stepping out into the early morning.

"Did you have a plan for today or is it just waiting around for Hakkon and his idiots to make a move?" Loke stretched his arms overhead, shoulders popping with the motion.

I turned my steps to the stables, passing the lodge Hakkon and his family called home. But no sign of him or the other warriors yet.

"I don't even know if I have a plan for tonight."

It had mostly been me saying I would protect Etran once he stepped into the lodge, but part of me still hesitated at the thought of going in. Father had trained us both on the ways a chieftain served, so I knew enough about the ceremony.

It just wouldn't ever be me performing it.

Every time I thought about the ways I wouldn't be chieftain, the anger receded more and something like relief kept pushing up in its place.

I had always done better on the training fields, out in the open, on a wolf with a spear in my hand and commanding riders. Not sitting in councils and debating.

A low *woof* announced Eska as he trotted around a lodge house corner. He usually spent the night around the lodge with the other wolves bonded to the warriors there, but I had a sneaking suspicion he'd been off to see a female with bits of brown in her fur.

Loke's greywolf followed, shoving a bulky shoulder into Loke's chest and rumbling until the warrior scratched at the thicker ruff around its neck. Eska dropped his head on my shoulder before withdrawing to watch me with his amber eyes.

"Later," I promised.

A huff escaped. In one way, we were the same. We preferred racing the mountains and valleys to sitting around and planning.

"I've never seen such betrayal in a wolf's eyes." Loke laughed, nudging his wolf away.

"He hasn't yet learned I have new duties that keep us from riding every day."

I turned to watch the greywolves meander off together before Eska pounced on the other to start a mock fight. Another warrior simply sidestepped the giant wolves and carried on about his morning.

"And how are you feeling about those duties?" Loke's voice stayed light, but his brown eyes leveled seriousness at me.

"I don't know." My response came honest.

"And you and Etran?" he pushed.

"At least wait until breakfast to weigh me down with questions," I snapped.

He didn't react, just jogged a step and swept up two practice swords from a basket outside the training lodge. I caught the one he tossed me, fingers curling around the carved wood. We stepped out onto the training field, leaving cloaks draped over a low pole built for that purpose.

"I was surprised to see you coming from his lodge last night." Loke settled into a fighting stance.

"Jealous?" I swung the sword a few times to test its weight before I did the same.

Loke allowed a shrug. "Maybe I am just curious as to what you will do, since you can no longer continue avoiding him."

He probed forward and I moved back, settling back into a crouch.

"He's always avoided me." Spirits, I sounded like a child.

Loke's eyebrow arched in judgment. I scowled and attacked. The crack of wood against wood shattered the quiet of the field. An irritated squawk from some bird sounded up the nearby mountain.

He used his unfair height against me, forcing me a few slipping strides over the icy snow before I disengaged and spun around him to attack. But he backed off, starting the dance all over again.

"And maybe I'm just wondering how you are taking the decision."

"Should we be having this discussion over our weaving by the lodge fire instead?" Irritation rushed in.

He broke his stance a moment, blocky features twisting in concern. "Comran…"

I didn't allow him to finish, charging forward and forcing him to block with his blade. What followed was inelegant at best. Boots slipped on the thin patches of ice cast by the night, and he lost his sword after a lurch down to his knee. I tossed mine aside and tackled him.

Foolish, because Loke never lost in the wrestling ring.

Two minutes later, we both stared up at the cloud-spotted sky from our backs, its blue deepening with the continued rise of the sun. Cool began to seep through my thick shirt, driving away some of the heat of the fight. The battlewolf medallion was a small circle of pressure atop my chest.

"I thought I would be angrier. Instead, I think I'm relieved." I spoke softly to the sky. "I think it stung the worst hearing Mother say she knew I wouldn't be chosen."

A low whistle cut from Loke. Ice crunched as he shifted to sit and stare down at me. I refused to meet his gaze.

"Did your father say anything?"

My chest wrenched with a scoff. "Like he would?"

At least Etran had seemed as surprised as me at the choosing. I worked my hand in and out of a fist, daring to admit more.

"He said he didn't choose me because he had a dream where I died in battle as chief. And he didn't want to see that happen."

"Afraid you might have to admit he cares a little?" Loke prodded.

I tilted my head to glare at him. "Then he said Etran is quicker with his mind and that is really why I wasn't chosen. So no, I don't think he does."

Loke's mouth puckered in a frown, but he didn't argue. He'd seen it often enough growing up, how starved I was for any sort of acknowledgment from my father. But at least he had a loving memory of his father to carry him through after his own fell driving off one of the giant grizzlies who'd come from the high meadows around the yellow cliffs years ago.

"And what of Etran?"

"What about him?"

The eyebrow rose again, and I rolled my eyes, shoving myself up before the cold froze my sweaty shirt to the ground. I dusted snow from my hair. Last night had caught me by surprise.

"I don't know. He is my only chance at a brother, and I don't think he's ever wanted it."

"What am I, then?" Loke pulled back, righteously offended.

I pushed his shoulder. "I know, but tell me you don't have something different with your own brothers, and not just this one you adopted?" I jabbed a thumb at my chest.

"You are easier to beat on the field." He nodded.

I grabbed him in a headlock, which he easily maneuvered out of.

"Maybe you should give him a chance now that you have no one hovering over the both of you."

"Nothing's changed in twenty-three years, Loke. I doubt it will now."

I had wanted some sort of bond with him since I'd first learned we shared a father, even though I wasn't quite old enough to understand why he had a different mother. But between Father's indifference, and the chill lingering between our respective mothers, he hadn't made any attempt to reach out. But neither had I.

Loke opened his mouth, on the verge of an argument, but I pushed to my feet and offered a hand down to him. Clasping it, he let me haul him up.

"Let's make it through tonight first," I cut him off again.

He glared, annoyed that I'd side-stepped his attempts to nudge me to better myself.

"Should we go back and see if Stian is awake?"

A grin spread across his face. "No, let him wake up and think we've been dragged from our beds to be murdered. Maybe that will make him think twice about sleeping so soundly."

I laughed. "Your lodge for breakfast it is, then."

Still, a bit of relief nudged my heart when we passed back into the wide circle and saw Amund step out with Etran. Amund jogged over to join us, dragging a hand through his hair and bringing it to some sort of unruly order.

"Nothing all night," he reported through a yawn.

"Then I have a feeling tonight won't be as calm."

Acceptance settled inside. One way or another, it would be settled in the spirit's lodge. Etran met my glance and gave a small nod.

He said he trusted me. I hoped it wasn't misplaced.

# EIGHT

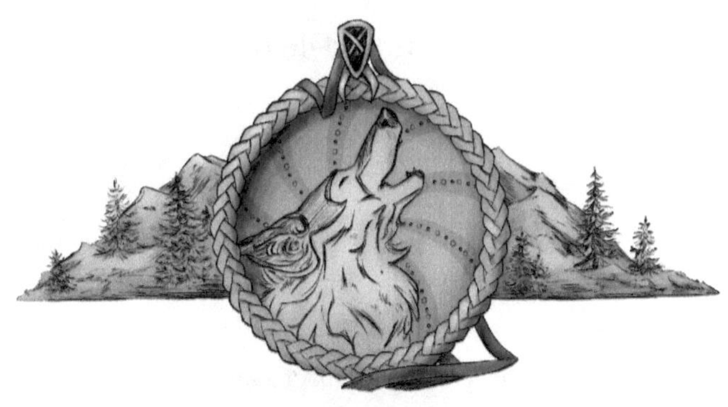

## COMRAN

The bits of dinner I'd managed to eat churned restlessly in my stomach. Hakkon had invited himself to the lodge and had spent the meal sneering at me from beside another warrior who supported him. I had attempted to ignore it, but the entire lodge seemed to hold its breath as glances darted between us.

And now, as the sun's light vanished over the western hills, my unease loomed higher and higher. Etran would be preparing. Jens stayed with him—not a surprise. I leaned against the outer wall of my lodge, one boot propped up, as I tossed a well-worn leather ball for Eska.

Also not an unusual sight.

Loke drifted up to join me, cloak drawn tight about his shoulders to hide his sword and extra dagger.

We couldn't wear our armor for fear of alerting the conspirators.

And we had to catch as many as we could. The thought of potentially going into battle unarmored made me even angrier at Hakkon.

"Ready?" Loke murmured.

I shifted, wiping Eska's plentiful drool on my trousers before throwing the ball again.

"Not really."

A glance up to the center of the lodge circle showed lights glowing from the spirits' lodge. The *talånd* came to take his place at the fire now crackling in a low pit before it. His colorful cloak waved in the evening breeze.

Other men and women had begun to step out to watch Etran as he entered the lodge, some staying up to gather around lodgefires to add their own supplications to the spirits and All-Father for the coming year.

More eyes to see if Hakkon and his followers decided to strike at Etran.

"Everyone in place?"

Loke nodded. Amund and another warrior had gone off after dinner under the pretense of running their wolves and should be hidden in the trees behind the lodge. Two other warriors whom Etran trusted had assisted with building the fire outside the lodge and lingered still by the pile of wood. One had kept the fire burning all night the winter before for Father, so it wasn't strange he and his brother had claimed the honor again.

Tribe tradition included the battlewolf accompanying the chief up to the lodge doors. That got me close, but not quite inside.

My fingers loosened the leather cords wrapped twice around my left wrist. I extended it to Loke, and he traded his cord for mine. We refastened them around our wrists. Braided leather and fire-hardened clay beads etched with our runes and greywolves would mark our bodies if we fell in battle one day.

We traded them before every conflict.

Loke held up his left fist and I knocked mine against his, feeling a little better for the action.

Movement stirred and Etran stepped out. I shoved away from the wall and strode to meet him. He wore the wolf cloak, face painted as chief. No weapons, as such a thing was not allowed in the house of the spirits. Another reason I feared what the night might bring.

Loke's comforting presence drifted up on my left. Etran gave a small nod. I returned it, sweeping my gaze to Jens, who inclined his head. All well so far.

"No one's been in or out all day except the *talånd*," I said. Two warriors watching for me had reported throughout the day.

"Ready to get this over?" Etran murmured.

I mustered a small smile. "More than."

He shifted, tugging at the soft tunic and adjusting the wolf cloak.

"I'll be staying by the fire." I had made the decision earlier. Birgir had done it often enough for my father that it might be assumed I followed in his footsteps. It might also be a deterrent to any who might be foolish enough to enter the lodge.

"You know the signal?"

Etran's jaw clenched as he darted a glance up at the spirits' lodge. A hand strayed to a belt empty of weapons. I listened to the sudden urge and rested a hand on his shoulder.

"We're watching your back. Focus on the duty inside."

Green eyes widened as he stared at me. A breath exhaled along with something else it seemed he didn't say.

We walked side by side up to the fire where the *talånd* waited. He inclined his head to Etran and his gaze settled on me for a moment. Warning, caution? Father stood there, too. But I stepped back as he leaned close to Etran. I stared at the curling flames, clenching my fist, ignoring the way he looked at Etran with pride.

"Comran." His deep voice jerked my head up. Approval lurked in the rigidness of his face. It was nearly more unsettling than the whole night.

My voice lost, I could only stare at him before Etran shrugged back into motion.

The *talånd* extended a hand to guide him to the lodge. I turned back to watch those who had gathered, seeing no sign of our enemies. The brothers ghosted closer to the firelight, looking to me for orders or reassurance as the door to the lodge closed.

Following tradition, it would not be re-opened until sun's rise. "Keep ready."

Nodding obedience, they and Loke moved off to assigned positions. I'd prefer to keep Loke at my shoulder, but he was needed opposite the fire where the lodges curled toward the spirits' house.

I stayed at the fire.

Nothing stirred for an hour besides a chill wind kicking up bits of snow to skitter around boots. New frost crept in, curling up the base of the lodges and freezing my cheeks. I circled the fire again, moving a few steps away to bury gloved hands in Eska's fur to warm them.

A glance to the spirits' house showed nothing other than the gentle light still spilling out from under the door.

Maybe I'd gotten it wrong and Etran would be lying in a pool of blood, waiting to be discovered in the morning. But no signal had come from inside, and nothing from Amund or Stian or the others who'd been watching all day.

But I still held back from entering to make sure everything was fine. Would doing so really bring the spirits' wrath down on me or the tribe? How would the All-Father Himself look on all our actions tonight?

Midnight approached, and I stifled a yawn. Poor sleep the night before and now a restless night on watch. I'd happily sleep till spring if the night went well.

A low growl from Eska brought alertness back. The wolf shifted to his paws, head stretching low and teeth baring at a threat in the darkness. Loke backed up into the fire's light, sword drawn against three men approaching.

I drew my sword in an instant. The brothers fell back as well, weapons out against the threat. Hakkon emerged, smug grin firm on his face.

"Well, Comran. I had hoped I wouldn't have to plan for you. This suits me just fine, though."

Eska crouched low, growl rumbling deep in his chest. I whistled low, the signal to wait to attack until I did.

"Etran is taken care of, and you've proven yourself to be too easily swayed. Time for a new leader to take the tribe, and tonight will see it done." The grin slipped from his face to show pure anger.

But I didn't care. *Etran is taken care of.*

The *talånd.*

A keening whistle ripped from me—the signal to attack—and I turned and ran for the lodge. My shoulder slammed into the door, breaking it open as swords clashed behind me.

Etran whirled from his place before a low altar spread with the bounty of the valley. A low spring gurgled in an open space in the floor before diving back into the ground to feed the river down the mountain. Torches cast the open room in shadow.

He was safe. No one besides him and the *talånd* inside. The *talånd* rose, anger twisting around him. He grabbed a knife from the table and raised it high.

"Etran!" I sprinted, clearing the spring in one jump.

Etran half turned, throwing himself to the ground as the *talånd* struck over the table. Off balance from missing, the *talånd* couldn't defend as I lunged to tackle him.

It took me across the table, scattering the offerings with a clatter. Arms wrapped around him, I rolled and took him to the ground.

His scream of rage burst in my ear as he wrestled against me. A punch to my stomach loosened my grip, allowing him to squirm free. I grabbed him around the waist again, hands slipping against the smoothness of his robe. He wrenched around and a stinging sensation ripped across my ribs.

Growling in anger, I grabbed his wrist as he pulled back for another wild strike. But he'd ended up half-atop me, throwing all his weight behind another attempt.

I strained against him, the knife hovering above my chest until Etran appeared, grabbing the *talånd* by the arm and wrenching it behind his back. The knife clattered to the ground and the *talånd* stumbled back, controlled by Etran's tight hold.

Scrambling to my feet, I located my sword.

"Comran!" Loke burst into the lodge.

"We're fine," I reassured. "Get some rope for this traitor."

A twinge cut through my ribs and I winced. The *talånd* sneered at me as Loke and Etran hauled him to his feet.

"The spirits will still make a judgment tonight."

I waved him off and Etran and Loke shoved him to the door. Outside, Hakkon and his followers knelt or lay in the snow, circled by Amund and my men. More warriors than I remembered stood around as well.

"Some came running the moment they heard swords," Loke said.

The world slid sideways with my nod, and I staggered a step. Bits of blood stained my hand as I drew it away from my chest. Not a deep cut.

"What about the rest of the ceremony?" Jens murmured to Etran as the bound *talånd* joined the others in the snow.

Doubt clouded Etran's features. "Find his apprentice. Maybe he knows enough to get through tonight."

Jens nodded and hurried off. I tried to take another step and fell to a knee. Stinging pain cut through me and I barely locked a cry away.

"You don't look so good, Comran." Hakkon's laugh grated on my ears.

Raging fire burst in my chest, and I curled to the ground, a cry escaping this time.

"The spirits have judged!" the *talånd* shouted. "Anyone who follows this bastard will be condemned!"

More shouts surrounded me. The fire spread, taking over, and my limbs thrashed against it. Darkness rushed in to cloud the stars overhead. Weight pushed against my shoulders, along with incomprehensible words. Dampness filled my mouth and a frantic wheeze escaped.

Cold touched my cheek and I choked a breath. The fire rushed back, scorching though my veins. A keening sound filled my ears. Shouts turned more frantic and then darkness.

# NINE

## ETRAN

As I stumbled out into the snow, holding the *talånd* tight, adrenaline gave way to fear. If the *talånd* himself was against me, was I truly fit to lead?

Jens brought me back to the night and the snow with a question about the rest of the ceremony. I looked back over my shoulder at the lodge door hanging open, gaping wide in horror that the night had been so disrupted. I'd tried to always pay deference to the spirits, but would this be something they would overlook?

"Find his apprentice. Maybe he knows enough to get through tonight."

Jens tapped a hand to his chest. Loke took the *talånd*, pushing him down into the snow beside Hakkon, who glared at me with anger brighter than a wildfire. Then it shifted away, and he turned a triumphant sneer beyond me.

I turned to see Comran collapsed to a knee, face pale in the firelight. The *talånd* screamed an imprecation behind me, blurred in my alarm as Comran crumpled to the ground. Loke's shout urged me to action, and both of us crashed down beside Comran as he began thrashing uncontrollably, blood and spittle dribbling between his lips.

"Get him on his side!" Loke ordered.

Together, we wrestled him over and he gasped a breath. But his limbs didn't stop their frantic twitching. A hoarse cry ripped from his straining throat.

"Get the healer!" I finally found my own voice.

Bits of blood stained his tunic, ripped open to show a shallow cut. Not enough to cause a reaction like that. Unless…

The *talånd's* words came back. *"The spirits will still make a judgment tonight."*

*No. Not him.* My hands shook against Comran's shoulders.

"What happened?" The healer knelt beside us. Comran's struggles grew weaker, arms and legs jerking sporadically as his head lolled to the side.

"He just collapsed!" Loke's stern voice held panic.

"What caused the cut?" The healer stayed calm, his hands tugging at Comran's tunic, lifting his head and opening his mouth to make sure he still breathed.

I shook myself, trying to remember. "The—the *talånd's* knife, I think."

"Get it." The healer looked to someone over Loke's shoulder. "Get him up and to my lodge."

He didn't seem to care that he ordered the chieftain, but at the moment, neither did I. The memory of my duties faded, and I slipped hands underneath Comran's shoulders as Loke took his legs and we lifted.

A moan cut from him as he moved, his head tipping back against my shoulder. The healer pushed through the gathering crowd of onlookers. I caught a glimpse of Father standing there, an expression I had never seen on his face.

Fear.

Heat from the healer's lodge hit as we entered and laid Comran down beside the sunken pit of heated and steaming stones.

"Take his tunic off."

Loke and I obliged. The door creaked open, bringing a welcome burst of cold to wash against the sweat already beading my forehead. Amund carefully held out a knife. The healer took it by the handle, sniffing, then cautiously licked the blade.

My heart stammered at the sight.

"Red spear." He spat into the fire. "He'll have to sweat it out."

He disappeared, leaving Loke and I to stare at each other. Another shaky cry from Comran warned us before he started thrashing again. This time his eyes flew open, pupils wide as he screamed around his clenched jaw.

I slammed hands on his shoulders, keeping him down before he could roll to the fire. Loke pinned his hips. A rattle tore from his throat.

The healer burst back in. "Tip him over!"

Racking coughs tore from him, more blood beading his lips from where he must have bitten his tongue. A girl in an apprentice's tunic followed in the healer's wake, eyes blurred with sleep. But she set about building the fire higher and fetching the supplies he called for.

Once Comran subsided, we rolled him back over, keeping hands pressed against him.

"Keep holding him."

We obeyed again as the healer began to spread a paste over the cut running ragged over his ribs. Five heartbeats passed, then Comran tried to wrench away, another scream tearing from him. His hand clawed at my arm.

"Hold him!" The healer grabbed Comran, helping keep him

contained as we moved him closer to the fire.

"This will help?" Loke demanded.

The healer stared at Comran with grim focus. "I haven't seen the effects of red spear before, and all I have are what the scrolls say from the old healer. I'm doing what I can, but much depends on him. How strong he is."

Loke turned a helpless look on Comran, an expression mirrored in my heart. The knife had been coated in poison. The knife I would have used to nick just above my wrist to let blood flow over the offerings—lending my strength and life blood to the tribe.

It should have been me lying there. Or dead within the lodge.

Comran's grip shifted on my arm. I'd barely noticed him still holding it in a vise.

"Etran?" My name trembled as a question. Unfocused eyes stared up at me in confusion. I tried not to let it hurt. Why should he expect me to be there?

Sweat poured from him, tinted red. Tremors raced through him and a whimper broke.

"Just breathe, Comran," I said almost helplessly. He tried, but another breath sent him arching in agony.

Loke closed his eyes as he kept holding Comran down. His lips moved, but I couldn't find any words to plead with the spirits myself.

"Etran." Father's voice came from the door. Cool air stirred again, drawing another shudder from Comran. "You need to return to the spirits' lodge."

Reluctance stirred and I stared down at Comran, at his hand gone limp around my arm. Loke lifted his head, debate clear on his face before he met my gaze.

"Amund," he said past me. I turned to see the warrior sitting against the far wall, eyes locked on Comran. "Stay with him."

Loke released his hold. "I'll go with you, Chief."

I opened my mouth to protest. Someone needed to watch Comran.

"I am not letting you back into the lodge without someone at your back." Loke's jaw clenched. "He wouldn't want it."

It took another moment to unlatch my hold from Comran's shoulders and let Amund slide in. I staggered back to the door, wrenching away as Amund and the healer lurched to hold Comran as another fit swept in.

The frigid night air threatened to freeze sweat in beads on my forehead. I shivered at the sudden change from the overheated lodge. Warriors and tribesmen and women stood outside still, clustering and whispering in groups as they stared at me or past to the healer's lodge. No sign of the traitors at the spirits' lodge.

"They have been locked in the guard house." A strange bit of deference came in Father's voice.

"Thank you," I said almost numbly. I hadn't thought of what to do with them in the panic at seeing Comran fall.

His hand touched my shoulder. I looked at him and found the fear still there, better hidden now. But it brought a sort of relief. Maybe he did actually feel something for at least one of us.

I stepped into the lodge, Loke at my back and Jens pushing up to guard the broken door itself. The apprentice stood at the low altar, hands shaking as he picked up the offerings and tried to arrange them again.

"Chief!" He nearly dropped the bowl of dried berries.

I searched for his name in my memory. There was a time when I'd thought knowing everyone's name would make things easier for me among the tribe.

"Mikkel."

He dropped a salute too deferential for a servant of the spirits to make to a chief who ranked below him.

"You on his side, boy?" Loke's growl came accompanied by the rasp of a knife from its sheath.

"I didn't know what the *talånd* was planning!" He clutched the bowl tight to his chest. "I didn't…" His hands shook.

"It's all right." I lifted a hand in reassurance. The apprentice came from a family who had always looked favorably on me. And he wasn't so much a boy. He'd reached his twentieth year at least, apprenticed since his fifteenth.

"You know what to do tonight?" I indicated the offering still clutched in his hands.

He glanced to the altar, jaw opening and shutting a few moments as the same helpless look I felt flitted across his face.

"I wasn't supposed to start helping with this until next midwinter. But—but I think I can." Mikkel nodded once, then again to himself.

"Then we'll muddle through this together." I managed a smile, and he relaxed a fraction.

Mikkel set the bowl down and ran a hand down his face. "Where were you?"

Loke moved back to the door to stand with Jens as Mikkel and I worked through where to restart the ceremony. He wasn't the only one to stumble through the supplications and motions of offerings and prayers, but mine came from distraction, thinking about Comran lying in the healer's lodge.

When it came time for me to mix a bit of my blood, I hesitated over the knife Mikkel extended to me. Quick strides announced Loke again. He wordlessly took the knife from the apprentice and set it aside.

"Is there any rule for the knife used?"

Mikkel wordlessly shook his head, not about to argue with the looming warrior.

Loke then held out his own knife to me. I took it and continued with the ceremony. The next time I requested protection from the spirits, I hesitated, then added in my own request for Comran, begging for him to have the strength to fight the poison.

*It should be me lying there in the lodge.*

Why had he jumped to protect me?

So it went, over and over until the candles dimmed and Mikkel went around to extinguish the torches, plunging the lodge into darkness for the last few minutes before the sunrise.

I waited, drained of energy and emotion, hoping that somewhere the spirits had deigned to hear me. That I hadn't doomed the tribe by standing in the lodge or daring to wear the chief's cloak.

Light crept over the window ledges, freed from their wraps by Mikkel. Dawn had come and, hopefully with it, another year of the spirits' favor. I sat back on my heels, letting my head bow low and pull at the tense muscles in my neck and back.

"Etran," Jens said softly.

I pushed to my feet and made my way over.

"Amund was just here. Said he pulled through."

Loke leaned against the doorframe, relief drooping through him. I braced a hand against the wall, exhaustion and the same mess of worry and panic for Comran pressing over me.

"Where is he?"

"Healer's lodge still."

"Thank you for staying," I told Loke. "You could have been at his side instead."

Loke tilted his head, regarding me with a thoughtful look. "He would have been here. I am honored I could stand in his place."

I swallowed against a parched throat. I'd never much spoken with the tall warrior, but he was nothing if not brutally honest with everyone. The need to leave the lodge and walk in the clear air came over me. They both stood aside as I left, Jens still trailing me as I headed for the river.

The rising sun began to wash the tops of the evergreens in gold as its light swept down the mountainside. Holes had been re-broken in the river's crust by someone already up and about to fetch water. I sank down to sit atop my cloak, and discovered I had another shadow.

Frea padded up, dropping to her stomach and stretching her head to me. A smile found my face and I scratched under her jaw. She whuffed and inched closer and closer until I stretched out my legs for her to place her giant head in my lap.

I leaned over, resting my forehead between her ears.

"What now?" I whispered.

She was the only one in the tribe who knew all my fears and doubts. She huffed a breath. Always so sure I could do no wrong.

All I wanted was to eat, to sleep, and maybe wake up and not be chief anymore. But I would have to plan for a trial of the traitors, decide what to do with them. Risk sentencing a *talånd* along with them. Keep holding my head high, even when half the tribe looked at me with hate or disregard.

"I don't think I can do it."

Frea pushed up, forcing me to straighten. She snuffled again, dabbing a cold nose against my cheek. She regarded me with amber eyes, stretching her nose forward again when I didn't move.

"I wish I had your faith in me." I rubbed along the side of her jaw. She closed her eyes, leaning into the touch, a wolfish grin showing at the corners of her mouth. I sighed and began to gain my feet.

Before I did anything, there was one thing I needed—wanted—to do.

Frea tagged along as I headed to the healer's lodge. Eska sprawled outside and Frea meandered over. They sniffed at one another cautiously until Eska thumped his tail against the ground and Frea batted at his head. Eska rolled over, jabbing paws at her.

They settled in to scuffle, and I passed around and pushed open the lodge door.

"Through here, Chief." The healer's apprentice beckoned me to a side door.

I followed and entered a smaller room filled with a few low cots. Comran slept in one, blankets tucked up around him, face still pale and drawn under the bits of hair clinging to his forehead. But the sight of his mother drew me up short.

Inger sat beside the cot, hand pressed on the edge, watching the rise and fall of his chest. Feeling intrusive, I made to leave. My boots scuffed and she turned to see me.

"Etran."

Somehow, I'd never understood why, Inger always had something like a smile for me. It didn't change now, even though she sat at her son's bedside, him laid low with a wound that should have been mine.

"I just—I just wanted to see how he was." My tongue twisted like a child's when admitting guilt.

She looked back to Comran, her smile softening.

"The healer said he will be all right with more rest. He has a strong heart." Her voice wavered and she blinked hard.

I slid away a step, not wanting to intrude further.

"How are you?" Inger regained control and looked at me much like a mother would.

"Me?" I stared, battling the thought that my mother would not have been so gracious should our places have been exchanged. If I had been wounded, instead of Comran.

"It was a long night for you as well." Inger turned to face me more. "And I remember…your father's first night in the lodge."

"I had to finish with the apprentice," I blurted. "I'm afraid I got it all wrong."

She nodded, biting at her lip before looking me directly in my eyes. "I think the heart matters more to the spirits than a perfect ceremony with words in careful places."

A bit of tension released from my shoulders. But that wasn't the only reason for my fear.

"I'm sorry he is the one here," I said.

"I think he would prefer to be here."

My gaze dropped to my boots again. Why? Why would he care about me? Why should she be so kind to me?

"I should go…" I stumbled back.

"Etran." Her voice halted me again. "I'll tell him you came when he wakes. If you want."

My jaw worked. I couldn't decide why it was important to me.

"I think it would mean something to him to hear it."

Like her son, truth shone bright in her eyes. I jerked a nod and fled from the lodge.

# TEN

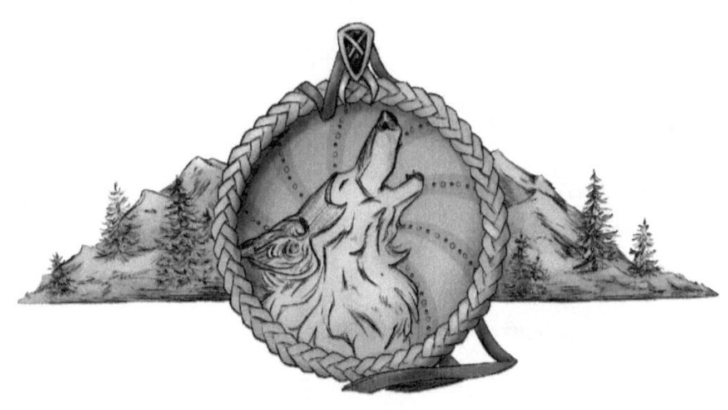

## COMRAN

Consciousness came in like a prodding spear. I tilted my head to the side, wincing against the effort of peeling my eyes open. I managed and found the earthy walls of the healer's lodge staring back.

A faint rustle brought my head rotating painfully to the other side. Everything ached and the bits of light flickering from candles pricked at my eyes. Mother sat at my side, slender fingers pausing in the midst of weaving a new basket.

"Comran!" She hastily set it aside and leaned over me, pressing a cool hand against my brow. I tried to speak, discovering a parched mouth. She slid her hand behind my head to help me drink from the beaker pressed to my lips.

"What happened?" The hoarse words ground from my raw throat. Bits and pieces flashed in my memory.

"The *talånd* tried to attack Etran last night, but you stopped him. The knife was poisoned."

Blankets pinned my arms, but I managed to move one enough to touch the bandage wrapped around my ribs. I didn't think it had been that deep of a wound.

"You're still fevered." She pressed a hand to my cheek and forehead again. "How are you feeling?"

"Awful."

Her smile came gentle, and she helped me get an elbow under me and sit up. Dizziness threatened, and I hunched over, shivering a little as the blankets fell away and chill rushed in against my bare skin. The battlewolf medallion slid on its leather cord, tugging at my neck as it fell back in place against my chest. I picked at a stray thread coming unwound from the blanket.

"And Etran?" I couldn't quite meet her gaze, unsure how she would feel about me asking.

"He was here just after dawn to ask after you."

My head jerked up. "He was?"

A soft smile teased her lips. "Yes. He finished the ceremony. I think Loke stayed with him."

"Hakkon and the others?" Now that it was done, I did not want to think of what might become of them.

Mother pressed her hands tight in her lap, lips flattening. "Etran called a council this midday to pass judgment."

My head flew up and I strained to search for any natural light outside. "What time is it?"

"Almost midday."

I pushed at the blankets, trying to free my legs, but finding a weakness lurking in my limbs.

"Comran…" She reached to stop me, hand pressing against my shoulder.

"I need to be there with him."

He needed his battlewolf alongside him to support his decision. I managed to get my feet off the edge of the cot. Mother sat there looking at me in helpless confusion.

"Comran."

I froze at the stern voice. Father stood in the door, watching me.

"You should be resting."

I shook my head. "If you were attacked by a tribesman and stood in judgment, where would you want your battlewolf?"

Father's face creased into a familiar frown, and I fought the urge to look away from the disappointment sure to follow.

He sighed. "Beside me." He gave me a small nod. "I'll get your armor."

My mother stood, shaking her head. "Then I will bring water for you to wash so you don't look so awful."

A chuckle rasped from me. "Thank you, Mother."

She leaned forward to plant a kiss atop my head as if I were still a child. "Stay put."

I promised obedience, not sure if I could stand by myself anyway. She returned a few minutes later with the healer's apprentice—a young girl who checked the bandage and frowned at me as if I didn't know getting up was a horribly poor decision.

Father arrived after I'd managed to splash some water over my face and chest, and through my hair. It was a more humiliating task to have my parents help me change into the clean clothes my father brought. Mother laced up my boots as he began to lay out my armor.

I took a breath, willing my body to stop shaking from the little effort expended thus far. Father watched with any thought hidden behind his stormy grey eyes. I finally reached for the bracers and managed to get them on my forearms before my mother laced them up, shaking her head the whole time.

The breastplate settled heavy over my shoulders and against my chest. Heavier even than the first time I'd put it on at fifteen years old. Father scooped up my sword and looked to me in question.

I tightened the last strap of the breastplate and extended a hand. He hauled me up to my feet, taking my weight as I listed into him. Mother was there in a moment, steadying me on my other side.

"You don't have to do this, Comran," she said.

Getting my feet under me, I released my grip on her and fished the medallion out to rest over the breastplate. Father belted my sword on, managing even with his curled fingers. He kept a hand on my shoulder as he looked me over again.

"Come."

I started for the lodge door, his hand under my arm. Mother hurried before us to open it. I leaned on the frame a moment before gathering the strength to keep walking. Weak winter sunlight scorched my eyes, and shivers raced down my arms. A weight descended on my shoulders and the thickness of fur cut the breeze but added another beat of hesitation to my steps.

The tribe gathered in the lodge circle, a more somber gathering than the announcement of chief mere days ago. Father stayed at my side as we made our way up to the head of the circle, where Etran sat facing off against a line of men kneeling in the snow.

Whispers dogged my steps, and I managed to stand straighter and with less help. Father fell back a half step the closer we got to the chief's seat.

Etran caught sight of us, his jaw dropping a moment before he regained control. Loke shook his head, rolling his eyes with a look of exasperation. A bench was brought out for me, thankfully before I reached Etran, so I could lower myself with bare grace onto it.

"Sorry I am late," I said.

"What are you doing here?" Etran leaned closer, the question hissing from him. "You look like death."

"By strange coincidence, that's what I feel like."

A reluctant smile spread over his face, and he shook his head.

I managed to make myself more comfortable on the bench, though each breath pulled at the wound, and fatigue from fighting the poison pummeled my body. Hakkon glared at me from his place on the ground. The *talånd* stared straight ahead, tight-lipped, after a startled glance at me.

"Surprised to see you here, *cousin*," Hakkon sneered.

"I told you before that if you moved on Etran, you moved on me," I said coldly. "I have no ties to you anymore."

His lip curled in contempt, and he turned his gaze away again.

"I've given each of you a choice," Etran said, his voice impressively even. "If you swear to me as your chief, then I will show mercy."

"And what of me?" the *talånd* spoke up, a hint of pleading in his voice.

Etran's jaw clenched. "You confirmed me in this position, then plotted to kill me and would have invoked the name of the spirits in doing so. You will bear the punishment without choice."

Horror and fear swept over the *talånd*, and he looked to me as if I would help. As if I hadn't almost died myself.

"You threatened the chief after I went to you for help in the matter." I impressed myself with how steady my own voice rang out, though shivers began to wrack my body. "You would have killed him. I will stand by his decision regarding you."

But my tongue could not quite be quelled. "And since I spent a rather miserable night because of you, I've even less sympathy."

Standing guard behind the men, Loke pressed his lips together and gave me a roll of the eyes.

"What would the punishment be, Chief?" One of the other men spoke quietly, eyes downcast.

I knew him from the wolfriders. He had a wife and two young girls. Another child on the way come spring.

But Etran didn't flinch. "What was your part in this?"

The warrior's shoulders hunched more. "I was to help keep the lodge clear of any who would help you."

"*Scata* job you did," I muttered.

Etran cleared his throat, and I felt a bit of sympathy for having to put up with me at his side through this.

"And you?" He turned to the next man in line.

All those except one said much the same. It seemed Hakkon wanted to be the one to finish either me or Etran. Whoever didn't fall to a blade or poison. Though it seemed he had not truly expected me to come through on my promise to defend Etran.

When he came to Hakkon, my cousin drew himself up, shrugging his shoulder against Jens's grip.

"I'm the only one not coward enough to stand up for what is right. You have no right to bear the chief's position, bastard."

He spat the word like a curse. Etran didn't flinch, though from my place at his side, I saw his fingers curl into the folds of his cloak.

"And you! You have forfeited any place of honor by throwing in with him." Hakkon's wrath fell to me.

"It's honor we're talking about now?" I braced myself to lean forward. "I gladly share blood with him when the traitorous likes of you stains what it is to be Greywolf. I'll wield the blade over you myself."

Maybe that way, his family could hate it less. There was a certain honor in someone close wielding a blade over you in judgment, rather than some nameless warrior.

"No." Etran stirred to life. "The wilds will choose."

Silence further deadened the lodge circle.

"Those who do not swear to me and pledge their swords and those of their children to me and my line, will walk out of this village and never come back. No greywolf and only one pack and a sword for each man. Never to return."

It was as good as death in the middle of winter. Especially without a greywolf to help share the burdens of the cold and hunting to stay alive. But maybe a little more merciful than the sword. There was at least a chance of survival.

Faced with that choice, all but Hakkon and the *talånd* chose to swear loyalty with the knowledge that any move they or their children made against the chief would lead to the same punishment.

The *talånd's* apprentice came forward from where he'd stood off to the side, huddled in a cloak and looking near sick with anxiety, and oversaw the swearing of the oaths.

The *talånd* stared at him the entire time, an odd bit of pride in his glance when Mikkel performed everything correctly.

Warriors went with Hakkon and the *talånd* to their lodges to fill packs. I stayed where I sat, not daring to move for fear I'd fall straight on my face into the snow. Another breeze ruffled the furred collar, sneaking down the back of my neck despite the cloak.

A tremor racked more forcefully, sending my stomach clenching.

"Are you all right?" Etran leaned over me, concern bright in his eyes.

"I'm grateful you'll at least be quick about these sorts of things. I might have misjudged when leaving a perfectly comfortable cot to come out here."

A grin cracked his face. "We'll have you tucked back in in no time."

I would have chuckled, but a grimace came out instead. I'd gone from cold to hot in an instant.

"How far do we have to walk?" I cocked an eyebrow. "I'm new to the idea of banishment."

Amusement vanished back into concern. "Just to the training fields. You do not have to come."

"I'm already grieving my mother enough as it is. Might as well finish."

Etran rubbed his forehead, as if unsure as to how to argue with me.

"He's always like this, Chief," Loke's wry voice cut in. "You might have made an error naming him to sit beside you."

"Is that a sign you'll miss the sunshine I bring to councils?" I grinned up at my swordbrother.

"No, I'll be glad to focus."

"Not with me leading them now."

"Chief, can I take his position with your blessing?" Loke turned to Etran.

I smiled to see an understanding growing between them. I was glad Loke had stayed with Etran for the rest of the ceremony.

The reappearance of Hakkon killed the lighthearted jibes. Loke helped me to my feet, and we watched in silence as his family bid him farewell. The *talånd* didn't have family other than his apprentice, and he rested a hand on the young man's shoulder, speaking softly to him, before a warrior nudged him to move.

I forced my feet into a step, grateful to Loke for staying at my side. A guard of five warriors followed us, all of whom I knew to support us both, their spears lowered to keep distance between them and the new outcasts.

Boots crunched the snow and murmurs followed us as the tribe filtered out through the lodgehouses to watch.

At the border of the training fields, where a scattered trail of pines stood guard between the village and the wide expanse of the valley, we came to a halt.

Hakkon didn't look back, but the *talånd* did once. His colorful cloak had been taken from him and he was left with one of plain design. It was strange to see him in it, after my whole life looking to him as the bridge between us and the spirits. He looked smaller, human, without it.

"Your lives are forfeit if you are seen within a half day's journey of this village," Etran declared. "No one may welcome you in camp or in lodge. Maybe in their mercy, the spirits will one day welcome you into the All-Father's lodge."

Hakkon pushed forward, striding off with sure steps. A moment more, and the *talånd* followed. We watched until they were small spots trudging south across the valley.

My knee buckled and Loke grabbed my elbow.

"Have you finished proving your own idiocy to yourself yet?"

"The day's still young, isn't it?"

"Come." He turned me and I made no resistance. My feet began to drag and the armor weighed more oppressive than before.

Etran stayed at my side as we walked back through the crowds. Many regarded Etran with respect, others undecided, and some still shook their heads with a bit of a sneer. And now, some of those discontented gazes turned on me.

It seemed we'd unite the tribe, one way or another.

We made it back to the lodge circle and I pulled to a halt, trying to drag a breath into my lungs. Loke hovered over me like a fretting mother over a newborn.

"Any chance you might carry me the rest of the way?" I

eyed the distance still to the healer's lodge.

"Sure your pride could take it?"

"I could swallow it in this one instance."

He tightened his grip on my elbow, and Etran did the same as I stumbled again. A bit of a wheeze strained in my lungs. I wasn't moving from that cot again until the world decided to stop spinning and stay one temperature.

"Do we need to stop by the hot springs on our way? You stink." Loke gently nudged his elbow into my side.

I rolled my eyes, wincing as my knees wobbled beneath me. "Next time I tread at the dark wood's border, I'll make sure to ask the spirits to send me back smelling like your mother's fragrance."

I snickered as Loke shoved my head down.

"Only because you're injured am I not sending you into the next drift."

Etran steadied me again, a faint twinkle of amusement in his eyes. Two figures waited as we neared the lodge. I wasn't sure which was more frightening—my mother's frown or the healer's. Either way, they didn't let up with their quiet judgment as Loke and Etran both helped me inside and I half-collapsed on the bed.

"Stop mothering!" I swatted at Loke's hand as he pressed a hand to my forehead.

"See if I care next time, then." He began yanking at the straps of my armor.

My mind was too fuzzy to be shocked anymore as Etran removed my bracers and set my sword carefully to the side.

Once done, they stepped back, leaving me shaking and gripping the edge of the cot with all my strength as the healer pushed in to poke and prod at me. Once I suffered through some vile concoction he forced down my throat, I lay back down to be smothered in more blankets. The healer raised a forefinger more threatening than spears leveled at me.

"Do not think about leaving this cot. The village can be in flames and under attack, but you will not move, understood?"

I stifled a yawn. "What if *this* lodge is on fire as well?"

The healer tossed a hand and Etran turned away, but not before a smirk betrayed him.

"Inger, he's your son!"

Mother turned a fondly exasperated look on me.

"I won't leave," I promised meekly, burrowing further under the blankets as another flash of cold struck.

"Best not," the healer muttered. My mother ushered Etran and Loke out, touching both their shoulders in thanks.

There was something I wanted to say to them, to Etran, but my eyes were already sliding closed.

# ELEVEN

## ETRAN

Comran's fever returned and lasted until the next sunset. For a few hours, the healer worried it was too much as he slipped into fevered dreams where nightmares chased. Loke, Amund, and I took turns checking on him. His mother never left his side, though she always found a welcome for me when I slipped in.

I never could stay long, the feeling of intrusion weighing heavy every time. It felt even worse when Father stepped through the door in the late afternoon. The healer had done away with the pouches filled with ice and snow to try to cut the heat raging in Comran's body and covered him again in blankets. He slept fitfully, with occasional flashes of lucidity before his eyes glazed again with fever.

Father stood by the cot, hand resting on his wife's shoulder as they watched their son. The pang I'd felt all my life sharpened. They were a true family, and I was an outsider, always on the fringes.

I would never see him like that with my own mother. He seemed to ignore all of us in public, but in privacy the love he felt for Inger showed clear. I'd just never seen it.

I left quietly and headed for the stream. A few minutes' walk from the village, the river never froze over a bundle of stones. Crossing them, I sat on the drooping spruce branch which had grown over the years to still hold me, even as I'd also grown.

Leaning forward on my knees, I stared down at my loosely-clasped hands. I'd survived twenty-three years without either of us showing anything toward each other. Why was it suddenly so hard to face the sight of Comran in the healer's lodge?

If Mother had a say, I should be glad, rejoicing even that the spirits might yet take him. But I'd never managed to feel the vitriol she directed at him and Inger.

"Etran?" A soft voice brought my head up.

Maren stood on the other side of the stream, hands tucked into the pockets of the furred vest laced over her dark green dress. I straightened, standing as she crossed the stream and accepted my hand to navigate the last rock slick with ice.

"Were you not going to tell me that Hakkon was planning to kill you?" She lightly punched my shoulder, but there was more than a little fear buried under her irritation.

"We agreed that it would be better to keep it to a few people."

It was a poor excuse, and we both knew it. Maren's brow arched and her glare didn't diminish.

"So I'm left to find out when I hear swords outside my lodge and rush to see what has happened in the dead of night?"

"I'm sorry." Perhaps I had been too eager to follow Comran's advice and keep the knowledge of the plot between the few of us.

Her frown faded and she tucked her hands into her side against the cold. "How are you?"

"I don't know."

Her dark eyebrow raised, and it drew a smile from me.

"The last few days haven't quite seemed real," I admitted.

Strange to think that it had only been a few days since my choosing as chief. So much had happened since.

"Did you really think he might not choose you?" Maren's brown eyes always held a wealth of belief in me. It frightened me some days.

I lifted a shoulder, afraid to voice my fears, even if it was just the two of us and she'd come to know me better than most.

"Why would he?"

"Because you're his son." Her voice held the flatness of irritation.

I turned my focus to the chuckling stream before it dove back under a sheet of ice. His son, yes, but born outside of a marriage bond. Looked down on by so many my entire life. Comran had to fight for the same affection from our father, but I'd had other battles to fight.

"Etran!" Her hand against my arm brought me back to face her. "You have to stop thinking so little of yourself. You are a good man, a strong warrior, and now chief."

"Then tell me how to shake twenty-three years of being looked down on as something less. As his…"

I couldn't say the word. I hated it.

Her hands gripped my upper arms, and she shook me a little.

"Then start with knowing that I believe in you. I always have. And so has Jens."

I couldn't deny it.

"Maybe it's remarkable to me that you do."

"I'll make you believe it one of these days." A faint laugh threaded her words.

"You would make the All-Father change his mind if you wanted," I said with the start of a smile.

Her grin grew. "Is that a challenge?"

I shook my head a little and reached to tap her hand in thanks. She released me and gave me a little more space.

"And what of Comran?"

"Are you so determined to make me admit things today?" I kept my voice light.

Her scowls were almost as fierce as an angry greywolf. "You're right. I should hold you feet first over a fire."

That earned her a roll of my eyes. It might be easier than she thought to get a confession from me. If she asked again, I was in danger of telling her everything.

"I know you've been going to check on him." The question was back.

"It's...I..."

"It is not such a bad thing to be concerned for him."

"Maybe I just wonder if he'd care as much in my place."

She tossed her head, sending a few of the small braids woven through her long hair tapping against her shoulders.

"Do you even know him?"

I tilted my head, fixing her this time with a raised eyebrow. Frustration gleamed bright in her eyes.

"What will it hurt to at least get to know him?"

Nothing.

"You made him battlewolf for spirits' sake. You'll have to."

"I know."

The admission stuck in my throat. She wanted me to show some bit of myself. Maybe if I did, it would restrain the fear.

"I—I've always wanted some sort of friendship with him, but it's never seemed to be. And he likely wants nothing to do with me, especially after I almost got him killed. But who wouldn't take the battlewolf position if it were offered?"

But Comran had turned right around and offered to protect me. *Had* protected me.

"I was given the position we both thought would be his."

Her gentle tug on my forearm stopped my rambling words. "He protected you. Do you think that means nothing?"

Part of me wanted to argue it was technically his duty as battle-wolf to defend the chief, but he could have just as easily sided with Hakkon and taken the tribe.

"He even said at the trial he gladly shares blood with you."

"When the alternative is Hakkon, a proven traitor." I edged backward but she didn't release me.

"Maybe you are thinking too much and should do something, instead of trying to out-think it." She gave my hands a gentle shake.

I gathered a deep breath. "What is the sense in that?"

Her lips pursed to hide the smile. "Come. I'm getting colder, and you can walk with me back to the village."

And pass right by the healer's lodge if I was not mistaken. But I let her guide the way back across the rocks and retrace steps back down the worn path which would be filled in again overnight by the snowstorm blowing in from the north side of the valley.

The sun's weak light had already begun to disappear behind the western hills and the oncoming clouds raced to smother the last of it.

Maren slowed her steps by the healer's lodge, pushing me in its direction. I frowned. The apology in her smile came half-hearted. The door swung open and Amund stepped out. He came up short when he saw me and jogged the few steps over.

"Chief!"

Alertness and concern shot through me. But before I could work out a question, his face burst into a smile.

"The fever broke, and the healer got some broth down him."

A breath of relief jerked from me. "How is he?"

"Tired and sleeping now. But the healer says on the mend."

"Good." Even that word almost caught in my throat.

"Now we can finally rest easy." Amund clapped me on the shoulder before spinning on his heel and heading up into the lodge circle.

I stared after him. Comran's friends had been open with me in the last few days, taking their lead from him perhaps. Yet another strange thing. But he'd thrown himself right into working with Jens.

While we'd all trained together as warriors, there were still men who did not cross paths much outside the training fields, and so it had been with the friends we'd each gathered. Comran had reached across the gap with little effort.

Maybe I could do the same.

# TWELVE

## ETRAN

Despite my resolution, it was still another full day before I could bring myself to darken the lodge door. And I will admit I waited until Inger had left.

Knocking once, I pushed in. Candlelight flickered across the walls draped with weavings of the spirits and prayer runes. A larger fire burned on the hearth, bringing welcome heat even from my short walk across the lodge circle.

Comran sat up on the cot, back pressed against the wall and propped up with pillows. The reddish cast of the fire still did not hide the paleness in his face.

"How are you?" I tucked my hands in the folds of my cloak so they didn't wave uselessly about.

His fingers ran across the smooth weaving of the blankets gathered around his waist. "They say I have nothing to worry about except gaining my strength back."

I edged a step closer, trying to physically bridge the gap between us. It still felt like intruding.

"That doesn't sound like much of an answer."

He half-smiled. "Every muscle aches, and I can barely feed

myself. Mother has been trying to get me to admit my recklessness, but…"

I stared at him. The poison had hollowed him out, leaving dark
circles under his eyes and a weariness in the slant of his shoulders.

"Why did you do it?" I asked. "In the lodge?"

I needed to know. Somehow, it still didn't make sense.

"The purpose of the plan was to protect you, wasn't it?" A
faint quirk appeared at the side of his mouth.

I shook my head. "I know. But you could have let me take the
knife. In the ceremony or a fight—no one would have questioned
it. It could have been me lying here waiting for the spirits to decide."

"They spared me. You think they wouldn't have done the same
for you?" A puzzled crease furrowed between his eyes.

I shifted, suddenly restless on the cliff's edge of a confession.
"Sometimes I think they won't hear me. Because of what I am."

That fear had never been spoken aloud to anyone. Another
reason I feared being chief. How was I to lead if the spirits ignored
me? And it would only be as the days progressed that I would
know if they truly favored me.

But understanding shone in Comran's face. As if he knew the
same struggle.

"I did it because you are a good man. You'll make a strong
chief. And that's what we need."

So much lingered in his unspoken words. He didn't think he
was strong enough, good enough, to lead. In that moment, I
found that we were more alike than I had known.

"Thank you."

He nodded, his look revealing that he'd shared his own secret
with me. I would keep it, as he kept mine.

"I heard you carried me here." Comran clenched the blanket,
the unspoken question hanging in the air. Caution filled his glance,

just as unsure where we stood. A brief bit of hope flickered in my chest.

"I wanted to make sure you were all right." My tongue tried to twist and stumble.

"Just doing the right thing?" A faint hint of bitterness crept through, and his jaw worked as if he regretted the taste of them.

But I couldn't dredge up any of the same, not when it still confused me how panicked I'd been to see him fall.

"It's a stressful task, picking a battlewolf. I'd rather not do it again."

He paused, then gave a huffing laugh. My stance eased a little.

"How has it been since the trial?" Comran glanced up.

I froze. There was a friendliness there, but not enough for me to describe the pointed words thrown my way, frosty glances in the hours when it seemed possible Comran might not make it, as if the tribe blamed me for it. The number of times *"bastard"* had dogged my steps, more than ever, in the last few days.

"Fine."

Comran barely shifted, but I was caught in his somber stare and panic hit me that his grey eyes might see straight through me, the way only Father's could.

"Well." He spoke abruptly, bringing me back. "I will see how long the healer can last with me here, and then maybe we can get back to normal."

I offered a slight smile. "Normal?"

"Maybe with fewer murder attempts."

A chuckle pushed its way out. "That would be preferable."

His grin swerved across his face, followed quickly by a yawn.

"I'll let you rest." Part of me was torn, hoping maybe that we could keep this odd easiness between us, the other half shouting to retreat and not trust it.

He eased down against the pillows, a faint grimace twisting his face. But he settled before I could step over to help.

"Etran." He stopped me as I made to leave. "Loke said you prayed for me in the lodge. I think the spirits hear you."

Another knot of pressure eased in my chest. I gave a wordless nod and pushed out of the lodge.

# Thirteen

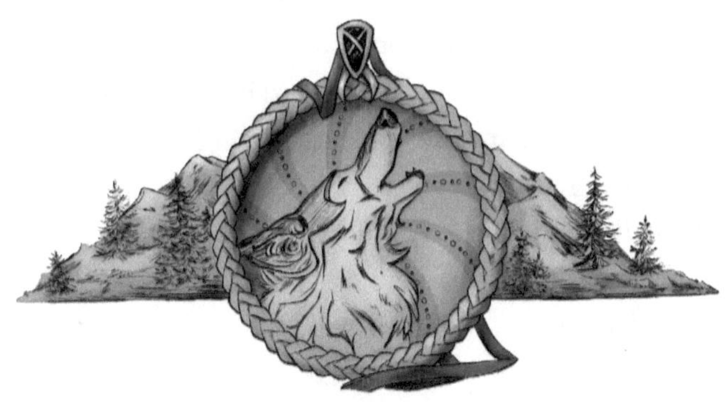

## Comran

Three long days later, I walked out of the lodge on my own two feet. Exhaustion still lingered just out of reach, but the healer had stopped fretting over me—or had finally gotten enough of my never-ceasing remarks and had decided to cast me out and watch me take my chances.

Eska was first to greet me, very nearly pouncing on me and sending me to the ground. He pushed into my chest, tongue slobbering over my cheek, whining and nosing at my chest and face.

"I am fine, you daft animal." I tried to push him away, but he circled me, sniffing harder at my chest where a bandage still lingered under my shirt and fur-lined tunic.

"He hasn't left the lodge since you fell." Loke laughed, and some of his lingering concern vanished with the sound.

Eska growled low in his throat, pushing his side against my shoulder, turning wide amber eyes to me in question.

"We'll run soon enough," I promised. First, I had to figure out how I'd gotten so winded by just standing there.

"The warriors will be glad to see you up." Loke clapped me on the shoulder, and I staggered forward a step. He frowned, the concern returning. Usually I could withstand his swipes with more of the grace of a mountain pine before a blizzard.

"I am fine," I said almost irritably. Not even the yellow fever as a child had drained me this much.

He offered a smile, but still hovered close as I began to walk across the lodge circle. My name was called by many, expressing happiness for my recovery. But I didn't miss the looks others shot me. Uncertainty, and anger. It was strange to see it in faces that had once shown support for me.

The healer had announced that the *talånd* had poisoned the blade, but maybe some still saw it as the spirits trying to express their will through the *talånd*. And now he was gone, and I stood as the man who'd seen him cast out. And defended Etran.

It didn't bother me so much among some men and women. It would be a different song among the warriors, where I might have to defend my position with the sword or spear. And the way my breath already ran ragged from walking half the circle, it might be another few moons before I could manage it.

"What's troubling you?" Loke shot me a sideways glance.

"Is it that obvious?"

"Your face is darker than a stormcloud."

Eska rumbled at my side, pushing up against me. I barely managed to stand my ground against it.

"I'd do it all again, but I fear I made both our positions harder by my actions in the lodge."

A huff broke from Loke. "Near a full counting later and you're just now asking that question?"

I shoved his shoulder. "How's Etran been managing?"

After his sudden confession, he had been by to visit once. It left more confusion among my already swirling thoughts.

"Most still aren't happy. But it is winter and there's not much to keep them occupied. Once he has his first true challenge, I think it will settle many."

My eyebrow raised. "Having a *talånd* and warrior plot your death isn't a challenge?"

Loke waved a hand dismissively. "An inconvenience."

"I think I need to find out what you call a challenge."

"Not you, spirits stay assured."

I had to jump a half step to get an arm around his neck and yank him down to my level. His laugh rang out again as he easily removed my hold.

"Comran." Stian joined us. He had a habit of appearing when not wanted and disappearing when someone needed something. "Your father wanted to see you."

My mirth vanished. Loke sobered just as fast. Eska nudged his head under my arm. I absently rubbed the side of his broad muzzle along the dark stripe.

"Where is he?" My voice had already taken on the even cadence I tried hard to maintain around Father.

"Home."

Loke wordlessly stayed at my side as we turned our feet to the lodge. I gripped the carved door frame to assist myself up the two steps into the large common room which made up most of the lodge. Mother saw me and came to press my shoulder with a smile, nodding at the back rooms.

Brushing the wolf's head medallion settled against my chest for strength, I made my way there. A thick deerskin hung between the main lodge and the narrow hall leading to the smaller rooms built on to shelter married couples, or to give a moment of privacy for a conversation.

Father sat in a smaller room filled with fur-covered benches and a small bundle of heated stones. Perfect for smaller gatherings and stories in the dead of winter.

"Comran." He pointed to the bench across the stones from him.

I took it, trying not to let slip how relieved I was to be sitting already. He studied me and I braced myself against the scrutiny, only to find with some surprise that I saw concern most clearly.

"How are you?" he asked.

My fingers tightened in the folds of my cloak.

"Well enough."

Conversation with my father never started with questions about my health. Even when I'd come back with a few bandages from a border skirmish.

"Good. I worried for you." Sincerity filled his voice, and I studied him just as hard.

"You did?"

He sat back a little. "Is that so hard to believe?"

A scoff betrayed me before I could hold it in. "Perhaps, when I've never much seen it these past years."

Father stared down at his hands, scraping a thumb against his palm. "Something your brother told me not long ago."

I wondered when I'd stopped flinching at the word.

"Maybe he had a point."

"I'm sorry."

I blinked. Maybe I *had* died, and this was some strange vision before I entered the All-Father's lodge.

A faint twitch of humor moved his lips. "Maybe that is a strange thing to hear from me. But I have seen that pulling away from both of you was wrong. But I didn't know how to change it years ago."

I couldn't do more than stare at him. It seemed a simple fix to me.

"And you think to change it now?" It burst from me. "We could have stopped some of this if we'd been raised together, instead of held up against one another. We would have learned better how to stand with each other."

Father regarded me with his frustrating grey eyes. The ones that saw so much and withheld more.

"I was never able to see him as a brother, even when that's all I wanted."

I pushed to my feet, unable to stay a moment longer. I might just risk taking Eska out.

"Comran." Father stopped me at the door. My shoulders tensed as I looked back over my shoulder.

"The way you stood for him, protected him…I was proud to see it."

I shook my head. "I didn't do it for you."

And I left, fighting a strange burning in my eyes. Eska didn't complain when I made it to the stables and grabbed his bridle. The saddle seemed too heavy, so I fixed the bridle, and he sank to his stomach to allow me to climb on.

To the dark woods with my duties, and possibly even my father. Eska padded forward, easing up to a gentle trot, feeling how I clung to his fur with one hand and poorly steered with the other.

In the end, we didn't go far. Beyond the village and to the lookout's peak—a taller spire of rock carved with handholds to allow warriors to climb it and see over the trees to the village and the valley beyond.

I slid from Eska's back and he settled to the ground so I could sit against him, drawing my cloak tight against the cold.

*What is he thinking?* Pooling anger began to rise up to replace the shock. It didn't make more sense the hundreds of times I replayed his words over and over. Did he think it would be so easy to set aside the way he had dealt with me, with us, over the years? Maybe for him, but not for me.

Eska's low rumble against my back drew me out of my thoughts. He changed the pitch of his next growl slightly higher to greet a packmate. Even seeing Etran standing there with Frea didn't seem shocking after all that had just happened.

"Father talked to you?" He slid the loose rein leathers through his hands.

I leaned my head back against Eska. "You've already heard what he tried to say?"

He nodded, searching off through the trees for something. Maybe understanding of what Father was thinking.

"What did you tell him?"

"Besides staring in shock at him trying to care?" My bitterness seeped out, and it felt strange letting him see it.

Frea sank down to her haunches and Etran kept running the leathers in his hands.

"I almost wanted to forgive him," he admitted. "But there are many things that others want me to remember, and…" His knuckles turned white around the reins and Frea huffed gently. He shook himself but I caught the twist at his mouth hiding the rest of his words.

"I was left to weather many things by myself," he finally said.

Once I might have relished a crack in his mask, but not now. Not when I thought I might finally understand.

"It's not your fault you were born." Certainty welled with the thought. "What came between you and me and what happened with the tribe was not *our* fault. Not entirely."

The way he stared down at his hands made him look like Father. But it was a different look in his green eyes when he glanced back to me. Not quite belief, but an attempt at it.

I did not hate him for being born. Maybe I resented him still, a little, for taking some of the attention from me and my birthright, but…I had made my choice, and it was getting a little easier with every day to be at peace with it.

"I'm sorry I never tried to reach out," I said.

"Going against those around you is no easy thing." He reached to scratch under Frea's jaw. It was said with a bit of dismissiveness, as if he'd rehearsed something like it a hundred times. But it still didn't make it right.

I tipped my head back against Eska's side and stared at the bits of blue sky peeking through the clouds. A sudden smirk tugged my mouth.

"I thought I'd died for certain hearing him trying to apologize."

A snort of laughter came from him, and I glanced to see him shaking his head. Chill rushed in with a new breeze threading through the pines from the north. I shivered and drew my cloak even tighter. Eska rumbled in concern, craning his head around to nose at my shoulder.

"Are you sure you might not yet after coming out here?" Etran tugged his furs tighter around his neck and scowled at the sky.

"Maybe I'll try to stay confined to the healer's lodge and continue to avoid all my new responsibility."

"Doesn't sound so bad." He clicked and Frea rose from the snow, shaking herself free of clinging flakes. "Though if I had known I'd be picking the laziest battlewolf in the history of the tribe, I might have considered different."

I grinned and used Eska's side to lever myself upright.

"You should have picked Loke. Very duty-bound, that one is."

"And quieter." He extended a hand to help me to my feet, as I couldn't quite manage it with just my wolf's help.

"Another poor strategy on your part. You're stuck with me now, one way or another."

"Maybe." He raised an eyebrow. "You don't quite look well enough yet."

I waved him off, trying not to grimace as I reached for Eska's reins. "Nothing a few more days won't fix."

Eska stayed down as I mounted again. Etran and I rode side-by-side back to the village, falling into an almost comfortable silence until the stables. We'd barely reined in before someone came to find Etran, calling him to settle a dispute as chief.

"Maybe I'll keep taking my time." I grinned down from Eska as Etran dismounted with something like a sigh.

He rolled his eyes and I laughed, sliding down carefully from Eska. We put up the bridles, and Etran paused at the door as I took longer to make my way back out. His eyebrow arched as if winning some argument, and my hand formed a rude gesture. A smirk twitched his lips and he said nothing as he stayed at my side.

"If I didn't know better, I'd think you were making sure I didn't do anything reckless."

Etran shook his head and the grin flickered again. "You act like that's such a surprising thing."

I chuckled. "Is Loke making you?"

He lifted a shoulder. "I told you, it's too much effort naming a new battlewolf now."

"Ah, wouldn't want to inconvenience you." I nodded seriously. It almost seemed the wrong thing to say, but he only paused a moment before speaking.

"That's considerate of you."

Snow crunched under our boots. Eska's nose jostled my arm. I absently scratched under his jaw as we walked.

"How has it been the last few days?"

"Nothing out of the ordinary."

The lightness matched mine, but I was starting to see more of him than I ever had cared to see before. And there was a wealth of things unsaid in him. I nodded uncertainly, pretending that maybe I believed him. He said nothing to contradict, and so we kept walking.

Stares followed us as we moved across the lodge circle. Murmurs and pointed words were easier to hear, and this time I caught the biting sneer of "bastard" as we walked past a small group of men and women.

Etran's jaw clenched but he kept walking. My feet paused only a moment to look back at the tribespeople, where some found something else to look at immediately and the rest met my glance with a look daring me to act.

I paused long enough to let them know I was thinking on it, and then caught up to Etran where he still walked without faltering.

Once out of sight, I caught at his arm. "Etran…"

"What?" He whirled on me, a rawness in his eyes that sent me leaning back. "You think that is something new? Something that I have only just now heard?"

"I…"

"You what?" He jerked a step away from me. "I don't want pity or anything from you. You think it was easy for me all those years in your shadow?"

Gone was the almost friendliness between us. Anger washed away the confusing mess of things I felt.

"My shadow? It was painfully clear that he favored you over me our entire lives!"

Etran's head jerked in a sharp nod. "Not just him. The entire tribe." His hand cut back toward the lodge circle. "My *entire* life held up against Comran, the *true* son of the chief. The one who could do no wrong."

A breath jolted from him as I stared. His hands eased from fists and calm fell back over him. Another way he was so like Father, able to master emotions in seconds.

"We both had our own battles, Comran. But don't tell me how to fight mine. I have never had the luxury of a quick temper or pride."

The words stung, followed up with the roiling mess of confusion at how I felt watching him walk away, shoulders now slumped a little.

I scraped a hand over my face, a harsh breath escaping. It was hard to admit that I did not like the way the word changed him. Or how uncomfortable it made me to hear it. Or that I was only just now aware of it.

The truth haunted me through the rest of the day, through a frosty dinner beside my father, and then back outside into the cold dusk.

Eska came to rest his head in my lap when I took a seat on the snow-covered bench beside the lodge. A few bright stars had begun to peek through the sky veil, bolder in the crisp nights when the night spirit kept the darkness longer before surrendering control back to day.

A few tribesmen were still out and about, walking across the lodge on the paths cut through the mud-covered snow. Torches flickered around the circle, waiting to be extinguished by the night guards. Wolves settled down around lodges, grouping closer together to share warmth among themselves.

The clack of the lodge door sent me glancing up to see Mother coming to join me. She wrapped her fur-lined cloak tighter around her and sat. Eska's tail thumped the ground as he turned soulful eyes on her.

She freed a gloved hand from her wraps and extended a piece of dried elk jerky. His body jarred my leg as he snapped it up.

"Mother," I *tskd*. "You'll spoil him."

"There is a saying, my dearest, about the salmon and the trout arguing if the river is wet."

I chuckled and leaned my head against the wall, watching my breath puff in front of me and waiting for her to say what she'd come to say.

"So what would you say to me if I told you I am proud of the stand you took?"

Tilting my head, I fixed her with a wry look. A quick smile flitted, but there was still the question in her eyes. I turned away from it, focusing on burying my hands in Eska's fur to keep them warmer.

"Are you truly?"

The cold air whisked the burst of her sigh away.

"At first, I wanted to hate him, even though I'd been some of the reason for him. But that started to change almost ten years ago now, when I saw firsthand what he dealt with." She shook her head. "And he took it in silence." Her hand squeezed my forearm. "And I knew you would not do the same."

I shook my head, agreeing. My temper would not have served me as well if our places had been changed.

"I did not know—or maybe just did not care to know—what he faces," I admitted softly.

It still sat uncomfortable with me. As did the thought that I still wanted to acknowledge that Father was proud of me, even though it was one of a few times I'd done something without thinking of him.

"And?" she gently prompted.

"And…" Eska tilted his head up to me when I stopped scratching behind his ear. "And I don't know how to feel that he does. We both spent so long intent on ignoring the other, but part of me is hoping maybe there's a chance we could be brothers."

My voice fell to near a whisper, still afraid of hurting her. But she tapped my arm again and I raised my head to see a sad smile.

"I am glad to hear it," she said. "I've hoped for years that you both might find a way to work together. You balance each other and will lead this tribe well."

I pushed Eska away to lean my elbows down on my knees. But he came right back and tried to wedge his nose between my arms to rest his head on my lap again.

"It seems plenty don't think that way."

"Then what do you think of your father?"

Eska grumbled as I pushed up to slouch back against the lodge. "He's had twenty-three years to show some sort of affection or pride to me—to both of us—and *now* he wants to?" My head jerked sharply. "I do not think I can forgive that."

Her hand found my forearm again. "I understand."

"Do you?" It snapped more bitter than a winter wind.

"Comran."

"I'm sorry. I'm…" I leaned back to my knees again, avoiding her gaze.

Her arm circled my shoulders, and I sank into her half-hug.

"I have no excuse for him," she said. "I did not want it for you, for either of you, how he decided to raise you. But do not tell me I did not see or know how hard it was for you."

She pressed a kiss to the side of my head, and I finally looked at her. The guttering torch caught the watery glint of her eyes.

"I am proud of you, and the man you became. You make a good battlewolf, and I think you will make a good brother, too."

"Thank you." I pushed the words past the tightness in my chest.

Mother stood, leaning down once more to kiss the top of my head as if I were a young child. "Do not stay out much longer."

"I won't," I promised. The cold deepened with the fading light, and finally I stood. Eska looked to me as I shook snow from my cloak.

"You know I would," I told him, more than happy to let him come inside the lodge if it were allowed. He grumbled and followed me to the door anyway. I nudged him away and he padded off to join the other wolves curled up on the sheltered side of the lodge.

As I reached for the latch, a pang struck deep into my side, sending me flinching around it. A bandage still wrapped my chest, but the healer had predicted it would come off soon. Maybe I had irritated it with the short ride that afternoon.

It did not come again, and I cautiously went inside, finding my sleeping place on the benches on the edges of the hall. My sword I kept with me, wrapped in the furs and blankets.

Sleep found me long after the rest of the lodge, kept awake by thoughts of Etran and our father. But I latched onto my anger at the way some chose to disrespect Etran still as chief. That I could change. And it would start with the warriors.

# FOURTEEN

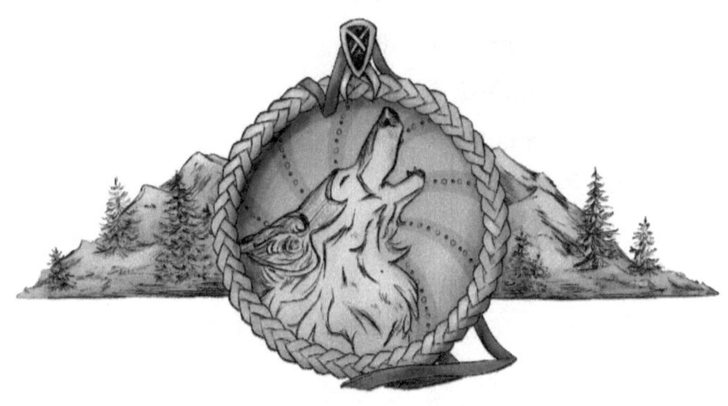

## COMRAN

Moving from my blankets the next morning felt like crawling out of a mud pit. I scraped grit from my eyes with clumsy fingers. Pulling on a new shirt and overtunic, I pushed up to standing.

"You all right, Comran?" A warrior paused beside me, pulling on his own tunic.

"I'm fine." Exhaustion pressed heavy around me. "Must not have slept well last night."

"Might still be recovering." He nodded, buckling on his sword. "Still don't look quite yourself, if you don't mind me saying."

My hand fumbled a little picking up my sword belt and buckling it on. I'd felt fatigued since leaving the healer's lodge the day before, but not quite like this.

"See you on the training grounds, Battlewolf." He tapped his chest. I returned the gesture, still puzzling out the change. I didn't think I'd overtaxed myself the day before.

The woman who'd held charge over the cook fires since before I was born handed me my customary breakfast, smoked bison sausage wrapped in flatbread and toasted over the fire. I very rarely sat at the table to eat the morning meal with the rest of the lodge.

"You all right, Battlewolf?" She'd not stopped proudly declaring my title to me since my choosing.

"Better now." I lifted the meal.

Her light laugh followed me away from the cookfires. I stepped outside, the rush of cold enough to finish waking me up. Eska waited for his customary portion I tore from breakfast before we headed to meet Loke.

"You look terrible." Loke frowned at me over crossed arms.

"You're the third person to tell me that this morning," I mumbled around a bite of flatbread.

"Well, it's true."

I waved my half-eaten breakfast in warning as he made to reach for me. "Are we training or not?"

"Aye. Amund is already waiting. You took your sweet time this morning."

Eska hop-skipped beside me as we made our way to the training grounds. Amund leaned against the stables, spear resting beside him. He scanned me from head to toe and opened his mouth.

"He's more touchy than normal about his looks this morning." Loke spoke first.

I shoved the rest of breakfast in my mouth and glared. Amund raised his hands, but I caught the cadence of a question as I kept walking out to the open field.

Loke's younger brother jogged to meet us.

"Battlewolf." Kjell wore the cheeky grin of a little brother poking fun at new responsibilities.

"Here to finally learn something?" I asked.

"Thought I would just petition you directly to let me into the packs early." He backed away in front of me.

Loke scoffed. "You can barely hold a spear." It came with the teasing mockery of an older brother. Kjell's face twisted in scoffing retort.

He and Loke fell to feinting and jabbing at one another, until Loke finally caught him and spun him to drape an arm over his shoulders.

"So, Comran…" Kjell raised his eyebrow at me from Loke's other side.

"Soon enough, Kjell," I assured with a chuckle.

Loke scrubbed his hand through Kjell's hair to a squawk of irritation. Kjell darted away, scowling.

Loke shooed him off. "Go train, or I'll report you to your pack leader."

We kept our steady way onto the training grounds, and my breath stayed frustratingly short. Loke and Amund exchanged a glance with each other that I ignored. Their intended nagging was cut off by the arrival of Jens. He tipped his spear against his shoulder and fell in with us after a nod to me.

"First day leading the training." Loke stretched his arms overhead.

I tugged at the collar of my breastplate, the action sending the battlewolf medallion tapping against my chest.

"I've led training before."

I needed the reminder just as much. With everything that had happened with Etran and the threats, I hadn't yet truly stood in front of the warriors as the battlewolf.

"As a pack leader," Amund unhelpfully said, and raised his hands in apology when I glared at him.

"I haven't," Jens broke in, and his hand shifted around his

spear. I had held a position as a pack leader for at least a turning, Loke had filled in once, but Jens had not yet.

"It is not so hard." I shrugged. "Just stand there and look self-important."

"Something Comran does well." Amund snickered.

I slammed a shoulder into him, but Jens laughed and eased a fraction.

"Just do what you know, Jens. I wouldn't have named you *rokr* if you couldn't manage it."

He tipped a nod and relaxed again. Most riders greeted us as we continued onto the fields. But some stayed silent, others glared or hid their thoughts behind impassive faces. A divide was still clear, though this time it was just me who caused it.

A new feeling.

Amund moved off to go join his pack who slowly arrived on the field. Loke began a sweep among the warrior pairs training with spears. I waved Jens to join me, and I kept a slow pace toward a pack divided out to work with blunted swords.

Jens did not comment on my sedate pace, but perhaps he didn't know me well enough yet. The pack leader looked up and made no effort to hide his scowl.

"Need something, Battlewolf?" He made the title sound more like a curse.

My fingers curled into a fist at my side. "Making some rounds, Kay, as I have been somewhat preoccupied this last counting."

Kay sneered a little. "Aye, too busy banishing good wolfriders and protecting that bastard."

"The *chief* has a name," I snapped. "And you would do well to remember it."

"Should I?" He crossed his arms.

My greatest instinct was to convince Kay with a fist, but another heartbeat only faintly calmed that impulse. I was battlewolf now. My heart stammered with the next thought that if I failed this test, then I would fail the position entirely.

"Or maybe you've forgotten it, along with the oath you swore to him. Something not taken lightly by me or the spirits."

Movement came from some of the wolfriders, looking to one another. One of the younger warriors looked grimly pleased as he glared at Kay's back.

Kay opened his mouth, but I pushed on. "You clearly have some sort of intelligence, Kay, as I did not see you in the line of warriors on trial. Do not make me question your capabilities any further."

And I strode away, the anger raging against my chest for a moment before beginning to calm. Boots crunched up to walk beside me.

"That was interesting," Jens said.

"It was." I hooked one hand over the collar of my breastplate, the other still bunched in a fist, as we took a wider path to get to the next pack.

"It will not be the last time."

"I hadn't thought of that," I snapped, then sucked in a breath. Jens regarded me with one eyebrow raised.

"I am sorry."

He shrugged. "Nothing more than what I've already heard from Etran."

I worked my hand out of the fist. "And how is he handling it?"

The quick bitterness rose up again, its tang coating my heart before I willed it away. We were not competing anymore, and we had vowed to work together. But years were hard to forget no matter what words had passed between us.

The look Jens turned on me next was one of slight scorn and

disbelief. "You think this is the first time he has been challenged like this?"

Bitterness gave way to the uncomfortable shame that I had no idea how often he'd endured the hate. Jens turned away and we walked in silence for a few steps.

"I am sorry if I spoke out of turn," he said.

"No." My jaw shifted. "No. You did not."

I halted and Jens pivoted to look at me in faint concern that grew the longer I paused.

"I do not know you well, Jens, but I know you've stood by Etran for many years. It seems that I do not know him at all."

Jens waited in silence, crossing his arms.

"I…" A faint laugh huffed from me. "It seems I would like to, and standing closer to him since the choosing has opened my eyes to things. Things that do not sit right with me."

The *rokr* nodded, understanding giving way to some threads of respect.

"Good," he said. "I admit I thought poorly of you for keeping your distance these years."

My hand tightened over the collar of my breastplate. "I could give excuses, but some of the blame lies with me." Perhaps more than I wanted to admit. "But I'd be grateful if you would let me know of any challenges that come his way."

His expression fell back to something I couldn't quite make out. "Why?"

The protectiveness came through clear in his voice.

"I think I can guess correctly that he wouldn't tell anyone."

Jens allowed it with a wry tilt of the head. The toe of my boot dug through the snow, unearthing a bit of dead grass. Spirits, why was this so hard for me to admit?

"And I would like to make things easier—"

"He doesn't need pity." A snap edged Jens's voice.

"It's not pity." My anger reared up. "Maybe there was a chance for the two of us, but it got stolen long ago. Maybe this is my way of making some things right."

A light breeze stole some of the heat from me and left me with a quick shiver. Jens didn't notice, still intent on staring at me, weighing my words. Finally, he nodded.

"He needs more friends, but won't let himself."

The "why" almost left my tongue, but the answer slammed in quicker. Jens gave a sad smile.

"Why would you try if you think you know the answer?"

A faint curse escaped.

"I will tell you when I hear something," Jens said. I gave a quick nod of thanks.

"It hasn't been easy these years by his side," the warrior continued. "But I'm glad to see you trying. I think it will be good for him to have someone else. He is not so aloof as he seems."

We continued walking in silence until we reached the next pack. Amund saluted with a grin and the rest of the warriors and the pack leader offered the same to both me and Jens. Of the three other packs on the training grounds, one gave the same frosty reception as Kay's, but no outright challenge.

I passed on from them and went to the trainees. I let Jens take lead in ushering them through forms, pacing through and making corrections as they went. Some cast wide-eyed glances to me, as if they'd never seen me walk the training grounds or take my fair share of bruises during sparring.

Finally, I retreated a little and leaned against Eska when he padded up beside me. The world tipped a moment before I shook my head and it corrected. The same twinge as the night before hit my side, harder this time, and I leaned closer to Eska. He growled and nosed my arm. I reassured him with a pat, though I didn't feel the same confidence.

*Maybe it just needs more time to heal.*

His growl turned threatening and I straightened to see Kay leading his pack by. The look he gave me promised that he was not quelled by my words. There would be a challenge from him yet.

# FIFTEEN

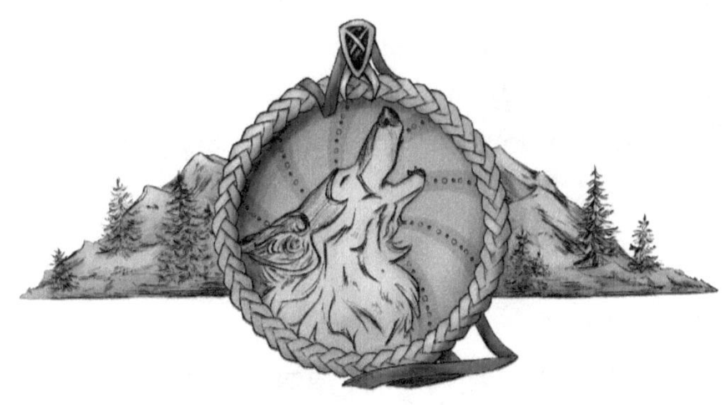

## COMRAN

Two days later, I stood on the training field, hand hooked into the collar of my breastplate, the other propping a spear against the ground as I stared out at the valley. Waiting for the first group of warriors to arrive for training. Loke came to stand beside me.

"Out with it," I sighed after a few moments of silence.

He lifted a shoulder. "You have that look like I should maybe be worried recklessness will follow."

The corner of my mouth tipped up. He knew me well.

"It's Etran. Standing with him these last countings, I've heard and seen more than I have in the past."

My throat tightened, remembering the look in his face days ago when we'd heard the word. The spear dug a hole through the snow under my force. I'd been avoiding him despite my words to Jens.

But when I didn't speak again, Loke did.

"Trying to right something?"

The spear worried the hole wider. "Maybe I care more than I thought I might. Maybe I ignored too much…" I swallowed hard. "I told him what was or wasn't between us was not entirely our fault. But it seems we both wanted to be brothers our entire lives, and did not feel we could. Some fault lies with me, too."

Loke did not turn his somber gaze from the valley in front of us, waiting for me to finish.

"I don't know." I shook my head. "Maybe whatever I do is too little, too late."

"Maybe a little compared to just saving his life over a counting ago."

A roll of my eyes, and he sobered again. "I do not think it is so little a thing to start sharing someone's battles."

I turned to face the warriors coming over the snowy field toward us and hoped Etran might see it the same way.

Three packs had come out to train under the rare sight of the winter sun. Loke and I made our way over. Like Birgir, I wasn't much needed to help train the experienced packs. That duty came with the younger men and women who would be out in the afternoon.

It was Jens's old pack, one he might ride with to battle should it find us, though he now held a higher position than the pack leader. A young woman stood with the warriors, a little off to the side.

"Maren," Jens reminded me. She wore hair bound back in warrior braids and handled a spear with ease.

"Battlewolf." She tipped a nod which I returned. I'd seen her often enough on the grounds, training with those a turning younger than Etran and I. But she did not have warrior cords at her wrist.

"Have you decided to join the pack yet?"

Maren shook her head. "I am waiting before I make the decision."

Jens shook his head with a slight smile, like he knew why she waited. I moved on, confident that Jens could lead the pack through the training they needed.

The next pack sent my fingers squeezing tighter around the spear. Kay. The youngest warrior among them sported a bruise to his cheek that had not been there a few days ago.

"Well, Battlewolf, any words of wisdom for me today?" Kay sneered.

Unfortunately, my restraint had not yet woken for the day. "Maybe how to pull your head from your *atcha*. Though it might take several lessons."

His face darkened. "You think this will earn our respect?"

I leaned a little closer. "Respect goes both ways."

"I used to have some for you, Comran. Did the bastard get you thinking that you are better than all of us?"

I shifted the spear in my hand, snapping it behind my back, point down, in a resting position.

"It's not hard to do when you insist on acting like a tantruming wolf pup. And you will speak of the chief with more respect."

Kay squared off against me. "And who is going to make me."

*Finally.* I tossed my spear to Loke. "Me."

Iron rasped as he drew his sword, features contorted in a snarl. "Then maybe I'll take that battlewolf medallion from you."

I ripped my sword free. "*Try.*"

The clash of iron on iron sent focus honing through me. The pack hurriedly backed away to give us room. Kay bulled forward, trying to use his bigger bulk and height against me. I moved quicker, staying a fraction ahead of him, returning strike for strike. Voices rose around, the other packs rushing to see the fight.

Sunlight glinted off a patch of ice a few steps away, and I angled toward it, feigning retreat. He came more confidently, especially as I slowed to make sure I navigated it without incident.

Then his foot hit the ice and, unprepared for it, he lurched to try to correct. I tilted my blade, smashing the flat of it into the side of his thigh. His leg buckled with a sharp cry of pain, and I sidestepped a wild swing of his blade.

Blocking his next strike, I stepped inside his guard, and plowed my knee into his chest, knocking him to the ground. The sword clattered from his grip, and I kicked it away. He froze as the point of my sword hovered above his throat.

Then I stepped back, twisting the hilt so the flat of the blade rested against the back of my arm. Kay gained his feet, knee slightly bent beneath him, not trusting his weight entirely to it. We regarded each other for a wary moment.

"You think to rule the packs with a heavy hand?" He spat off to the side.

"You are the one who challenged me. And I do not care if I am liked or not." Though an annoying bit of me protested otherwise. "I do not care whether you wanted me as battlewolf. Our father considered Etran a valid choice for the place of chief. And so do I. He has my sword. And any move or word against him is against me as well."

That caught his focus. More than just he and his pack had heard it. Had heard the words before the fight. Anyone going against both chief and battlewolf was a special kind of idiot who might see themselves following Hakkon out of the village.

"But…" Another warrior spoke up hesitantly, licking lips under my new attention. "What of the spirits?"

"The only mark of disfavor against him has been of mans' making," I said. "Not of the spirits."

Turning back to Kay, I considered him. "I will not take your position. Not unless you prove different to me. If this tribe has to ride to battle, I would prefer to have you leading a pack instead of seeing your skill and ferocity wasted."

The warrior's features didn't change from their grim slant, but he jerked a sharp nod and limped away. Some of his pack followed, others stayed and, with cautious looks at me, started into training forms.

Sword still unsheathed, I moved to the outer edges as the two other packs fell into pairs to spar. Loke stepped up beside me, leaning comfortably on my spear.

"Well," he said meditatively. "How do you feel?"

"Tired," I admitted. The bout had stolen more from me than I'd expected, though I'd woken with more strength the last few days. A pang struck my side and I winced, pressing my hand over it and trying to convince myself I didn't feel dampness spreading through the bandage.

Loke's eyebrow arched, and I moved my hand away, pretending it was nothing.

"Then I might need to stop going easy on you during sparring."

I gave a sarcastic laugh and sheathed my sword. He passed my spear back to me.

"One thing is certain. Life is going to be a little too exciting with you as battlewolf."

A smirk spread across my face, and I tapped his arm with a fist. "I wouldn't ever want you to be bored, Loke."

"It might be nice for one day!" he called after me as I strode away to make a round through the training pairs. The sight of Etran standing at the edge of the training grounds caught me by surprise. Jens stood with him.

"All right, Battlewolf?" Kjell's question brought my hand away from my side again. It hadn't stopped aching since the fight.

"Fine." I prodded his feet with my spear. "Check your foot-work."

He rolled his eyes, but fell back to his forms. I hesitated a moment more before striding toward Etran. Sudden cold wracked through me and I stumbled a step, pushing the heel of my hand hard against my breastplate.

"Comran, what is wrong?" Loke appeared at my side, Amund not far behind him.

"Nothing."

Etran had noticed and took a hesitant step forward.

"It's not nothing," Loke growled. "You're paler than a ghost."

"Seen many ghosts recently?" I snapped, almost cursing at the stab into my side. My knee buckled. A hand grabbed me under my arm and Etran was there, concern taking over.

"Lodge," Loke ordered, taking my other arm.

Etran looked between us. I jerked away from their hold, and my legs decided to hold steady as I pushed into the nearby training lodge. Faint beams of sunlight snuck through the open window slits.

"What is wrong?" Loke tapped my shoulder until I sat on a bench.

Amund, Jens, and Etran stood beside him, looking at me with the same expression. I tossed a hand.

"I don't know!"

Loke tilted his head, mouth flattening in a line. The uneasy twinge in my side prodded again. Disquiet took over my irritation. I set aside my sword and armor and pulled up the tunic and shirt. Loke helped me undo the bandage around my chest.

He rocked back on his heels with a soft curse.

"I am no healer, but shouldn't that be mended?" Jens frowned.

I stared down at the shallow cut across my ribs. It had been well over the full nine days of a counting. More than enough time for something so insignificant to have closed. I hadn't thought much of it in the days since I'd defeated the fever, but now…

"We're going to the healer's lodge." Loke abruptly stood.

"What, all of us together?" I said wryly. The others looked in no hurry to leave.

"Fine. Amund, go get the healer, please."

I opened my mouth to protest, but Etran nodded his agreement. Amund disappeared out the door, and I slumped back on the bench. Etran tapped Loke on the shoulder and some message passed between them. Both *rokrs* stepped outside, leaving Etran and me alone.

Spirits, I was wary of him again. His boot scuffed at the floor, and he gnawed at his lower lip.

"I saw your challenge," he blurted.

I shifted, bracing myself for the disapproval or rebuke our father might have given.

"Jens told me some of what was said…" He flicked a hand at the door.

My hand curled at my side, waiting for the same anger I'd seen before. But instead, his face held a look of lost confusion.

*He's not so aloof as he seems.*

His lips parted, closed, then he spoke.

"You do not think the spirits look in disfavor on me?" he said softly.

I lifted a shoulder. "Well, if they do, then it extends to me too, and I happen to think that's a terrible waste of my talent."

A tentative grin flickered at the corner of his mouth. But the wariness fell back between us. The arrival of the healer broke the tension. And created something new. After a quick inspection, he confirmed the fear budding in the back of my mind. The cut was not healing. He rubbed his jaw and stared at it, as if that would make it close.

In the end, he rebandaged it and told me to come by his lodge later.

Maybe it was a mark of the spirits' disfavor. Perhaps it was just taking its time to heal.

But as the days marched on, it stayed open, sometimes oozing, and refusing to turn to a scar. The healer even tried stitches, but it still did not close and became infected. So he just shook his head and trained me how to keep it bandaged, telling me to keep coming for more paste to spread over it.

Not many knew. It didn't trouble me, except for some mornings when I'd wake up feeling exhausted and was forced to struggle through the day like my limbs were caught in mud. Eska fretted, but I think it was more because my duties kept me busy, and he had no one to run him.

Kay was not the only pack leader to challenge me, with weapons or with words. Etran had fewer physical battles than I to fight as the countings turned to months, but he still kept his head up and threw himself into the task of chief, shaking his head sometimes when I'd confront someone I'd heard muttering curses at him.

But many days, the years of habit were hard to break, and I automatically avoided him. Only the tradition of meeting at least once a day kept us talking and trying to keep bridging the valley between us.

Maybe I could admit someday how I came to appreciate his more level head. Or admit that some days I tried harder to make him smile or laugh when cares weighed his shoulders down or I caught the look in his eye when he'd quietly pushed through barbed words from others.

Through the rest of the cold months, it began to come a little easier between us, but when warmth began to prick through the air, it brought more than just a new season.

# SIXTEEN

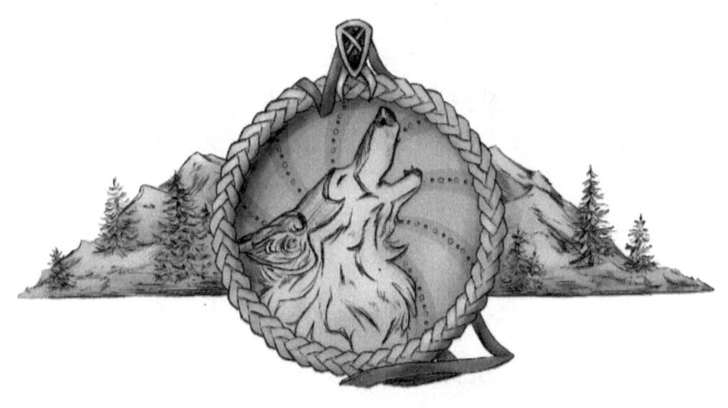

## COMRAN

The season's change hovered in the air when I discovered signs of intruders in our valley. I'd led a small pack of wolfriders out to refresh our borders and to hunt the lower valley where the great-elk had begun to gather with the promise of spring and tender shoots and leaves beginning to push through the layered snow.

We'd camped by our discovery and waited for Etran to arrive after sending two wolfriders back for him and more warriors. He'd want to see it for himself. I let my cloak fall about my shoulders, protecting me from the nip that still threaded its way through the air. Spring might be on the way, but winter maintained her jealous hold.

The warriors ranged in a ring around our small camp, their wary attention turned to the deceptive peace of the valley. A signal went up announcing the arrival of Etran and a new pack.

Eska rumbled deep in his chest and rose from his hindquarters to give Etran room to join me.

"What is it?" He glanced my way.

I merely pointed in answer. A worried frown twisted his features as he stared at the paw print. Too big and too far across the valley for the tawny mountain lions that occasionally came down from the high peaks to hunt or come after a lone rider. My first suspicions had been confirmed as soon as Eska bared his teeth at the lingering scent.

Sablecat.

I picked the bits of black hair that had been brushed off by the grasping thistles.

Etran took them from me and rubbed them between his fingers. "Saber tribe?"

"They're a long way from home." I nodded my head to where Half Peak was a smudge no bigger than my thumb to the southwest. And the border stones were still over twenty miles away at the rapids and low hills before the valley fell into more open plains and sulfur springs.

"It wouldn't be the first time."

But this was more than border spats. They had not come this far into the valley in a long time.

The Saber tribe had been keen to expand its territories into the valley for years. I'd gotten my first battle scars from them in a border skirmish three autumns ago.

"Think they intend the same as they did to the Blackpaws?"

After nearly wiping out the tribe eight years ago, the Saber tribe had gained a foothold in the hills across the river and up by the lake in Blackpaw territory, but hadn't given us much trouble since.

Etran frowned again as he pushed to his feet. "We can't stay out of the fight this time."

I raised an eyebrow. I didn't know he felt the same as me regarding the past.

"Scouts are out looking for more tracks. This is too far into the valley."

Etran swung onto Frea's back. "Make sure our borders are clearly marked. I will call a war council when you return."

I gathered the reins and mounted Eska, taking my spear from the warrior beside me.

"Yes, Chief."

Five warriors took the game back to the village, while the remaining ten accompanied me on a run of our borders. We carved runes of warning into the towering pines, while the greywolves left their scent behind.

It took the rest of the day and well into the next to mark the borders we shared with the Saber tribe before heading across the valley, splashing through one of the river fords, and loping the remaining twenty miles to the village.

Eska proudly ran at the head of the pack, broad paws leaping across the thinning snow. The bite in the wind rushing over my face sent another nudge of foreboding through me. The Saber tribe lived farther south among hot springs, petulant geysers, and meadows that would already be shaking off winter.

If they felt confident enough to start scouting our borders and into our territory, it meant that war might not be far away. Winter hadn't given up in the higher valleys and mountains. We'd have more snow before spring came for certain, and it was no easy thing to go to war in the snow.

The Blackpaw tribe had been driven deeper into the low mountains and hills around the western lakes eight years ago, the Saber tribe pushing farther north to take over their hunting grounds. Not even the Coyote traders who came through in groups of three or five had seen much of the Blackpaws since.

And now the Saber tribe felt confident enough to move against us.

The village came into view in the curve of the mountain's roots. It was sheltered enough on the far side of our territory. The sun's light had begun to fade as we loped into the village. Warriors gathered in groups, watching us, worry creasing their features. Women clustered together in the midst of work.

I shifted my grip on my spear as Eska padded along, trepidation rising at the way focus turned to me. As battlewolf, I would have the most responsibility, whatever happened. I would lead packs into battle.

A small part of me wanted to turn the medallion back to Birgir. He'd know better than I how to lead. Etran stood with Father, discussing something below the shadow of the main *tåkn*. He glanced up as we rode through and gave me a small nod.

We'd figure out how to stand together.

"What are you thinking?" Loke asked as we leaned spears against the stable walls and turned to unsaddling our wolves under the eaves of the stables.

"About?"

"The general weather and how many more countings until spring." Loke rolled his eyes. "What do you think, Comran?"

"I think at least another month of countings."

He smacked me across the back of the head like a small child. I grinned as Eska idly growled at him.

"Do you have a plan for the council?"

Anxiety settled back over my shoulders heavier than the exhaustion I'd fought off that morning to climb back on Eska like nothing was wrong.

I'd sat in the council of war Father had called eight years ago when deciding whether or not to help the Blackpaws against the Saber tribe. And then hidden in the shadows listening to him and Birgir argue the decision to keep the wolfriders in the village.

The yellow fever had taken a toll on the valley that year, and Father did not think it was wise to extend more of ourselves in a war that had not come to us. There had been no need for such a council since.

Tossing my saddle over the low rack, I brushed Eska's clinging fur away from the leather before taking it inside to clean it.

"Bigger packs running patrols and more frequently."

Eska's rough tongue swept up the piece of dried elk meat I held out and he wandered away. Loke and I brought our saddles and bridles inside the building to clean and store them.

"If it comes to battles, draw them out into the open valley." The sablecats had more advantage in the trees, whereas we stood strongest in open areas with the strength of the pack against an enemy.

"A good place to start." Birgir's voice brought me automatically moving to salute him as battlewolf.

He walked up the narrow path of the stables, a half-woven rein in his hands. Taking a seat on a stool, he kept lacing and tightening the leather as we settled in on other stools.

"What else would you do?" I asked, not caring if Loke heard my uncertainty. He wouldn't think less of me. And, as one of my *rokrs*, he'd need to know the best ways to lead as well.

"Make sure we have more warriors training to fill empty saddles," Birgir said.

I swallowed hard. I didn't mind going to battle. In the saddle with a spear or sword in my hand, I always found calm. But there were plenty who had people to care if they fell, who would leave families behind. And there would be time to mourn, but we'd need warriors in saddles before that time came.

"And what if the chief and I don't agree if it comes to war?" My fingers twisted at the cleaning cloth.

Birgir nodded, tightening the braid he wove. "You will have to find a way to compromise. Though, traditionally, in times of war when the spear is passed, a chief will defer to the battlewolf. Unless such a plan will lead to sure ruination."

"How often did you lead the packs in war?" I leaned forward on my knees, forgetting the saddle.

"Three times. Once against the Saber tribe before you were born, when their current chieftain and your father and I were young. Another when the Coyote traders thought to band together and claim some territory in the northern mountains. And the third time alongside the Blackpaw tribe when a strange tribe came over the hills from some lands farther west, riding savage creatures they called wolverines."

"And still you would not ride to their aid eight years ago?"

Lines creased deeper in Birgir's weathered face. "I wanted to. I'd made friends with some of their warriors in the countings we rode together against the invaders. But your father would not be gainsaid and he would not pass the spear to me." His hands paused in his work. "It's one of the regrets I will bear with me to the All-Father's lodge."

I straightened and dabbed another bit of oil on the cloth to spread over the saddle, keeping it supple enough to form to Eska's sides. It was just one paw print. What if Etran decided to do nothing about it, even when unease stirred around my heart?

"The Saber tribe has pushed enough," Birgir said. "Etran should understand we need to push back. Their chiefs and battlelions are always eager for war, which is why we've tangled with them often enough. I just wonder, why now?"

My unease rose further. "What do you mean?"

"Their chief is getting on in years. Why is he choosing now to scout our territory?"

I pushed to my feet, needing to move. The Coyote traders passed freely among the tribes, having a sort of immunity to violence from all of us, but more than willing to carry news of all the tribes to each other.

Birgir was right. We'd yet to hear that their chief had passed the mantle to someone new. But they would have heard of the change in our tribe. Maybe they thought a new chief and new battlewolf would be weaker. Birgir and my father had long held strong against any assault on our lands in their years. Etran and I were both untested.

"Etran is calling a council of war. Will you come?"

The council of elders, my *rokrs*—I was willing to wager Father as well—would be there. I wanted an extra voice of reason on the side of the wolfriders if it came to it. But I had a feeling Etran would lean the same way I did.

"I'd be honored, Battlewolf." Birgir dipped his head. "Trust your instincts. You are a good warrior, Comran, and have done well these last months. I'll trust you to lead the packs into battle any day."

I nodded thanks for his words, though they didn't do much to assuage the fear sneaking up on me. It was one thing to lead a small pack in a border spat, and another still to command all the packs and defend the entire valley.

Loke's face bespoke the same trust. I slung the saddle over my rack and ran the cloth over Eska's bridle before storing it away as well.

*"I had a dream."* Father's words came back. *"You led the tribe to battle as chieftain. We fell to the enemy. You died."*

Since I wasn't chieftain, maybe it would not come to pass. But that's not what I feared most.

What if I failed?

It sent new restlessness through me, and I left Loke and Birgir behind. Loke wouldn't push. He knew me better than myself some days and knew when I needed time. My feet took me across the lodge circle, veering me toward the *tåkn* before I fully realized where I'd instinctively headed.

To find Etran.

He still stood by the *tåkn* with Father, and I slowed. Since that day Father tried to talk to me, I'd attempted to stay as far away as possible, even within the narrow confines of our lodge. Etran didn't have much of a choice, as his duties still took him to Father for advice.

"Comran."

An unfamiliar wariness filled Father's eyes, as if, for once, he was the one unsure. The sternness had left him most days when I came face-to-face with him, leaving me with a sense of uncertainty. Maybe he had been serious about wanting to change the way things were between us.

I still didn't want to let him.

"You have your plans ready for the council?" he asked.

I automatically stiffened, ready for him to tell me I'd done wrong, and exactly why.

"I do." I didn't offer more, not wanting to admit it wasn't much.

"Anything I can assist with?"

The words made me draw back, and I saw the change in his face. Like it hurt him. Like he cared.

"I've already spoken with Birgir for advice." My words came with a snap, unable to hide the brittle anger inside.

Etran swept a wary look between us.

Father inclined his head. "He will have sound council."

But it seemed like the words pained him.

Good.

"Could we have a moment?" Etran spoke up, moving a little closer to me.

Father regarded us. Me with hands still fisted at my sides, and Etran slightly between us like a peacemaker. He dipped another nod.

"I will see you in the council, then." He touched Etran's shoulder like a father might a son.

I didn't say anything, not trusting my tongue to the anger and scraps of desperation for his attention swirling in me.

"Well?" Etran said.

I took a long inhale, relaxing my fists as it whispered back out. "Seems you've forgiven him?"

The words held a bite I regretted only a little. Etran offered a small, rueful smile.

"Maybe a little. But I feel guilty at how much I now have his focus and attention. And how he now treats me as an equal."

I crossed my arms over my chest, digging a boot into the dirty snow.

"I'm not telling you to forgive him as well, Comran. But know that he is trying."

Shaking my head, I looked off to the woods. He'd had plenty of time our whole lives to try.

"And maybe I'm worried it might drive something between us again."

My eyebrow arched at Etran's sheepish expression. He dragged a hand across the back of his neck. I gave a half-smile.

"It's too much effort to start hating you now."

Etran gave a slight roll of his eyes. "Then can *I* ask if you have plans for the council?"

I allowed a laugh and we turned to the council lodge, outlining the things I'd spoken with Loke and Birgir. He stopped short.

"I think we might have to go to war." It rushed from him and he stared past me to the *tåkn* like he wasn't quite seeing it.

I lifted a shoulder. "If they truly are making a push for our lands, yes."

"No. I…" A tremor crossed his face. "I think I dreamed it."

My arms crossed again, and I leaned in closer. Usually only the chief would be granted such a gift from the All-Father. The chief, and the *talånd* who could help interpret. I tried not to let the fact needle home the point that I was truly not meant to be chief.

"What did you see?"

"At least one battle in open fields. Snow melting to spring. You."

A shiver of unease cut down my arms. "Me?"

The uncertain look remained on his face, and he shook himself a bit. "I'm not sure what it was trying to tell me."

Father's dream hovered on the edge of my tongue, but I held it close.

"Did you speak to the *talånd?*" I asked instead.

"Not yet."

Though perhaps young Mikkel wouldn't have the same advice as his predecessor.

"Etran." I touched his arm as he made to keep walking. Before we entered the lodge, I wanted to make sure he knew where I stood. "The Saber tribe has tried to take some of this valley before. I will not let them take any more. I'm ready to fight."

Even if he didn't command it.

Etran nodded slowly, jaw clenched. "What if I make the wrong decision in calling for war?"

"Then I'll make it alongside you. And won't regret it."

His shoulders relaxed a fraction. "Then we convince this council that we need to begin sending out the packs."

I nodded, eager to be doing something and maybe keep proving myself. But just as fast apprehension came nipping at its heels. Father and Etran had both dreamed of war.

Why did they also dream of me?

# SEVENTEEN

## ETRAN

*It's started.*

I watched Comran lead two packs from the village, spears held high, war paint smeared across faces and wolf pelts. And tried not to think about the dream that had come back to haunt me over the last two nights since the council.

Everyone had agreed that extra packs needed to be sent out to patrol our borders. Watching and guarding for now. And Comran had thrown himself into the preparations once I'd handed him the red-painted spear in front of the tribe—giving the decisions for war over to him along with it.

I watched with some jealousy how effortlessly he commanded warriors and they answered. How quickly the tribe began to look to him as he took over. How fast any remaining disputes died in the face of war.

He would have made a good chief. Perhaps he didn't second-guess himself at every turn.

Mother came to stand next to me. She said nothing, but disapproval radiated off her. She still didn't think I should let Comran do his duties as battlewolf. Even after he'd saved my life in the spirits' lodge, nothing had thawed her toward him.

And the fact he came to our lodge more frequently had maybe made it worse, something I didn't know was possible.

"He will try to overthrow you," she said with certainty.

"He's had plenty of chances," I reminded her.

Starting with the spirits' lodge. He tried to pretend the wound was nothing, but I knew it still pained him some days. He wasn't so hard to read, and Loke and Jens reported on him anyway.

She sniffed in derision, like I was still a trusting child. I turned, seeking space away from her. My eyes roved over the crowd, trying to find Maren and maybe a few moments of distracting conversation. But I found Comran's mother instead.

Inger stood with arms pressed tight against her stomach, leaning into the light breeze as if she could follow along with the pack as they loped into the valley. She had always radiated assurance and poise as the *dronni*, but now she looked like the other mothers whose sons had ridden out with Comran.

Mother hissed under her breath as I turned and made my way over to Inger. She tilted her head up as I came to stand by her, that same small smile in place.

"He'll be all right," I said, unable to find much else to say.

Her arms tightened over her stomach and her dark eyes stared at the vanishing puffs of snow marking the pack. For a moment I thought she might hate me for sending her son away.

"It is a mother's place to worry. Yours will when you ride out." Some of the strange wistfulness I sometimes caught from her lingered in her eyes again.

I risked a glance to Mother. From the burning stare she gave me, it seemed she might not be too sad to see me leave.

"Thank you, Etran." Inger flashed a brighter smile, and she reached out to tap my forearm before leaving with a last glance over her shoulder.

"What could you possibly have to say to her?" Mother hissed as she swept up beside me again.

I moved my shoulder out from under her grip, weary of it all. "She's worried for her son. And maybe I worry for him too."

Mother's glare at me could have melted ice, though her tone was colder than a glacier. "He's not your brother."

"Maybe that's for me to decide. And I should have stopped listening to your anger a long time ago." I didn't back down, matching her with the intensity she'd taught me.

"Then you will see yourself regretting placing your trust in him." She gathered herself up, tucking her cloak around her. "And I will not mourn if he falls."

She swept away, taking her bitterness with her. I turned back, but the pack had disappeared. Reluctantly, I headed back into the village. Settling in to wait.

Five days later, Comran rode back in, one wolf following with an empty saddle at the rear of the pack. I met them in the center of the lodge circle. Bandages were in evidence, and a wolf limped on a wrapped paw.

But concern faded at the sight of Comran's face.

He dismounted from Eska and rammed his spear into the ground.

"What happened?" I asked.

"We found the Saber tribe," he said. "Fought them at the boundaries across the river. I left riders there to watch."

"But?" I prompted, unease stirring in my gut. There was something else.

"I know why they're making a move on us."

I swallowed hard.

"Hakkon was leading their pack." He heaped another curse upon the traitor.

I didn't know what I'd expected. But hearing that Hakkon had made his way to the Saber tribe was not it.

"*Scata.*"

He arched an eyebrow. "I was more vocal about it, but yes."

"This is not a border fight." The very small sliver of me that had hoped for that vanished quicker than smoke on a windy day.

"No. They made it clear they are coming for our lands."

Heaviness settled over me, another burden weighing on me. I saw it on Comran as well. He'd seen battle and would see more. Lead more than one greywolf back without a rider.

"Muster the packs. We're going to war."

# EIGHTEEN

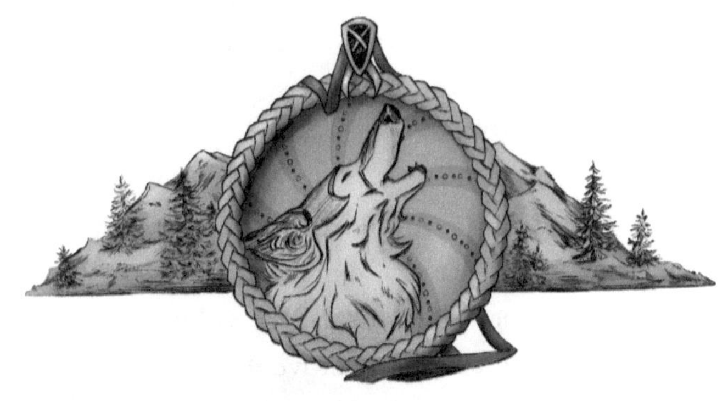

## COMRAN

"Saber tribe spotted, Battlewolf!" A wolfrider loped up, spear held high.

I launched into the saddle, other riders following my lead. The rider wheeled his greywolf and led the way out of the trees and across the open plains toward the small tributary stream beginning to shake the ice.

Two countings of sporadic fights, and here we were. A mixed pack of twenty riders followed at my heels. Our wolves' broad paws leapt across thawing snow and emerging greenery. Eska strained forward, head stretching low in his eagerness. I reined him back. I didn't need him to exhaust himself before we clashed in battle.

The rider raised his spear again, but I'd already seen. A line of sleek black figures racing our direction.

My call sent the pack staggering in a line with two peaks. We lowered spears in readiness. The sablecats bounded forward, their guttural roars sending Eska's ears flicking back. He snarled in response, and Loke's wolf bayed a challenge.

I fixed my sights on the lead rider on the largest sablecat. I'd come to know his name over the last two countings. And his cruel streak.

Kamil. The Saber tribe's Battlelion.

*He's mine.*

Under the challenges from the animals, paws whisked across the ground, then all fell silent a moment before we clashed. The sablecats tried to come under our wolves to bite at throats with long curving fangs, but our spears drove them away.

Most of our riders made it through the line, turned, and headed back to battle as the Saber tribe did the same.

I left my spear in the haunch of a sablecat and drew my sword. It yowled in anger, mouth parted wide, lower jaw unhinging to show the two long curving teeth from its upper jaw. I moved with Eska as he dodged the teeth and came at the rider from the side.

The Saber tribe forced their iron into curved blades to mimic the sablecats' dangerous teeth. My straight blade shrieked down the curve of my opponent's sword. Eska's bark of warning came too late, but his dropping crouch didn't as a black shape lunged at my side.

The sablecat's teeth missed my throat, but its chest knocked me to the ground. Eska whipped around, burying teeth in the cat's shoulder, giving me time to scramble to my feet. The wounded cat swiped with a paw at my head, its rider goading it.

I slashed with my sword, the blade cutting deep into the paw. It screamed again and I drove my weapon through its throat. The rider jumped free as the cat collapsed, and charged me.

I dodged his first swiping blow and followed up with a strike. Eska guarded my flank as I fought the warrior, finally finding my opening, and delivering a final blow.

A pained sound came from Eska. I darted to him, trading my sword to my weaker hand, and grabbed my spear from the dead sablecat's haunch. Spear leveled, I jabbed it at a prowling sablecat as Eska hop-skipped backwards behind me, blood staining the snow from his forepaw. My turn to protect.

The battlelion sneered down at me. His long hair was drawn back with leather cord at the base of his neck. Eyes nearly as dark as his lion's pelt watched me carefully as I deterred another threat from the animal. Red paint streaked in four diagonal lines across both tanned cheeks.

"Battlewolf." His voice matched his proud features.

"Bastard," I returned, my medallion tapping against my breastplate in time with my circling movements as Eska kept my flank and the sablecat kept crouching. Not three days ago, we'd found the tortured body of a wolfrider scout and mutilated form of his greywolf left behind by the battlelion.

His medallion glinted in the sunlight—roaring sablecat with curving teeth and a small red gem set in the eye.

"I do not see your chief anywhere." Kamil made a show of looking around.

I shrugged a shoulder. "He's not bothered enough by you to even pick up a spear."

A flash of anger distorted his face, and his sablecat swiped with a paw again, batting at my spear. I moved it in a small circle, dodging the grasping reach of its claws.

Another dark shape prowled forward to my exposed right side. I moved into a different defensive pattern, spear swinging between both new threats, sword ready in my left hand.

"And what about you, Battlewolf?" The title came with a veneer of condescension. "Worried about me?"

I tossed a smirk. "Maybe I'm just worried about how much—courage—you have, needing another rider to help you face me."

His sablecat growled deep in its chest, and Eska responded in kind with a hackle-raising snarl.

"I'll cut you down without a second thought."

"Go ahead and try. I thought we were dancing here."

Too late the thought came that my mouth was getting me into more trouble than I already was. The sablecats crept closer, lowering on their paws and preparing to spring.

Eska edged forward, teeth snapping a warning. I bent my knees as I decided my target.

The cat to my right sprang a split second before the battlelion. I whipped my spear up, thrusting to meet its pounce. The impact of sablecat onto my spear shoved me backwards, bearing down on my arm. I dropped the spear and twisted to the side to avoid the dead weight. Eska lunged to tangle with the battlelion, yelping again as he earned another wound on my behalf.

"Eska!"

I managed the whistle to send him retreating as I yanked my leg out from under the dead cat. Scrambling to my feet, I passed my sword back to my strong hand as the rider, who had fallen to the other side, sprang over the dead lion at me.

Already off-balance, I crashed to a knee under his assault. Yanking a dagger out of my belt, I jabbed it into his thigh. His mouth dropped open in shock and he stumbled back to press against the gushing wound. A force crashed into my shoulders, throwing me down.

Kamil's laugh echoed as I twisted under the paws of his cat. Its jaws opened above me. I rammed the pommel of my sword against its jaw, driving it to the side to save my throat. But one of the curving canines still scraped my cheek.

A savage growl and split second later, I lay staring at the clear sky, chest free of the weight of a sablecat paw. Eska crouched beside me, guarding.

A breath gasped from me, and I turned my head to see Loke's wolf half atop the battlelion's cat, pushing them backwards as Loke struck down at Kamil.

The cat managed to wriggle out from under them, and the battlelion sounded a retreat. I kept my head up long enough to make sure they indeed fell back across the tributary river, before letting it thud back down to the ground.

My heart still hadn't slowed from the feel of the sablecat's breath and the sting from its tooth across my cheek.

I lay there until Loke's face appeared upside down above me.

"Are you dying, or are you going to join the rest of us real warriors?"

I rolled my eyes and extended my hand. He came around and helped me to my feet.

"Thank you."

He clapped my shoulder before taking hold of my jaw and turning my cheek to see the cut.

"How much more handsome am I now?" I wiped my sword clean on my trousers before sheathing it.

"Still as hideous as ever."

"Perfect." I gently dabbed at the oozing blood, likely just smearing it into the green battle paint on my cheek.

Wolfriders started to gather, sheathing weapons and picking spears back up. Wolves crouched or lay, licking their wounds. A younger wolfrider circled through the warriors, bringing bandages for them.

A few bodies lay on the banks, red staining the patchworked snow and grass. Two sablecats and a wolf wouldn't rise. We'd be carrying two wolfriders away for burial. Already one wolf crouched beside her fallen warrior, a keening howl filling her throat.

I swallowed hard and turned away. It was always hardest to see the animal mourning the rider. The Greywolf spirit had seen fit to give us a bond to his creatures, and it hurt when it was severed.

I shuddered to think that one day it would happen between me and Eska. Either in battle, or in old age. The wolves did not live as long as us. Turning to him, I ran a gentling hand down his neck. He stilled and let me brush at the blood-matted fur around his wounds.

"And thank you," I murmured to him.

He snuffled and turned his head to nose at my hair. I scratched under his chin, scraping at some of the battle paint in his fur. One circle around his left eye, and two lines down the right side of his muzzle, mimicking the battlewolf's lines on my right cheek.

The young warrior delivered bandages, and I used them on Eska instead. I'd taken no significant injury.

"Gather the dead," I ordered.

Another wolfrider took up the reins of the female wolf, dancing back a step as she snapped and settled in closer to her dead warrior.

Eska hobbled to them. He lowered his nose to the female and whuffed in her ear. She whined and looked up at him. Eska rested his chin atop her head a moment before nudging at her, pushing her away from the body.

She nosed at her warrior one more time, the lines of her body sloping in defeat. The wolfrider gently tugged her away, turning her so the body could be lifted up and placed across the saddle.

I cast one more look across the river to make sure no sablecats lingered in the bits of treeline scattered this far out into the valley.

We'd held so far, but they were becoming bolder as they crossed over our border stones and made for the great river.

Loke came to stand beside me. "They're pushing harder."

I gnawed on my bottom lip. "We need more riders out."

"Who do you want me to send back to the village?"

A brief thought entered my head of going back myself. But besides my mother, anyone I truly cared about was already out with me.

Except Etran.

"Sander." I named the young warrior standing not too far away, staring white-faced at the ice-crusted water.

I moved to his side, startling him with a hand dropped on his shoulder.

"Battlewolf!" He dragged a hand down his cheek, smearing his war paint.

"First battle?" I said, though I knew it was true. He'd just earned his place with the warriors before the winter started.

He nodded, drawing in a shuddering breath.

"I lost my breakfast and I think the meal from the night before after my first fight." I matched his stare over the river.

He darted a quick glance at me, eyes wide in question as if I should be admitting that fact.

I grinned. "Ask Loke if you don't believe me."

A shaky smile formed, bringing some color back to his face. I nudged his shoulder.

"It's all right to feel shaken. It's no easy thing to ride into battle."

"You make it seem so," he said.

I paused. Did I? It seemed easier to me, more natural than anything else I'd tried my hand at before joining the warriors.

"Experience," I finally said instead. "I need you to ride back to the village. Tell the chief we need more riders out."

He nodded, but something else crossed his face. Shame, perhaps.

"Your wolf appears to be less injured."

His features cleared just as quick, and he dipped a nod. "Yes, Battlewolf."

"Go on then." I nudged him. He left me to stare across the small river to where border stones were a mere two miles away.

As I went to collect Eska, a pang lanced through my side. I pressed a hand against the smoothed leather of my breastplate. A dampness clung to my ribs, bringing a scowl. The cursed wound had broken open again during the fight. I'd need to bandage it, or it would keep a slow, steady drip of blood.

"Mount up!" I called out, hauling myself up into the saddle.

Eska glanced back over his shoulder. I reassured him with a pat and nudged him into a limping walk. We were a less impressive sight leaving the river than charging to defend it. Sander and his wolf loped away up the valley, followed more slowly by the warriors Loke had sent back with the dead.

I twisted once in the saddle, staring back at the red staining the ground. Not long into this war and I'd already lost good riders. The death did not shock me the way it did Sander, but it didn't stop it from weighing on my heart. How many more times would we ride away with empty saddles to build graves in the village or in quiet groves? Gather around the farewell fires?

The Saber tribe was showing themselves just as intent at taking our valley as we were to defend it. Another breeze, warm with the oncoming spring, ruffled through Eska's fur. No time to linger on the battle just behind. Time to focus on the battles to come.

# NINETEEN

## ETRAN

"Chief!" Jens met me at the camp, smiling, his hand raised in greeting.

I slid from Frea and tugged the reins over her head to lead her on. Tents were pitched in a circle throughout the trees, wolves sitting or piled atop each other beside them. Warriors sat around, sharpening blades or restitching leather.

For the first time since taking the mantle of chief, I relaxed a fraction. I'd rather ride with the warriors than lead from the lodges.

"Where's Comran?" A quick glance around didn't locate him.

"Asleep." Jens reached for Frea. "He's been pushing himself hard."

A frown quirked my lips. He'd sent the call back for more warriors, relentless in leading battles along our boundaries over the last few countings. He hadn't been back. Which made Jens's statement a little more concerning.

"How is…" I didn't finish, afraid of the warriors around me.

Jens shook his head and leaned closer to lower his voice between us. "He would have collapsed this morning if Loke hadn't made him go sleep."

I shook my head. A nagging thought surfaced again that the wound might make Comran unfit for duty as battlewolf. It was a time of war and I needed someone strong leading the packs.

But just as fast, I shoved it away. I didn't trust anyone else.

The late afternoon sun slanted through the pines and spruce. Hopefully, he'd had a few hours of rest, but I did need to speak with him.

"Where is he?"

Jens pointed to a tent off to the right between two towering pines. No sign of Eska around. A bit of warmth tugged my chest. He hadn't even pitched his tent in the center or at the head of the circle as was the battlewolf's right. Or maybe he just didn't feel confident enough still.

It made me feel a little easier since I also had not been able to harness much confidence myself in my position.

I paused at the entrance and no sound stirred on the other side.

"Comran?"

Still nothing. I shrugged and tugged the flap aside to step in. And stifled a laugh.

Comran lay sprawled on his stomach in his pile of blankets and pelts, asleep. And somehow Eska had wormed his way in to stretch out by his side, one giant paw resting over Comran's shoulder. His armor and weapons lay neatly on another blanket opposite them.

I eased further into the tent. A breeze snuck in with me to ruffle at Eska's fur. Comran flinched and burrowed further into the pelts.

"Go 'way, Loke," he grumbled.

"I would, but I'm not Loke."

Eska lifted his head to blink slowly at me, then yawned with a faint squeal at the back of his throat. Comran emerged slightly and cracked his eyes open.

"Etran." It came out more a question than statement. "You're here."

"Don't sound so disappointed."

He turned over to his back, rubbing his eyes and pushing Eska away as the wolf snuffled at his face. A bit of concern spiked at the sight of blood crusting around a shallow cut across his cheek.

"I told the battlelion that you'd stayed home because you weren't worried about him. Now it looks like I was lying."

But a grin swerved over his face. A laugh teased my chest.

"Am I meant to be surprised by this?"

His grin became a slight wince as he sat up, covering it by ducking his head to comb a hand through the unruly bits of curl in the dark hair we both inherited from Father.

I dropped to a crouch. "How are you?"

His hand strayed to his side, and again the thought snuck in that I needed to find some way to send him home. Find a battle-wolf who didn't suffer from an unhealing wound.

"It's fine." But the growl in his voice wasn't completely for me.

"And how did you get him in here?" I kept my voice light, jerking my chin at Eska who hadn't moved at all, instead settling back down with nose on paws.

The grin raced across Comran's face again. The tent was barely big enough for two warriors to share, let alone a massive greywolf.

"It is unfair they can't fit through the doors into the lodges."

"I think it was on purpose."

He laughed and clicked to Eska. The wolf huffed and cautiously rose to his paws. In a routine that seemed more than a little familiar, Comran scooted to the side and Eska padded around him to push out of the tent.

Seconds later, Loke swatted the flap open.

"Again?" He glared at Comran.

Comran shrugged. "He's quieter than you two."

Loke rolled his eyes before dipping a nod to me. "Chief."

I returned the greeting. Comran shifted again, hand braced against his side. Loke scowled and pushed past me. Comran matched the expression, then relented and pulled off his shirt. I reached behind me and grabbed the pouch Loke indicated.

The *rokr* took it and shoved it in Comran's chest.

"Ow." Comran huffed, digging into the bag and bringing out the small box of ointment and a roll of bandage.

"How is it?" I asked quietly.

"Same as always." He jerked the bloodstained bandage off from around his chest. The wound still didn't look like much—a slice across his ribs. Enough to jerk me back to the frantic seconds of Comran bursting in to defend me. More bruising and cuts stained his shoulders and chest. Evidence of the battles he'd been fighting.

"It might be better if he didn't let a sablecat pounce on him every chance he gets," Loke said.

I leaned forward in concern, even as Comran rolled his eyes.

"I had the battlelion right where I wanted him."

Loke grunted. "Yes, about to kill you."

"Any other sign of Hakkon?" I cut off whatever retort Comran had prepared.

Anger stirred in his grey eyes. "Only once. And the coward didn't stick around long once their cats ran scared."

"But they seem to know where best to strike and how to fight against us," Loke butted in.

I scraped a hand over my jaw and muttered an imprecation.

"I told you I'm the more creative one, Loke," Comran said.

The *rokr* huffed a reluctant smile. "Only because you're always running that mouth of yours."

Comran wrapped another bandage around his ribs, again showing complete ease with the process, before pulling his shirt back on. He pointed past me in question, and I handed him the bracers.

"How many riders did you bring?" He tugged the laces snug against his forearms.

"Another four packs. Birgir is training more as fast as he can." I prepared to hand the leg greaves over.

He shifted to better strap them over his boots while sitting.

"Are you here to stay?" There wasn't annoyance in his voice.

"For some time, at least. I had Father step back into my place while I'm here." I fiddled with the buckle of his breastplate before handing it over.

"A good plan." He paused and waited until I looked up in relief. I'd been afraid it might seem weakness to have the old chief step back into the role while I left. But he nodded.

"Why do you think I had Birgir start the training?"

"Laziness, pure and simple." I tilted a grin.

They both laughed and Comran pushed up to his feet, stooping a little under the low ceiling, and pulled on the armor. He buckled on his weapons as he stepped out of the tent, standing tall and showing no sign of favoring his wounded side which had clearly been bothering him.

We went first to greet the new packs that had ridden in with me. Comran knew most names and shared more than one laugh as they settled in. It helped me shove away my previous thought.

I needed Comran as battlewolf.

And when he looked at me with a bit of trust, and something I dared name as relief that I'd come, I wanted him as a brother even more.

# TWENTY

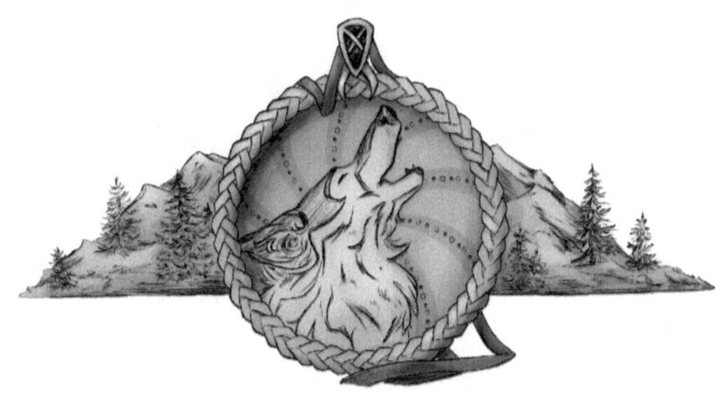

## COMRAN

Loke handed me a bowl of white war paint and I passed the dark green paint to the warrior next to me. Two green lines running down my right cheek, and the single line drawn under my left eye marked me as the battlewolf. Dipping a finger into the white paint, I streaked three bands down my left cheek, one down the outer edge of my right jaw, and a broad stripe across my forehead—bands of mourning for those we'd lost.

Every warrior had begun to add white paint around their green war paint.

Lastly, I inked the mourning rune on my breastplate over my heart. There were too many dead for all the names to fit. Loke's chest bore the rune for a member of his own pack who'd fallen the day before. We'd carry them to battle with us one more time.

I wiped my hands clean and loosed the warrior cord around my wrist. Loke did the same, and we wordlessly exchanged our cords, tapping left fists together once back in place.

Picking up my spear, I surveyed the camp. Each lodge provided a pack of warriors between ten or fifteen riders, depending on the calling the lodge-members felt. Thirty packs total, and twenty-two had ridden out to don war paint and go to battle.

The rest remained to guard the village, and Birgir kept training the younger warriors. I prayed to the All-Father Himself the trainees would not be called out. That Loke's young brother would not have to face battle yet.

"Ready?" Loke came to stand at my shoulder.

I nodded, checking sword and knives. Eska waited nearby, green paint streaked across his fur. At my whistle, he came to my side, walking with me as we went to each pack who'd be riding with us.

A younger warrior stood with hands wrapped tight around his spear, staring at the ground. His head jerked up at the hand I dropped on his shoulder. He swallowed hard, eyes a little wide underneath the paint drawn in shaky lines across his face. But he gave a nod in response to my wordless question.

I moved on, pack leaders tapping fists to chest, verbalizing their readiness to follow. When I got to the last pack, I paused. Kay tilted his chin up as I came to stand in front of him. I arched an eyebrow, waiting. While he hadn't challenged me since our fight, he'd still found small ways to dissent.

"Don't worry." He gave a grim sort of smile. "I find I don't mind following orders."

My lips quirked slightly. "That might be the nicest thing you have said to me."

He shook his head, jaw working to hide some expression. "I thought you did not care what others thought?"

I tapped his shoulder. "I lied."

He was still shaking his head as I backed away and gave the call to mount up. Wolves heaved themselves to paws, growling and snapping in readiness as warriors swung into saddles and gathered up reins.

Eska's growl trembled through the leathers as I settled my spear in my left hand. Scouts were reporting larger sablecat packs. The Sabers were pushing their way past our boundary stones at the mouth of the valley and in the stolen southwest corner. Twelve wolf packs were ready to follow me and try to push the Sabers back from the two miles they'd gained in the last counting.

The packs moved out in lines, snaking around towering pines and oaks that spilled from the hills, marching down into the valley in narrow bands. Scouts darted away at my signal, their lean wolves leaping quicker through the trees and across the open spaces.

We rode on, quiet lingering other than the whisper of paws across the snow still spotting the darker sections of the wood.

Scouts raced back, bringing word just before I saw myself. Packs of sablecats broke from the tree line. I raised my spear and howls answered. Eska surged into motion. Greywolves fell into spearheaded formations, pack leaders at the head.

A hiss warned me of danger coming from above. I shouted an order, and slid to Eska's left side, hand bracing through a strap at the top of the saddle, and spear tucked up tight against me. The Saber's cursed arrows hit around us in bursts of snow or dirt. Cries brought me looking over my shoulder. Most had made the same transition as me, but at least two saddles were empty and a tumbled pile of grey fur fell behind as we raced on.

Eska hop-skipped, nearly undoing my grip as an arrow bounced off the saddle seat. But still I held the position against his side, waiting as the sablecats kept coming and we came under range of their bows. Then, with my own howl, I pulled myself back up, and reset my spear.

Eska shook his head, lunging even faster. Howls followed mine as the packs re-mounted. I picked my target, heart steadying, thudding six calm beats, and then our lines met with a rending clash.

Cries and the screams of animals shattered the air. But calm still held inside. This was where I was most confident. Where I felt most at home.

Even when Eska collided with a sablecat and I lost my seat, Loke and I joined forces on the ground, swords flashing as we kept pushing.

The sun cast shadows at a slanting angle to the east when the battle ended. The Saber tribe retreated from the field. I watched them go, arms hanging by my sides, blood dripping from my sword and a dozen other places my leather armor had not protected.

The battlewolf medallion tapped my chest as I began to walk the field, helping pull wounded warriors up or kill injured sable-cats who had not been able to leave the field.

Their wounded had been taken from the field with retreating warriors, though reports said the battlelion and some other leaders would often leave the injured. But those who would not survive long, I gave orders to see to them and to let them pass in peace.

I stood over one warrior, his red-painted features twisted in agony as blood spread around him. One hand grabbed the pelt of his dead sablecat beside him. Resignation glinted in his eyes. We both knew he was dying.

We were all just men when it came our turn to walk through the dark wood's veil and meet death. Maybe he'd find the path to the All-Father's lodge lit bright with torches for valor and good deeds. Maybe he'd hunt forever in the darkness.

Either way, I had no joy in watching him die. Even if he might have killed some of my warriors. If it were my blood watering some place far from home, I'd want a friendly face when I died.

I crouched beside him. Fear took over as he stared at me, breaths taking on a rattling sound.

Placing a hand on his chest, I said gently, "Go in peace. May the All-Father welcome you home."

His shaking and blood-stained fingers pressed over mine before he jerked one more breath and went still. A thin scrap of cloth around his wrist fluttered. It stilled between my fingers, threads marking runes of protection and images of sablecats, different from the beads we wove onto our warrior cords etched with signs of strength and protection. Requests of the All-Father who still chose when to call us from this world despite prayers and runes.

I pushed back to my feet, standing a moment before I smeared the warrior's blood from my hand onto my trousers. Battle held no fear for me, but my heart felt its weight in the moments afterward. Swallowing the tightness in my throat, I picked my way towards a thrashing greywolf. By the time I reached its side, it had stopped, sides heaving as it lay on its side, defeat in its eyes.

A faint movement brought me moving quicker. Kay lay half-pinned under the wolf, his eyes unfocused under the blood streaking his face. One hand grasped at the ground in a fumbling attempt to pull himself out.

"Easy." I touched his hand. He blinked unsteadily. Crouching beside him, I tried to see if he was wounded anywhere else. It did not seem so.

Hooking hands under the straps of his breastplate, I heaved. The wolf gave a mighty groan and tried to roll away, lifting its side enough so Kay's legs slid free. The wolf's head thumped back down. I held onto Kay's armor, keeping him sitting.

His head lolled until I got a hand up against his cheek and brought him up to face me.

"You with me?"

His hand lurched up to clench around my upper arm. He blinked again, taking a few shuddering breaths, and nodded.

His gaze shifted past me, taking in his wolf, and his face twisted. I released him, letting him lean over its shoulder, brushing a shaky hand over its fur. A low whine came from its bleeding muzzle.

Kay ran a tentative hand down its belly, shoulders hunching more when he saw the wound. The tightness grew in my chest when he pulled a knife. He plunged it into the wolf's throat with a strangled cry.

My hand clamped on his shoulder as another hoarse scream shook him. Eska padded up, amber eyes taking in the sight with the strange brightness sometimes caught in a wolf's eyes.

Eska pressed his nose to the dead wolf's, then softly huffed at Kay's neck. The warrior stilled, then touched Eska's cheek in thanks.

Kay took the hand I offered and let me help him to his feet. We stood regarding one another for a moment, then he slammed a fist into his chest. I nodded, and let him go, heart clenching again as I watched him stumble away.

Movement at the distant tree line drew my attention. A mounted Saber warrior emerged, bow fastened to his back. I tensed, hand falling back to my sword. But he just watched for a few minutes before he turned his lion and vanished.

# TWENTY-ONE

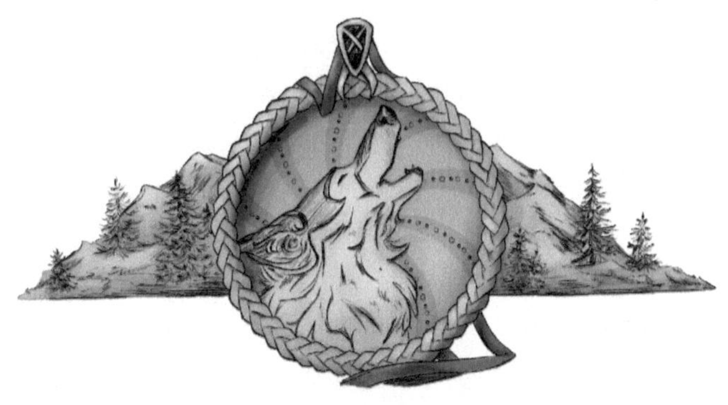

## COMRAN

"Hold still!" The healer shoved my shoulder back down, ignoring my glare.

Etran stood nearby, wrapping a bandage around his wrist where it had been twisted under a sablecat. The needle stabbed my leg again and I cursed the healer, which he also ignored.

"Stop being such an infant," Loke reprimanded. Another warrior cleaned a cut across the side of his scalp, water dripping to mess the green and white paint.

"This hurts worse than the spear that did it." I thumped my head back against the ground.

"It wouldn't if you'd hold still," the healer groused.

"Then hurry up. You're moving slower than my grandmother, may she rest in honor in the All-Father's Halls."

The healer glared. "I'm about to send you to the All-Father's Halls myself."

"Good. Then I won't have to suffer your attempts at healing."

Irritation suffused his normally calm face, and I swear he stabbed the bone needle harder than necessary into my skin again. I jolted and scowled at him.

In truth, I would do anything I could to forget the way we had to retreat the field in the last three battles, giving way before larger packs of sablecats. And losing nearly five miles of our territory.

They had pushed east towards the lower curve of the river. Even with the additional packs Etran had brought with him almost two countings ago.

At least winter was steadily giving way before spring, though snow still littered the ground under the trees in the spaces where the sun didn't reach. The nights were still cold, bordering on freezing, but the sun had been gaining strength.

Ice retreated from the river and its tributaries more and more every day.

Finally, the healer finished the bandage and left me to go attend the next rider. Etran extended a hand and helped me gain my feet. He shifted in surprise when I leaned an arm on his shoulder to help balance, and then kept it there as we began to head away from the healer's area.

"It's not your fault," he said quietly as my feet stopped at the sight of the wolves and riders clustered around, nursing wounds and looks of defeat.

"I'm the one who led the battle."

"You can't win every fight," Etran said wryly.

"That sounds illogical." I allowed a faint smile.

It faded again at the sight of the wrapped bodies waiting for burial. More white paint to add to our faces and armor to keep bringing the fallen with us to battle.

"And you can't protect everyone."

I heard some of my own pain in his voice.

"If I hadn't banished him, this might not have happened." The low words held something akin to distress.

I shifted, turning to watch him. Etran stared unseeing ahead as he crossed his arms over his chest. Was that what he thought?

"The Saber tribe might have attacked anyway. They have been pushing the boundaries since summer."

Uncertainty and anguish filled his eyes as he met my stare. "But do you know that?"

I didn't, and for once couldn't find words.

"What would you have done in my place?" he asked.

That I did know. "I would have killed him as a traitor. But that means you likely chose right." The mirth I tried for didn't make it to my voice.

Etran studied me more intently. "Why do you sell yourself short?"

I huffed a humorless laugh. "The day you were chosen, I was told that I lead with my heart, but the mind was clearly the better revered between us. It appears it's not my strength."

He shook his head. "I wish I had the strength to make decisions with my heart, instead of weighing every option countless times. You know what you want. I don't."

"I want many things, but I think we might need your steadiness instead of my rashness, especially if we keep losing ground."

We'd suffered more than one defeat in the last counting, our packs beginning to give way east back toward the river and north along the hills, and it frightened me that I might be failing with each choice I made.

"Then why did you side with me?" Etran tilted his head in puzzled confusion, still contemplating the matter of Hakkon.

I fought within myself to reveal the truth. "You needed my support. A decision had to be made. I wanted the opposite, but that did not make it the right choice. And they need to see us in agreement."

A quiet chuckle broke from him as he shook his head. "You might be a better man than me. You would do the right thing. I would do the best thing."

I propped my arm on his shoulder again under the pretense of needing support. "Perhaps you sell yourself short."

Loke and Jens began to make their way toward us. Amund would join us later with scouting reports. We needed another council among ourselves, determining our next strategy. The Saber tribe had taken a corner of our valley. If they pushed us back across the great river, it would be harder and harder to hold them.

"I think I could use some help from that mind of yours," I admitted. "I'm not sure what to do next."

Understanding filled his eyes, unfairly seeing the way the words stung my pride under the careless way I'd said them. He dipped a nod.

"We'll find a way to hold the valley," he said.

I wished I could have his assurance, because not so deep down, a bit of doubt had begun to stir at our strength, and my own ability to lead.

# TWENTY-TWO

## ETRAN

I rubbed the aching knot forming under the left shoulder strap of my breastplate. It had appeared the night Father had named me a chief and had yet to leave, the muscles knotting tighter and tighter with each day and decision I second-guessed.

Frea padded up and nudged her side against mine as she *whuffed* low in her throat. I left off trying to manage the muscle and sank my hand into her fur instead. Her muzzle parted in a happy pant as I found the spot at her shoulder she always begged me to scratch.

Around us the camp had begun to stir. Comran was not up yet, which sent a flicker of concern through me. He was usually up and about with the dawn, but last night at the council fire, he had winced more than once. It had not gone unnoticed by me or Loke.

And he was supposed to be leading out a pack today to ride the southern paths and mark new boundaries where the Sabers had pushed us back in the last days. The thought of more ground lost to the enemy sent my shoulder clenching tight again.

Frea rumbled, slamming her side a little harder into me. I frowned, but she successfully stopped the spiraling of my thoughts.

"Chief." One of the warriors passed by and tipped a small nod. My tongue seemed to freeze and I barely managed a nod back.

I had been eager enough to join the warriors, to fight with a blade instead of words. The men and few women who rode the wolves were blunt and didn't care to hide their feelings. Most had kept their same ambivalence toward me, but the bits of respect now cropping through were almost stranger.

"Etran." Jens's voice snapped my attention back. His head tilted in slight confusion as my face held the bewilderment I felt.

"What?"

He studied me a moment longer, then shrugged. "Comran is up, but…does not look well enough to be riding out." His voice stayed between the two of us and Frea. "Loke is having no success trying to get him to stay, so we thought you might try."

"Me?"

It was the closest I'd seen to Jens rolling his eyes at me. "Yes. If not as chief, then maybe as…you."

That did not make things clearer. This time Jens did roll his eyes and huff.

"He respects you at least, Etran."

My tongue froze. Comran and I had been getting along more these last countings, perhaps becoming more open with each other out in the valley and away from Father and the eyes of many of the tribe.

Before I could attempt to speak or move, Jens's hand clapped over my shoulder, and he pushed me forward. I frowned and shook myself free. He raised an eyebrow and extended a hand in invitation to keep walking.

Resisting the urge to childishly stick out my tongue at him, I kept moving to Comran's tent. He still had not taken the place at the head of the tent circles, and I had not either, both of us preferring to keep tents closer to our own friends.

The low hiss of voices guided me around the tent to where Comran and Loke stood with Eska. Loke lifted his head, something near relief breaking over his broad features. Comran stopped whatever retort he'd been making to check the source of Loke's attention. I almost flinched.

His face was painfully pale and drawn, and sweat clung to the edges of his hair despite the cool of the morning. His shoulders hunched under the weight of his armor, but Eska stood steadfast under his hold, doing more to keep Comran upright than his own legs.

Uncertainty forgotten, I strode forward. "Are you all right?"

"Yes," he growled, and offered no other words, a sure sign he was not.

Loke shook his head, eyes raised to the sky as if asking the spirits for patience. Comran tried to push up taller, but his knee wobbled. Eska gave a little yelp and shift as Comran's grip on his fur became white-knuckled.

"Comran, you cannot go today." I almost reached out.

He sucked in a breath, ready to argue. Loke was already shaking his head again, but I gave a small wave of my hand. I knew enough about Comran by now that a friend telling him no would only make him do it more. But perhaps he would listen to the chief.

Loke dipped a small nod and retreated, leaving us. Comran had yet to make his reply, but a small tremor racked his arms.

"Comran, you don't have to prove yourself," I said softly, understanding a little of what might be driving him.

"Why? Because we all know you're better than me?" he snapped.

I barely flinched. He twisted his head away, hand fisting before he gently tapped it against Eska's side.

"I'm sorry, that's…"

I offered a faint smile. "Not like I didn't tell you the exact same thing not so many countings ago."

He sucked in a breath, then turned to look at me, a tentative rise at the corner of his mouth. "It should not be surprising you see it more than Loke."

"We are not so different, the two of us." I reached out and tapped Eska's side. The greywolf craned his head around and offered me a lopsided grin.

"I suppose not." Comran shifted again, feet appearing to be a little steadier this time. "So maybe you'll see why I feel I need to go."

"And if the places were exchanged, you'd be telling me I should trust those around me to lead the patrol."

The glare he sent me was halfhearted, but we both knew I'd won.

"Did the spirits make you the most irritating man in the tribe?"

"I was going to ask the same of you," I said.

He huffed a laugh, raising his head to look over Eska's back into the forest. It took a moment before he nodded, acknowledging his defeat. I dared place a hand under his elbow. He freed his hold from Eska and latched on to my upper arm to keep himself steady.

We managed to start taking the few halting steps back to his tent.

"You lead the patrol, then," he said.

I didn't shift my gaze from our boots, making sure the ground stayed clear of other obstacles. "Me?"

"You are so determined to make me stay in bed like an ailing grandmother, so you get to do the boring work." A shadow of his normal smirk was back. I rolled my eyes.

"You're already dressed for it." He managed to tap my leathers with his free hand, the other still painfully clenched around my arm. "And it won't hurt for you to prove what you can do to some of these warriors, either."

My head snapped up to find the faint, rueful grin in place. We did know each other after all.

"Fine. But only because the battlewolf outranks the chief in war," I finally said, sweeping open the tent flap for him.

"Of course." He nodded seriously.

I helped him inside and down to his pile of furs. A sigh of relief eased from him as he settled. I crouched and took his armor as he slowly undid the buckles, setting it on the other side of the tent in what I thought was a close approximation of his exact piles.

"How is it?" I helped lift the breastplate off.

Sweat dampened his shirt collar and he wiped more from his forehead with his sleeve.

"It's not been this bad in awhile," he admitted.

"Do we need to send for the healer?" Concern had me shifting.

Comran shook his head. "He is only going to tell me the same thing he has since that night."

The night he jumped to save me without hesitation.

"Loke was going to ride with me. He should be getting the pack ready to go." Comran started to unlace his boots, then gave up and lay back with a faint grimace.

I did not mind riding with the *rokr*. "Get some rest."

He made a noise of assent, eyes already closing. Hesitation slowed my hand before I reached and took one of the neatly-folded blankets to spread over him. He didn't stir, breath evening out in sleep. The nudge at my heart came again, the one that wanted so desperately for us to acknowledge each other as brothers.

Pushing it away, I left the tent. A grin appeared at the sight of Eska hovering just outside the flap and blocking my way. The wolf lowered his great head, eyes looking at me almost guiltily. A glance over my shoulder, and then I stepped aside, holding the flap open. Eska paused once, then nosed his way inside, settling down beside Comran. At the brush of fur against his face, Comran rolled toward his wolf, a sigh settling through him.

Eska nosed at Comran's hair before resting his head down on the ground and shifting more comfortably. Shaking my head, I closed the tent flap and asked the spirits to send Comran some rest.

"You shouldn't encourage him," Loke said, exasperated smile on his face.

"What?" I attempted innocence.

Loke snorted. "It's why I won't share a tent with Comran. Try waking up half-smothered by that excuse for a wolf."

A laugh threatened this time. "He asked me to take the pack instead. You were to ride with him?"

Loke affirmed, no argument at my first statement. "The pack will be ready when you are, Chief."

"I'll get Frea."

"Etran." He halted me before I strode away. He flicked a hand to Comran's tent. "Thank you."

I tipped my head before escaping to find the familiarity of Frea and pulling my walls back up in preparation for riding with the pack.

Dusk was falling when we returned, creeping its way under the spreading branches and filling up the smaller spaces in the forest. We'd encountered a Saber pack on the ride and a short skirmish had seen us maintaining our borders. Some riders had wounds, but all the saddles stayed full, and no wolves had been lost.

Comran strode to meet us, moving as if he hadn't been about to collapse hours ago.

"How was it?" he asked.

"We skirmished at the borders and held." I slid from Frea.

Relief shone bright in his eyes. He moved past to knock fists with Loke.

"Cook fires have been waiting for you." He gestured farther into camp.

Frea settled down to rest her paws as soon as I had the saddle off. Another pack rode in as I finished and made my way to the fire we'd been sharing with the *rokrs*, placed midway between our two tents in some sort of truce. Jens was already there, and Loke not far behind him.

I held a plate of food and watched Comran move around to greet the new pack, clapping warriors on the shoulder or roughly patting wolves. From there he went to each cookfire, spending some time at each, laughter and smiles following in his wake. His was the loudest and it seemed even the stars perked up at the sound, everything, including him, seeming to forget how terrible he'd looked just hours before.

Even the wolf riders and pack leaders who might have once given him trouble made space at their fires for him. It dimmed my appetite a little to watch him effortlessly moving between each place, accepted so quickly, extending himself so easily in a way I never could seem to do with anyone.

A hand dropping onto my shoulder startled me from my intent study of my food, which I'd yet to touch.

"Thank you for leading the pack." Comran lowered to the seat beside me—the rough tree trunk hauled there when we'd set up camp.

I nodded, shoving a bite into my mouth to avoid speaking, the bit of bitterness still lurking at the back of my tongue.

"I heard it was an efficient fight with you at the head." Comran still looked to me.

"That's because he does not hurl himself from his wolf every chance he gets," Loke put in dryly from his place across the fire.

A smile snuck onto my face as Comran scoffed.

"You have always been critical of my technique."

"What technique?" Loke scooped more hash onto his plate.

"Finely-crafted strategy." Comran leaned closer to me as if re-assuring. A faint snicker came from Jens.

I had to agree. Comran fought with wild abandon, but still somehow focused and intent on a goal. It wasn't hard to see why he'd gained the respect of the packs so quickly.

"No respect." Comran shook his head, continuing as if not noticing that I'd yet to contribute to the conversation. Jens and Loke filled in the spaces, keeping conversation going as they discussed the patrol and where we had encountered the Sabers, and the most recent reports brought in by Amund and his scouts.

I kept eating until silence fell and I looked up again to see Loke and Jens walking off, Comran still beside me. He rested his elbows on his knees, hands loosely clasped, and looked at me expectantly.

Placing my plate aside and dusting my fingers off, I searched for something to say.

"You look better."

He shook his head. "We've already discussed me enough

today. You, however, look like you smelled something sour."

My palms scraped together. "Just worried about everything that's happening." That seemed the safer option.

Comran nodded thoughtfully and picked up a jug, uncapped it, and gestured for my cup. Warily, I handed it over.

"Never thought I would figure out that you are a terrible liar." He poured clear liquid into the cup. From the smell, it wasn't water.

I swirled it around as he poured himself a share.

"Trying to get a confession from me?" It came out more bitter than I meant it as I lifted the cup.

"I prefer the truth in most matters," he said. "And while it still stings in some ways, I am finding it easier to accept many things out here away from the village."

Away from Father. It didn't take much to fill in the gaps in his words. I tossed back some of the drink, its warmth burning down my throat. Normally I didn't care much for the draw-off taken early in the brewing of spruce ale and kept in small jugs in dark hollows, but it was a welcome distraction right then.

"How much of this have you had tonight?" I took another bolstering sip.

He chuckled and drank. "My first cup."

The silence fell back between us. It only served to press harder against the feeling of alarm at seeing him in such a bad way that morning.

"I've always wanted a brother," I blurted. My stomach clenched, dreading his reaction.

But he sat back, staring at me. It didn't make the knot loosen at all.

"I've always wondered why we weren't," he finally said. "We *are*, but…"

Realization filled the space between us, and I almost laughed in pure relief.

"Spirits above." Comran shook his head. "I thought for years you hated me, and maybe just were tolerating me recently."

"You have more reason to hate me."

I'd tainted everything for him.

"I suppose." A wince creased his face as he shifted. It brought me leaning slightly towards him, but he only drank, the expression passing. "There were days I wanted to. But I just never could figure out a reason to start."

I tipped my cup back and forth, watching the gentle sway of the liquid. "Even with Father?"

It had given me some triumph over the years when I caught the extra favor bestowed on me. But it soured the moment I saw Comran struggling just as hard as I did for the next drop of approval.

Comran's gaze focused on the fire, and he turned the beaker slowly in his hands. "Maybe that is not a failing on either of our part."

I shifted to watch the dancing flames as well, the heat somehow stretching to sting at my eyes.

"But maybe it *is* a failing that I did not see the difficulty of your path." The words came slow and methodical from him. "I followed those around me."

I forced my hands to stop moving and dragged my gaze to him. I knew why I had kept away for years.

"Do you remember when we were no more than six?"

His head tilted, no memory stirring yet.

I swallowed. "Just before midwinter. The ice was thick on the river. You and some others our age went out on it to play."

Recognition began to dawn in his face, but I pushed on.

"You called me to join. We'd played together before, and no one had said anything about it. But I think maybe, even then, I knew there was something strange about us and Father."

I'd started to notice the whispers and looks directed at me when I moved through the village, but didn't understand them just yet.

"Mother always got quiet when she saw you around," Comran said softly. "At least in those years. But I didn't see her or your mother. Just someone else to even out teams."

I nodded. Maybe that was Comran's way. Finding a way to include others.

"I went, excited to be a part of it. I—I'd looked up to you even then." Heat singed my cheeks at the admission.

His eyes widened in shock and his mouth dropped open in question, but I hurried on.

"When we came back, Mother saw us together and called me over. She was upset, but I didn't know why. She grabbed my arm and pulled me away, telling me I shouldn't play with you. And for the first time I saw her hatred directed back at you, and the way she and your mother looked at each other."

My fingers curled into a fist. "She told me the reason for my birth that night."

There had been other pointed words I'd understood later, but didn't care to say now.

"I remember seeing the look she gave me and wondering what I'd done wrong," Comran admitted. "Mother told me I should look for friends in other lodges."

Setting the cup down beside my boot, I laced my hands together. It wasn't just our mothers. I knew he'd seen the divide, the way we were regarded differently among the tribe, even still.

"So what now?" I asked.

Now that the wound lay open and raw between us.

"You're not the only one who wanted a brother his whole life," he said, and hope lurked in his eyes. "But even if not, Etran, I did swear to protect you and stand by you as battlewolf."

And he'd proved it, nearly with his life. He was proving it every day spent warring with the Sabers. What might he do for a true brother?

"I am honored." I pushed to my feet, needing to breathe clear air and pick back through his words.

"Etran." He halted me before I left the circle of firelight. "I think he chose right. You make a good chief."

Heat blossomed in my chest, warm and reassuring. "I couldn't have chosen better for my battlewolf."

My feet stayed long enough for me to see the bit of pride lighting in him before I left.

# TWENTY-THREE

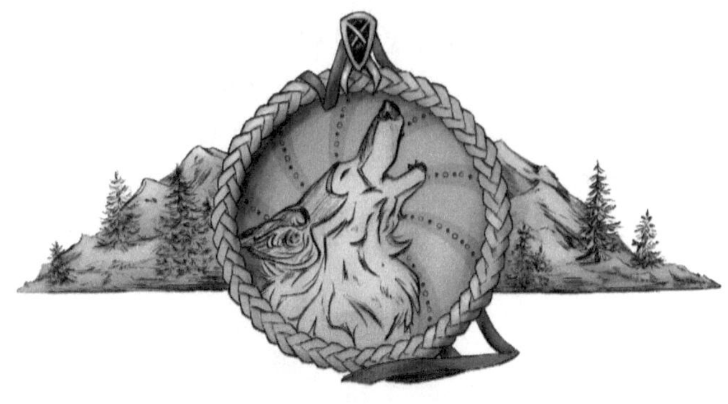

## COMRAN

I stared into the darkness after Etran, barely able to comprehend what he'd said. He'd looked up...to *me*? Had always wanted a brother...in *me*?

It drove an incredulous laugh from my chest. He rarely showed emotion, but I did not think the fear in his eyes when he'd admitted his truth could be faked. And the story he'd told, I remembered as well. Though it seemed my mother had been gentler in her reaction to seeing us play together.

Maybe she had been gentler in many ways in how she'd brought me up. It was a wonder Etran truly didn't hate me. I didn't hate him, either, I'd just tried to ignore him for years, determined that he didn't think much of me and unwilling to let someone else find less worth in me.

I leaned on my knees again, frustration prodding along with the nagging pain in my side. It didn't seem right to sit and think on it by the fire. It was the sort of tangled thing to be pulled apart while racing the mountainside on Eska's back.

But the mountains were miles away and the threat of the Sabers was always lurking. I swallowed sudden restlessness. Eska would at least lend a listening ear. Loke would just ask too many questions and maybe even give a smugly knowing look.

What did this mean for us? I had not lied when I told him it was getting easier and easier to see him as the chief.

And maybe, somehow, we could figure out how to be brothers, as it seemed we'd both wanted all our lives.

The next morning saw us moving camp, pulling back a few miles and digging in on the western side of the river. Our lines were strung out across the valley, and I wanted to bring our camp to the center of our territory.

I sent Amund out with his scouting pack. He'd always been a swift rider, but he was proving a canny spy and tracker, and had picked out the other lean riders and wolves who could do the same.

The rest of us turned to setting up camp. I held back, waiting for Etran to pick his spot first. Our conversation the night before had followed me through every waking moment, bringing with it new awkwardness I was glad to avoid by riding and making sure the packs were moving.

Etran set his packs down, Frea sinking back on her haunches and giving a wide yawn. He still did not take the place at the top of the tent circles, but neither was I. Eska snapped at a drooping pine branch trying to tickle his ears as I halted him beside Etran.

I pulled the packs off and dumped them on the ground, saying nothing. Eska's leathers came next, and he threw his weight against the pine, scratching against the bark. Crouching, I undid the straps of my tent, starting to roll it out and shoving Eska's nose away as he came to investigate and beg for elk jerky.

Finally deterring him, I glanced up to see a more well-mannered Frea still sitting behind Etran, who watched me with a raised brow. I shrugged like I didn't know the reason for the bit of disbelief in his face and kept working. When I looked up again, Etran had turned to pitching his own tent, but a bit of a smile crossed his face.

Less than two countings later, we'd lost more ground to the sable bastards. I fought and I fought, but their numbers were always greater. Scouts reported new packs in their ranks. And with the warriors we lost every encounter, the eventual outcome of the war became more and more grimly apparent.

The night after we managed to hold our ground, I met Etran's somber stare across the fire. We'd fought the Saber tribe in pitched battle in the hills, and lost ground once another pack had appeared and rained cursed arrows on us.

They had been making headway north along the border we shared with the Blackpaws, if the lynxriders even haunted the deep hills anymore. The border stones we could find were overgrown and unmarked except for the stench of sablecat.

"We have to hold here," I said.

Our packs stretched across the length of the great river, forming a barrier on the western bank which had not yet fallen, even if battles in the hills were going differently. I needed to ride and check on them, lend my strength to Jens and their pack leaders and make sure they could keep standing. But it seemed to me, and to others as well, that the brunt of the fighting had become focused on our packs when Etran had arrived.

It wasn't so hard to see why. The battlewolf and the chief, together in one place. Strike them both down in battle, and the tribe loses its heart. You take the valley with little resistance left.

Etran nodded. He knew it same as I.

The night was quiet, the roar of a waterfall cascading down from the yellow hills into a tributary river a distant clamor behind the usual nighttime noise.

"We can do it."

I rolled a pine needle between my fingers before flicking it into the fire. I wished I shared his confidence. But fatigue from more than countings spent camping and fighting, and from fresher wounds, weighed on me.

Every morning brought a new exhaustion from the red spear wound. Every morning, I fought through it, determined to keep standing tall beside Etran and for our packs. Five days ago, I might have fallen in battle from sudden weakness and pain from the wound if not for Jens and one of his packs.

"You need to rest, Comran." Etran's green eyes shone bright in the flames. Eska grumbled from his place off to my left, just far enough from the flames.

"There's enough time to do that in the All-Father's lodge." I tried for a smile, but none stirred his face.

"Are you sure you can keep doing this?"

My spine snapped straighter. "What do you mean?" I growled.

His head tilted, and I knew what he meant. Keep fighting through the wound. The doubt needled at me again. He needed someone stronger, smarter, than me to stand as battlewolf. It was a good thought he had of naming me months ago, but clearly he'd had more than one chance to regret it.

I'd done well enough in the first few countings, but every mile I lost hammered away at my confidence. I was failing to stop an invasion, and I was failing as a warrior. Yet again, I wasn't strong enough.

"You want me to give it back?" I jerked to my feet, a winter storm of anger and shame and doubt raging inside.

He rose, stepping around the flames closer to me. "No, I—"

"It's the right choice, Etran," I spat. "Find someone better than me and you might save the valley."

"Comran, that's not…"

I jerked from his outstretched hand. "Not what, *Chief?*" The voice in my head rebuked me for not being fair, but the bigger one whispering my failings echoed louder.

He recoiled a little.

"It's clear to me. It has been clear my whole life that I'm not as good as you. Do what you need to do to save the tribe. I'll bend the knee again." I couldn't keep the hurt in, and I hated showing that much of myself to him.

"Stop." His command came sharp as I turned away.

My feet treacherously obeyed, when all I wanted was to leave the circle of firelight behind. He came up beside me, enough space between our shoulders that firelight spilled through onto the ground.

"I wasn't questioning anything you've done here," he said softly. "I'm just worried for your wound. I see you struggle with it. And that makes me worried in battle."

I stared at the ground, at the small three-petaled flowers gathered in clumps we'd use in the morning to make new war paint.

"Maybe you're not questioning me, but I am. It's becoming more clear to me that I'm not the one to lead here. You should find a new battlewolf."

"Comran!" He jerked in surprise, and for a brief moment it

warmed my heart that he might actually believe in me.

My hand settled around the medallion over my chest, but he stopped me from pulling it over my head.

"I'll think on it." His words still sent a stab through me. "Keep it for now. We'll speak again in the morning. Go get some rest."

"It's the best thing to do, Etran."

Etran didn't turn away from my gaze. "But is the best thing the right thing?"

"It seems to me it is." I walked away and he didn't call after me.

# TWENTY-FOUR

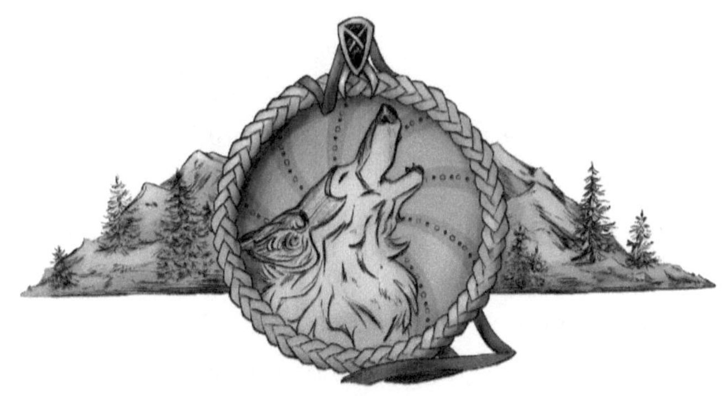

## COMRAN

But the next morning, Etran said nothing. I didn't either, afraid to think he might have seriously considered my words and waited for the right time to reclaim the battle-wolf medallion and pass it to someone else.

We doused fires and saddled wolves, waiting for the sign from the scout. I crouched on the opposite side of camp from him, Eska sitting behind me. Loke waited with me, saying nothing in his frustrating patience.

"Etran told me," he finally said.

"He tell you who he chose in my place, then?" I darted a glance at Etran. He stood talking with another warrior, a bit of laughter escaping every now and then.

"No one is blaming you for all this," Loke said, an unfamiliar bit of anger creeping through. "I wish you would stop blaming yourself and pinning your own self down."

"Maybe I'm finally admitting reality."

"Comran." The anger flared brighter in Loke. "Do not make me beat some sense into you."

"You should take it," I said. "You might have a better head for it."

Loke shook his head, tossing a hand in frustration. "Do you honestly not see how the packs look to you? How we all trust you?"

I studied the laces of my bracer, sliding my finger underneath to test their tightness. The looks of dissent or hate had all but disappeared within the first few countings of the war. And since the day his wolf died, Kay had been one of the first to answer my calls for packs and battle.

"Some of the older warriors are saying you are just as good or better than Birgir," he said.

I had no response, daring to glance up at the gathered packs. Riders settled by their wolves, a deceitful air of relaxation around them. Hands drummed against sword sheaths, or checked blades for the thousandth time, or tapped the spears lying next to them. War paint, freshly applied, glistened on faces and the white bands and runes had been repainted around the green or on armor. Wolves sat alert, noses lifting every few moments to sniff the wind.

And, now that I looked, more than one glance was thrown my way or to Etran. No doubt, no anger, maybe confusion that we weren't standing together as we had been the last few countings, just waiting for the signal to follow us into the next battle.

I swallowed hard. "Maybe it's hard to see."

Loke softened and reached to tap my shoulder. "I know you've felt overshadowed by many things your whole life. Etran trusts you, looks up to you."

A familiar confusion rushed over me, like when Etran had admitted he looked up to me as a small child.

"He wouldn't have chosen you as battlewolf if he didn't think you could do it."

I spun Loke's bands around my wrist. We hadn't traded back since the fighting had become more frequent and the countings stretched on. Part of me wanted to argue that Etran had chosen me to make sure the tribe didn't divide itself into infighting.

The scout rode in, his wolf panting as it sank to the ground. He slid off, looking for me, and finding Etran first. I froze, waiting to see what Etran would do. But he looked directly at me and lifted a hand.

"Battlewolf!" he called.

Loke's hand jarred my shoulder again, and I rose to my feet. As I walked toward Etran, the riders pushed to their feet, adjusting weapons and girths.

"They've made camp by the red-rock tributary," the scout reported. "Not far away."

"Numbers?"

"Near thirty cats as I saw."

I glanced around. We had almost the same number after sending a smaller pack to reinforce Jens farther south two days before.

Etran waited on me. I frowned at him. The scout darted a look between us, unsure about the frosty silence as he'd reported plenty of times to the both of us and we'd not been this distant. For a moment, we were both back under Father's training, him waiting for us to make a decision and see who was wrong.

Etran crossed his arms and arched an eyebrow, still waiting. I glared, matching his stance.

The scout eased back a step, not sure what he was between.

"Fine," I practically spat. "We ride to ambush them."

"Good." Etran didn't relax. "Muster the packs, then."

Part of me wanted to stubbornly refuse, but the other part, just as stubborn, made me turn and begin to give orders.

We rode in short order, tracking a path single file through the trees as the scout led us back through the bits of forest spreading over the rising hills. Amund and his wolf ghosted from the trees and joined us. The rush of the tributary river where it cut a deep path from a distant waterfall through the western hills masked our approach, but it also hid theirs.

The Saber tribe pack had broken their camp and had begun to move as well, making their way from the sheltered place in the hills, when we came face-to-face.

A moment of silence lingered, paws whispering to a stop when I first met the eyes of an approaching Sable warrior. His mouth opened to call to his pack, but I'd already spurred Eska into motion. My riders followed without a second's hesitation.

Our wolves swept forward over the low ridge to leap down atop the sablecats and their riders. I left my spear in a sablecat's gut and drew my sword, cutting past another warrior. Loke pushed up beside me and we fought on until a sharper cry jolted my attention away.

Amund sprawled on a hillside, jabbing at a crouching sablecat with a broken spear. Etran was also un-mounted, locked in battle with a warrior. I recognized the bulk of the battlelion. And saw his sablecat creeping up on Etran from behind.

"Loke!" I shouted, knowing he'd follow when he could. Eska leaped forward, snapping jaws and my sword clearing us a path to the hill which rose up before dropping off the side into the tributary river.

The battlelion pushed Etran back and back, closer to the edge. Amund shouted again, a bit of hopeless defiance in his voice as the sablecat knocked away his spear. I jumped from Eska and gave the command.

Eska raced away, tackling the sablecat away from Amund. I sprinted uphill, time slowing as the sablecat sprang, bearing Etran to the ground. But it didn't strike, just backed away, leaving Etran stunned and at the mercy of the battlelion.

I angled my approach, fear pounding through my heart.

*He can't die.*

A scream tore from me as I crossed the last feet and threw myself into the battlelion, knocking both of us into his cat and away from Etran. The battlelion came up fighting. We scrambled to our feet, blades meeting in a crash. I held my ground, hammering away at him, driving him back downhill and away from Etran.

Blood ran from a cut on my thigh and on my upper arm from his blade. He staggered to the side as my sword slashed above his knee. He backed away a step, giving us both a chance for a breath.

I glanced around for Etran. He was pushing to his hands and knees a few paces away. Relieved, I focused again on the battlelion, only to find a smile on his face.

Weight descended on my shoulders and another scream tore from me as pain speared through my left shoulder. His sablecat's front paws hooked around me, pulling along with its fangs embedded in my shoulder. My feet slid backward, my body too stunned from pain to react.

The roar of the river overcame the pounding of my own heart. I twisted my sword and rammed it back into the body behind me. Its squeal of pain didn't make it release its hold in my shoulder. Instead, a weightlessness took over, and I had a heartbeat to see my feet slip off the edge of the overhang.

The last thing I saw before darkness took me was Etran staring down at me in horror, one arm flung over the edge of the cliff as if he could stop me from falling.

# TWENTY-FIVE

## ETRAN

I stared down at the rushing river, bloody foam swirling away in its haste to cover up Comran's fall. He didn't resurface.

The rocky cliff pressed against my chest and chafed the underside of my arm where it dangled over the edge, as if to reach down into the river twenty feet below and pull him out.

"Chief!" Hands pulled me up, shaking me free of my shock.

The Saber tribe was in retreat, their cats spread out as they raced through the sporadic trees back down the valley.

Amund skidded to a halt at the edge, staring down into the river, before fixing me with wide eyes. I shook my head numbly. Even if we could find Comran, we had no time. We needed to pursue the Saber tribe.

I could leave a few men behind to trace the river gorge down to where it formed banks, or comb the various waterways spitting off it, maybe even down to the nearest lake, but this far out there was a chance they wouldn't return either.

We needed to stay together. Protection within the pack.

"Move out."

The words rumbled harsh from my mouth. Amund's gaze

melted to horror and anger. Loke restrained him, his face twisted in the same disbelief, but understanding lurked beneath. He knew what I did.

Even if Comran survived the fall and the cold, so much blood stained the ground where he fought the battlelion and the sablecat. Where he'd fought them to save *me*.

I could never forget the way he screamed when it bit into his shoulder, him driving his sword into its gut seconds before it dragged them both over the edge.

The spirits' lodge and now here.

It should have been me.

We pursued the Saber tribe, but their fleet sablecats outstripped us. We managed to bring down three more of their warriors before we halted, their lithe black forms kicking up faint puffs of dust as they vanished into the distance.

I left a patrol of twenty wolfriders to range through the hills. The rest of us turned across the valley, a numb thought pounding at my mind that I needed to be the one to deliver the news of Comran to the village.

A savage growl and shout jerked my attention up. Eska fought with the rider who held his reins. He'd known to run with the rest of us, but he must have sensed we were not going back to the river.

A wild and dangerous light shone in his eyes, and his lips curled back in a feral snarl. The rider and his wolf barely managed to dodge away. Eska did not respond to the usual calming words.

It wasn't Comran speaking them.

Eska's struggles grew wilder until Frea growled. I dismounted and let her lunge forward. She pinned Eska to the ground, snapping dangerously close to his muzzle. He snarled back, ears pinned against his head, fangs bared to their fullest. Frea's threat rumbled and Eska reduced his snarl to a growl. She backed off and he rolled to his feet, his tail lowered in slight deference. Barely obedient.

My heart plunged deeper in my chest. Comran would not have hesitated to go back.

I mounted Frea as she returned to my side and checked to make sure Eska tolerated a new hand on the reins before we moved out. Loke rode beside me in silence for the hours it took to cross the valley.

Cries went up from the village when they saw us approaching through the fading light. Cries of welcome that would soon die to those of grief when the fallen were noticed. I pulled Frea to a halt in the lodge circle where the villagers had begun to gather. Mother strode towards me, glad welcome on her face, but I didn't look at her.

Comran's mother had come to an uncertain halt. Father halted between us. My legs were stiff as I went to Inger, feeling as frozen as the ground beneath my feet, still yet to fully thaw under the mountain's shadow.

She looked up at me with questioning eyes, hope of some other explanation achingly plain in her face. I opened my mouth, but no sound came. Her chin trembled and she lifted a hand to my chest to brace herself.

"I'm sorry." The pathetic words ground shakily from me. We didn't even have a body to bring back.

A keening sob broke from her and she bent under the weight of it. I wrapped steadying arms around her, for once not afraid to defy my mother's biting words about the woman who had chosen to respect me in spite of everything.

"I'm sorry." My voice broke with the effort of keeping my own stinging pain from showing.

It was my fault.

He'd tried to protect me and had paid the price. Again.

Father touched my arm and I surrendered her to his hold. He soothed a hand over her greying hair and looked to me with shocked eyes. Perhaps, like me, he had thought Comran would never be the one to fall.

It hadn't happened in my dreams.

"He fell. Protecting me." The admission jerked from me. "It should have been me." I stumbled back a step, the world finally snapping into focus again.

"Etran." Mother stopped me. There was no grief in her face. Only joy that I was the one who had come back.

I pulled my arm from her grip.

"Come inside. Clean yourself. Rest."

I shook my head, suddenly desperate to get away.

"Etran." A sternness took over her voice, as if she didn't believe it should have affected me so.

I turned on her. "He's dead! My brother is dead." My shout echoed across the circle.

I left her standing there, desperate to find some place to harness the choking emotion.

My brother.

I never had a chance to call him that. Would never know if he truly felt the same. Never had a chance to thank him for saving my life. Never have a chance to tell him I believed in him as my battlewolf.

Would never have a chance to repay him.

My feet brought me to the river by the village, a gentle stream fed by the melting snows and glaciers high on the mountains above us. Not like the raging torrent that had swept him away. Comran's face had been one of shock—and, for a moment, acceptance—before he'd vanished, the sablecat still wrapped around him, weighing him down.

I pressed a hand against my forehead, trying to drive it away. If I'd seen the sablecat behind me, if I'd gotten up faster to protect him before it sank its teeth into him...

*I should have gone back.*

I'd made the right choice.

*He could still be alive.*

The river had claimed him, the sablecat had bitten deep.

The words flitted in and out as swiftly as the water in front of me.

"Chief?" A hesitant voice broke through. I turned my head to see a wolfrider there. "It's Eska," he said apologetically.

My heart fell further.

"We all said you should be the one to decide."

I forced a nod and followed him to the stables. Snarling and snapping teeth sounded from one of the larger pens. Most of the wolves lay or stood to the side, watching Eska struggle against his leads. Their eyes and muzzles betrayed almost sorrowful expressions, as if they knew what had broken him.

Froth dripped from Eska's teeth as he paused for a moment, flanks heaving. Three riders surrounded him, two spears lowered to keep him at bay in a corner. The saddle skewed over his back, one rein leather on the verge of breaking.

Loke waited for me. He crossed his arms, staring down at the mud for a long moment.

"We've tried to calm him. He won't. His eyes are changed."

I swallowed hard. Eska had gone wild. Losing Comran had shattered him.

"Can we get the leathers off him?" I asked.

"He won't let anyone near enough."

I stepped closer, ignoring Loke's sharp intake of breath. Maybe I sounded or looked enough like Comran to do the job. Eska tensed as I got closer, a growl rumbling deep in his chest. He kept one baleful eye on me, muzzle forced away by the point of a spear.

"Careful, Chief," one of the warriors cautioned needlessly.

I whistled out softly the way Comran did to him. One ear pricked up, but the bright light didn't fade. He stilled enough for me to touch the saddle leathers. I undid them in two quick twists.

"Open the gate."

The growl throbbed lower in intensity as men began moving. Eska pushed back against the spear.

I whistled again. Murmuring nonsense words, I gingerly approached his head. One swift move and I'd be dead or at least missing an arm. But Eska still held. The warrior shifted his spear to nudge the dripping teeth farther from me. The rider holding the reins leaned further back on the leathers, keeping him in place.

"Ready?"

I received nods in reply.

Whispering a prayer to the Greywolf spirit, I reached up and tugged the bridle loose. Eska whisked away, shaking his head and snapping at the spears. We retreated to allow him a clear path to the gate and the forest beyond. Pausing once, he turned to look at me, eyes sorrowful and understanding for a moment, before turning wild. He ran through the gate and disappeared into the woods.

A strangled sound drew my blurred vision to Loke. He stood staring after Eska, the back of his hand pressed against his mouth, smothering a cry. Anguish bowed his shoulders. Amund was there in a moment, gripping Loke's shoulders, tears tracking down his own face.

Loke pressed his head against Amund's shoulder a moment,

his body shaking with suppressed sobs. Then he wrenched away and strode off, head bowed and shoulders curled around his grief.

The riders still present glanced to one another, made a sign of respect towards the woods where Eska had disappeared—as close as we would get to paying honor to Comran—before slipping off until only Amund and I stood there.

Amund gave me one long look, his war paint smeared across his face, before he, too, left. I don't know how long I stood there, staring at the woods, somehow waiting for Eska to come back. Refusing to believe I would have no way to remember Comran.

*He can't be gone.*

"Etran?"

I turned to see Maren. I lifted a hand helplessly, finally feeling the tears tracking down my face. She strode forward and pulled me into a hug. Burying my face against her shoulder, I held tight and wept. She didn't say anything, just rested a hand against the back of my head, until I finally regained some control.

"I don't...we weren't close...I don't know why..."

She shifted her hands to my shoulders, bringing me gently to meet her gaze. "But you were starting to be."

I rested a hand around her forearm. "Maybe. I'll never know. I only ever wanted him as a brother, and..."

"I heard he fell protecting you," she said gently.

I nodded miserably.

"First the spirits' lodge, and now this. I think he must have cared to do so much for you." She searched my face.

The thought struck that Comran would have done it for anyone. But then the remembrance of his doubt the night before, his willingness to give up the position of battlewolf...

I'd still believed in him, and I hoped he knew it before the end.

"I left him behind." The admission whispered from me.

Her hands shifted to give me a small shake. "Sander said the river was too fast and deep there. You couldn't have found him."

Sander. Her younger brother. The one Comran had looked out for after his first battle and sent back for more wolfriders. The young warrior who I knew regarded Comran almost as a hero of old. Something Comran probably hadn't recognized in many of the other warriors. Hadn't heard the way they told stories around the fires about his ferocity in battle. The way he could turn to laughing just as easily.

He only saw what he thought were his own failings.

"That doesn't make the guilt I feel any less."

"I know." She pulled me back into her arms. "And I'm sorry he's gone."

I drew a deep breath, taking in some of her strength. "Thank you."

"I'm glad you're back, Etran. I've worried for you."

"I won't stay for long."

Understanding and a bit of disappointment appeared in her eyes. Something else stirred in my chest. Something that had appeared before when confronted by her and, just like now, I wasn't sure I wanted to give it a name.

Instead, I scrubbed the corner of my eye with the heel of my hand, looking more closely at her. Training leathers molded against her body and she wore weapons easily.

"How is training?"

Maren offered a small smile at my attempt to turn my mind for a second.

"It's good. I have a wolf now."

We now had spare greywolves to bond with new warriors. And that meant one thing.

"When?"

"Birgir said soon. There are almost enough ready for a new pack. And then I'll ride out."

The tightness twisted harder in my chest. "Is he sure?"

Maren tilted her head against the sudden contention surfacing in my voice. "He was battlewolf for years, Etran. I think he knows."

My boots shifted restlessly against the ground, and I glanced off to the woods again. Her hands found her hips and she arched an eyebrow at me.

"You don't think I can do it after years of encouraging me on the fields?"

"No, that's…"

"What, Etran?" A dangerous light glinted in her eyes. Daring me to say something, and it seemed we both knew.

"It's war…"

"I know. I'm watching warriors leave and come back to be buried, same as everyone else."

"Maren!"

"What, Etran? What is it?" The challenge hadn't left her.

"I…" My hand lifted and fell back to my side. "I can't lose someone else. I don't have many friends."

Friends wasn't the right word, but she'd already risked so much years ago becoming friends with the bastard. I didn't dare ask for anything more.

But the arch of her brow was unforgiving. "You might have more if you reached out, Etran. You cannot hide yourself for-ever." Her lips flattened as she paused another moment. "*I will not wait forever.*"

Then she was gone, striding away, her warrior braids tapping against the leathers. I stared after her, not daring to think too hard on her last words.

Just before sundown, the farewell fire was lit in the lodge circle.

The words came uneven from me, aware of Father and Inger standing close together, new tears streaking her face. They seemed pitiful now, a rote prayer and request for mercy at the All-Father's lodge for the fallen warriors.

Silence fell and those who'd lost loved ones began to move forward. I stared at the flames, watching as leather cords or precious items were cast into the flames. But nothing for Comran. His cord had fallen with him.

"Etran." Loke's voice pulled my head up. He extended his hand, bits of braided leather trailing from his palm.

"Comran's?" I asked dumbly.

He nodded. "We exchange them before battle."

I swallowed hard. Sword brothers. I didn't have that bond with any of my friends. He kept his hand extended to me.

"You called him brother. You should do it."

I gave a tight laugh. "I don't think he felt the same of me. It's not my place." I tried to push his hand away.

Loke's smile twisted in grief. "He wanted nothing more than to hear that. I know he did, though he never said as much."

My chest squeezed tighter. Loke placed the cord in my hand and stepped aside. I looked to the flames again, extending my hand to toss it in. My fingers wrapped around the cord. Waiting.

I couldn't throw it in.

My hand fell back to my side. I couldn't yet admit that he was gone.

Loke's eyes didn't hold any judgment. Even some relief and understanding that I hadn't given him to the flames just yet.

"We need a new battlewolf." The words stuck in my throat,

reproaching me for speaking them this soon.

Loke nodded, his gaze never leaving the flames.

"Will you take it?"

He took a short breath, slowly turning to look at me with haunted eyes. "Yes. At least until you find someone better suited."

The unspoken words lingered between us—he'd give it up if somehow, Comran came back.

Once the fire had consumed the memories, we turned inside to the meal. Loke came with me at my request, though I hated to take him from his own family. I needed him beside me.

The meal went on about me. Food lay untouched on my plate. Conversations buzzed around me, bits and pieces coming to my ears.

"I heard he left Comran behind."

"He went into the river. There was nothing to be done."

"Chief's mother doesn't look too upset."

"Chief does."

"He's already named a new battlewolf."

"We need one."

Accusations and defenses were tossed around. I didn't raise my head to contradict or support any of it. The same arguments buzzed around my head.

The leather still twined about my fingers. I couldn't let it go.

"Do you think there's a chance he might have survived?" I turned abruptly to Loke at my right.

His shoulders slumped further. "I don't know. I keep waiting for him to barge through the door, red-faced at being left to walk the entire way back."

The thought brought a faint laugh to my lips. But both of us knew it was so unlikely.

I held out the cord. "You should have this back. He entrusted it to you."

Loke regarded it for a moment. "No. I think he would want you to have it." Brightness filled his eyes. "You should have something to remember your brother by."

My throat closed. "So should you."

"Keep it, Etran. And when you decide it is time to burn it, then I'll believe he's really gone as well."

I dipped my chin in a nod. It would likely be a long time before I could.

# TWENTY-SIX

## SASHA

Water trickled by, chuckling as it celebrated freeing itself from the last vestiges of winter as it headed through the hills toward the lake. Sasha stood balanced on two rocks, spear poised above its chill embrace, waiting for the darker shadow of a red-tailed trout to swim by. Quiet lingered between her and her brother standing a few feet away.

A tendril of scarlet distracted her from the hunt, and she glanced upriver. Her breath caught and she stepped across another rock to tug at Lukas's sleeve. She pointed. His eyes widened.

They retreated to the bank, spears at the ready, sliding cautious feet forward. The tangled lump in the river shallows didn't move. Silence reigned.

"Sasha!" Lukas hissed, tugging at her sleeve as she stepped closer.

She jutted her chin, jerking a hand at the figure. He took a quick breath, watching the forest again with keen eyes before nodding.

Sasha stepped into the river, shivering as the water skidded around her fur-lined boots. Lukas's boots disturbed the flow of the river in low *plunks* and she breathed easier knowing he stood at her back.

She prodded the mass of black fur with the point of her spear. It didn't move. She curled a lip in disgust.

*Sablecat.*

A step closer showed its fangs lodged in leather and a human hand buried under the water.

She beckoned Lukas closer. He went around the sablecat to better look. Raising an eyebrow, she pointed at the animal.

He crouched and pushed. The bodies shifted to reveal a young warrior. Remnants of green and white war paint smeared across his features. Water and blood beaded his face. Blue tinged his lips and fingers.

"He's a Greywolf." Lukas's voice pitched higher in surprise as his fingers slid over the leaping wolves etched into the leather breastplate. He pressed a hand to the man's throat. "And he's alive. For now."

They stared at one another. A Greywolf. Maybe only a little better than finding a Saber in their river.

Sasha lifted her gaze out to the trees. He must have come from somewhere upriver and been swept away. Likely from a battle. Rumors of war in the valley had been whispered around lodge fires. Scouts reporting movement from the Sabers on the stolen side of the lake, and skirmishes between sablecats and greywolves along the border stones purposefully left unmarked. Howls echoing in the night.

Tightening her fingers around the spear, she regarded the unconscious warrior again. Young. Injured. And likely to not last much longer in the frigid water trying to push its way past her insulated boots. If he were a Saber, she might think harder about leaving him in the river. But her conscience was already prodding.

She pointed to the man and then over her shoulder. Her brother nodded, reluctance a bit more obvious in his face.

"We can try." Maybe hoping he wouldn't survive anyway.

He pried the teeth from the man's shoulder with difficulty as the cat's jaw had stiffened in the cold. The curved fangs came free, stained in blood, and the man stirred.

A groan tumbled in his chest, and he shifted away. Lukas caught him before he could turn his face into the water. As if that were a signal, he began to shiver. His eyes flashed open and closed. Blood matted the side of his head.

Lukas pulled him farther away, revealing a sword lodged in the cat. Its other paw snagged on his armor and he shoved it loose.

Lukas pursed his lips in a trilling whistle. A soft growl answered as their lynx stepped from the shadows of the oak trees leaning over the riverbank. Sasha pulled the sword free and shoved it through her belt.

They hauled the warrior over to the bank. Sasha took off her outer jacket and draped it over him. He shivered harder, his hand stirring to pluck the pitiful warmth it gave.

The lynx crouched to the ground, and they wrangled him up onto its back.

He coughed and groaned again, river-water and blood dribbling from his lips. They exchanged a concerned glance.

"We need to hurry," Lukas said.

The lynx padded without a lead as Lukas kept a steadying hand on the warrior. Sasha walked beside them, spear still at the ready, sweeping the forest with cautious eyes.

Ten quick minutes later, the first of the circular lodge houses came into view, settled deep into the forested hills. Two more lynxes regarded them from where they lounged against the walls. A few warriors came up when they noticed the load their lynx carried.

"Greywolf," Lukas said. "Found him in the river. Sablecat took him down."

"Any more of the sable bastards around?" a warrior spat.

Sasha shook her head. She pointed to the ground. The warrior nodded. He jerked his head to the other lynxrider and they set off back down the path to cover their trail.

Sasha hurried ahead to the lodgehouse near the center of the circle and pushed the door open. Her mother looked up from the firepit, concern lighting her eyes at the strange sword in her belt.

Sasha brought her hands together, rapidly signing. <Found a man in the river. He needs help now.>

"Where?" Her mother rose to her feet.

<Lukas is bringing him.>

Her mother pushed through the door to where Lukas had halted the lynx. She circled around to the man's head.

"Sasha, go to Tyra and get all the blankets you can hold. Lukas, help me get him inside."

When Sasha returned, they had moved the man onto the spare bed drawn up beside the fire pit, where he shivered frantically. Sasha placed her armload of blankets on the floor beside the bed. Lukas shut a trunk and brought some of his clothes over.

Her mother undid the man's sword belt, pulling it away. She reached for the straps of his breastplate and stopped. She slid her fingers along the collar and brought out a leather cord. A circular pendant rested in the palm of her hand. Sasha looked closer at her mother's sharp intake of breath.

A wolf craned its head to howl at the sky.

"He's the battlewolf."

Lukas froze and tilted a worried look up at their mother. She pulled the cord over the man's head and tucked the pendant away into her skirt.

"Lukas." The customary briskness returned to her voice. He lifted the man's shoulders to let Sasha and her mother pull the armor away.

The Greywolf groaned again as his shoulder jostled. Red stained his shirt, creeping down his chest and stomach. As his body warmed, more wounds appeared.

"Looks like he's been in quite a fight."

"Sablecat was still attached to his shoulder in the river." Lukas pulled at his shirt. Sasha took over, tugging it over his arms as Lukas lifted him again. Her mother moved in, wrapping a bandage around the man's upper arm, blocking her view of a very muscular chest.

As soon as her mother finished with the bandages, they pulled on dry trousers and a shirt, then began piling blankets over him.

A whimpering cry broke from him as Lukas accidentally jostled him. Their mother soothed a hand across his forehead, and he quieted. Sasha pointed at his shoulder.

"He needs to get warmer first."

His eyes flew open, and he jerked against the confines of the blankets. Panic sharpened his features.

"Easy. You're safe." Her mother repeated the words over and over until he settled back onto the pillow, his eyes glazed and unfocused.

"Etran?" he mumbled in a hoarse voice.

Sasha exchanged a concerned look with Lukas. There had been no one else in the river.

"Where's Etran?" he repeated when they did not answer.

"Not here." Her mother pressed a hand to his chest as he tried to move. "But I'm sure he's fine."

That could be a lie for all any of them knew, but it seemed to calm him. Another shudder wracked his body and he coughed—rasping sounds that tore at Sasha.

"Get me some yellowflame," her mother instructed.

Sasha pushed past the leather wall hanging separating her mother's workspace from the rest of the house. Bundles of dried yellowflame hung from the rafters. She pulled several blooms and placed them in a bowl before bringing it out.

Her mother grabbed it and began twisting the pestle to grind it into fine dust.

"Water," she instructed Sasha. "Lukas." She didn't take her eyes from her task.

Lukas went to the lodge entrance and peeked outside. "No one yet. The chief will be here soon, Mother."

Their mother carefully measured out a few fingerfuls of ground flower into the cup Sasha held. She stirred it and turned to the man. Sliding a hand under his head, she propped him up. His eyes flickered open again and he reflexively swallowed as she poured the liquid into his mouth.

"A little more," Sasha's mother prompted when he tried to stop. He began coughing on the last sip. She turned his head to the side, allowing him to spit it out instead of choking.

He made a sound like something of an apology. Her mother smiled and settled him back down.

"Rest," she said.

His eyes closed, but flickers of pain still crossed his face as he shivered.

"Mother," Lukas warned and stepped away from the door. Their mother wiped her hands and set the bowl aside as the chief and battlelynx stepped in.

The two women looked at the man for a long moment before turning to them.

"Lukas, you and Sasha brought him here?" the chief asked, her green eyes not nearly as stern as her voice.

"Yes, Chief." Lukas spoke for both of them. "Sasha saw him in the river, tangled with a dead sablecat. He must have killed it somewhere upriver before it carried them here."

"That's too close," the battlelynx snapped. "You shouldn't have brought him here. What if the Saber tribe finds us again?"

Sasha stepped past her brother, already signing, but Lukas held out a hand. "We made sure we were the only ones at the river. Two warriors backtracked our trail."

The chief moved closer to their mother. "He's a Greywolf, Zoya?"

Zoya nodded, keeping her hands away from the pocket where the medallion rested. The chief stood by the cot and looked down at the unconscious battlewolf.

"He's young. Will he survive?" A bit of dispassion coated her voice.

"His body is fighting against the cold, but I'm afraid the water got to his lungs. He has several other wounds as well. It will be a hard few days for him, but he looks strong."

Sasha glanced at the man again, amazed he'd survived as long as he did in the river. He was young. It could be Lukas lying there. He probably had family somewhere who likely thought him dead. She crossed her arms and rubbed her thumb over her lower lip.

Maybe a brother too. Or whoever Etran might be.

"Do we want a Greywolf to survive?" the battlelynx spat.

The same anger creased the chief's face, echoed in Zoya and Lukas's eyes, and deep in Sasha's heart. The older women had all lost husbands, and Lukas and Sasha had lost a father, in the war with the Saber tribe when the Greywolves had abandoned them.

But they'd pulled him from the river and brought him here. Zoya sighed and reached into her pocket.

"We might want this one to survive." She held up the medallion.

Shock creased the women's faces, and the chieftain grabbed the wolf's head.

"The battlewolf? But he's so young!" A different emotion clouded her eyes.

"That means Reidar stepped down as chief," the battlelynx said. "He has the look of the chief about him. So is this one his son or his bastard?"

They all stared at him, before Zoya stirred. She rested a hand on the side of the cot where he shivered under the blankets.

"Do I have your permission to care for him?"

The chief worked her jaw, clearly torn. She jerked a nod.

"Yes. But I want to speak with him as soon as he wakes."

Sasha's mother dipped a nod. The chief and battlelynx left and Zoya turned back to them.

"We'll need to make sure he stays warm. And keep giving him more yellowflame. I don't like the sound of his lungs already."

Sasha nodded, used to helping with her mother's patients. But Lukas sighed and tipped his head back. Sasha sent a sympathetic smile and tapped her brother's shoulder. He tossed her a grin.

"You're offering to take first watch, right?" He was already to the door, fumbling with the latch.

She formed a gesture which had him laughing. Her mother's frown sent her meekly pulling up a chair and propping her chin on her fist. Zoya leaned in to kiss her forehead.

"I'll be in the next room mixing more yellowflame. Let me know if he gets worse."

Sasha nodded and settled in to watch the Greywolf.

# TWENTY-SEVEN

## ETRAN

The morning brought no great relief. I dressed and stepped out into the early dawn. Only a few wolves and riders stirred, pacing the boundaries on watch.

Frea heaved to her feet, coming to press her head into my chest. A low whine built in her throat. I pressed my forehead to hers, scratching under her jaw. The memory of Eska flashed again and she grumbled as my hand tightened in her fur. I couldn't bear the thought of losing her too.

She paced by my side as I turned to the spirits' lodge. No smoke stirred at the *talånd's* dwelling. Mikkel was not yet up and about, though I didn't think he'd have much in the way of advice for me.

Instead, I slipped through the door and lit a candle on the low table before sinking to my knees beside the bubbling spring in the center of the room.

The faint scent of smoke lingered from offerings past. Bobbing light from the candle tried to reach the corners, not quite succeeding. I rested back on my heels, hands pressed against my thighs.

It still wasn't yet clear to me if the spirits had decided to grant me favor. I'd doubted it ever since Comran had first seen the sablecat print. And now…

I bowed my head. "Bring him safe to the All-Father's lodge. But if, somehow, he's still alive…"

I couldn't finish the prayer. The rivers ran cold through the valley. If he'd survived the initial fall, and the wound from the sablecat, the river would have drowned him, or the cold would have killed him.

"May he forgive me."

The floor creaked behind me, and Father lowered to his knees beside me. He said nothing, and I turned my focus forward. A bit of guilt resurfaced that he had begun to actually show emotion toward me, and Comran hadn't seen it himself. But I still didn't know how to reach out to him as a father.

"How is Inger?" I looked down at my hands.

Father gave a surprised inhale. "I did not expect you to ask after her."

"She's shown me kindness these past few years."

"I'm glad."

I rubbed the knuckle of my right thumb.

"She's mourning the loss of another son."

My head jerked up. "Another?"

Father finally looked to me and gave a small smile. "I know your mother told you the reason for your birth, but perhaps not all of it. We would have had two children before Comran, but they did not make it to this world."

He took a deep breath. I stared, heart aching more for her.

"And when we did have a son together, I pushed him away. I…" His voice broke.

Eyes stinging, I rested a hand on his forearm.

"I thought I would protect myself from more heartbreak if I did not let myself love him—love both of you—as I should have." His free hand pressed to his eyes.

I had no words of reassurance. I'd come to see that Father could love in his own way, but Comran hadn't.

"I'm sorry," I said instead.

With a deep breath, Father regained control, shuttering away his emotion like he'd done our whole life. It made me want to shake him, to make him keep showing it.

"You said it was your fault," he said.

My hand fell away. "How could it not be? He fell protecting me from their battlelion."

Father's hand settled on my shoulder. "Inger has always said that Comran's heart beats fierce. He loves and protects. And though I failed in many ways as a father, I could still see that about him. He would not want you to blame yourself. It was his choice."

"He wanted to give up the medallion," I whispered. "He thought he was failing me—failing the tribe. He died thinking that."

Father's fingers dug into my shoulder for a painful moment as he took a shaky breath. "Then make sure his sacrifice for you was not in vain."

"Will you keep watch here for me again?"

Father nodded. I pushed to my feet. As he'd said, I wouldn't let Comran's sacrifice be in vain. I wouldn't let the Saber tribe take our valley and let his spirit linger with the knowledge that we hadn't been able to hold the line.

"Etran." He halted me at the door. His rise to his feet was not so quick as mine, and I realized with a pang that he was not as tall as I'd always thought.

"You called him brother. I was happy to hear it."

Sudden shame cut through me that I'd been too afraid my whole life to stand for those I wanted to trust.

"I should have chosen to side with Comran years ago." My fingers touched the new leather cord wrapping around my left wrist above my own bands.

Father's face creased again, and he dipped his head again.

"Tell Inger we will honor him."

Outside, Loke's voice began to muster the riders. I paused once outside, looking to the *tâkn* and the howling Greywolf atop it. *Keep guiding us, please. May I not fail again.*

# TWENTY-EIGHT

## SASHA

The Greywolf was stirring. Sasha reached over and pressed a hand to his forehead. Still chilled, his body still shivering despite the hours he'd already been under the blankets and the fire that had led her to cast aside her fur-lined overtunic long ago.

Lukas had yet to return. Still avoiding his turn to help in the lodge. She rolled her eyes and stood to go find her mother.

"How is he?" Zoya kept her voice low, mixing a new ointment to give to Sanne for her aching joints.

Sasha rubbed her arms. <Still shivering.>

Zoya frowned and led the way back out into the main lodge room. She did the same as Sasha and felt the man's skin. Her lips didn't turn away from the frown as she pulled back the blankets.

Spots of red stained the cloth over his shoulder. He flinched against her touch as she undid the shirt laces to better pull it open to see his bandage.

"He needs to get warmer."

<But it's bleeding.> Sasha pointed to it.

"I know." Zoya re-did the laces and tucked the blankets back around him. She stared down at him, hands on her hips.

"Go get Raya."

Sasha allowed a small grin and tugged her mother's sleeve. <Desperate?>

Her mother shooed her away. "You're getting in there with him."

Sasha squinted a glare. <Why not Lukas?>

"Because he's conveniently disappeared. Go on!"

Sasha went to the door and gave a low whistle. The dark shape of Raya leapt down from the roof and padded up to the opening. A rumbling purr sounded in her chest and her tufted ears twitched as she eased one giant black paw in at a time.

The lynx crept around the circular wall to the bed, stretching out her head and sniffing cautiously at the Greywolf. Golden eyes studied him, then she gave an inquisitive chirp.

"He's all right, Raya," Zoya reassured. She helped Sasha bring over another cot to shove next to the Greywolf. Raya hauled herself up onto the cot and snuggled in close to the man. At the brush of fur against his cheek, he turned his head to her, visibly relaxing.

It made Sasha smile a bit. She'd only seen a greywolf once, and from a distance, but maybe he felt as close to his wolf as she did to Raya.

Zoya tapped her shoulder. With another sigh, Sasha tugged the blankets up and slid in, back to his side, lending her warmth to him.

With another smile, her mother disappeared. Sasha stayed on her side, staring at the fire, listening to Raya shift again. Gradually the Greywolf's shivers abated between the hacking coughs tearing through his body. She turned to check on him each time he coughed, until in a longer period of quiet where she could still feel him breathing, she fell asleep.

# Twenty-Nine

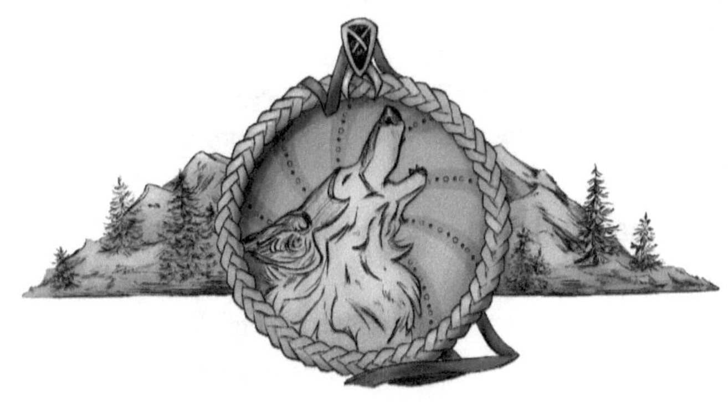

## Comran

Heavy ceiling beams stared down at me, flickering light casting trickster shadows. I blinked, but it did not clear the slight blur to my vision. Warmth cocooned me. Too much warmth.

And I couldn't move.

Sudden panic set in and I tried to jerk free of the tightness wrapping around me. The movement rubbed against the roughness in my lungs, and they seized in a cough. It tore at my chest, but I couldn't clear my lungs, couldn't move. I could barely turn my head to look for help.

Motion stirred on both sides. First, a mound of black-spotted fur shifted and rose. Golden eyes blinked down at me from a feline face. Its mouth parted in a yawn and my heart jolted before I registered the lack of oversized curving fangs. Only extra fur framing its jaw like a beard.

A more human noise competed for my attention, and I risked a glance away to see a young woman standing and straightening her dress. She rubbed sleep from her eyes and brushed dark hair from her face.

She froze in my stare and a tentative smile emerged.

"Where..." My voice scraped hoarse from my throat. "Where am I?"

Last I clearly remembered, I was falling from the cliff.

She held a hand toward me, palm out.

"Where am I?" I demanded more strongly.

She glanced over her shoulder, lips twisting in a frown. Digging an elbow into the softness beneath me, I tried to shove myself up. Heaviness smothered me, but I fought against it and the new cough nagging at my chest.

"Who are you?" I managed between ragged breaths.

She clenched hands in frustration and dug in a pocket of her dress. I tried to rise further.

"Answer me!"

"She cannot speak," a new voice interrupted.

My neck protested as I turned to see another woman coming around a curtain. I glanced back to the younger woman. Her hands had paused, and she offered me a slight rise of her shoulders.

"I'm sorry," I told her.

"You didn't know," the older reassured. "Lie back down, please."

Her tone came calm and soothing, so I obeyed. Her hand pressed cool against my forehead.

"How are you feeling?"

"Confused?"

It got me a startled eyebrow raise, then a smile from the

woman. "My name is Zoya. You are in my lodge."

Lodge. I glanced around again at the rounded room, woven blankets draping the walls with different shapes and patterns than I was used to. The large feline hopped off the cot next to me and stretched long limbs before padding around to rub its jaw against the younger woman's shoulder. Tanned fur riddled with black spots, and four black paws.

"I'm grateful a Blackpaw decided to take a Greywolf in," I said.

Zoya softened again. She tilted a glance over her shoulder to the younger. "Sasha and my son found you in the river and brought you in."

Sasha offered the smile again.

"Thank you."

The weight of the blankets was peeled away to free my limbs. Zoya slid a hand behind my right shoulder and urged me to sit up, assisting with surprising strength. I hunched, fighting dizziness and sudden nausea. Pain stabbed from all directions, my side and shoulder harshest of all.

A cough tore through me again, dredging up fluids from my lungs this time, leaving me lightheaded as a bowl appeared for me to spit.

"I need to see to your wounds now." Zoya's voice cut through the haze, and I made no resistance as the shirt lifted over my head, care taken around my shoulder.

My hand pressed against my chest, missing the familiar weight of the battlewolf medallion. It seemed I'd get my wish. Etran would have to appoint someone new to the position now.

Regret clenched around my heart. They likely thought I was dead. Unless the Sabers had killed them all on that hill.

"When you found me, were there any other Greywolves?" I managed to lift my head to look at Sasha.

Slowly, she shook her head, and held out one finger upright, then to me.

"Only me?" I guessed. Another slow nod.

Good or bad, I didn't know. Only that it was likely I had been left behind, might even be remembered at the fire some night. Loke, Amund—Etran—I thought they'd still been standing.

But from the look of myself, I wouldn't be finding out anytime soon.

"What's the damage this time?" I tried to keep my voice light but couldn't stop my flinch as she pressed around my shoulder.

"This is the worst." Zoya pointed across the room and Sasha disappeared behind the hanging, returning with bowls and the scent of herbs. "You sound as if you're not surprised to wake up in a healing lodge poked full of wounds."

I chuckled, a raspy sound that triggered another cough. "This is not the first time."

Sasha handed me a cup. I regarded it a moment, trying not to breathe in the bitterness wafting from it before downing the contents.

"That is for the cough and something for the pain," Zoya told me over the sound of my coughs again. "Sasha."

Sasha's hands pressed against my chest and back, holding me steady as Zoya began to thread a needle. I glanced away, hand curling into the blankets. The hand against my back lifted for a moment.

"She asks what your name is."

The needle pricked my skin, and I forced my head to turn and look up at Sasha.

"Comran."

She gave a half smile and nodded.

"Nice to meet you, too," I said.

A faint sound like a laugh came from her, barely above a whisper. The needle pulled and aching pain stirred in my shoulder. Forcing my attention from it, I tried to find something else to say.

"You let your lynxes come inside?"

"Only for some extra warmth for us. And you needed it hours ago."

"I have tried to use the same argument at home, but could never convince anyone to let our wolves in." My half-smile at the thought of Eska died.

What had happened to him? He'd gone after the sablecat about to attack Amund. But after?

A tap on my chest brought my eyes back up to Sasha. Her lips pursed and she tilted her head.

"I do not know what might have become of my wolf."

"What happened to bring you into the river?" Zoya asked gently.

"We stumbled into a Saber pack up among the hills. One was going after—our chief. Bastard's sablecat got me and pulled us both over." I cleared my throat. Mother had never liked the rougher words. "Sorry."

Zoya set the needle aside and began packing some sort of poultice around my shoulder. "We share the same sentiments around here."

I stared at the wall in front of me as she lifted my arm and began wrapping a bandage. It was a spirit's blessing that they'd decided to bring a Greywolf into their lodge after what we'd done.

"And I'm sorry for that, too. I didn't think we should have held the packs back."

Zoya's hands paused. "You don't seem old enough to have ridden with the warriors then."

"I wasn't." My hand reached for the medallion again before I remembered it was missing. "Doesn't mean I didn't think what my—chief ordered was right."

I did not yet want to let them know who I truly was. The medallion must have come off in the river. For all they knew, they just had a wolfrider in their lodge. Not the son of the man who'd spelled their doom by withholding aid.

Zoya's attention turned to my side and her voice turned abruptly brisk again.

"What happened here?"

Her touch at my side sparked another pang of discomfort and I shifted away. The wound maintained its steady weeping.

"Old wound," I said dismissively.

Zoya caught me in a severe stare, one similar enough to my own mother's look that I wouldn't dare disobey as a child.

"I was injured by a blade laced with red spear."

Sasha's intake of breath joined her mother's.

"When? How did you survive away from the village?"

I hesitated. It would mean showing the tribe's difficulties to an outsider. But after she pushed again, I answered.

"I was in the village when it happened. By all accounts it was a miserable night I had in the healer's lodge."

Zoya sank down to the cot to better look me in the eye. "What was happening for someone to use red spear within the village?"

Sasha's hands shifted, keeping their steady support. I offered a half smile.

"I was trying to protect our new chief from those who thought he wasn't a good enough choice."

Understanding broke over Zoya's face, and a little bit of pity, and she shook her head. "Reidar chose his bastard as chief?"

Ire flared in me, escaping through my words.

"He's not…" But he was, technically. "He's a good man. A good chief."

A better chief than I was battlewolf. *Who did he choose to replace me?*

Zoya nodded, her lips parting in a breath of hesitation before she spoke again. And it seemed it was not what she intended to say.

"When did this happen?"

I tried to stay tall under the gentle pressure of her hands around the wound.

"Midwinter night."

She paused again. "And you've been living with it like this since?"

Some days "living with" seemed generous. "I'm here, aren't I?"

"You're…" She sat back, shaking her head.

"Stubborn is the word most often used, I believe. Right after flaming idiot."

A smile creased her face, and the whispered sound came from Sasha behind me.

"I haven't seen red spear used since the war with the Saber tribe, and never a wound this old. I will see what I can do for it." Zoya cleaned it and bandaged it again.

She gathered up the old bandages and bowls of herbs she'd used. "Do you feel up to eating something?"

I nodded, thirsty more than anything. Sasha tentatively brought her hands away and I kept myself propped up on my un-injured arm. By the time I managed a few sips of a broth, and downed a cup of water, my arm shook with effort and new ex-haustion pressed against my shoulders.

Zoya gave me something else to drink and helped me lay back down. "Get some rest. Our chief and battlelynx want to meet with you, but I'll tell them tomorrow."

A pang of misgiving struck. So far Zoya hadn't cast me out. But what would the chief say? I had no idea where I might be in the valley, but a Blackpaw village was as far from Greywolf territory as I could be.

But she only pulled the blankets back over me with a slight smile. Sasha cast a glance at me then moved her hands in a dizzying flash of motions. Her mother replied in kind, before taking Sasha's shoulder and moving her out of my sight to continue the discussion they were having. Most likely about me.

The ceiling beams stared down at me, clearer than they had been at first. A Blackpaw lodge was the last place I'd expected to wake up. Honestly, once my feet had slipped from the ledge, I'd expected to not wake up at all. The Blackpaws weren't enemies, but they weren't friends either. Not after what we'd done to them.

But not much more I could do for now besides rest.

# THIRTY

# ETRAN

Loke and I watched the new pack ride in. His whispered curse mirrored in my heart when I caught sight of Maren riding in the middle of the warriors. But Loke's gaze was fixed on another rider.

A young man dismounted and flashed a grin at Loke, tempered only slightly by the pack leader, looking barely advanced from training spears himself, standing nearby. My new battlewolf shook himself and strode forward, clapping the warrior on the shoulder.

"They sending out the scraps now?" His voice was light, but I knew him well enough now to hear the strain.

The rider puffed his chest and made some reply. Loke shoved him away, but the man's face turned somber and he asked something else. Loke stilled, then nodded and nudged the warrior back to his wolf.

The pack leader got his attention next, and I forced myself to join, tearing my eyes from Maren, who'd yet to acknowledge me.

"Chief." The pack leader slammed a fist into his chest, and I almost winced for him at the force of it.

"There will be a place for your tents beside Gunnar's pack," Loke said. "Get settled for now. Meet at the council fire tonight to get assignments for tomorrow."

The warrior saluted again and gave the order. His pack followed without question, all giving us some deference as they led greywolves past.

"Chief, you won't mind me giving them easy patrols for a few days?" The strain crept back into Loke's voice.

I shook my head. "I know someone in the pack, too."

"Probably not your little brother." Loke mustered up a smile.

Something closer to a strangled choke than a laugh answered him. Maren was more, much more, but I was too much of a coward to face what that might be. I'd tell Loke to keep them all on patrol duty on the furthest lines from the Sabers forever, but that would dishonor them.

Loke's solemn eyes studied me, trying to parse out what I meant by the sound, but I mustered myself. "None of them look to have battle experience. Work them in as slowly as you can."

The battlewolf rubbed his chin. "Aye, Kjell shouldn't have gotten his spear for another year at least."

I uttered a curse under my breath. For him to have a brother out in the fight so close on the heels of losing Comran—and if riders had been sent out early, that didn't mean good things for our fight.

"I named Amund as *rokr*." He looked to me with a bit of apology.

"He'll be a good fit," I said.

It seemed petty to care about naming someone to *rokr* who had supported either me or Comran now that we were at war, and he was gone.

"He is out with patrols. And will hopefully come back with

better news."

But by the look in his eyes, he wasn't hopeful.

"Go see your brother," I said.

It had been three days since we'd left the village and the remembrance fire for Comran, but Loke had barely seen his family since the war began. He'd been down the tributary river with Amund and another warrior. To scout, he said.

But I knew the truth. Looking for a body. They came back empty-handed. I tried not to be disappointed, though I'd expected as much.

Loke replied with a tight smile, but he moved off, leaving me alone. He looked back over his shoulder once, but I quickly shifted my attention away. It fell to the bands around my wrist instead, and I wondered if Loke felt as lost as I did without Comran.

The new pack did not get much of a chance to settle in. The scouts brought in word of three Saber packs crossing the boundaries. With many packs out and the others too wounded to put together a full pack, Loke had no choice but to call them.

I joined the wolfriders Loke mustered, and we rode out together.

The fight we found was short and sharp and left more wounded than whole when the lines pulled apart, and the boundaries even more murky. Loke led a small group to scout after the retreating Sabers, and I took the rest back to the camp.

Frea loped along with a slight hitch in her gait. A distant howl brought my attention up across the valley, waiting for any answering howl. Nothing came, and a lump surfaced in my throat. Any lone wolfsong drew my mind to Eska and the memory of him, eyes wild, as he disappeared into the wood.

A low growl brought me back to Frea and her grey coat stained with bits of blood and green paint. I'd inked a white rune for Eska into her fur, tracing over it like I did the rune for Comran on my breastplate every day. The cords stayed on my wrist, and I'd caught Loke checking every morning. I couldn't let him go yet.

We made it to camp, and I gave the orders to disband and rest.

"Chief." Maren's voice stopped me. Frea growled a greeting and Maren's war-painted features split into a smile as she reached past me and scratched the greywolf's jaw. And it seemed that the bit of frostiness between us since I'd last seen her in the village melted away.

"You're all right?" It was one thing seeing Maren on the training field, but now seeing her fresh from a fight, blood spattered on her leathers—it tangled up my throat.

Her shoulders rose and fell, finally lining up with another breath.

"It was worse than I thought it might be," she admitted, tilting her chin enough to let me see a new hollowness in her eyes.

"If we all knew the truth of war," I said, "no one would want to go."

Her face faltered. "Some would."

It punched through my heart. Comran would go. I'd been there the day he picked up his sword, freshly made for him, the first time. He'd changed that day, though I don't know if he knew it. Like he finally found the thing to make sense of the restlessness the All-Father had given him.

"How are you holding up?" she asked quietly.

The question stormed the walls I'd shored up since Comran had vanished under the waters. "Fine."

Her hand found mine and she squeezed. "You are not very good at lying, Etran."

"Maybe you're just better at seeing the truth."

She tilted her head, a bit of surprise leaking past her warpaint. It was as close to an admission as I'd ever made to her.

"You should get that taken care of." I indicated the wound just above her left bracer, and pulled Frea around her, hoping to escape the uncomfortable, tongue-tied feeling.

The camp settled into quiet around fires as darkness began to fall. Loke and his scouting pack rode back in. My heart had not stopped jumping any time someone announced the battlewolf, as if it still hoped it would be Comran, and not the man I had picked to replace him.

I waited by the fire, but Loke went to each pack first, spending some more time with the wolfriders who had accompanied us today. Faint guilt stirred that I had not done the same once we'd returned. I did as I'd always done—retreated from everyone, keeping the physical boundary of distance in place.

Finally, Loke came to sit down with me at the council fire. He splashed some water over grimy fingers and worked a blood-stained bandage free. I silently offered him a mug of ale when he'd finished replacing it with a clean cloth.

A brief bustle marked the return of another pack, and Amund came and dropped down on the seat he'd claimed three days ago. He stretched his legs out in front of him, circles heavy under his eyes. He didn't need to tell us the news. We could read it in the lines of defeat etched into him.

My glance turned to the two empty spots. Jens was not supposed to return for two more days. The other we had yet to try to fill, or move makeshift seats closer together in an attempt to erase the lurking space. Comran's tent was still pitched beside mine, and the cup he used still sat beside the fire.

None of us had suggested it, and mere days later, it didn't seem right to keep removing pieces of him.

"Kjell's here?" Amund finally stirred, shifting his feet under him to better grab a stick and prod the fire.

"Yes." Loke stared at flames snapping higher.

"*Drakr.*"

Loke grunted. Amund stabbed at the coals, face twisting harsher in the shadows cast by the flames. I looked away, seeking out the pack and Maren where she sat beside Loke's brother and shared a mug of ale. It twisted my heart to see it, but I made no move toward them.

"Worried for Maren?" Loke spoke, bringing me back to the campfire and my more somber companions.

"She's a friend." But it came out a little stilted, like I didn't quite believe it.

Loke's eyebrow raised, and he exchanged a glance with Amund.

"Think he's noticed how much she stares at him?" Amund cleared his throat, forcing a smile onto his face. "It's almost disconcerting looking around and finding her watching our every move."

I treated him to a withering glare.

Loke held up a hand like he was thinking. "So are you the reason she's turned down at least three offers since last winter?"

The look I turned on Loke didn't seem to affect him. And it was only one offer. That I knew of. Amund chuckled as he knocked a coal side to side with his bit of wood.

"Who am I to offer her anything?" My fingers broke apart a fallen piece of bark.

"The chief?" Loke said in bemusement.

A scoff tore sharp from my chest. "You know what I mean." I tossed the bits piece by piece into the flames where they glowed bright before turning to cinders.

"I think you'll find that's mattering less and less to many," Loke said softly. "Especially out here."

"Is it?" I flung the last fragment at the fire. It drifted short, landing on the stones containing the fire instead.

It had always mattered.

"If you bothered to look, you might see." Loke's voice crept the closest to irritation I'd ever heard. My gaze found Maren again. His words were not far from what she'd told me.

I swallowed down my retort. Easy for them to say, harder for me to actually live it. Pushing to my feet, I said a sharp goodnight instead.

But as I turned, Comran's empty place snagged my eye. I would have listened if he'd said the same. So why couldn't I trust the words of his friends?

# Thirty-One

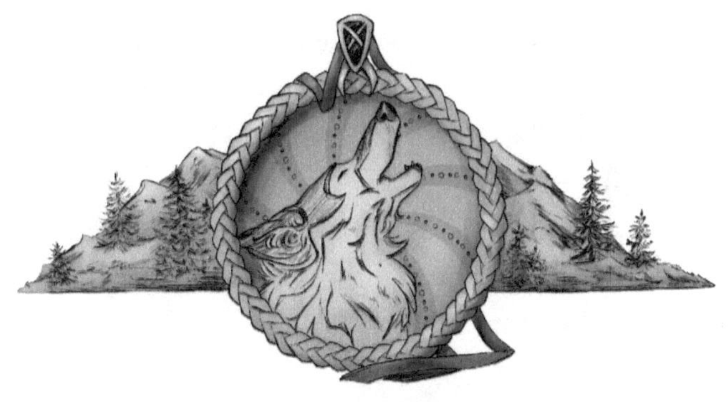

## Comran

A scraping noise accompanied my return to wakefulness. A young man, not much older than me, sat beside the bed this time, his knife carving its way through a block of wood.

He glanced at me and sheathed the knife. "Finally."

I blinked as he stood and left. The ache plaguing my body had lessened and I maneuvered myself up into a sitting position. No one was there to stop me, but the movement spurred another round of coughing which had prompted a restless few hours of sleep. A soft growl alerted me to the lynx curled against the wall opposite.

Gold eyes ringed in black stared somberly at me, urging me to stay on the bed and not attempt anything else.

The fire crackled in a pit inset in the center of the lodge room. The entire room did not look big enough to hold more than one family. Benches and trunks were shoved up against the walls. Two other plain hangings of deer skin gently moved in a phantom wind, marking different rooms.

My gaze fell on a small table set with candles and carved figures of the valley's spirits. A narrow hanging woven with prayer runes and a man's name was placed above it. I swallowed hard. The runes declared he'd fallen in battle. And I had one guess what war and to what enemy.

A hanging brushed aside and Zoya appeared. She pressed her hand against my forehead and tugged at bandages, a preoccupied frown between her eyes.

"Your fever's down a bit."

My lungs decided to spasm again and her frown deepened at the ragged sound.

"Wait here." She vanished again.

But I gingerly moved to bring my legs off the bed to rest on the wood floor, warmed this close to the fire. The lynx watched me, barely blinking. Giant paws flexed slowly against the floor.

"I won't try anything," I reassured around another cough.

Movement stirred and Sasha appeared. She raised an eyebrow at me.

"Don't worry," I said wryly. "I'm not going anywhere."

She raised her hands, then paused, curling them slowly into fists and lowering with an expression of apology. We stared at one another, not sure how to communicate.

"Could I have a shirt?" I finally found words.

It got a nod and faint smile. She turned to a trunk and dug one out. I reached to take it from her, but her frown sent me meekly allowing her to help pull it on.

"Thank you."

Palm facing her, she touched fingers over her heart before moving her hand away. *You're welcome*, I guessed.

A knock sent her spinning away to answer.

"Sasha, is your mother in?" A female voice.

She stepped back and two women filed in. I hesitated under their sudden scrutiny. They both wore dresses and plain over-tunics, embroidered with swirls and diamonds in red thread—a color Mother bemoaned the lack of on our side of the valley. Why, I'd no idea.

One, slightly older, stood tall and imposing, grey streaking her hair. The other, maybe a few seasons younger, wore a long dagger on her belt. Her dark hair had been pulled back, smaller braids tucked into one longer one running from the crown of her head down her back. Similar to how the women of our tribe who trained with spear and wolf also wore theirs.

"So, you're the Greywolf Zoya said she had in her lodge," the older said, voice sharp and brittle.

"Yes."

Sasha eased back a step, making for the hanging. I watched the way the warrior stood a pace behind the other in deference. The way they both sized me up like a potential threat. The way women might stand when they'd lost too many men to a war and had to fill the positions somehow.

"What's your name?"

"Comran." I pressed fingertips to my forehead in deference of a position above my own. "Chief."

The woman arched an eyebrow. I looked to the warrior and tapped my chest with closed fist. One warrior to another.

"Battlelynx."

The warrior tipped an impressed frown and crossed her arms over her chest. Zoya came around the hanging at that moment, steps pausing at the sight of the women.

"Aelita," she greeted the chief.

"He's guessed, Zoya," the chief reassured. "I am surprised to see the Greywolves still have some respect left in them."

"My mother taught me not to underestimate anyone." I managed a smile around the irritation the comment stirred.

"And what did your father teach you?" The sharpness in the chief's eyes cut me. "To do what serves him best?"

"What?" I stared.

The battlelynx pulled something from her pocket and thrust it out between us. Firelight glinted off the howling wolf's head swinging from the cord bunched in her fist.

"Were you planning to lie, *Battlewolf*?" she snapped.

"I thought it lost in the river." My fingers itched to take it, pull it on and feel the reassuring weight of it.

"That does not answer my question."

"It is no hard guess why you took the positions you hold. Not hard to know why he fell in battle." I pointed to the prayer hanging. "It was my tribe that caused it to happen. Perhaps I thought to gamble another day before I attempted the trek back across the valley to my people."

The chief started a fraction. "You think we would turn you out?"

"Why not? Small revenge for what you've lost." I lifted my shoulder. "I wouldn't hold it against you."

A faint scoff brought my glance darting to the other side of the room. Sasha leaned against the wall, hands tucked behind her back, watching intently. The young man from before leaned in the doorway beside her, arms crossed over his chest. He'd made the noise. They looked enough like each other and Zoya to tell me it was their father who'd been lost.

"Perhaps." The battlelynx's hand fell to her side where she turned the medallion over and over between her fingers. "Maybe I think it would serve some sort of justice for Reidar to lose as I did."

This time I stared at her. They, too, had guessed correctly, except they didn't know the full truth.

"Best find some other way to do it, then." I forced a laugh. "It wouldn't pain him much."

The horror and pity in their faces was too much and I looked to the fire instead.

"Zoya said he chose the bastard as chief."

My own shame disappeared in a burst of anger and my head snapped up. The battlelynx regarded me in surprise.

"You'd defend him?" she challenged.

"Yes. Etran did nothing wrong by being born. He's a good man." He'd believed in me. "It took me long enough to see it."

The chief smoothed an invisible wrinkle from her tunic. "Who chose you as battlewolf?"

"Etran. We agreed to stand together to keep our tribe from splintering." Restlessness churned through me. "Though I managed to fail again and let the sablecats into our valley."

Another cough ripped from me along with the confession. Zoya hastened to my side, steadying me as I hunched forward under its force.

"Here." Another beaker of medicine appeared before me.

I choked it down, managing not to spit it back up as my lungs continued their fight. A faint moan caught in my throat as my body settled, leaving stabbing pain in my shoulder.

"That does not sound as if you will be going anywhere soon," the chief said.

I managed to lift my head, still trying to calm my breaths. "I'm sure there are plenty who'd be vindicated after years of telling us not to swim before summer came."

A faint quirk disturbed the iron set of the battlelynx's features. I took it as a small victory.

"Zoya?" The chief looked to her.

Zoya pressed a hand to my forehead again. I shuddered against the chill of her skin, the shiver racing all the way down to my toes.

"He's still fevered, and the cough is fresh. He'll need time. Not to mention the wounds."

I watched the fire, sneaking a glance up every few seconds as the chief and battlelynx conferred in hushed tones. Sasha and her brother leaned forward as if they could hear. He frowned at me when I started coughing again, as if I could help it.

The chief turned to me. "I cannot in good conscience cast you out. You may stay until you are healed and able to travel. Then you will leave this place."

"Thank you, Chief." I pressed fingertips to my forehead again.

She left in a rush of chill air. The battlelynx hesitated a moment more before crossing to me. The cool of the medallion pressed into my hand. Her warrior callouses pressed against mine as she gripped my hand.

Understanding shone in her dark eyes.

"My own husband, an experienced battlelynx, could not hold them off. We are not so blind and deaf here as some might think. From what we have heard, you led well."

"Perhaps that is not good enough, when I keep seeing warriors fall and ground lost under their boots."

I had no idea if she'd led packs as a battlelynx, but there was no mistaking the hollow-eyed look of a warrior about her. I guessed she had been alongside her husband every step of the way.

"Maybe there is no stopping them," she said softly.

This time I clenched my fingers around hers. "If there is still a battle to fight when I leave here, I will find a way to take it back and send every last one of them to the dark woods."

But her ferocity softened to sadness. "I thought the same once. And here we are."

Her hand fell from mine and my fingers curled around my medallion as she left, a slight stoop to the proud shoulders.

Zoya touched my shoulder, lifting her chin to urge me back to bed. But her son stirred in the door beside Sasha.

"You think you could defeat them?" he asked, challenge in his voice.

"I don't know," I said. "But one of their cats threw me off a cliff. I'm even more angry now than before."

A faint smirk stirred his lips and he nodded. "Well, then. You'd best get some rest. Wouldn't want to hold you up."

He shoved out the main door, turning to click to the lynx and showing a glint in his eye that, if I didn't know better, might mean he planned to do something reckless.

# THIRTY-TWO

## ETRAN

"Well?" I asked Loke as I slid from Frea.

Loke scraped a hand across his forehead, smearing dirt and blood. "We're holding for now, Chief."

One counting since Comran had fallen and we'd managed to hold the Saber tribe in place at the river.

I ran a finger under the leather cord wrapping my left wrist above my own bands as Loke and I strode side by side to check the warriors. One counting. Nine days. It seemed both yesterday and forever ago that I'd watched him fall.

My confidence had fallen along with him. Thank the spirits for Loke's steady hand. Steady, but lacking Comran's burning fire. A good warrior to have at one's side. But Loke made the safer decision every time. Comran attacked, and Loke defended.

*Maybe the steadiness is what we needed.*

Betrayal prodded my heart at the thought. We'd held the ground, but that's all we'd done.

*Give him time.*

The warriors respected Loke, but he'd been thrust into the role with no training and little preparation. I could hardly expect him to win a war overnight.

"How are you, Loke?"

A sharp chuckle came from him. "Well enough."

"That doesn't seem much of an answer."

"For all his doubts, Comran was better than me." Loke gnawed at his lower lip as he stared out over the packs.

"And how many times did you tell him not to doubt himself?" I raised an eyebrow.

A reluctant smile formed on Loke's face as he shook his head. "Is it a burden always being right?"

"One of the many benefits of being chief. I can be more smug about it."

Loke shook his head with a small laugh. We made our way to his tent, where he ducked inside to retrieve the map of the valley. I took one end as he unrolled it, keeping it stretched between us.

"We're holding here at the river." Loke's finger traced a wobbly line along the length of the river. "But they have begun focusing their strength here." He pointed to a smaller area of the river's curve that, if crossed, would allow the Sabers a straight path across the valley to the village.

A soft curse whispered from me.

"We just don't have the warriors to drive them back," Loke said softly.

It was a reality I'd been hoping to avoid. Somehow, even after war on the Blackpaw tribe eight years ago, the Saber tribe still had plenty of warriors.

We had more wolfriders in training and would be bringing young warriors into the field before they had finished their training. Warriors like Kjell.

"What do you need from me?"

Loke slowly rolled up the map. When at war, the chief could stand second to the battlewolf. And it gave me a bit of relief to not be making all the decisions.

"We need another patrol out on the southern banks."

It came out more of a question. But I nodded.

"Who's freshest?"

Tapping the map against the palm of one hand, he looked out over the warriors again. Most had evident bandages and a general air of exhaustion. Loke beckoned me to follow, and we picked out a small pack of six riders to go with me.

All but one rose readily to their feet, checking wolf leathers and swords. Sander took an extra moment, hands clenching as he stood. Loke had already turned away, so I went up to him.

"All right?"

Sander forced a nod, and a smile emerged on his pale features that resembled a grimace.

"Sander." I kept my voice quiet.

His fingers fumbled as he jerked the saddle leathers tighter. His female greywolf turned her head to regard him with dark eyes. An inquiring huff came from her. It sent his shoulders into a slump and his hands braced against her side.

"I just feel shaken about everything," he admitted in a trembling voice. "I don't know that I have what it takes to keep riding with the packs."

I gripped his shoulder. "You do, Sander. You keep riding, keep fighting. Courage has many different forms. We all feel shaken, one way or another."

He tilted a look over his shoulder. "How do you do it? How did he do it?"

*He.* Comran. I swallowed. No one saw Comran's self-doubt as intensely as I had the night before he fell.

"I have an entire tribe to look out for. And that is an intimidating thought to wake up to most mornings."

A faint smile appeared in response to my lighter tone.

"And it is also what keeps me going, no matter what I feel. And Comran…" I paused, words sticking in my throat as if I were unworthy to speak of him. "Father says he had a fierce heart. He protected. That's what drove him."

That, and a desperate need to prove himself. Something I understood all too well.

Sander drew in a deep breath and stood a bit taller. I clapped him on the shoulder and left him to his preparations, now moving with a bit more sureness.

A whistle brought Frea back to my side and I checked her leathers, undoing the spear strapped to her side before mounting. Aron, one of the men in the patrol, nudged his wolf closer to me.

"We've been worried about him the last two days." He nodded over to Sander. "He needed whatever you told him, Chief. It's what Comran would have done." Aron tapped his chest in respect, and for once I didn't feel the sting of comparison.

Once Sander joined us, I led the way from the camp, Frea easing up to a lope once free of the trees stretching along the side of the river. Out in the open valley, we fell into a loose formation, staggered to watch in all directions as we rode south along the river.

A small herd of bison raised their heads, wary and edging back in a milling commotion as we neared, then falling back to an uneasy peace as it became clear we would pass them by. An eagle swept overhead, circling once before speeding north.

Green grass spread out across the valley, only faint bits of snow remaining. The frost brought on the night before had already melted away under the sun, emerging flowers and sweet clover reaching back out toward the warmth.

For a moment, as Frea snapped mid-stride at a butterfly, I could imagine we were just on a run and could ignore the weight of the spear in my hand.

A low bay from the wolf on my right shattered the illusion. Black forms raced towards us. At my shouted command, our wolves pivoted and charged the sablecats.

New rage filled me at the sight of one of the sablecat riders. Hakkon, riding the lion with ease. A hoarse curse burst from the rider next to me.

I lowered my spear to sweep low at the sablecat coming for me. The Saber warrior yanked up on the reins, swerving around the spear. I twisted in the saddle, throwing myself down against Frea's back to escape the returning swipe of the sword.

It seemed we'd both been practicing the maneuvers used against us.

Frea turned and charged again. I brought up the spear to strike at the warrior instead, trusting Frea to deal with the sablecat. They connected with a lurch, and I shifted my weight in the stirrups, rising up with Frea as she grappled.

Spear of no use anymore in close quarters, I tossed it away and drew my sword instead. Frea had the upper hand, wrestling over the sablecat's shoulders and biting down on its flank. The warrior swung at her exposed neck and I blocked, iron shrieking against iron.

He pushed against my blade, attempting to overcome with brute strength. I dropped the reins and pulled a knife. Kicking free of the stirrups, I threw myself sideways, connecting with the warrior and knocking him free from the saddle.

We hit the ground hard, but as intended, he did not rise, my knife buried in his neck. Yanking it free, I sprang to my feet, slashing out at the dark blur on my edge. Hakkon's cat skidded backwards, mouth wide and teeth bared in a hiss.

He jabbed forward with a spear and I retreated, ducking away from two successive strikes.

"You should have killed me," he snarled. "I won't make that mistake with you."

Twisting away from another strike, I tried to get closer inside of his range, but the cat swiped with a heavy paw.

"All this just to get back at me?" I jabbed my knife at the fight still around us.

"Maybe the whole tree needs to be razed for something better to grow in its place. And they will give that to me."

The words sent a shock through me, nearly freezing my legs and leaving me open to a new attack. Backtracking swiftly, I readied my sword again.

"You think the Saber tribe will leave anything standing? They want the valley for themselves." I swatted away the spear and lunged in to strike at the cat. Its thick fur turned the knife blade, leaving me with nothing but a dribble of blood on the iron.

Back again from the snapping fangs.

"Kamil has promised it to me."

"What can a battlelion promise?" I sneered.

A smile crept over Hakkon's face. "Much. He is chief in all but name and this will solidify his claim. But he will give me the honor of killing you."

"You won't get a chance, traitor." Sander's voice growled stronger than a wolf as he appeared on my left. His greywolf dropped to a crouch, her ears back and teeth bared. Blood stained his spear.

"What's a scared youth like you going to do?" Hakkon sneered, but his sablecat backed away, hackles raised and muscles tensed.

Sander's spear didn't waver in my periphery as I stayed focused on the cat and traitor in front of me. Frea's triumphant bay sounded behind me and a smile crept over my face. Her comforting growl came up behind me and she mirrored Sander's wolf in stance. The sablecat backed away again, a threatening hiss not deterring the wolves.

As one, we took a step, driving Hakkon back again. The sablecat's tail whipped back and forth. An unfamiliar voice shouted and Hakkon pulled back.

"With Comran gone, how long do you think you'll hold out, bastard?" His cat turned and they raced away with the two survivors.

I stared after them, jaw clenched and hands gripping my weapons painfully tight.

"Chief?" Sander's cautious question shook me free. He looked to me in worry. I mustered a smile, hiding the way the word left me shattered every time.

"Muster up," I said, sheathing my sword and grabbing Frea's reins.

A quick check revealed a bit of torn fur and clotting blood on her chest and flank. But she'd taken down the sablecat. A wolf-rider lay on the ground, a rasping sound in his throat as another tried to staunch blood. I knelt beside them, resting a hand on the dying man's shoulder before he shuddered and went still.

Lifting blood-stained hands away from the dead man's chest, the warrior sat back on his heels, a frantic curse breaking free from him as he stared after the departing Sabers.

"Dark woods take that traitor!" he snarled.

I wasn't going to argue.

He scrubbed his hands clean on the grass, scarlet smearing across the green. I took the blanket Aron handed down and helped wrap up the body.

"Sander told us what Hakkon said." Aron looked to me as he tied off a leather cord.

My hands paused in their task.

"I don't agree with what Reidar did. But you're here and making a good chief." Aron tested the strength of his knot. "Word will make it back to the village and you can bet that every man and woman will throw in behind you now."

He flashed a grim smile. "Or we'll make sure there's nothing left for Hakkon to rule over."

# THIRTY-THREE

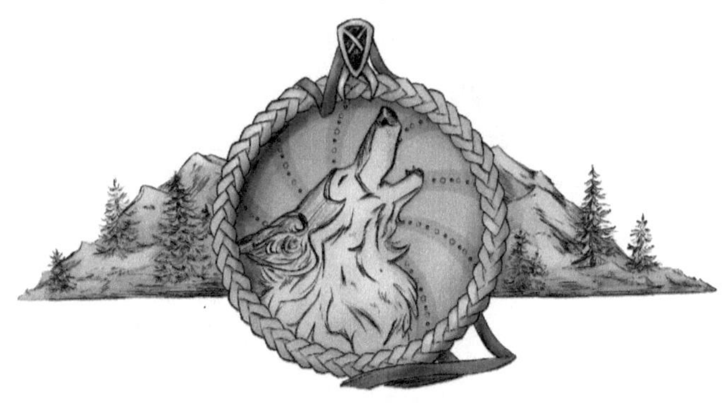

## COMRAN

I tipped my head back and soaked in the light sneaking through the branches surrounding the circular lodges. One counting. Nine days since I'd been pulled from the river, and Zoya had finally allowed me to step outside.

Fresh air. Something other than the round walls and woven hangings and smell of herbs mixed with wood smoke.

"I don't know why I'm the one who had to walk with you," Lukas grumbled at my side.

"Maybe because you can tell me to sit down instead of just glaring at me." I stretched my neck side to side against the pull of the sling keeping my wounded arm tight against my chest.

A huff escaped Lukas—something suspiciously like a laugh. "And I thought I was the only one who could annoy them so much."

"It's a talent." I winked.

And looked for somewhere to stop and sit. Nine days of being confined to a cot. Nine days of a cough slowly leaving and strength returning as my body healed from the sword wounds and where the sablecat's teeth had punctured my shoulder.

Apparently not as deep as Zoya had thought, but it could have fooled me with how much it hurt. Walking even ten yards had left me breathless. Lukas frowned and pointed me to the low bench set against the outer edge of a lodge house. I lowered myself down, stretching my legs out and tipping my head back against the wall insulated with rough bark.

Unlike ours, the village didn't follow a circular design. Instead, the houses were scattered under the trees in no pattern I could tell, with paths worn through the grass to each. A *tâkn* stood in the middle with the Lynx spirit glaring out at any trespassers.

Lukas dropped down beside me and pulled out the small carving knife and block of wood he'd been working for the last counting. He was one of the few younger men in the village. There was a notable presence of older men with greyed hair or limping gait, a few of middle age who carried themselves in a manner that bespoke old wounds, which had maybe prevented them from joining the warriors again. And boys just coming into their training in their chosen trade.

From what I'd overheard as the family gathered around the fire in the evenings and talked, and now what I watched as the village went about their day, it seemed maybe half the size of ours and missing more than half of the warriors' strength.

"It's been hard here since…?"

"Why do you care, Greywolf?" He scraped the knife across the wood with a bit of force.

"Maybe because I do not want this to be my village in a few countings' time." I leaned forward. Watching, looking for the warriors. Many of the women wore their hair in warriors' braids and carried knives along with bracers strapped to their forearms.

"What are you looking for?" he asked warily.

"You have a training area?" The short break had sent energy pulsing back through me to swirl together with the restlessness.

"Why?" He regarded me more cautiously. "You're not near strong enough to start back yet."

"Maybe I just want to see?" I shrugged my good shoulder.

He rolled his eyes, but sheathed the knife and pushed to his feet. I followed more slowly, biting back the depressing thought that I'd stood up like a man of over eighty winters.

"Just to see?" He frowned at me, and I nodded.

No harm in just looking. And walking more would help. Everyone knew that.

We made our slow and steady way down the twisted road between the lodges—having to stop to rest twice more—until we came to an open area among the trees. The grass had been worn down and a smaller building stood under a towering oak. The training lodge. Conveniently, buckets of wooden swords sat out.

I angled toward it and Lukas made the growling noise of disapproval in his throat, but did not stop me. There were no other warriors about to say anything different either. And no sign of the battlelynx.

"What are you doing?" Exasperation leaked through his voice as I pulled a sword out and tested its weight.

"Just looking."

He huffed. And took up a sword himself.

"If you're going to insist on injuring yourself again, let's get this over with, so I can get you back to the lodge before Mother finds out."

I grinned and moved out into the training area. "That's the idea."

Lukas huffed, but didn't seem too anxious about the idea of

me hurting myself. Maybe I should have felt a bit more concerned, but an ache had set in the pit of my stomach, filled with restlessness and anger and failure, growing louder with every second since I'd first woken.

I really needed to hit something. Or get hit. I didn't much care.

We took up stances opposite each other. The sword felt heavier than normal, and I swung it with a low growl of frustration. He blocked easily and followed up with a simple strike.

Back and forth we went, like two boys on our first day in the arena. Barely swallowing my pride, I kept at it until sweat soaked my shirt and my arm trembled with effort. Lukas didn't even have the decency to look winded. He extended his hand, and I gave him the sword before scrubbing my sleeve across my forehead.

"How are you feeling?" Lukas frowned.

"Refreshed."

He shook his head, but the faint amusement flickered again. "Come on."

I limped after him as he jogged over to return the swords and then returned to my side.

"Thank you," I told him after a minute.

He inclined his head. "I won't tell if you won't."

I chuckled. "We'd get in that much trouble?"

"Mother has very specific rules when it comes to her patients. And I am fairly sure we broke at least three. We were not supposed to walk more than back and forth to the first lodge a few times."

"She wouldn't be the first healer to be angry with me," I admitted. "But my lips are sealed."

"About what?" Zoya came around the corner to confront us.

Thankfully, we had made it closer to the boundaries she'd originally set. Lukas looked to me in invitation to explain. I narrowed my eyes a bit, but it had been my idea and I might as well take some of the blame.

"I might have reached a bit far today," I admitted.

She studied me over crossed arms and nodded. "You're exhausted."

Now that she mentioned it, yes.

"Go rest. Lukas, help him, then come assist me in the sweat lodge. We'll need more stones for later."

"What's later?"

"We're getting rid of the last red spear in your wound," she said matter-of-factly.

Taken aback, I asked, "We are?"

A brusque nod and clap of her hands to dismiss us, and she left without any other explanation. Lukas shrugged in response to my questioning glance and prodded me back to the lodge.

Sasha met us at the door and took over shepherding me to back to the cot, which four days ago had been pushed back against the wall when my body had finally decided to hold a steady temperature. She brought a cup of water and refilled it twice for me before I handed it back.

"Thank you." I tapped my chest twice.

She paused, looking at me in surprise.

"That is how you do it, correct?"

I'd been watching her signs since regaining consciousness and had picked out some familiar patterns. But this was my first attempt. It had taken a few days to work up the courage to even try.

A slow smile spread, and she hesitated before bringing her hand to her chest, a slightly different angle than I'd held, and tapping twice. I mimicked it and she nodded, her smile a little wider.

"Tell me if I have these right." I went through the signs for what I was sure was please—hand to my chin. Then held my hand palm out.

"Done?" I guessed.

She nodded, hands toying with each other in front of her waist. An air of uncertainty hovered around her. With a bit of a smirk, I twisted my hand in another gesture I'd seen her and Lukas toss at each other frequently enough.

"I think I can guess this one."

Her cheeks flushed pink, but her lips parted in a smile. She tucked a stray bit of hair back behind her ear and pulled out charcoal and a sheet of birch bark from the pocket of her dress. Scribbling a moment, she re-read over it before handing it to me.

-You learned some of the signs?-

"It's not so hard to pick up if you watch." I handed the paper back. "Not that I'm watching you, or…" Spirits, when had my tongue decided to stumble over itself?

A small smile and she wrote again. -Not many have tried to learn it.-

I paused over the words, darting a glance back up at her. She seemed hesitant, fingers twisting around the charcoal stick as if maybe she regretted sharing. I'd already been about to ask, but it prompted the words a little faster.

"Could you teach me more?"

Her eyebrows arched and her hand stayed in the middle of reaching for the bark again. At her head tilt, I offered a smile.

"I don't have much else to do right now."

A smirk twisted up half her lips and she bent over the paper again, writing furiously.

-What about swinging swords in the arena?-

I jerked my head up, making a hushing sound, though it was her words I'd read. Brightness filled her eyes and I chuckled in response.

She tapped her lips with a finger and shook her head.

"Best not," I warned.

She drew up a stool and wrote again. -I can show you some more.-

"Perfect."

In the end, it was harder with one hand free and the other still wrapped up against my chest. But I managed a few that only required one hand for full meaning and remembered them when she tested me out of order.

She jumped up when Zoya and Lukas came back through the door. Zoya glanced between the two of us, but said nothing. She passed back into her healer's room where she'd come from often enough with mixtures to force down my throat or coat my wounds.

Lukas slouched on the bench by the wall and resumed his carving. Sasha went over to him and signed rapidly. This time I picked out two of the signs she'd just taught me, but nothing else from Lukas's blank expression and the flurry of his hands.

When Zoya came back, she had a large bowl propped on her hip and sleeves rolled up to her elbows.

"Come." She beckoned.

I stayed right where I was.

"And what exactly is happening?"

She paused and chagrin filled up her face. "Sorry, I got caught up in preparations." She shifted the bowl. "But I have determined that there is still a bit of red spear caught inside the wound, which has stopped it from healing. I don't know why it didn't all come out."

She'd pressed for information on what the healer had done to treat me right after the injury, but, given it was all a blur of heat and pain, I didn't have much for her.

Her words filled me with faint misgiving. "Do you think it

would have been hard to tell if it all had come out the first time?"

Zoya paused, and a bit of understanding brightened in her eyes. "I cannot say for sure. But it was not so hard to tell that some is still in your wound."

My hand clenched around the edge of the cot. Did the village healer truly not know, or did he think to do his part to weaken to tribe? Either way, he and I would have words when I got back to the village. Maybe I'd been too hasty in thinking getting rid of Hakkon and the *talånd* would put an end to conspiracies.

"What is your plan to clear it?"

"You'll have to go back to the sweat lodge. I have another poultice prepared that should draw the last of the poison out. We have different herbs and plants this side of the valley, which we use to effectively treat a red spear poisoning."

That reassured me a little. Maybe the healer just didn't know.

"Sounds like a miserable time for me."

Her features softened in apology. "This is why I wanted to wait until you were stronger to be able to push through it. But it will keep slowing the healing for your other wounds, so it should be done sooner."

Shifting a little on the cot, I lifted a shoulder. "We could keep waiting."

A snort came from Lukas. "Scared, Greywolf?"

I narrowed my eyes. "It's a miserable experience having red spear drawn from your blood."

Sasha eased up beside her mother and asked some question. Zoya nodded.

"He will be strong enough." She looked to me. "It should be easier than last time. But still expect a few hours in the lodge."

With a sigh, I levered myself up. "Then let's get this over with."

It wasn't just my fatigue that slowed my steps to the sweat lodge. Perhaps she didn't know what she was promising me in a cure for the cut that had plagued me for months. I did not know what I'd do if her cure didn't work.

Once inside the lodge, she nudged me to sit against the wall. Carefully undoing the sling, she helped bring my shirt off overhead. I hissed a breath as my injured shoulder twinged under the movement.

"You don't have a cure for this shoulder in there, do you?" I settled back and cradled my arm.

Zoya offered a smile as she undid the bandage around my chest to expose the wound. Sweat already trickled down my skin from the steam rising from the heated rocks in the center of the lodge.

"Sorry. Spirits' own time for that one."

She took my boots and shirt and set them outside. I tried to relax, but my muscles stayed rigid under the thought of what was to come. The poultice spread cool across my skin at first. Then came the first twinge driving deep into my side, feeling like it punctured my lungs.

A touch on my arm brought my eyes back open. Zoya watched me with a look I'd seen in my mother's face often enough.

"Just breathe through it," she said.

I tried to draw in a breath, but it came jagged as another wave hit, scraping through my veins.

"Why did you decide to help me?" I managed.

She rocked back on her heels, a thoughtful look on her face. "The spirits tasked me with helping those in need. But I admit I did hesitate when I saw your medallion."

The medallion still laying atop the extra shirt I'd been given.

"Then I saw how young you were. I thought of my Lukas

maybe laying somewhere and someone refusing to help him. I'd never know how he died. Wouldn't have his body or cords to offer to the spirits."

Loke's cords were still wrapped around my wrist. I wondered if he'd thrown mine to the fire or kept them as I knew I'd keep his if he fell.

"My mother likely thinks she lost a third son and the one she thought would survive." The words trembled not just with the pain thrumming through me.

Zoya's hand was somehow still cool where she pressed it to my chest.

"Breathe," she instructed.

I tried again and this time a rough curse escaped me as the lodge walls swam in and out of focus.

"You're strong, Comran. You can make it through this."

It loosened something in my chest and extra moisture dribbled from my eyes. I didn't think what everyone did. That I was strong. That I could lead. That I could make it through.

How could I believe it when I could not even believe in myself?

# THIRTY-FOUR

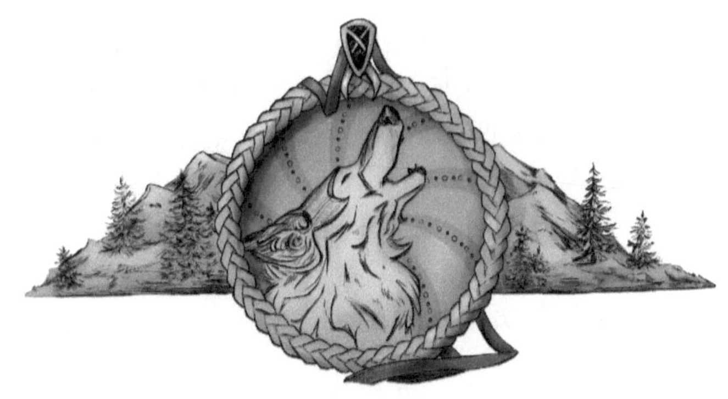

## COMRAN

Quiet filled up the lodge around me. Faint embers flickered in the pit. I turned my head, barely making out the lump of Lukas against the opposite wall. Swallowing against a dry mouth, I levered myself up.

Zoya had been right, and two hours in the lodge had finally yielded the last of the red spear. Or so she hoped. She and Lukas had to help me stumble back to wash and dress in new clothes, only to collapse into bed and sleep like the dead.

Nothing stirred and no light seeped under the hide-covered windows. Stifling a grunt of pain, I bent over and wrangled my boots on. Managing to stand on my own, I straightened my shirt and limped to the door.

Stars winked bright in the sky. A breeze sighed through the trees and the darker shape of the lynx prowled around, reducing the need for human guards.

Spring had a stronger touch on the western side of the valley, but a hint of cool still stirred. The waning moon caught a few sparkles of frost on the pine needles and grass blades. My hand supported my other elbow, keeping it up against my chest.

I looked down at myself, a heavy sigh catching in my throat. I felt like a failure, but still wanted to be back with the packs. Turning to the east, like I could see anything through the darkness and the forest, my fingers clenched tighter in my shirt sleeve.

What was happening out there? Was Etran still standing tall? Who led the packs? Were they doing a better job than me? What had become of Eska?

The faint shift of a door opening behind me sent me rocking back to see. Sasha stood in the gap, shawl tucked tight across her chest. A question formed in her brow and she ghosted a step closer.

"Did I wake you?"

She nodded, but waved her hand to cut off an apology. Coming closer, she tapped my chest with a finger, the question still lurking in her eyes.

I turned away again, looking east. "Just restless."

Sasha circled around to face me again. Pointing to my side, her head tilted.

"Everything just aches."

Her hands slid back among the folds of her shawl. We stared at one another a moment, before she shifted and pointed back to the lodge, a challenge in the positioning of her jaw.

"I will," I promised with a small smile, but still made no move.

She didn't either, staying facing off with me. But after a moment, she softened a fraction and came to stand beside me, but not leaving, as if worried that I wouldn't go back in.

A faint howl echoed on the night air. I stiffened, leaning

toward the noise. A lynx growled softly in response, but didn't shift from its curled position by a lodge.

Sasha touched my elbow gently. I wondered how often they'd heard the howls since our packs had been out in force. And how far it was. The still air could carry a sound for miles and you'd never know the difference.

Who was out there?

"Have there been scouts out from your people?" The question burst from me.

She slowly nodded, her hands still tucked away.

"Not good news then?"

A shrug.

My fingers pilled the shirt sleeve as I stared at the soft cloth. Why would she know? I'd have to speak with the battlelynx and chief to learn anything. A touch on my shoulder drew my gaze back up.

She pointed at the lodge and closed her eyes a long moment. Then pointed at the sky, then to the east before arcing her arm up to indicate the sky again. Lastly, she pointed somewhere in the village.

"Wait until tomorrow to ask someone else?" I guessed.

A warm smile and nod. She tried to prod me back to the lodge. But when I didn't move, she narrowed her eyes and her lips pursed.

"Your mother's look is more intimidating."

A faint quirk to her lips accompanied her eye roll. It drew a smile from me.

"I promise I will go back inside in a moment."

A disbelieving eyebrow raised.

"On my honor as a warrior."

The expression didn't change, but she didn't push further. The howl hadn't come again, no response from another member of a pack. But there was no such thing as a lone wolf. Not in our tribe.

Well, Hakkon was now. But he'd thrown in his lot with the Saber tribe. His family hadn't taken the news well. I think maybe they had been angry at his banishment, until the news that he was marshaling an enemy against us.

A dark shape padded up, the hint of moonlight glinting off golden eyes. Countings of fighting sablecats sent me reaching automatically for a weapon at the feline shape. Sasha held up her hand, though I didn't even have a knife on me.

Their lynx regarded me calmly, blinking once before rubbing its jaw against Sasha's arm. Her lips curved into a smile at the throaty rumble coming from the lynx. She freed her hands from the shawl and buried them in the thick ruff of fur, leaning to rest her cheek atop the creature's head.

It reminded me too much of what I would have done with Eska if he'd wandered over to check on me. I turned away to try to swallow the sudden lump in my throat. A touch on my arm brought me back to Sasha.

Head tilted again and brow furrowed, she nudged my arm again.

"You're close with your lynx?"

She nodded and smiled, leaning on the cat as it circled her, butting her fondly with its head.

"My wolf, Eska, and I are close." It sounded a foolish thing to be concerned for a wolf when warriors were bleeding and dying. "I just worry about what he's done since I've fallen."

I didn't think he'd take to a new warrior, even as friendly as he was. Sasha's hand caught mine and I let her move it to the lynx.

The cat watched me, nose twitching at my outstretched hand. Sasha kept her hand on mine and made a *shh-shing* noise, which sent the lynx's ears pricking in interest. Another cautious sniff and it stretched its head forward to let me touch its fur.

Softer than a greywolf's pelt and twice as thick, my hand disappeared into the ruff of fur. A few tentative brushes elicited the curious rumbling noise again. Sasha smiled and scratched at the lynx's shoulder. The familiar motion and feel of fur beneath my hand eased something in me, the thing which had broken open in the sweat lodge only hours before.

Every bit of me felt wrung out and raw, but something about the moonlight and pale frost helped steady me on my feet. A shift drew my attention back to Sasha. Maybe the Blackpaw woman who'd decided to show me some kindness when she had no reason to was part of it.

She'd pushed to bring me in from the river. Her family had decided to help me when they didn't have to. The bits of moonlight caught her in a halo of light. I'd find some way to make it up to her. To the family.

This time when she indicated the lodge, I turned and made my way inside. She softly shut the door behind us, and we waited a moment for our eyes to adjust back to the darkness before we parted. Me back to my cot and her to the room she shared with her mother.

"Sasha?" I whispered.

Her faint outline paused.

"Thank you."

Footsteps brushed lightly over the wood floor and her chill hand closed around mine and squeezed before she retreated again.

Sinking down onto the cot, I curled my hand around the memory of her touch. I couldn't remember noticing someone as much as I had her the past few days. Slipping my feet from my boots, I tucked back under the blankets, waiting as the beams above me became darker streaks in the wash of blacks and deep greys.

It was nothing more than being confined to the same walls for days on end. Nothing to do with the way she'd somehow found the thing I needed a few minutes ago with the lynx.

Slamming my eyes shut, I frowned at myself. *Focus on healing. Then getting back to the fight.* That's all I needed to do.

# THIRTY-FIVE

## ETRAN

Sablecat roars reverberated in my chest, competing with the shriek of iron on iron. Frea swerved to the side, taking me out of the path of a seeking spear. Twisting mine, I wheeled her around on hindpaws and stabbed at the Saber warrior. He fell with a cry and the fresh smell of blood. My spear wrenched free, and we turned for another enemy.

Scarlet stained the frosted grass, spreading in wide stains beneath fallen figures and animals. Three wolfriders had become encircled by Sabers. I kicked Frea and we bolted forward. Settling my spear and grabbing the strap on the saddle, I braced as Frea hurled herself at the nearest rider, shoving him and the sablecat to their side.

One of the wolfriders took out the warrior as I stabbed down into the sablecat. A sharp cry jolted through my heart. Frea's head wrenched around faster than mine, a savage growl in her throat.

A riderless sablecat had thrown Maren backwards with a headbutt. I did not have to signal Frea—she leapt on her own, going straight for the sablecat's throat instead.

Once it went still, I turned, relief crashing over me to see Maren pushing up on her elbows. Frea trotted over and I reached down, offering Maren help to stand. Our bloody hands met, and I pulled her to her feet. Once up, she hunched over slightly, free hand pressed up against her stomach.

I could not force my fingers to let her go and something of the same flickered in her eyes. Battle faded for a moment. Then it rushed back with a shout and a call for me. I squeezed her hand and she stepped back, taking up a fallen spear to salute me.

Amund and his wolf galloped up, blood streaming freely from both.

"Chief, their center is weakening."

A quick glance confirmed it, and hope stirred that we might actually be able to take the day and maybe some of our land back.

"Muster up." I lifted my spear. Amund stood in his stirrups and whistled. A horn rang out in response. Wolves howled and warriors began circling.

One glance back at Maren showed her grouped with the other unmounted riders, the wolves still standing beginning to make their way over. But we couldn't wait. She gave me a tight nod, and I turned.

Amund flashed a bloody smile and drummed heels into his wolf's sides, matching Frea stride for stride as we led the charge. Our lines met with a rending sound. Snarls and shouts came up on its heels.

My spear was wrenched away by a falling warrior, and I unsheathed my sword. Amund no longer rode at my side, but the saddle on his wolf was empty. Horror slammed through my panic as I pulled Frea up looking for him.

Amund picked himself up, only for his feet to slip on the bloody ground as he tried to twist away from a Saber warrior. The warrior kicked him in the chest. Frea jolted under my sudden kick. But a force slammed into us. Frea twisted, sinking her fangs into the sablecat, but not before she pinned me to the ground.

I struggled free as Frea kicked at the dead weight with her hind paws. Amund had gotten halfway up, but no more as he blocked an overhead strike. I pushed through a jolting pain in my knee and charged the warrior.

Amund's arms shook as he kept the Saber warrior's strike from cleaving through his head. Panic overrode any rational thought I might have had, and I tackled the warrior away from Amund.

We thudded to the ground. He grabbed my sleeve as I tried to roll away, stabbing awkwardly at such close quarters. The sword point snagged against my breastplate, but I had no good angle for my own strike.

Another blade plunged down, stilling the warrior. A strained gasp broke from me, and I pushed away from the dead warrior, rolling to find Amund over me. He extended a hand and hauled me to my feet.

"You must really be his brother, pulling a move like that." His fist slammed into my shoulder. "Thought it was him for a moment."

A faint laugh trembled, and my hand fisted against his breast-plate. "You good?"

"Don't worry about me, Chief. We've still got a battle to win."

Our wolves loped up and we struggled back into the saddles, turning once again to the fight.

It didn't last much longer. Our wolves stood on the field, staring at what barely felt like a victory. The orders to gather the dead and send out what patrols we could came from my hoarse throat. Frea limped along behind me as I helped clear the field.

"Etran?"

I whirled at the voice. Maren's braids hung lank and bloody and her warpaint was smeared, but she was the most beautiful thing I'd seen. Stumbling a step, I hauled her into my arms. She returned the embrace just as fiercely.

"You're all right?" I whispered and felt her nod against my neck. I'd kept my distance since her pack had arrived, and it still shook me to my core every time she rode out.

"You?"

"I love you," I blurted.

She pulled back and my stomach knitted in terror, but she only smiled and pressed a hand against my cheek, resting her forehead against mine.

"Finally admitting it on a battlefield was not what I expected from you."

A shaky laugh answered her, but as she hadn't released her hold on me, I guessed she felt the same. Her lips on mine confirmed it.

"I wasn't planning on doing that on a battlefield either," she said, drawing back slightly. I brushed tangled strands of hair away from her cheek.

"I don't mind."

Her eyes came alight with her laugh, and I stole another kiss.

A gruff cough brought our attention flying away. Amund stood leaning on his spear, one eyebrow arched.

"*If* you two are done finally declaring feelings for each other, could we get back to this mess?"

Maren backed away, a laugh still in her eyes. I reluctantly let her hand go and watched her head back to her pack, grabbing the reins of her wolf as she went.

"Don't worry." Amund clapped me on the shoulder. "I think only half the packs saw."

Heat found my cheeks and I took Frea's leathers again. "Shut up."

"Almost made my cold heart believe in love."

He staggered under my shove, but I smiled and shook my head. For a second, it seemed like Comran was there. The thought made me sober again, but couldn't stop me looking for Maren every spare second as we began the ride back to camp.

The healers rushed to meet us as we rode in. I cared for Frea, waiting my turn as they tended some of the more serious injuries. Jens and Loke still hadn't returned by the time riders began to settle. Amund was half-asleep on his feet, and I made him go to his tent to rest.

Cookfires were lit and packs gathered around. Even though we had taken the field, there were few sounds of victory. A buzz still filled me from Maren's kiss hours earlier, and I couldn't yet sit still, even as the healer wrapped bandages around my wounds.

He left me and I pushed to my feet. Amund's words came back. *"Thought it was him for a moment."* Comran wasn't here. Neither was Loke. But some still glanced my way. Frea nosed at my arm as I began to limp to the nearest campfire.

Even the injured warriors still gathered around to share a meal. Most looked up, the others already asleep. Hesitation locked words in my throat, and they stared at me almost expectantly.

"Doing all right?" I finally managed.

"Aye, Chief." A man with his arm bound up in a sling answered. "You?"

A nod was all I seemed capable of, but they accepted it. I shifted, leaning my hand against Frea as I prepared to move on.

"You led strong today, Chief." The pack leader tapped his free hand against his chest. "Seems the Greywolf has been looking out for us all along."

I swallowed hard, afraid to read too much into his words. Others echoed the sentiment in their tired nods and quiet taps to their chests. His features softened a little at the hesitation and confusion I knew had leaked out across my face.

I limped to the next fire. Some packs offered bare words, others had more to say, but it all echoed what the pack leader had said. It became a little easier each time to find words.

My knee ached and I leaned heavy on Frea as I made it to the last fire, where Maren sat with a slight, knowing smile. Forcing my gaze from the sight, I managed to ask after the pack. Kjell pushed to his feet as I made to leave.

"Chief, do you know when Loke—the battlewolf," he hastily corrected himself, "might be back?"

I shared his glance out in the darkening woods. Loke and three packs had been gone for two days. If they did not return by the morrow, I would start to get worried. But it already shone clear in Kjell's face.

"Tomorrow at the latest." I tapped his shoulder. "I'll make sure he finds you when he gets back."

Relief broke before Kjell tried to shutter it away. "No, it's…"

I forced a smile, wishing my brother still rode with the packs. "I'll make sure."

"Thank you, Chief." Kjell eased back down to his seat, and I almost had to look away from the respect in the other wolfriders' eyes.

"Get some rest," I said and made my way back to my tent, stopping once with the pack leader in charge of sentries.

The same continual exhaustion lurked around him, but he tapped his chest in salute. Frea settled in beside my tent. Pausing once in the entrance, I cast a look back at the camp now falling to sleep. Wolves settled down in tight bundles within their packs.

Sentry wolves and riders paced through the woods as silent shadows.

But for the first time in a long time, I felt settled in my place as chief. I tipped a glance heavenward, finding the Greywolf leaping across the stars, hoping I'd done enough to honor Comran's memory. It was a start at least.

# THIRTY-SIX

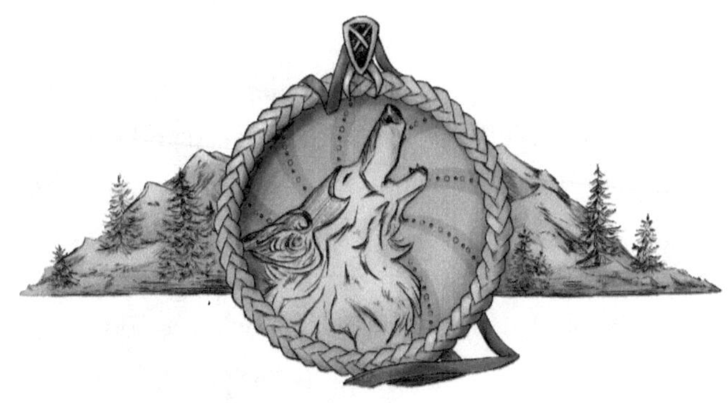

## COMRAN

Breakfast had barely settled in my stomach before I asked if I could see the chief. Zoya's lips flattened in a frown, but Sasha interceded with a string of signs. Zoya propped hands on her hips, not softening as I gave my best smile and a promise that I would not overexert myself.

Clearly, she did not believe me.

After another argument from Sasha, Zoya relented.

"To the chief's lodge and then right back."

I dutifully promised, but it was not enough to drive the glare away.

"Sasha will go with you to make sure."

At least Sasha didn't seem as upset by the declaration as Lukas would have been. She beckoned me to the door, and I joined her, easing around Zoya's arched eyebrow when she noticed me already in boots and ready.

Sasha kept a sedate pace down the paths, pausing every few yards to point to a bench with a questioning look. Each time I shook my head. I already felt stronger than the day before and had eaten more at breakfast.

So I was not ready to admit that my legs shook a bit when we finally reached the chief's lodge. Sasha knocked and stepped back beside me, offering me an encouraging smile. It made me think I wouldn't get good news.

The door swung open and the chief herself stepped out.

"Ah, Greywolf. I wondered when I would see you."

"Chief." I offered her the sign of respect.

"What is it you need?"

"I wanted to ask if you'd been sending out scouts, or knew anything about the fighting?" My hand messed with the sling keeping my shoulder steady, afraid and eager for news all at once.

The chief crossed her arms. "We have warriors patrolling our boundaries, but no news that would mean anything to you."

I tried not to let it needle at me. But I pressed on with another request.

"What about sending someone to my village or the warcamp to let them know that I am alive."

The creases around her eyes softened, but she shook her head.

"I thought you might ask. But I cannot risk a rider across the valley, not when the Saber tribe is out. And I cannot risk a rider being followed back here. They have pushed again at the new boundaries they claimed at the lake, but have not found our village in years. I would keep it so."

It was logical, I knew it. It just hurt to know that my mother would keep thinking I was dead. That the packs were another warrior short.

"Zoya says you are healing," the chief offered. I brought my gaze back up to meet hers.

"Not fast enough." I attempted a lighter tone to try to hide the swooping restlessness and bits of anger from her declaration. "But I was never very patient."

Her mouth turned up at the corner. "Zoya is the best healer this village has seen in many a year. You will be fit soon enough."

With another respectful gesture, I took my leave. Sasha jogged a few steps to catch up to me. Her touch on my arm turned my attention to her. She started to sign, then flapped her hands in frustration, and pointed to me instead.

"I am fine." But my feet didn't stop their quick pace.

She tugged at my sleeve again and gave a disbelieving look. I ignored it and instead looked over my shoulder, trying to remember the way back to the training court. Sasha's finger in my chest and her blocking my way with a frown as soon as I turned again only slightly quashed those plans.

She pointed emphatically back to their lodge. I tried a smile again which left her narrowing her eyes.

"All right!" I relented. "But I need to do something. I cannot go back to sitting inside."

Tilting her head, she thought a moment, then beckoned me on. She led me around the back of her lodge where a bench and several long staves rested. She picked one up and handed it to me, lifting a finger on her free hand and frowning severely.

"I'll be careful," I quickly promised as I took it.

About as long as a spear, it sat lighter in my hand without the iron tip. And like our training staves, it was made from a lighter wood. I hadn't used one that simple since my second year of training.

She picked one up as well, handling it with familiarity. I tested the wraps on my injured shoulder, making sure it was secure against my chest before I moved into the simpler forms.

"You are not going to tell on me for this, are you?" I pulled back from a lunge, my legs wobbling a little from the effort already.

She shook her head, still watching me as she tossed the stave from hand to hand.

"Or are you just waiting for me to collapse in exhaustion?"

She lifted a shoulder with an innocent look, drawing a laugh from me. Her lips parted in a grin. Another lunge and back to jab in an overhead motion. It still managed to pull at my shoulder, and I winced.

Sasha cleared her throat and I frowned at her. "Not a word."

Lacing both hands around her staff, she smoothed her features into a blank slate.

"If you have time, I am betting there's more signs you could teach me."

A nod.

"And it would probably get us into less trouble if Zoya happened to see it."

But in reality, my body already protested after only a few forms.

Stepping back, I offered her the stave. She made a show of clapping her hands in approval, earning her an eye roll from me. A nose-wrinkling grin scrunched her face as she took it and set it back against the wall. Waving me to follow again, she moved around to the sunnier side of the lodge and we took a seat on the bench there.

Sasha pulled out a clean sheet of birch bark paper and charcoal and set them neatly on the bench between us as she turned to face me, leg tucked up under her. Pointing to her eyes and then her hand, she waited until I promised to focus.

Thankfully, she'd made me promise to focus on her hands, instead of her smile. I shook the thought away. The fall might have injured my head after all, despite Zoya's assurances to the contrary.

She scribbled a word on the paper, showed me, then demonstrated the sign. It came a slower process as she taught me new signs and, admittedly, had to re-teach some from the day before. But it was worth it when, after an hour, I could understand a simple response to a question.

And her triumphant smile had nothing to do with it either.

-You need two hands for most everything else.- She offered the paper with a bit of an apology which I waved off.

"Soon, though?"

A shrug.

My lips flattened. "You help Zoya, so I have a thought you might know."

An eye roll and scribbled message. -She's trying to keep you patient.-

I laughed. "Good luck with that. My own mother couldn't manage it."

Her cheeks scrunched with her silent laugh. -Do you have siblings?-

The question quieted my mirth for a telling moment. She pulled her hands back into her lap in hesitation at the response.

"My mother and father thought they would never have me. So they—agreed—my father could have a son with another woman."

Her brows drew together, and lips parted in surprise. I gave a tight smile.

"But they also had me. I'm actually two months older than Etran. We weren't close our entire lives until he was chosen as chief and named me battlewolf."

It came spilling from me. I barely knew her, but here I was, unable to stop talking. Maybe finally trying to work through it all myself.

"I'd always thought he hated me or saw me as a challenge. But really, I just wanted a brother. Something like what you and Lukas have. Or what my friend Loke has with his brothers. It wasn't until Etran blurted out that he felt the same that I thought maybe we could."

Her gaze hadn't moved from me, even though I'd shifted to stare out at the woods. It was odd to admit it all to a near stranger, when I'd barely admitted it to Loke months ago.

-You asked after him when we brought you back.-

"I did?"

She nodded. My fingers fell to worrying at the edge of my shirt.

"I never called him brother. I think I'm scared to, for some reason." Again, I wondered at the fact I was confessing all this to her. Maybe because I wouldn't hear the pity in her voice with any reply.

-It can be hard to change a way of thinking.-

"I suppose." I moved to lean more comfortably against the lodge. "Was it hard to change your thinking and bring me here?"

This time she paused, catching the corner of her lip in her teeth. The charcoal twitched in her hand as she stared down at the paper in her lap. Finally, she wrote. A bit of nervousness stirred as it took longer than before, and she flipped the paper over for more runes.

-At first, Lukas and I hesitated. But maybe bitterness is not as strong as hate. The Saber tribe took so much. Perhaps you can redeem your tribe to us.-

My thumb smeared the last few runes as I lightly touched the thought she had written.

"Your thought or the tribe's?" I handed it back.

-Mine,- she admitted, and extended her hand for the paper again, taking a moment to think through her next words. -I think you've surprised us by being more passionate than I'd heard your father to be.-

"That's not hard to do," I scoffed. "And I know I am not the only one who disagreed with him. Our old battlewolf told me himself that he would have ridden to help in a heart's beat. I'm truly sorry."

Her hands twisted together a moment before she tapped over her heart twice. Thank you.

"Do you miss your father?"

-Not as much as before. It fades more and more each turning. I hate that it has, but time wears things smooth.-

She pointed to me, brow raised in question. I shook my head. Then amended it with a shrug.

"I don't know what I would feel if my father died. Etran said he's trying to be better, but I can't quite forgive him yet for shoving us both away our whole lives."

I cleared my throat and brought a smile. "Now that I have spilled my darkest secrets…"

Sasha tossed her head with a smile, and shifted to lean her shoulder against the lodge, still facing me.

"Can I ask why you don't talk? Unless you do not want to tell me."

She waved it off and began writing. -Fever when I was ten years old stole my voice. The talånd's mother was deaf. He taught me signs. Lukas and I made others.- She smirked a little, and I didn't much have to guess which ones she meant.

-It was hard at first. But my family learned with me.-

"There have been days some wished I had no voice," I said with a grin.

She shook her head, and I caught the sign for "I like" before she curled her hand in a fist to stop herself. Red tinged her cheeks and I grinned again before leaning back against the wall.

"I will give you a few more days stuck with me in the lodge before you change your mind."

She nudged my shoulder with a roll of her eyes.

"What is this?" Zoya appeared around the edge of the lodge, hands propped on hips when she saw us sitting. The frown she leveled at me must have been the one sent by the spirits for all healers to wear.

"We went to the chief's lodge and then right back." I looked to Sasha for confirmation. She nodded, a bit of a grin still on her face. "You did not say anything about going back inside."

Zoya's mouth worked as she crossed her arms. "I see I might have to be more specific with you."

I tried for something contrite, but ended up with most of a smirk. Zoya shook her head and waved her hand.

"Come along. I need to check your shoulder. Inside." The sternness still in her voice brought me up to my feet faster than the day before, but not by much.

"It will come," she reassured in response to my quick sigh.

I didn't argue, just followed her back in to sit on the bench close to the fire and the extra candles she and Sasha brought over.

"This is healing well," she assured as she poked and prodded.

I craned my neck to try to see the wounds left from the sable-cat's teeth. "It feels like it went all the way through my shoulder."

Zoya tapped the back of my head with a finger. "Don't be dramatic. Your armor stopped it from biting too deep."

I looked questioningly to Sasha, who lifted a shoulder and tilted her head. I treated her to one of the signs she'd taught me.

Another rap on the back of my head from Zoya, along with a,

"Language. Sasha, what have you been teaching him?"

Sasha's hands flitted together airily. Zoya snorted and went back to tending my shoulder. A paper appeared under my nose moments later and I flashed a grin up at Sasha when I read:

-It's not my fault you are a quick learner.-

It turned to a flinch as Zoya pressed something against my shoulder.

"I will take the stitches out in a few days, and then you can begin to use it. Slowly."

It would be a spirit's blessing if she didn't knock me out with how many times she'd rapped me over the head.

"On my honor."

Her snort sent the message that she didn't believe me.

"What happened to my armor?" It hadn't much crossed my mind in the last few days, but now with the promise of soon being able to move more freely, I needed to start making my plan for leaving.

"Sasha." Zoya tilted her chin at the hanging.

Sasha disappeared and returned first with the vambraces and greaves, then again with the breastplate, setting it all on my cot. Zoya helped me pull the shirt back on and fastened my arm back in the restrictive sling with a warning glare.

Sasha stood a step away as I picked up the smaller pieces of armor. A faint ripple in the leather marked the time I'd spent in the water. Rubbing my thumb over the distortion, I cursed softly under my breath. It would do until I could get back to the village and get new armor.

The breastplate was in no better condition. The same water damage to the leather, and then the puncture marks and blood-stains in the left shoulder. The sablecat's teeth had ripped through the shoulder buckle.

I had my work cut out for me. Maybe find some way to patch over the holes and make a new buckle to keep it on.

Perhaps it was a good thing Zoya would be keeping me around the lodge for some time yet.

"Lukas can help if you need," Zoya cut in, studying me as I slowly laid out the armor as I would in my tent. Sasha cleared her throat, a raspy sound.

My focus fell to the sword she held out in both hands. Taking it, I rested the point on the cot, rubbing a thumb along the leather where the hilt met scabbard. A bit of rust flaked off the iron. Pulling it free, I let the scabbard fall to the cot. I'd need a new sheath, but like the bracers, it could serve until I returned to the village.

A breath of relief escaped that the rest of the blade had eluded rust and damage from the river.

"Sasha cleaned it the night they brought you back."

"You know how to take care of it?"

Sasha rubbed her arms, shrugging.

"Her father taught her and Lukas both." Quiet filled up Zoya's voice, and she and Sasha shared a look filled with ache.

I managed to slide the sword back into its sheath. "Thank you."

She nodded, and slipped away, returning with some cloths and a small box. The familiar smell of oil surrounded it and it made me relax a bit more.

Sasha set it all on the cot and took out her paper and charcoal. I waited, focused on the paper, still sensing Zoya's scrutiny. A hint of red touched Sasha's cheeks as she handed the message to me and flicked a glance to her mother.

-If you need another hand to help, I can.-

A mother's stare might be a bit more unsettling than a healer's. I kept my focus on Sasha with an effort and nodded.

"I would appreciate it."

Her smile sent something odd through my chest, and I swallowed hard. If I wasn't careful, there might be something I'd miss when I left.

# THIRTY-SEVEN

## ETRAN

When I dragged myself from my tent after mid-morning, weary still to my bones, Loke had not returned. Exhaustion had settled over the camp countings ago and had yet to let up. Many warriors were still wrapped in their sleeping furs and wolves lounged around, as grateful as their riders to have a few hours of rest.

I limped my way on aching knee to speak with the pack leader on duty, rubbing at the knot in my shoulder. Even a change of clothes and hasty wash in the frigid stream had not helped me feel any more awake.

"No sign, no scouts back either."

A curse hovered on the edge of my tongue at the somber report. We looked out into the forest like they'd appear in the shadows just by us wishing. I twisted to glance into camp.

"Jens is not back either?"

The pack leader slowly shook his head. This time the curse did escape. The creases deepened around the wolfrider's eyes, lips turning down in a frown. Loke had ridden for the border, intent on salvaging some of it. If he did not make it back, it might mean the worst.

An hour came and passed with no sign. The light murmur of voices became a little louder, holding a few more edges as the same feeling of unease spread across camp. Finally, I pushed to my feet, Kjell already up and coming to meet me by the time I made it to the center of the camp.

Warriors looked at me, but for once hesitation had no place in my heart.

"I want two packs ready to ride. We're going to look for Loke and the others."

I would not lose another battlewolf.

"I'm coming too," Amund said, but he staggered worse than me. The healer shook his head.

"Chief, he has a fever and has lost too much blood recently. He needs rest."

Amund's pale features were drawn tight, and he hunched to the side, but determination filled his jaw.

"I'm going."

"No," I said. "You need to rest."

Amund's eyes sparked bright, but it did not deter me.

"I need someone here in the camp. Jens hasn't returned either, and if he does not, I need someone here."

He stared at me. "So why are you going?"

It stung, even though I had braced for it. I was not Loke's friend or swordbrother.

"I am not losing another battlewolf." Even if I was barely tolerated as chief, I could do this. It was what Comran would have done.

Amund backed down, but still stood looking after us when we rode out minutes later. Kjell and Maren rode behind me, several others in their pack saddling up without question. The rest were those healthy enough from other packs.

I led the way southwest to where three small tributaries formed one larger, rushing stream to pour into the river. We cut across the valley, loping fast where we could and slowing the wolves to pick through the mess of streams pouring from the hills, scouting any small growth of trees or reaching forest for Sabers.

The boundary marker was a new one we had established in the last counting, miles east of where it had originally stood on our border with the Blackpaw tribe.

We lost ground daily. Not much longer and we would be pushed back across the great river.

Hours passed until finally the river's rush sounded ahead in the lurking twilight. Foam spilled over ledges worn by the river over the years, dropping down from the hills to merge into a gushing mess that sorted itself into a calmer passage down to the great river.

The early moon glinted off the calmer water and the empty hills. Nothing. No sign of Loke or the packs.

Frea shifted on her paws, sampling the breeze that rustled the trees across the rivers. A growl started up in her chest as unease crept down my back.

"Back up," I ordered softly.

Frea's caution spread to the other wolves and fangs glinted in the light. But the wolves responded to our cues and backed away from the rivers. Once back where the river didn't mask so much sound, I looked back to the towering trees.

A lithe black figure dropped from the branches. Yellow glinted for a moment in the sablecat's eyes and its warrior stepped out, arrow on bow.

Frea pulled against the reins, ready to take on the threat. But night was the sablecat's territory more than anything, and they blended into the darkness better than cursed shades in the dark woods.

"Head upriver," I said, keeping Frea to a slow walk between the pack and the scout. Some grumbled at the order, but most complied, knowing what I did.

It was not the time to engage in full battle. Greywolf eyes did not fear the dark, but we warriors were not so lucky. We walked away, letting the scout and whoever else was watching know that we would be back.

We pushed for another hour until I began to raise my spear to signal the halt. But Frea lifted her head, ears swiveling. Hope stirred and I urged her on. Kjell leaned in the saddle, letting his wolf lope faster.

And in the last of the fading light, we found them.

Kjell gave a sharp cry and only an order from me kept him from racing forward. Five wolfriders peeled off at my next command to ride a scouting circle around what was left of the packs staggering in an uneven line.

Warriors walked beside wolves, others rode, but too many saddles held limp figures draped across, or hunched over.

Kjell made straight for the pair in the lead, though in the rapidly falling darkness it was hard to see who supported whom. But one sagged against him in a tight embrace. Frea edged up and I carefully dismounted, my knee aching worse for the hours cramped in the saddle.

"Etran?" Loke's voice held a bit of confusion. Blood stained the side of his face and more covered his armor. I reached out, but he shifted his grip onto Kjell's shoulder.

"Hardly any is mine," he said.

"What happened?"

Loke's frame slumped even further. "They're across the boundaries. We couldn't make it more than a few miles at a time without being attacked. This morning was the worst of it. We finally got enough distance."

"Or they let you go so they could take the rivers' meeting." Realization came cold.

A vehement curse broke from Loke. "Jens?"

"He was not back yet when we left to find you."

Kjell grunted slightly as Loke re-shifted his weight. "You came?"

I nodded. "Amund needed the rest." I paused, seeing Loke's bare wrist where his cords should have been. I needed my battle-wolf, but it was more than that.

Loke waited, his silence prodding the final answer from me in a frustrating way. The darkness made it a little easier.

"I left him behind. I couldn't do the same to his friends."

"His?" Loke's voice rose in question. "And what do you think you are to us?"

I stared, trying to see more through the poor light. "What?"

"You had us as friends as soon as Comran swore his oath, Etran." Loke's hand descended on my shoulder. "I'm only sorry I didn't do it sooner."

The leathers stuck in my hand. I didn't know what to say. One hand could count the number of friends I'd had my whole life.

"And I'm sorry we lost ground." Anger and fatigue competed for dominance in his voice. I reached to tap his shoulder.

"Let's get you all back to camp and make a new plan."

His nod was bare movement in the dimness, and Kjell helped him onward. I stood back with Frea, watching the procession of wolves and defeated riders move past. The distant forest was a bigger strip of darkness under the emerging starlight.

If we'd lost the border and the river tributaries…

A touch against my hand brought my quick glance to Maren standing beside me. She returned the tight squeeze of my fingers, staying with me as I turned back to watch the packs.

I wished for Comran. Wished for him to have some sort of plan to strike back before we gave up the land. I couldn't do it on my own. I led with my mind, seeking the best alternative. Loke was a good warrior, but he also played the defensive hand, likely why he and Comran fought so well together.

And I knew Loke would agree with me. If the Sabers had gotten this far, we had to withdraw across the great river to keep our packs and camp safe, and draw a line of defense for the rest of the valley that could not fall.

# THIRTY-EIGHT

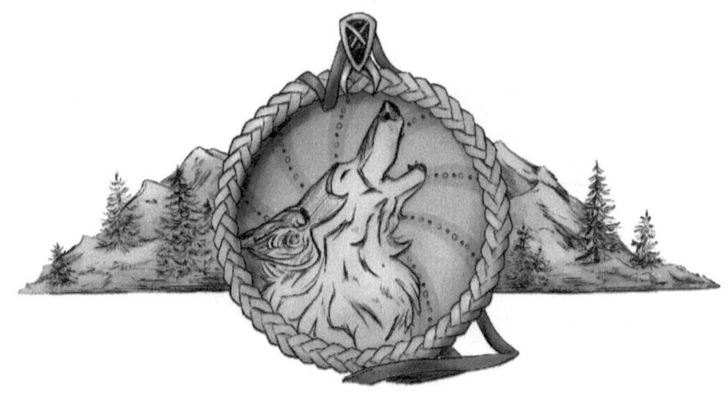

## COMRAN

Water surrounded me, pushing down, forcing its way into my throat. All while something dragged at my left shoulder. I tried to fight against it, but cold seeped through me, slowing my limbs and freezing my reactions.

Panic started to set in, but water smothered my cries.

Something heavy knocked at my other shoulder, shaking me, shattering the icy water holding me prisoner. With a jolt, I opened my eyes to stare into golden orbs hovering above me.

Reflex sent me scrambling away and the cot rocked precariously beneath me. It took a moment before I made out the shape of Raya in the darkness of the lodge and my heart steadied.

Her humming rumble sounded, and a cold nose pushed at my shoulder.

"Thanks." I reached a hesitant hand out to brush her fur. She padded away to settle at the foot of Lukas's bed across the lodge.

I pushed myself the rest of the way into sitting, letting a breath fill my lungs with air and not imagined water. I thought I hadn't remembered anything from hitting the river to waking up in the lodge, but it seemed my body did.

"Did she scare you?"

The embers of the fire in the center of the room helped me focus on the outline of Lukas's head raised to look at me.

"I've had one too many sablecats that close to my face," I replied in the same low voice.

A light rustle came from him.

"I wouldn't know." Bitterness laced through his voice.

My fingers rubbed at the blankets pooling in my lap. We weren't that different in age. But I'd seen more battle.

"It is not always as glorious as old riders make it out to be."

He huffed. "Perhaps. But I feel I'll never have the chance to see. I don't fault the chief and battlelynx for what they've done. The tribe has survived under them. But…" A sigh cut from him and I turned to try to see him a little more in the darkness.

"The other lynxriders my age—we were all young during the war. Not old enough yet to ride into battle, and the battlelynx forbade it. We'd be the last defense and we had to keep the tribe safe somehow."

A lump lodged in my throat. Young men and women would not finish the warrior training, learning that it wasn't for them. Others might be taken to fill out the packs too soon and perhaps be sent to the All-Father's Halls much too early.

"You are going back to fight?" His next question caught me off-guard.

"Yes." Fight and swear an oath to whoever Etran had named battlewolf. Maybe give them the medallion still tucked away.

"Do not misunderstand me, none of us have fondness for your tribe."

I did not try to protest.

"But we are tired of living in the shadows of the woods. Hiding. And now the Saber tribe is out again and trying to take more of this valley. I think the need for vengeance has cooled in many of the warriors who fought in the war."

"But not you?" I guessed.

"No." It came with finality. "I can ride, and I can fight. And there are others like me who would as well."

"And what would your battlelynx say?"

"Would she have to know?" he said stubbornly.

A faint smile barely pushed away the misgiving inside. "Speaking as a former battlewolf, I think she would notice. And it's no simple thing for warriors to leave the village in packs when not sent."

"What would you do, then?" He scoffed. "If you'd lost a father you loved and saw friends lose fathers and brothers and sometimes sisters and mothers? If you had to wait eight years and be told to live in hiding and keep your distance."

He shifted and propped himself up on an elbow and I could feel the weight of his gaze through the dimness.

"What would you do if your enemy reappeared and you had a chance to fight?"

I didn't hesitate, because I knew what I'd do. "I would fight."

He settled back. "Mother says she will take out those stitches in two days. Then it won't be long until you'll be strong enough to leave. You might have some company when you trek east across the valley."

I flexed my wrist as if to feel the weight of my sword or spear in hand again. I would not turn down more warriors on our side in the fight, or ones with a grudge against the Saber tribe already. But there was something about the lodge, the way the three of them interacted as a family. The way they included me in a few things, like I was more than just a Greywolf they'd allowed into the lodge.

It made me want to keep Lukas far from the war. And keep his family from feeling more loss.

⌒

The morning followed the same routine I'd grown used to over the last counting. Lukas and Raya vanished out the door. Zoya came to check my bandages and reassure me my wounds were healing. Sasha and she made breakfast as I finished dressing. Lukas reappeared with fresh water in two buckets. Sasha beckoned me over to the table as she had every day since I had been allowed out of bed.

Lukas ignored me like the conversation in the late night hadn't happened. I slid into my seat at the table, trying to ignore my sudden awareness of Sasha, which had appeared over the last few days, intensified when she pulled out her paper and charcoal and taught me more signs in some of her spare time.

The meal began in silence after Zoya offered a bit in the hearth for the spirits. I stretched the fingers of my left hand where it was still bound up in the sling. Every morning my strength returned fractions more and I became increasingly restless in the shadow of the lodge.

"Is there anything I can do to help today?"

Zoya's hands paused in the middle of tearing a piece of bread. "You feel up to it?"

I nodded.

"You should still be resting."

Breaking off a piece of dried salmon, I shook my head. "I've rested enough. I need some way to start gaining my strength back more quickly."

She tried a different tactic. "You are a battlewolf and a chief's son. You do not have to."

I offered a slight smile. "I'm not above getting my hands dirty. Or hand."

A faint flicker of amusement shone in her eyes. But it was Lukas who spoke up first.

"You can help me gather wood."

Zoya's eyes narrowed this time and Sasha darted a glance between us both. There was a bit of challenge and sincerity in his voice. I inclined my head.

Zoya extracted a promise from me to rest when I felt strained. It didn't stop me from eagerly joining Lukas when he pushed away from the table and jerked his head for me to follow.

"Thank you for this," I said as I fell into step with him.

"The faster you heal, the faster you leave." He didn't break stride. But then he turned enough to flash a sly smirk. "And it means less work for me. We will be bringing in wood for several lodges."

"Several?" I raised an eyebrow. "Then I'm afraid I have to go back to rest."

He shook his head, hearing the jest. "Too late, Greywolf."

The training lodge yielded axes and another young man who sized me up a long moment before Lukas started walking into the treeline again.

"So, you're the battlewolf." The warrior shouldered his axe as we followed. "You grow shorter over on that side of the valley?"

I adjusted my grip on the axe Lukas had given me, feeling off balance with my left arm still tied against my chest. My height had never truly bothered me, even when I stood shorter than most of the warriors in the village.

"The spirits knew I wouldn't need as much room for my pride as some." I didn't look at him as we picked our way down the narrow trail.

A smile quirked his mouth. "Though maybe not big on brains, then, for being dragged over a cliff by a sablecat."

"I had heard that extended baths in icy rivers were good for one's health."

"And?"

"Rejuvenating."

He tossed his head with a laugh. "I am Arkadi."

"Comran," I offered, then raised my voice in Lukas's direction. "Though I also respond to just Greywolf."

Lukas raised his hand in a reply, and I smirked. Arkadi apparently knew what it meant and chuckled.

"You think you'll be able to keep up?" The warrior nodded to the sling.

"I have never been one for sitting still," I said. "Though I think I am a little afraid of Zoya, so we'll see how much work I can do today."

Arkadi chuckled again. "Then I will make sure to stay far away. I have been the subject of her wrath before, and it is not pleasant."

"That is not reassuring."

Coming to a small clearing where several trees already lay felled, we set to work. Lukas and Arkadi chopped off larger branches and split more, and I, with my one working arm, broke off small branches to place in a pile for kindling.

It felt good to be swinging something again, though I did have to stop every few minutes to catch a breath. Once done, we set to carrying wood back. Lukas gave me a few logs in my arm, which took some shifting before it was comfortable. He and Arkadi eyed me, as if wondering when I'd give up, but the work and the sunshine and warming air had me feeling better than I had in a long time.

Though maybe it was also due to not having red spear still lurking in my blood.

An older woman with grey-streaked hair met us at the first lodge. Her smile died to a scowl at the sight of me and she crossed her arms tight. Lukas silently took the wood from my hold and stacked it neatly.

I offered a nod to her and followed them back for more. If the Blackpaw village was anything like mine, everyone would know of me, even if they hadn't seen me out and about yet. The second trip back, she hadn't changed her posture, though now another woman stood with her, dark shawl wrapped around her shoulders.

"Bastard," she spat.

My shoulders tensed and heart quickened in fight. Until Etran's face flashed in my mind. Setting my jaw, I kept my silence as Arkadi helped me unload. One time I'd been on the receiving end of that word. And he'd had a whole lifetime. It had never occurred to me until he said it, the battle he'd faced every day from some of our tribe.

Lukas flicked me a glance as we headed back for more. I mustered a lighter expression.

"They won't avoid that wood out of spite for me, will they?"

A glimmer of approval sparked in his eyes as he shook his head. "Sanne keeps a lodge of widows and orphans. I didn't think."

I stooped and tossed a small, willowy branch into the growing pile of kindling. "I assume it would not be hard to find those in this village. You are sure you'd ride out to battle alongside a Greywolf?"

His jaw tightened and he slammed his axe into a tree trunk. "Not to help you."

Arkadi began gathering the last of the logs we'd cut, but his gaze had fixed on Lukas.

"My father says vengeance is a weighty thing to carry before the spirits," he said.

Lukas swung again with a savage intensity, the axe cutting deep into the tree. He yanked it free. "At least you still have a father to tell you such things."

Arkadi didn't rise to the sneer, his expression open and a little mournful. Instead, he picked up a log and beckoned to me. The two of us returned to the village with wood while Lukas stayed to take out his frustration on the tree.

The women thanked Arkadi and glared at me.

"That does not bother you?" He slid me a glance.

I lifted my already aching shoulder in a shrug. "I can hardly blame them, can I?"

He nodded, gnawing on his lower lip.

"It does not bother you to be walking side by side with me?"

"I will not say it doesn't. My father rode with the warriors. On the coldest days of winter, he can barely walk, his leg pains him so much. But we didn't lose as much as some families."

He sighed. "It doesn't rest easy with many knowing that the chief and battlelynx allowed you to stay, or that Zoya is caring for you."

"I will leave as soon as she allows me," I promised.

He shrugged. "But maybe I am surprised you are here working alongside us."

"I would be long dead in a river if not for Lukas's family. And it is spirits' mercy your chief allowed me to stay. That's a mighty thing to repay, so I'll do what I can."

Arkadi shook his head. "And here I was thinking Greywolves only cared about their pride and mangy pelts."

I allowed a brief smile. "Spirits assured, there's some of those in the village."

He chuckled and tilted his head in acknowledgment. "There's some here too."

By the time we made it back, the dark clouds had cleared from Lukas's face and we set to work again.

Sweat drenched the back of my shirt as we took more wood to the village, this time to a different lodge. A man with the same bulky shoulders and broad nose as Arkadi met us, leaning heavily on a carved wooden cane.

"Taking your time today, boys?" His smile dimmed a little as he rested eyes on me. He set aside the cane and helped them stack the wood neatly in a pile.

"No thanks to Arkadi and his weak arms," Lukas said.

Arkadi rolled his eyes as he and Lukas both grabbed the wood from me. I couldn't stop a short breath of relief as they took the last log and my throbbing arm fell back to my side.

"Sit down and rest." Lukas pointed to the bench a few paces away. I opened my mouth, but he shook his head. "I am not coddling you when you take a turn for the worse."

I darted a cautious glance at Arkadi's father, unsure what his reaction might be.

"Sit," he agreed.

Obeying, I eased onto the bench, feeling the weight of his stare as Lukas and Arkadi began the trek back again.

"Been a long time since I've seen a Greywolf in this village," he said.

"I assured Arkadi I will not be here long."

"I hear you are the battlewolf." His burly arms crossed over his chest, weight still shifted off his bad leg.

"A poor one." I offered a tight smile. "And have likely been replaced by my chief."

There seemed an unfair amount of perception in his dark eyes as he watched me. So much so that I struggled to keep his gaze.

"You took over from Birgir?"

I nodded. "I only held the position for a few months, but leaned on his advice. I wish he still held the medallion. Maybe we would be doing better against the Saber tribe."

"He was a good battlewolf," the man agreed. "We rode together against the Lox tribe."

"He told me he counted many in the Blackpaw tribe as friends. And that it is one of his greatest regrets he did not lead the packs to aid you."

And looking at the village and the men and women left, I wondered how much more he would regret it if he saw the aftermath.

The man's features sharpened. "Your father made that decision, did he not?"

"He did." I lifted my chin. "And I did not agree with it, though I was not allowed to ride with the packs yet."

"Maybe your tribe is paying for it now."

"It has crossed my mind."

And more than once again since being in the Blackpaw village, while also filling me with an extra desperation to rejoin the fight, so our village might survive without so many ghosts lurking in the corners.

The man limped to sink down beside me. I inched away an extra space. He turned his cane between his hands.

"And what do you hope to do here while you appear to help this time?"

The words stung and I focused on where my fingers picked at the sling. It was getting a little wearying having everyone question my motives, but losing my temper wouldn't help me.

I could occasionally think with my mind.

"A bit of repayment for the kindness shown me. And to gather my strength as quick as possible so a Greywolf won't darken your lodges for long."

It still snuck through.

There was something else I wished I could ask, but didn't think I'd get far, no matter how Lukas burned with the desire to go fight.

He tilted his head to regard me better. "Aye, there are many who don't want you here."

"I noticed."

I slumped a little more against the lodge, wondering if that was how Etran had felt his whole life. Not wanted by half the tribe, not even by the one who did want to call him family.

What would I tell him if he stood there before me? *Sorry* seemed too pathetic a word.

Footsteps and voices preceded Lukas and Arkadi's return. The old warrior and I pushed to our feet and helped stack the wood. I followed them back without a word, still feeling the weight of the man's stare on my shoulders before we disappeared into the trees.

# THIRTY-NINE

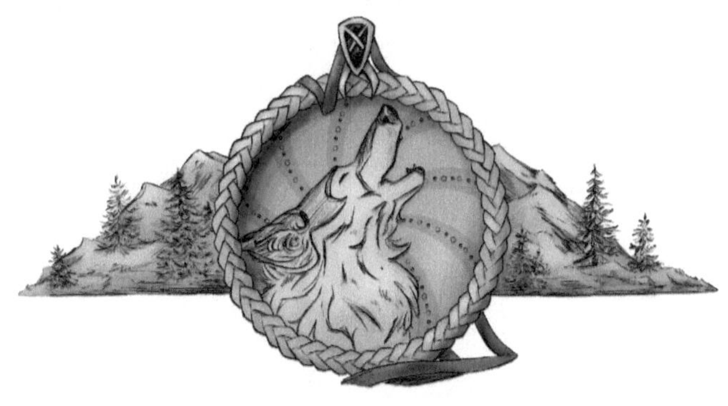

## COMRAN

"Sit still," Zoya reprimanded.

I forced my limbs to still, a little nervous at the knife she held so close to my shoulder, preparing to pick the sinew threads out. A half thought wormed in that she'd stab me then and there and be done with Greywolves, even though she'd taken the time to stitch up my wounds in the first place and make sure I recovered.

Another blurred memory flashed of the sablecat biting into my shoulder and I shifted again. Zoya's lips pursed, and she withdrew the knife.

"I'm sorry." But it didn't much sound like it. Restlessness stirred. Just a few minutes and it would be done. I could say good-bye to the sling and begin using my arm again.

A light touch brushed my hand and brought my focus over to Sasha. She rotated her hand and, placing caution aside, I closed my fingers around hers. I focused on the sight, flinching a little as the knife brushed my skin, a slight tug, and the first stitch was cut.

Sasha's free hand tapped my arm, and I watched the slow signs she formed. She had to repeat it once before I grasped the meaning.

<Yes.> I signed back.

She grinned and it sent a little jolt through my heart.

"You have learned quickly." Zoya's voice held a little something like disapproval. Sasha darted a glance at her mother.

"She's a good teacher."

And it didn't bother me to sit still and learn the signs with Sasha.

Zoya hummed, and didn't say anything else, until the tugging at my shoulder stopped and a softness pressed that brought a sting just after.

"It healed well," she said, wiping the area again. As she reached for a new bandage, I snuck a glance.

Fresh red skin puckered in places on my shoulder, surrounded by darker spots where the stitches had come out. A bit of clear liquid beaded around, wiped clean again by Zoya before she wound the bandage around my shoulder.

"It will still be tender. Do not overwork it."

Even Birgir could not hope to attain the iron in her voice. Sasha's thumb tapped the back of my hand and I promised Zoya I would be careful. She watched with narrowed eyes as I pulled my shirt on by myself, moving my left shoulder.

It fell back to my side with a faint huff of frustration from me. Weaker than I thought it might be. Zoya softened and she tapped my right shoulder.

"Keep being patient."

Left fingers fumbling a little, I got an overtunic and my belt on. Sasha beckoned me after her as I gained my feet. A new warning shone in Zoya's eyes before she stepped out of my way. I swallowed hard, afraid of it and my own eagerness to spend time with Sasha.

Sasha paused around the rear of the lodge first and retrieved a spear, handing it to me as she adjusted the bag across her chest.

"I'm flattered you believe I could fight anyone like this." I held it in my left hand, noting the way my entire arm shook under the light weight.

She rolled her eyes and I switched it to my stronger hand.

"Where are you two going?" Lukas appeared, eyes narrowed in suspicion.

<Out to gather more…> herbs or plants was what I guessed from her hands.

Lukas pointed at me.

Sasha treated him to a pitying glance and her hands flew. Lukas didn't look chagrined in the slightest. He swept up another spear and announced he was coming along. Sasha shrugged and set off without a backwards glance. Lukas invited me to follow and fell into step with me.

"How is your shoulder?"

I swung my left arm in gentle arcs, feeling the slight pull to muscles that had been cramped for almost two countings.

"Better now that I can move it."

He grunted. After working alongside him for the last two days, performing tasks around the village, it seemed he fluctuated between bouts of words and silence. And didn't seem to mind my inability to keep my mouth shut.

"Anything new from the scouts?" Maybe he'd be more willing to tell me than the chief who'd gently rebuffed me again yesterday.

"They stay content to just watch the borders and bring back

bare whispers of the fighting." Lukas tipped the spear against his shoulder, the frustration I felt plain in his voice.

I jabbed the spear butt into the ground with each pace. "I am afraid there won't be fighting left when I finally make it out of here."

Sasha fell back to my left side, mouth pursed in sympathy. I offered a slight smile. Her eyes slid past me and she hurried a few steps to begin gathering some broad leaves from a smooth-barked tree.

Lukas and I waited, him tapping fingers against the spear held loose in his hand.

"Could you show me how to fight a sablecat?" he blurted.

Sasha whipped her head around, staring at him in surprise and a little apprehension. He looked straight head.

"I've never been in battle," he admitted.

I tapped my spear against the ground. "I can. Though it will be from a Greywolf's perspective. I don't know how a lynx would go against a sablecat."

"That I can help with." The set of his jaw didn't change.

Sasha tapped his arm and they fell into some argument, maybe even shouting as their gestures grew broader and more expressive. It seemed Lukas won, and Sasha's expression mirrored his own stubbornness as she looked to me. Her forefinger tapped her chest.

"You want me to show you, too?" I asked.

She nodded, signing something else.

"She says so that she can pick up the fight when I get myself killed."

My heart wrung at the brother and sister not budging an inch from each other in shared obstinacy.

"Lukas," I started. "I can, but your battlelynx and chief, they have chosen to stay out of fighting. I—"

"Do not tell me what I can and cannot do. The Saber tribe cost me dearly!" He slammed a hand into his chest.

"And don't tell me that I haven't lost either!" I hissed. "I led men to battle, and I saw them killed. I have buried warriors and knew that I failed them." My voice had begun to rise, and a bird fluttered away in nervousness. "Maybe I don't want to see another family ripped apart when I could prevent it."

"We were ripped apart long before you came!"

"And what would you do now?" I leaned closer. "You would just leave? You cannot go against your battlelynx."

"You said yourself that you would go fight if in my position." He shoved my shoulder, knocking me back a fraction.

Sasha's hands planted on both our chests, pushing us back a pace. Her lips tightened as she looked back and forth between us. The tension left me quicker than Lukas. It took another few seconds before his shoulders sloped and he backed away another pace.

"I'm sorry," I offered first. "It's just…"

For once I could not quickly find the words I wanted. Lukas dug his spear in the soft forest floor.

"You have more of a family here than I feel I've had my entire life." The admission spilled from me quicker than a rushing river. "I do not want to tear it apart."

They stared at me, united now in shared sympathy.

"I think the spirits made me for war, Lukas. But it is not something to charge into without thought."

"Perhaps," he admitted. "But is it not your duty as a battlewolf to make sure warriors are ready for battle when it comes?"

The challenge was back. I shook my head against a smile.

"If you fight as well as you argue, maybe you'll do fine."

Sasha quirked a smile and Lukas nudged her with his elbow. I relented with a show of sighing heavily.

"Tell me what I need to know about your lynxes."

He grinned in triumph and Sasha turned back to her task, walking alongside us as we trekked the forest, listening attentively as Lukas and I shared battle strategies.

When we returned, Lukas paused outside the lodge while Sasha went in to deliver the sack full of plants to their mother.

"Are you tired?"

Shifting between my feet, I took stock of myself. My left arm was tired, but the rest of me could head to the training circle for a bit. Helping Lukas over the last few days had done wonders for my strength, but I had far to go before I could ride and fight like I did before the fall.

"Not overly so."

He nodded, biting at his lower lip.

"Will I need this?" I hefted the spear. The corner of his mouth lifted.

"And you hear me promise not to do anything with my left arm?"

The curve grew. A light whistle brought their lynx emerging around the lodge. It still brought a jolt through my stomach the way the lynx just seemed to appear and disappear. I was used to wolves padding around, ready to push their way into your face, instead of crouching atop lodges or in small spaces watching the unsuspecting go by.

We turned our steps to the training circle, painfully aware of how Lukas took a meandering path to avoid certain lodges or tribespeople out and about. Light footsteps sent us both turning, but it was Sasha coming to join us, spear in hand. I made way for her to walk by our side.

Once in the training area, I jabbed my spear point down in the dirt and swung my right arm to loosen it, relaxing a bit with the familiar pull on my muscles as I went through the motions we'd learned day one in training.

"Is there a way you can show me how the lynx attack? It might help me to better see it and compare to the Saber tribe."

Lukas nodded, beckoning to Sasha. They vanished into the training lodge and emerged with a grass-stuffed dummy attached to a pole. Familiar enough. We used them as spear practice when learning to control both wolf and spear.

Their lynx sat alert on back haunches, tufted ears pricked as it watched the process with unblinking eyes.

"Raya." Lukas held a fist out, fingers toward the lynx. She rose to a crouch, settling in, great paws kneading the grass and dirt. Eyes darted to Lukas before focusing on the dummy. I stepped back a pace with Sasha.

Lukas kept his hand out, waiting, waiting. Then dropped in a quick sign. Raya sprang to a run, crossing the distance in three great leaps, before launching herself. Paws sank into the cloth and jaws found the throat. The staff snapped under the weight of her sudden attack, and she bore it to the ground. One more twist of the head and dried grass sprayed in an arc.

I swallowed hard, that grass for a moment becoming blood.

A whistle from Lukas and Raya left the destroyed dummy behind, padding around and licking stray grass from her muzzle. Lukas grinned and Sasha went to the lynx, picking away a few more bits of grass and threads of cloth and patting her in reward.

But the urge to sit down ran through me. The memory of sablecat claws dropping on my shoulders flashed. Fighting a shudder, I turned away, trying to bring myself back to the present.

"Comran?" Lukas's voice rose in concern.

I took up the spear and turned back, smile in place.

"Not so very different from a sablecat," I said, and had them prop the dummy back up on Sasha's spear. I hesitated. "A grey-wolf will rush you and go directly for the throat of your mount. None of this ridiculous pouncing."

They shared a smirk. I took my spear and reversed it.

"Imagine Raya coming at you. You don't want to hold it high. Sablecats are quick devils. Angle low for the chest." I demonstrated by tapping Lukas on the chest with the butt of the spear. "The trick is to wait until they jump to expose their throat and strike there instead. Quicker death, but you will also lose your spear."

Lukas tilted his head back. "You can do that?"

I shrugged, suddenly awkward under Sasha's interested stare. "It's not so hard if you practice enough."

Lukas huffed. "Then I will find you a lynx and you can show me."

Raya settled down to clean her paws, and the sight made me wish for Eska. If I had him, I'd throw caution to the winds and ride across the valley back to the village. However, I was not so eager to climb on a lynx.

"Maybe in a few days. But with your lynx, you'll go up against a similar fighting style if you fight a Saber warrior."

"When," Lukas asserted, shifting the spear in his hands.

Sasha's lips flattened, but she didn't correct him. Neither did I.

"Then show me what you can do with a spear here on the ground," I said, and passed my spear to Sasha.

Raya pushed back up to sitting, watching with careful eyes, ready to spring to action should Lukas signal it.

"They said the Saber tribe did not often use spears," Lukas grunted around a form.

I shook my head, alternating watching both of them.

"They have two parts to a pack. One with spears and the other with arrows, which are harder to avoid, especially on open ground. They do not seem to use them as much if we can get them into the forests, but our wolves are better suited to attacking in open spaces."

But there had been more than one sniping hail of arrows from between trees to fell a wolfrider and wolf.

"But we've had enough practice dodging arrows during border spats, it was not hard to adjust."

"Is anything hard to you?" Lukas spun the spear in a block and pivoted to thrust into open air again.

I allowed a grin. "Watching you butcher that form. Here." I extended my hand and he passed his spear over with a frown.

"It is in your feet." I demonstrated slowly, cautiously, as my left hand closed about the spear haft. "Don't step, move smoother." My boot swept the ground. "Hold the spear closer than a woman at a dance."

Lukas rolled his eyes. Sasha watched with focused intensity, eyes darting to me when I said the word dance. It almost made me stumble, wondering what it would be like to dance with her at a summer's festival.

A prod in my shoulder warned me, but I did the sequence again, a beat quicker this time, before handing it to Lukas. He turned to the form again, better on his feet this time. It was a simple thing, something Birgir would have corrected instantly.

"Who do you train with?"

Lukas pulled out of a lunge, bringing the spear back to his shoulder with a snap. "Petya still runs training. She fought along-side her husband, the old battlelynx. Some other warriors help. But many are like Arkadi's father."

Too injured to help train the younger men. Lukas had been trained well. But I'd also been raised for leadership my whole life, ready to step in and make corrections. Different from someone thrust into a role and under orders to help keep the tribe hidden.

Sasha went next, performing the same drill. I stepped closer and tapped her left elbow.

"Keep it higher on the thrust. Gives you more power."

She nodded and tried again.

"Good. Now do it a hundred more times."

She frowned a little, but I gestured for her to continue.

"You too," I told Lukas.

He didn't appear much happier, but settled in to repeat. I hesitated, then went to grab the broken staff. Still long enough for practice. Keeping one eye on them and giving corrections as needed, I took the staff in my left hand, rolling it a moment as I paused one more minute to consider.

Then gentle motion forward, back, and to the sides, lifting the staff until my shoulder ached and reprimanded me. Which did not take long. I switched to my right hand, twisting it to rest against my shoulder.

Lukas finished his repetitions, and I nodded, more satisfied.

"Good. Now." I swung out with the blunted end of the broken staff. He backed away, quickly reversing his spear so the butt faced me. In a true fight, he would have the advantage with the longer weapon, but that's not what I wanted.

He parried and swept my blows away, returning with gentle strikes, still crisp enough in motion to reassure he knew how to make the actual strike.

Sweat beaded my forehead, grabbing at my shirt and making it cling uncomfortably to me in a way the walk through the woods hadn't done. But we finished a short round, and I beckoned to

Sasha. She was slower to engage, reversing her spear as well and sending me a look which I waved off.

"I will be fine for a few more minutes."

More hesitation marked her movements, and I ended sooner than with Lukas.

"You can't pause between strikes," I told her, trying to keep my voice even between the breaths fighting their heaving way from me. I hated being injured.

She set the spear to lean against her shoulder and began signing. Lukas stepped up beside me.

"She was worried about you hurting yourself."

But she flicked a glance at me, and I caught a glimpse of something else there. I didn't press, nodding instead and brushing sweat-streaked hair from my forehead.

"I might be done here for the day."

Apparently, they were just as eager to avoid their mother's wrath. I waited, leaning on a spear as they replaced the dummy and cleared away the broken staff. Raya sidled up to me, sniffing curiously at my sleeve, then my chest. I held still.

Were it Eska, he'd be distracted by my affection. But something like fear still stirred at the shape of the head and the golden eyes, even though her fangs were hidden, not curving down over her lower jaw.

Taking a shuddering breath, I gingerly reached out a hand. She'd let me touch her that night with Sasha, but what if she changed her mind? Raya moved, but into my hand where it hovered above her neck. Twisting, she pushed harder into my palm. Understanding dawned, and I began to scratch. Eyes closing, the undulating rumble began again in her chest.

It brought a slight smile and made the fear recede a fraction. It still lurked not too far under the surface. I wondered as I petted her if it would follow behind me into battle, and leave me shaking like I'd seen in some warriors who'd seen death himself stare them in the face.

Sasha's touch brought my hand away and Raya looked to me with slight betrayal. Almost the same look Eska would turn on me when I ran out of dried elk jerky or removed my attention.

<She likes you.>

Raya pressed her head into Sasha's chest, making me tense for a second before the rumbling began again. It sounded like the distant echoes of a mountain avalanche.

She asked something else, but it only made my brow crease in confusion.

"She asks what the greywolves are like." Curiosity shone in Lukas's eyes as well.

"More energetic, always scuffling with each other." A fond smile crossed my face. "Each lodge's wolves group together, and their warriors ride together as a pack. Easier to develop tactics if the wolves know each other. Eska, my wolf—we like to run the mountainside. Sometimes you'd think he hadn't a sensible thought in his head, but he does well in a fight."

Sasha smiled at the obvious affection in my voice. Lukas rested an elbow on Raya's back.

"You miss him?" He voiced Sasha's question.

My hand faltered where it brushed at Raya's fur again.

"I do not know what happened to him after I fell. I think he was still standing. I'd sent him to help another warrior, while I went to help Etran."

A breath and steadying press of my hand against Raya helped me continue.

"I have seen wolves broken after their warriors fell. But I have no idea if they think I am alive. If he thinks me alive. And it needles me a bit to think of another warrior riding him to battle."

Understanding showed in their faces and Sasha's hand rested close to mine in Raya's fur, a distant look in her eyes as if imagining what it would be like to lose her.

"We do not have so many lynxes here anymore, but I think I would feel the same about Raya." Lukas patted her shoulder.

The lynx looked pleased with all the attention, her rumbling deepening.

"What is this?" The battlelynx's voice rang tight.

All three of us turned as one, and a faint grumble came from Raya as if she, too, was now alert to sudden danger.

Petya stood, hands on hips, sword belted on, the same as the warrior standing next to her, frowning at us in disapproval as if we were young children caught with our fathers' swords.

"Battlelynx?" Lukas tried for innocent questioning.

Her hand cut through the air. "Do not play games with me, Lukas. Maks saw you out here with spears and this Greywolf."

I bristled. Gone was the apparent respect of battlelynx to battlewolf.

"Is it against the rules to train in this place?" Lukas asked, unruliness surfacing, and I almost nudged him to stop.

Petya's arms crossed over her chest. "With an outsider?"

"He only asked me what it was like to fight a sablecat, Battlelynx." I dipped my head in deference, but it did not appear to sway her.

Maks, however, shifted a hand to his sword, taking Lukas and me in with a look softening toward understanding. He looked old enough to have ridden against the Saber tribe.

"You have some here who could teach you," she snapped, "if that were a thing you needed to know."

Maks shifted and Lukas's chin jutted, a breath away from launching a full argument.

"He might have need of it sooner than you want." I cut Lukas off.

The full force of her glare turned on me. "And what do you know of such things?"

"Our war was not going well before I fell. I don't know what has happened since, as no one has the courtesy to tell me." Anger welled up, urged by the frustration at being confined to the lodgehouses. "And if we fall to the Saber tribe, do you honestly think they will continue to forget about you?"

I was a few paces away now. Maks shifted, ready to stop me if I threatened. Petya's face contorted in anger, but this time fear glinted underneath.

"As I heard it, there was no clear defeat or victory for either the Blackpaws or the Sabers. Do you really think that if the Sabers take our side of the valley, they will not turn again to the west?"

I tried to control my voice, but spirits, I could not imagine hiding away with my tribe, letting an enemy stalk their way through the valley.

"As you heard it?" She sneered. "I lived it, lost a husband and son to it. Let me tell you, *Battlewolf*, it was a defeat. And I will not lead warriors into the same again."

"War will find you again, whether you want it or not!"

"And you know so much of it, then? You who've barely been a full warrior for what, three turnings?"

It stung harder than it should have. And seven was the answer.

"I have fought more recently than you. And I am not one to hide and let them take over my home."

"Let me know when you think different after suffering defeat." She leaned close, eyes narrowed and tone biting.

I didn't back down. "I have tasted more defeat than victory these last countings, and my answer would still not change."

For a moment, I thought she might pull a knife and stab me right there for my words.

"Battlelynx," Maks's quiet voice interrupted.

She withdrew and inhaled a breath, chin still set in anger. "You will leave as soon as Zoya says you are fit. And then you will go back to your people and your high ideals."

I wanted to argue that it was simple fact, but the stubbornness in her words told me this was an old argument.

"And you will leave alone, with no help from us."

My fingers curled into a fist at my side as she whirled and strode away, spine rigid under the abrupt tapping of her warrior braids. Maks paused a moment more, lips parted as if he meant to say something. He nodded before following the battlelynx.

A breath hissed between my teeth, a poor escape for the fury all our words had stirred. With no look back, I pushed my feet to walk, taking me anywhere but there.

# FORTY

## ETRAN

Home at last.

Curls of smoke rose from the lodge chimneys, threading their way above the towering pines trying to keep the village from view within the arms of the mountain roots. Figures on the training grounds became visible the closer I rode. The small pack riding with me broke out in relieved murmurs, as anxious as I was to see home and a warm hearthfire again.

Some called greetings to me as we passed, but some of the familiar looks were still there—disapproval, hate, indifference. My hand tightened around the reins and Frea tossed her head a little, a grumble in her chest. I'd almost forgotten what it was like to face their disapproval after barely seeing it the last countings with the warriors.

The wolfriders spoke softly among themselves, lightness touching their voices for the first time in a long while as they unsaddled wolves and prepared to find their way home. I worked in silence.

"Chief." One warrior cleared his throat and I glanced over Frea's back. He gave me a small nod and moved away, slinging his pack over his shoulder. One by one, the others gave me small nods and farewells before they headed off.

The perpetual knot in my chest loosened, and I took some extra time working a brush through Frea's coat.

"Chief." Father's voice drew my attention from the task.

He strode toward me, stopping a pace away like he held himself back from grabbing my shoulders in an embrace. I could not help but tense at the thought. It seemed too much emotion from him, even though he had started to show more affection.

It might forever grieve me that Comran had not seen it for himself. Or had refused to. Not that I could blame him. And guilt followed quick on the heels of selfish gratitude that I had Father's attention for myself. A poor way to repay the friendship Comran had shown me before he fell.

"Father."

"Birgir will be here soon and will have a report on the riders."

Already to business. My fingers tightened around the brush.

"How has it been here?"

"There are a few things you will need to attend to," he said. I wondered if it had irritated him to make them wait for me. Or if it was another way for him to keep testing me.

"But we are all focused on this war. There is no time for many disputes."

Frea stayed obediently under the eave's shelter as I carefully unwound a bandage from her front leg. Father handed me a cloth and I gently scrubbed dried blood from her thick fur. She leaned into the rhythm with eyes half-closed.

"And what are the thoughts on this war?" I asked around a tight throat. No doubt many found some sort of pleasure that our failing might be my doing. Proving them, and Hakkon, right.

"A counting ago, a rider brought news that Hakkon thinks to

take over the valley in the Saber tribe's name. That did not sit easily with many."

I arched an eyebrow. That might be an understatement.

Father set his hand on Frea's shoulder, and she briefly turned to sniff at his hair. "You have their support, Etran." His words willed me to believe it.

Straightening, I stared at Frea's coat, focused on picking out a bit of paint still caught in the hairs. He sighed, frustrated, maybe, that I did not believe it. But I did not have the energy to tell him why when it might be partially his fault.

Finished, I tapped Frea's side, and she backed away from the stables, shaking herself in a cloud of dust and fur before meandering off. I followed her path, chest tightening again at the sight and wondering where Eska might be.

A few warriors had said they'd seen a lone greywolf in the woods or running across the valley. There was no such thing as a lone greywolf. Until now. It could only be Eska, and my heart ached that he was wild. My fingers found the extra leather cord wrapped around my wrist above my warrior band.

*I'm sorry.* But no matter how many times I thought it or prayed, words would not bring Comran back.

"Etran?" Father's hand settled on my shoulder. "Are you all right?"

Concern. Real concern. I shook myself a little, trying to break free from the thoughts that had crept after me my entire life as I fought for his attention.

"I am just tired." And I eased my shoulder out from under his hand.

A bit of pained understanding flickered in his face. Forcing a breath and even tone, I continued.

"Where is Birgir?"

"Training lodge. But I will have him come to yours if you want."

A sudden urge to avoid my lodge came over me and I shook my head. "No, I'll go to the training lodge."

Together we began to make our way there, when the sight of Inger stopped me. Father said nothing as I paused and took a few tentative steps as she came to meet us. Inger's smile wasn't as wide as it used to be, but she still managed one for me along with a hand to her forehead.

"Chief."

"How are you?"

"Managing." Inger's smile wavered. "Every day brings a new challenge. But we will make it."

It seemed she included me in that "we." She reached out and took my left hand, squeezing it with a strength I wouldn't have guessed from her. Her other hand reached over and touched the warrior cords around my wrist. No one else had noticed the extra bands, or they hadn't said anything.

"Keep him safe for me."

My throat tightened and I could only nod and wish that we could have brokered this sort of peace between us with Comran still alive and standing there. She released my hand and accepted Father's kiss on her forehead before she left us. He said nothing of the exchange, and we continued on our way, until the less gentle voice of Mother cut across the lodge circle.

"Etran."

I broke away and bent my steps to where Mother strode toward me. Placing her hands on my shoulders, she scanned me with green eyes. A bit of welcome, but most of all rebuke.

"You are home and you stopped to see that woman first?"

I shifted, nudging one of her hands away with the action, suddenly tired of it all. Wanting Comran to meet me in the training lodge, instead of Birgir. Because he'd know exactly what I felt.

"She is a kind woman, and she is still mourning the loss of her son."

Disapproval tightened her features. Like she didn't think I should be mourning as well.

"I need to go speak with Birgir about the wolfriders." A step backward slid my shoulder away from her other hand. Her jaw tightened, a sign she was about to argue.

"I will see you tonight." I gave a clipped nod and strode away. Blessedly, Father kept his silence, but I caught the faint motion of him looking back to her.

The news Birgir gave was only slightly better. There would be two new packs ready to ride out with me. Some older warriors who had re-sharpened their swords and dusted off leathers. But most were young men right out of training, earning their spears perhaps a turning or two early. And three women to lend ferocity to the packs.

"How is Loke doing?" Sadness lurked in Birgir's eyes as he asked the question.

I swallowed hard. "He does well as battlewolf."

But not as well as Comran had done.

"I know he might like to hear some wisdom from you," I said.

Birgir nodded, picking at the rough grain of the table. "There are some who can keep up with the training here, Chief. I am ready to ride with the packs."

Sudden panic hit me that I'd dishonored him by keeping him in the village. Naming someone else battlewolf, instead of him taking up the mantle again, like Father had done in the village while I'd been gone.

He must have seen it in my face.

"It was needed for me to stay here," he reassured. "But there is not much more I can do. Most of our ready warriors will be riding out with you again."

I sagged back into my chair. Some would be left as the last defense of the village. This was all we had. We were down to our last hope.

⌒

Two dawns later, I led the packs back out. We rode to meet Loke where he and I had planned the new camp on our side of the river. A few small packs still roamed as scouts, but most had come to the shelter of the trees where they stretched in a long line from the river toward the mountains.

One last defense against the Saber tribe.

Loke took the news that we had no more packs to bring from the village in silence. A salute, then he strode off alone, shoulders still rigid until he passed from the view of most. But as I followed his path away from the camp, I saw when his resolve collapsed, and he placed a hand on his greywolf's shoulder to steady himself.

I turned away with a curse that rebounded through me as I looked instead over the valley that had once been ours to ride without fear. Now we had only precious miles still claimed with our wolves' scent.

A small herd of great elk grazed cautiously downriver. They knew, maybe better than anyone, that danger lurked in the valley. They'd learned a new scent in the last countings, and sablecats were quieter hunters than greywolves.

For now, they had nothing to fear from us. Our cookfires and provision bags were full.

Jens came to stand with me. A red scar traced across his hairline and he'd wrapped a bandage tight around his left hand to help the broken bones heal while he refused to go back to the village.

"What are we doing wrong?" I asked.

"What?" He settled his right hand on the hunting knife in his belt.

"Here." I gestured out to the valley. "How is it we can hold the border when they push, but now we fall back every day?"

Jens spat away from our feet. "They did not have a thrice-cursed traitor giving them the secrets of the valley."

"Jens, I put him there," I whispered.

"Etran." His hand descended on my shoulder to give a mighty shake. "He made the choice to rise against you. You made a decision to spare him. He could have gone anywhere in the valley. But he was the one who chose to betray his own people."

"Comran thought maybe I should have just killed him." My boot nudged the ground.

"If you had, I might be sitting at home working up the courage to ask Lise to marry me come winter." He shrugged. "Or I might still be standing here."

My fingers picked at a stray thread on my shirt sleeve. "If she had any sense, she'd say no."

I rocked to the side under his shove as he snorted a laugh.

"When are you going to ask Maren?" He turned it back to me.

My head jerked up, and he rolled his eyes.

"You've been pining after her for turnings, worse than a mood-addled pup. Amund told me what happened on the field, and he still owes me for winning that bet."

I frowned at his triumphant grin. But he lifted a shoulder in honest question. A sigh broke from me.

"I don't know. I'd like more to promise her than a ruined village and me likely dead."

"How could a woman refuse that?"

This time I pushed his shoulder. "Maybe when this is over."

He snorted again. "It's a wonder she's kept waiting this long. You're worse than my grandmother trying to make a decision on Coyote wares. 'Just a little more time,'" he said in a reedy voice.

I had him in a headlock before he could dodge. He laughed and elbowed my side until I let up. He turned serious seconds later.

"There may never be a perfect time, Etran. She's a good match." He slapped my shoulder again. "So let's hurry and win this war. I'd love to get roaring drunk at a wedding right about now."

He retreated under my push. The bits of good humor he'd managed to revive didn't last long as I looked back out. The elk herd had moved on, but something had worried them as they milled about and then pushed into their loping run farther down the valley.

A howl went up from a scout and a pack raced out of camp in response. I hurried back to camp, checking armor as I went and loosening my sword in its sheath.

Frea acknowledged me with a gruff noise before returning to stare out after the vanishing wolf pack, lips pulled back from her fangs in a faint snarl. I set a hand against her shoulder, and she settled. The guard wolves maintained their alert position, testing the wind where they stood around the camp.

Warriors, only minutes ago finding rest, now sat alert, weapons closer than ever. Maren met my gaze across the camp where she sat cross-legged by the low fire she shared with her pack. Her hands ran over the smooth shaft of the spear in her lap.

Some of the younger riders leaned closer to each other, whispering, speculating. But when nothing else stirred after ten long minutes, most of the older warriors settled back in apparent reassurance.

But the twisting sensation in my gut refused to abate. I'd had a dream the night before. Dark and confusing, it had left me in a cold sweat. Something bad would happen.

But I could have sworn I heard Comran's voice in the dream.

# FORTY-ONE

## ETRAN

Loke didn't like me leading a pack out. But it had to be done, and I would not cower in the camp or at the village. My place as chief was with the packs.

And with every passing day, I held it more my duty to do what I could as the Saber tribe started crossing the river from their new camp just on the western side. I took Maren's pack of twelve and a few more riders and rode south, ready to remark the new boundaries and to engage the enemy.

We scouted almost three miles down along the river's curve to the clusters of blue spruce trees which marked the unofficial edge where they hadn't much shown themselves, preferring to keep striking through the center of the valley. I was not the only one glaring across the river at the emptiness there.

Passing around the block of trees, we began to cut east back into the valley. Chill swept down my arms and I pulled Frea in and twisted in the saddle. A greywolf behind me had also paused, his rider alert as well. Wolves took in the wind, padded forward a step, and tried again.

Misgiving tugged at my gut. The wind was coming behind us and they were not smelling anything. But a few countings of being hunted by sablecats gives a heightened instinct. I gave a low command and we turned greywolves into a protective ring, with spears and teeth facing out.

Looking back across the hundreds of feet between us and the spruce trees, nothing stirred over the grass and pale yellow flowers. Then, a dark shadow prowled from the trees. A human shadow emerged from the depths of the trees and came up beside the sablecat.

For a moment, we stared at one another, then the sablecat arched its head back and loosed a guttural roar.

Wolves snarled in return and strained against their leathers. Frea stood still, a baleful rumble vibrating through her chest to my legs. My hand tightened around my spear as more sablecats raced across the shallow riverbed.

"Chief?" a rider asked, fire in his voice.

At quick glance, we stood even for numbers.

"Form up." My command rang sharp, not even hiding the anger in my voice at the invaders.

The pack swirled into motion, re-aligning into an attack formation. Frea bayed and leapt forward, the other greywolves surging alongside us.

Frea bore toward a sablecat and I readied my spear. The warrior leaned down on his mount's back, red paint smeared across his face. Loke had suggested I not wear my chieftain's paint on patrol, but I'd refused. The white rune on my breastplate stood for Comran. The white lines on my face were for every warrior who had fallen.

I saw the moment the warrior realized who I was. He shouted something and another cat swept in behind him. I kicked Frea on faster, aiming my spear for the lead sablecat's chest. He pulled away bare paces from the shining tip of the spear. Frea didn't follow, she and I instead changing our target to the sablecat following up behind.

We met in a clash, my spear grinding its way through the animal. I released the spear, twisting, to let my armor take the brunt of the warrior's strike across my back. It still knocked the breath from me and two perilous seconds later, Frea ripped free from the tangle of man and sablecat.

Ignoring the throbbing across my back, I drew my sword. Frea turned and we met another warrior head-on, iron screaming against iron as I blocked his strike. The sablecat backed away and Frea planted her forefeet, ears pinned back against her head. The warrior and I watched each other warily, waiting for our mounts to make the next move.

The prickle along my spine warned me in time to move with Frea as she whipped to the side, rearing up to meet a second sablecat midair. Grabbing the thick fur around her neck to steady myself as I practically stood in the stirrups against her back, I reached around her head to stab into the sablecat.

My sword, combined with Frea's teeth, brought the cat down to the ground. We landed unsteadily, still half atop the fallen animal. She tried to jump free, but stumbled, knocking me further off-balance. Another sablecat sprang on my unguarded side and took me to the ground.

I tucked into a roll as my shoulder hit the ground, softening the impact. A heavy paw hit me, preventing me from coming up to a knee. I managed to get my sword up to bat away a spear strike. The cat pressed over me, paw snagging in the vambrace over my sword arm and pinning it under its weight.

My free hand went for my knife and I stabbed into the

sablecat's chest. The thick fur managed to turn it enough to keep it from piercing too deep. But the injured animal's roar ripped through my chest and ears, stunning near as much as its weight.

The dim echo of my name sounded. Twisting, I stabbed blindly again. The sablecat pulled away, but I skidded along the grass with it, a paw still caught in a strap of my armor.

Grabbing around its ankle joint, I stabbed into the paw. It reflexively opened and I shoved it away and struck again. A grey streak flew over me and Frea slammed into the warrior and sablecat, pushing them away under her fury and giving me precious space to finally scramble to my feet.

My sword lay a few paces away, but a low growl sent ice through my joints. A riderless sablecat watched me with golden eyes, tongue snaking out to lick around its curved fangs.

I clutched the pitiful knife and swallowed against my dry throat. I gave a step as it advanced one. Heartbeat after heartbeat pounded in my chest until, in the space between, I sprinted for my sword.

My knee hit the ground as I scooped up the sword and braced with both hands. The sablecat, mid-leap, had no chance to avoid the sword. It sank into the cat's chest, its claws still scraping my upper arms as I fell back to the ground under the weight.

Its last musty breath caressed my face and neck. A strangled sound of relief or belated terror escaped from me as I lay pinned under it for a long moment before beginning to struggle free.

As soon as I stood, I wished I hadn't. Another sablecat pack had joined the fight at some point and our greywolves were sorely outnumbered. A clear path stretched from me to the edge of the battle.

I scooped up my knife and gave a shrill whistle. Wolves and riders began to move, pulling back from fights, but many coming under attack again from more than one sablecat at a time. Forcing my feet to move, I ran toward the edge of the battle. Frea angled her path to come alongside me.

But ten paces away, she was borne to the ground under a sablecat. Sense told me I should leave her, but my heart refused, crying out with her as the lion bit into her shoulder.

Changing my path, I raced to her side. A furious scream scraped my throat raw as I plunged my sword deep into the sablecat. Frea shook it off and hobbled to her feet.

"Go!" I ordered. She began her slower retreat, scarlet rushing to stain the grey and black fur.

Another cry of pain caught my attention. A younger wolfrider lay pinned under his dead wolf. He struck gamely at a swiping sablecat as its rider laughed at his attempts.

I barely had time to reflect it was a poor time to begin thinking with my heart as I charged to help. My sword traded hands and I scooped up a fallen spear, taking two more steps before launching it at the sablecat. It collapsed, dead before it hit the ground.

"Chief?" The warrior stared at me, his face confused and bloody, as I sheathed my sword and hooked arms under him to pull him out.

"Come on." I grunted as I took most of his weight.

We began to hobble away.

"Etran!" Maren paused beside us, her spear poised and ready.

"Take him." I pushed the wounded rider closer.

She looked down at me, then reached down to take the wounded man's arm and haul him up behind herself.

"Go!" I drew my sword again.

They rode away, and I began to follow when two sablecats blocked my path, their riders aiming spears at my chest.

A quick glance around showed most of the wolfriders still alive had made it off the field. A few riderless greywolves followed, their empty saddles another stab in my heart.

Two other riders faced down sablecats like I did. None of us close enough to help the others. Our pack was in full retreat, not looking back. And even if they did, sablecat riders had moved to block off the gaps.

The two warriors watched me, unblinking, until another rider came to join them. He stared at me a long moment, and I couldn't detect any emotion past the lines of red paint across his face. From the way he studied me, my warpaint was still intact enough to declare who I was. Finally, he stirred.

"Take them all." He wheeled his cat and rode away.

Sense won out, and I followed the example of my other warriors and set down my sword.

Unmounted warriors moved in, yanking my arms behind me to bind with rough cords, before pushing me into motion to walk away from the field and from anyone who could help.

# FORTY-TWO

## ETRAN

We stumbled on for miles, spears prodding when feet faltered and sablecats eagerly sniffed at our heels. And through it all, the pack leader watching me from his sablecat as he occasionally circled around the packs.

"Chief." Aron, the older warrior at my side, leaned closer, bits of blood crusting his face. More stained his armor and shirt sleeve from a wound making him hold his bound hands awkwardly in front of him.

The only thing that had made our predicament worse was recognizing the younger wolfrider once they'd shoved us together. Kjell's jaw was set beneath the warpaint, and he still held his head high enough to glare at anyone who came close. I had no reassurance to give either of them. We'd all seen what happened to the few wolfriders taken before. And they might stand more of a chance than me.

The thought managed to weaken my knees, no matter how I tried to lock it away in iron bands. Was this how the valley was to finally fall?

Across the river, the packs angled back north, heading for the fringes of the small forest clustered around the western side of the river, where not long ago, we'd held a camp before retreating. The tang of woodsmoke filtered through the breeze, and the sablecats perked up, some jerking up to their bounding gait until riders pulled them back.

It didn't look so different from wolfriders and greywolves ready to make it home.

The camp emerged right within the treeline. Guards leaned on spears or held bows, watching with quiet eyes as warriors dismounted and pushed us onward. The pack leader strode ahead, calling out as he entered the main encampment where tents were pitched in no discernible order. Sablecats lounged beneath the towering trees, and heavier rustles marked more golden eyes peering down from the foliage.

"Stop." The pack leader held out his arm. Hands jerked us to a halt, and then helped us to our knees.

A tent flap opened and out strode the battlelion. His medallion tapped his broad chest with every stride. Dark eyes gleamed with interest as he prowled forward. I caught the moment he realized who I was, a smile began to spread, and he came closer to tower over me.

"Welcome, Chief." He bowed mockingly.

Some laughed, but the pack leader just watched.

"Go get Hakkon." The battlelion jerked his head at the pack leader. The man paused a moment, and irritation sparked in the battlelion's eyes before the warrior walked off, every movement purposeful.

The battlelion shifted to look at the others. He grabbed Kjell's head and forced it backwards.

"Scared, boy?"

"Not of you," Kjell managed around the tight angle of his neck.

The battlelion half-laughed. "Not yet."

"Battlelion." Hakkon's voice triggered a wave of anger that intensified like a flashflood as he made his way over. The traitor paused a moment, looking at all of us kneeling in the middle of the camp.

Recognition twisted his features in a snarl and he pushed forward, driving a fist into my face. Tumbling to the side, I barely managed to arrest my fall with my elbow. I was yanked back up by an armor strap and took another strike. Blood gushed from my nose and mouth, and the world swayed precariously.

It took a moment for the shouts to filter in. The wolfriders struggled against their captors. It took two to pin Loke's brother back down. Aron hurled abuse at Hakkon, calling him a thousand things worse than a traitor.

It took a kick in the gut to silence him.

"And you're so loyal to this bastard then, Aron?" Hakkon sneered down at the older warrior.

"Do not stand there and speak of loyalty, Hakkon," Aron spat. "You brought them here. You are destroying the valley. Chief should have just killed you."

Hakkon allowed a humorless smile and looked to me. "Yes, he should have. But now..." He stood over me, and I spat blood across his boots.

His smile turned to something colder. "Looks like I get to kill you instead."

"Not yet." The battlelion's voice interrupted, smooth and chill. "There is still a war to win and a valley to take. We need new information and I see three potential sources here."

"Do we need all three?" Another voice interrupted. The pack leader was back, staring with dispassion.

"So eager to kill them all, Davor?" The battlelion smirked, but it seemed forced.

The warrior sniffed and lifted a shoulder. "Three is more effort to guard, when one could do. Simple logic—brother."

The battlelion's eyes narrowed and surprise jolted through me. *Brother?*

Though the Coyote tribe traded in information as well, I still didn't know much about the battlelion. Or that he had a brother. And they didn't like each other, judging from the wary glares they gave each other.

I shifted on my knees, now noting something familiar. Division among the warriors. Most watched with interest, some with hands on weapons as the two brothers stared at each other. The pack leader shifted first, a bare sort of deference in the slight incline of his head. The battlelion lifted his chin, triumph glittering in his eyes.

But he missed the look Davor flicked as he turned away.

"Get them up."

They yanked the three of us to our feet. The battlelion pulled a knife from his belt, running the tip gently under his thumbnail.

"I do not need all three of you. But I do need information." He paced back and forth in front of us, pausing slightly in front of me. "I will even put aside Hakkon's thirst for vengeance."

The unchanging murderous look in Hakkon's eyes shouted he did not agree with it.

"I could kill two of you, but I think I have a better idea." He came to stand in front of me again. "Two go free, back to your packs, alive and well. And the third stays here." His grin spread as I held his stare, knowing what was coming next, but the words still hit worse than Hakkon's fist.

"And as chief, you get to choose."

"Chief." Aron didn't panic. My muscles locked me in place, and my neck jerked as I managed to look at him.

The wolfrider gave me a nod. Volunteering himself. Beyond him, Kjell kept his jaw clenched and shoulders back, but I saw a crack in his front. He was not yet to twenty years. And I could not take another brother from Loke.

Aron had a wife. Children.

The battlelion watched me, hateful smile in place.

"Two go free, all the way back to the lines unharmed?" My voice stayed even, demanding an answer from him.

He inclined his head.

"Do you have enough honor to swear it?"

His smile spasmed into anger before it smoothed out. "I will swear by the All-Father Himself." But his voice held a hint of mockery.

"I will see it done," Davor spoke up, and the battle renewed between him and the battlelion. This time the battlelion turned away first, jerking a hand to the pack leader.

"There. His word. So afraid for your own skin, Chief?"

Hakkon scoffed behind him.

Fingers dug hard into my palm, keeping my hands from shaking in their bonds, as I made my decision.

"No. I choose…" The world paused a heartbeat to listen. "Me."

A breath exhaled quietly with the word, and my next heartbeat thundered against my chest.

"No!" the greywolf warriors shouted together, renewing their struggle against the Sabers.

"Chief!" Aron protested, trying to push to me, but I wrenched my gaze away. They would carry the news back to the tribe. A new, better chief would be chosen. Maren could find someone more worthy of her. Maybe Father would even mourn me.

Loke might never get Comran's band back. It would likely not take long for him and Amund to recover from my loss. Jens…he would carry on.

A slow smile spread across the battlelion's face.

"Very well. The chief has spoken." He waved a hand and his men dragged mine away, their shouts still echoing no matter the attempts to subdue them. I didn't look back, staring straight past the battlelion.

"Davor, make sure their tribe finds them. I want them to know where the power now stands in this valley. And—" He grabbed my jaw and wrenched my head to face him. "Tell them they have three days to decide what to do with their chief. If they want him back alive, I expect a complete surrender. Though"—the cold iron of his knife pressed under my eye— "maybe they will be glad to finally be rid of him."

"I will tell them, Chief." Aron's voice came strong.

My heart hadn't stopped its pounding, and it fluttered a little to maybe hope the council would argue more than a few minutes for me. Chiefs could be replaced. An entire village, homes, families, could not.

My voice failed me, words staying trapped in my throat. Davor paused by me, and he tipped his head slightly before passing on and giving orders to ride out again.

"Take his armor." The order came and I managed to stand tall while they removed my armor and tossed it away.

"We will have some fun together, you and I." The battlelion smiled, knife flashing in his hand. "And I am sure Hakkon will be more than happy to join us." He lifted a hand in invitation and Hakkon pushed forward again.

A spear haft to my stomach sent me to my knees, gasping and defenseless. As more and more blows fell, my only thought was hoping I could last with some honor until I was sent to stand in judgment before the All-Father.

# FORTY-THREE

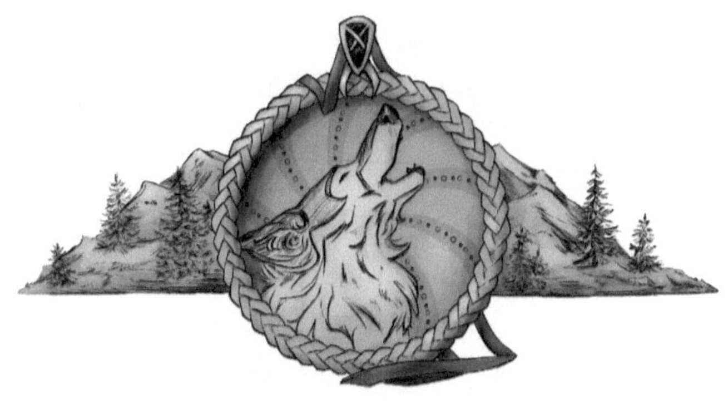

## COMRAN

"What is this?" My feet paused at the edge of the training area. Lukas nudged me.

"It is no crime for others to be out here to train."

Since the battlelynx had not ordered us to stop that day, a few other Blackpaw warriors had begun to find their way to the training area when I went with Lukas and sometimes Sasha.

But this…?

Near thirty warriors stood there, clustered in groups, some even having the decency to spar or work through routines while they waited.

"Lukas!" I hissed as he propelled me forward. "Your battlelynx will not like this."

"They are just here to train."

I blessed him with a withering look. He grinned in response, a bit of recklessness shining through. Though it was not in my nature to retreat, I began looking for escape. The Blackpaws had been tolerant enough so far, but I didn't think the chief or battle-lynx would hesitate to show me to the village boundaries if they heard of this.

"Battlewolf." The warrior who'd been with the battlelynx three days before—Maks, I thought his name was—offered me a sign of respect.

The sight sent a spear through my heart. I managed a smile. "I am not battlewolf anymore. My chief has likely replaced me."

And I still could not bring myself to slip the medallion back on.

"Nevertheless, there are some of us who would be grateful for your insight." Maks hesitated, hand clenched around his sword hilt. "I feared the day the Sabers would return. But it has been years since I have fought them."

My fingers curled tight around my sword hilt. "I will not over-step here. Not when your battlelynx has already expressed her displeasure."

I made sure my voice was loud enough for the entire training area. The warriors just looked back at me, some leaning closer to murmur to each other. But no one left.

"Yes, I did." The battlelynx's voice sent tension back through me. But I took some brief hope from the fact Maks's expression didn't change. I turned and offered her a salute.

"Battlelynx, I spoke the truth. I will not overstep."

A shift of motion at my side announced Lukas's displeasure.

The battlelynx crossed her arms. This time she wore trousers and armor like the others, hair pulled back in full battle braids. She looked around at the warriors, her fierce expression softening as she came back around to me.

"There were some angry words traded here between us a few days ago," she began.

I nodded, a heartbeat away from preparing an apology, but she lifted her hand to forestall me.

"I will admit, it took this long for me to work through my anger at you and realize it was also anger at myself." She wasn't speaking to just me. The words carried across the breathless quiet covering the training grounds.

"We all lost something in our war with the Sabers. And it shook me, harder than I thought. And for years, we focused on hiding and surviving, because it was the thing that would get us to the next day and then the next. And I did what a warrior should not do. Became complacent, dredged in the routine."

"You are not the only one, battlelynx." Another warrior spoke up, some bits of grey in his hair, and the same pain in his eyes that the rest of the village still carried.

She inclined her head.

"And while I still will not lead packs out to battle, we will need to re-learn how to fight them again. They have spread along the boundaries and move toward the great river."

Lukas had delivered the news the night before. I was fully behind the enemy's lines. They held the hills and had begun to lay siege to the river.

"And"—finally her lips quirked a fraction— "maybe we'll even deign to hear from a Greywolf."

I smiled, but it seemed my confidence leaked away with it. "I would be honored to work alongside you, Battlelynx."

Lukas's face quickly shifted to triumph as the battlelynx and I turned together. The warriors fell into training pairs, and the two of us walked side by side, spending time with each pair until we'd circled back and stood to watch.

"You make a good battlewolf," she said.

My hand edged to my chest before I remembered I didn't wear a breastplate to hook my hand into. I crossed my arms instead.

"Birgir taught me well."

"There is more to being a leader than just learning from someone."

I dug the toe of my boot into the ground, staring down at the rich darkness of the earth I turned over.

"Perhaps I can teach warriors, but when it came to leading packs and defending our territory, I'm afraid I did a *scata* job."

She tilted a glance at me. "How long have you been battlewolf?"

"Since midwinter," I admitted reluctantly.

"And you expect to win a war within days?"

My heart burned a little at the faint rebuke in her voice.

"Even experienced warriors and packleaders could not. Why do you think you must?" Her tone shifted to something like Birgir would use when asking me why I thought I must conquer every task.

"There has been little room for failure my entire life."

The words escaped around a tight throat. It was from Birgir I learned how to work with men and women and find skills and tasks done well first, before homing in on what was done wrong.

I couldn't meet her eyes as she shifted to face me more. She'd offered a truce between us, but it still rankled me that Lukas, and now her and many of the warriors, looked to me in almost the same way as my own wolfriders.

"Etran and I—we were held up against each other our whole lives. It wasn't until recently that we realized that neither of us truly hated each other. Etran extended the hand of peace first by asking me to be his battlewolf. He told me he trusted me. I feel like I have failed him as well."

"And do you know what he feels?"

I watched a warrior pairing fighting with blunted spears. Etran had refused to take the medallion when I'd been ready to offer it back. He'd blurted first that he'd wanted a brother. And while I felt the same, I hadn't mustered the courage to say it. Because what if I disappointed him as I constantly seemed to do with Father?

"Comran."

Her gentle voice called me back to the training grounds.

"Our scouts have kept an eye on this war between you and the Sabers. We heard from the Coyote traders as well when they came after midwinter. By all accounts you are respected within your tribe. And it is no failing to keep riding out every day, to keep leading packs, even when it seems like you are not winning."

"Are you sure it is not just sheer stupidity?" I tilted a wry eyebrow.

A slight quirk softened her angular features.

"The difference between stupidity and courage is sometimes a fine line. But courage keeps trying to protect, even when it feels impossible."

We stood in silence as I turned over her words.

"I tried to give Etran back the medallion. Told him he needed someone better than me."

The battlelynx's gaze did not falter. "And did he take it?"

I shook my head.

She nodded. "Then it seems to me that the issue lies not in your people not trusting you. But in you not trusting yourself."

My arms tightened across my chest. I didn't need her to tell me that.

"Warriors who lead with their hearts burn bright. And sometimes it is hard for them to keep their fire because they feel things more keenly than others." Her words came slow, thoughtful. "My son was one such warrior. But when faced with war, he did not flinch. I do not think you do either."

I shook my head. I didn't shy from battle, but I felt too battered and bruised from losses.

"You have those who trust you, even if you do not trust yourself?"

My gaze fell to Loke's warrior bands still around my left wrist. He had told me much the same even before we entered the training grounds together for the first time.

"They would be happy to hear your words right now," I said.

A low laugh came from her. "If I can learn to forgive a Greywolf, perhaps you can learn to forgive yourself."

"I think you might be asking a mightier task from me." But I allowed a slight smile. She returned it.

"How is your arm?"

Grateful for the change, I loosened my arms and moved my left for her to see. "Better every day. I do not think I will be darkening your village for much longer."

"Then, if you feel able to, I would ask that you spend as much time remaining here. We have one hundred and twenty-two warriors left in this village. Some cannot wield weapons anymore. And many are like Lukas and have not yet tasted the thrill of battle. Some will refuse to work with a Greywolf. But, if you are willing, I would still have them come in groups like this to listen to what you have to teach before you return to war."

While I wished I could ask for the Blackpaws' help, I did not want to shatter this new trust between us.

"I would be honored, Battlelynx."

"Petya." She offered a hand.

I clasped it, honored again by her allowing me to call her by name. "Thank you."

Petya gave another short nod before striding off in answer to a warrior's call. Movement on the edge of the training circle caught my eye.

Sasha stood alongside Raya, both watching the warriors intently. I jerked my gaze away from the way her thumb ran along her bottom lip. My traitor heart thudded in my chest when I glanced at her again and she caught sight of me and smiled.

I had never given many of the young women in my village much of a second glance, happy to focus on training instead. So why now, with so much at stake, did I find my attention divided?

"I heard you are going to be leading more training." Lukas still held a bit of the triumph from the day, even hours later over dinner.

I nodded, picking at the stewed meat in front of me.

"I thought you might be happier about that," Zoya observed from her place at the head of the table.

"No lecture about overexerting myself?" I gave a weak smile.

Her lips pursed, but after near three countings, I'd come to learn it was almost the same as a smile. Sasha flicked a glance between us, humor in her eyes.

"But?" Zoya prompted.

"I am happy to help where I can." I tore a piece of flatbread.

Lukas shifted as if ready to challenge my sudden change, but a tight shake of the head from Zoya stopped him. A tap against the table brought my attention up to Sasha. She slid a piece of paper across to me.

-Do you not want to?-

"No, it's—the battlelynx gave me some things to think over today."

Like the fact I would be leaving soon and should maybe stop my heart from feeling too much about someone I might never see again.

"Perhaps you can convince her to send out packs when you leave," Lukas said.

Zoya inhaled sharply, but I was already shaking my head.

"That is not my place."

Lukas's jaw clenched and I fought the frustrating thought that dealing with his stubbornness must be how people felt dealing with me. I finished the meal in silence and excused myself, feeling their stares following me from the lodge.

Outside, lingering rays of light painted the sky in vibrant oranges and reds to the west, while above me, blue faded to the darkness of night. A few stars began to appear, bright specks in the darkness.

Restlessness churned through me. I had managed to leave it behind for a few days, but since speaking with the battlelynx it had come back full force. I started to walk. First pacing around the lodge, then broadening the circle until I strode through the forest. I scooped a stick off the ground, swinging it in my left hand, daring the consequences of moving too hard or fast as I swung at trees.

Was I so afraid to trust others?

*Thwack!*

Was I so afraid to believe in myself?

*Thwack!*

What made me so afraid to return to the tribe?

*Crack!* The stick shattered with the last hit, and I tossed it away.

Fear that Etran might have realized he didn't need me? That I had truly not been the right choice? Had Father mourned me? My heart ached for my mother. Thinking she'd lost me when she'd fought so hard to have me.

My fingers slipped under the warrior bands on my wrist. And what had Loke done when he saw me fall? What had Amund done? Etran? It had been horror and helplessness on his face as he saw me fall. That I did remember.

I could leave now. My arm moved well enough. My strength had returned, but still lagged in the injured shoulder. Nothing stopped me other than Zoya telling me she wanted a few more days.

And I wanted to wait as well.

Never in my life had I wanted to stay away from battle. Fear kept me close to the village. Fear and…A certain smile flashed in my mind again and I slumped against a broad trunk.

Unless I was mistaken, she felt some of the same pull.

"Spirits, what am I doing?" I sighed, tilting my head back to the sky. The bright north star was visible, marking the entrance to the All-Father's lodge.

I wished the Greywolf spirit, or the All-Father Himself, would give me some sort of sign. Tell me what to do.

*It is never that easy.* The *talånd's* words echoed in my head. He had told me that since I was young and wanted things to be straightforward. Simple.

But then he'd gone and turned against both Etran and me. Maybe it was the spirits' way of judging the tribe for my father's actions.

*That is stupid.* I pushed away from the tree. It was Hakkon and him alone who had brought this to the valley.

I began my trek back, halting when I heard the distant cry of a wolf. Turning, I strained toward the sound, this time hearing a few echoes replying. A pack somewhere out there. It brought a smile and quelled the restlessness for a time.

Packs were still running, so the Sabers hadn't taken everything yet.

I made my way back to the lodge with more confidence than

when I had left. I had a few more days. I would train with the lynx warriors as Petya had asked. She had softened that much, maybe she might find her way to sending some willing warriors with me when I left.

# FORTY-FOUR

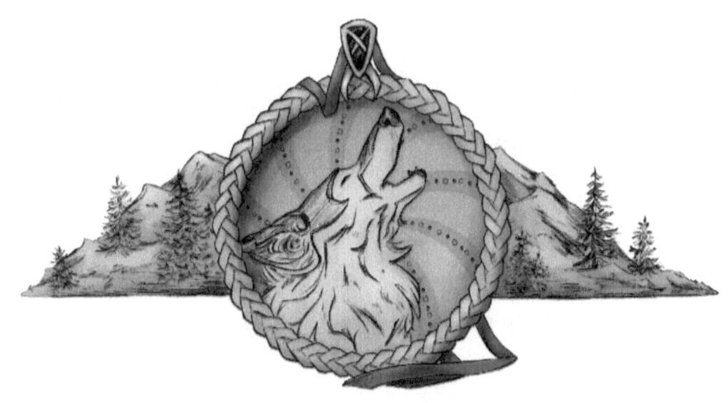

## COMRAN

"Sasha, I need more water," Zoya said as she cleared the remnants of the morning meal.

<How much?>

I was getting better at reading the signs, but most of what she said to her family still came a muddled mess.

"It will take several trips," Zoya said apologetically.

"I can help," I offered.

Lukas had already left before the dawn to take his turn on a patrol of the village. And I was not expected at the training grounds until the afternoon. Sasha nodded eagerly and beckoned me on. Zoya watched me again with the indecipherable look she'd taken to holding close over the days since she had removed my sling.

Buckets in hand, we began the short trek to the river together. I had gone with Lukas once before to help bring in water. And, just like the first time, I halted at the banks and looked out at the shallow ford where they had found me and the sablecat.

Moss-covered trees hovered close, leaning over the banks to admire themselves in the river. Water gurgled around the bigger stones it hadn't yet worn down to smooth pebbles in the riverbed. I tried to remember anything from hitting the river to waking up in the lodge, but still nothing stirred in my mind.

Except at night when I dreamed of drowning.

Sasha touched my arm and I smiled.

"I do not know if I'll ever look at a river the same again," I admitted.

She patted my forearm and waved me forward. Water swirled and gurgled around her boots as she walked in. Turning, she curled her fingers in invitation. I followed her lead, stepping into the shallow ford, cold still seeping through my boots even if they were protected from the water itself.

*How did I survive this?*

Most of the water in the valley came over the yellow cliffs in the north from the great ice fields only a few of our tribe had ever seen. And over three countings ago, winter had not yet given up.

"When we were boys, we used to dare each other to jump in the iced river in the winter." A red-tailed trout darted past my feet.

Sasha shook her head.

"I know. It seems an even stupider decision now." A chill shivered down my arms.

I bent instead and scooped up water in the bucket before taking it back to the bank to retrieve the third bucket we'd brought.

"I think I'll be happy if I never swim in a river again."

Her breathless chuckle warmed me inside as she stooped to fill her bucket with water. On the way back to the bank, pebbles shifted under her feet, sending her staggering.

I reached out and grabbed her arm to steady her. She flashed a smile and held onto my hand to take the last few steps to solid ground. We paused on the bank, a bare space apart, hands still clasped. For a moment, we both stared at the sight, then she lifted her face to me.

It made my voice vanish a moment.

"Sasha, I…" My voice barely came a whisper.

What was I going to say?

Understanding lingered in her eyes. Her lips parted as if she would try to say something, then pressed back together. The gentle squeeze of her fingers around mine brought a new tightness to my chest.

In her face, I saw all the things I knew myself.

She was Blackpaw. I was Greywolf. She was daughter to a healer. I was son to a chief. She was staying. I was leaving.

My thumb brushed over her skin. Even knowing it all, I did not want to let her go just yet.

For a long moment, we stayed, then she shifted and looked back up the narrow path back to the village. I nodded and slowly released her hand. Sadness filled up her smile. It took another moment of us staring at each other before we began to move again. Picking up the buckets and beginning a careful trudge back to the lodge houses.

Zoya thanked us both, but her gaze lingered a little on Sasha. It was about the time we would usually be going outside to sit on the bench for her to teach me more signs, but neither of us stirred that direction.

Instead, we both came to that same wordless agreement and took an actual step away from each other. I scooped up my sword and armor and the small kit they'd lent me and retreated outside to the bench. There, I turned my focus to cleaning and oiling the vambraces and greaves. It had taken several rounds of oiling and some re-shaping for them to return to near full use. I would still need new ones from the armorer back home before going to fight.

My breastplate was another story. I had yet to be able to fix the torn and broken straps or patch up the tears from the sable-cat's teeth.

But I could at least wear the rest to remind myself who I was and where I would be going in a few days.

# FORTY-FIVE

## ETRAN

There were more ways to inflict pain than I had known. And worse things to be called than bastard.

# FORTY-SIX

## SASHA

The riverbanks were quiet. A good place to come and think. She'd brought her light spear with her under the pretense of fishing. But really she wanted to get away.

A moss-covered rock two yards from the riverbank, hidden by a leaning oak tree, was her favorite spot. Big enough to sit cross-legged with her spear across her lap. Her gaze lighted on the spot where the river ran low.

Where she had found Comran.

Where two days ago, the feel of his hand in hers brought her heart soaring for two precious moments before it dove down to crack gently upon reality.

And she had seen the same in him.

Tipping her head with a huff of a breath, she stared down at the lines she'd etched in the spear on the other days she'd come to the rock.

The river was where she had come to mourn the loss of her voice. Where her tears had threatened to overfill the banks when her father did not ride back from battle. And a dozen other heartbreaks. She had conquered them here, and she would do the same again.

There was no fairness in it this time either.

She had resigned herself to what she had. A life where there were still enough young men her age, but who did not give her a second glance. Or those who might, quickly turned away from the effort of learning her language.

But not Comran.

From the first day he'd woken, fevered and confused, he had seen her. Two fingers could count the number of tribespeople who had bothered to learn more than a handful of basic signs. And he had learned some on his own, surprising her with his first attempt, and then his dedication to learning more just so he could· understand *her*.

A stinging blurred her eyes. Spirits, it wasn't *fair*.

But she drew in a breath, shutting her eyes tightly to prevent tears from leaking out. She hadn't meant to feel something for him. But it was so hard not to.

His smile, energy, willingness to learn, to help, and the hurt and doubt he tried so hard to hide until she wished she had something to say to banish it from his grey eyes.

Scrubbing a hand over her face, she took in another breath. As her hands fell back to her lap, she stared at them. They were her voice and maybe she'd be glad they wouldn't betray her the way her old voice might when he left.

But there was something she wanted to give him before he left. Something she had wanted to do before the day at the river. It might make everything hurt worse, but she wanted something to remember him by.

She wanted to give him his own sign.

But before her fingers could start piecing together something worthy of him, a rustle broke on the other side of the bank. Alert, she slid from the rock, spear at the ready as she backed farther into the shadows.

A shape broke through trees and her lips parted in surprise to see a greywolf coming to stand in the river, a warrior slumped on its back.

Swallowing hard, she forced herself to wait and listen. No sound of pursuit, and no sign of other greywolves. The warrior stirred, pushing himself up a little higher in the saddle, curling an arm to his chest, red staining his shirt sleeve and armor.

The greywolf dipped its head down and cautiously lapped up water, dark eyes watching the banks carefully. The warrior tapped its shoulder and began to look around. No paint lined his features, except for some odd discolorations across his left cheek.

He was young. And hurt.

And might have news for Comran.

There would be lynxes patrolling, but she did not know where one might be and there was no way for her to call one either. Trying to calm the frantic pumping of her heart, she slowly stepped out to the bank, spear still lowered.

The wolf's head jerked up and a growl threatened. Ears pinned back and mouth open in a snarl, and dropping into a crouch, it seemed nothing like how Comran had described his wolf. The warrior drew his sword in a rush, leaning slightly and ready for when his wolf would leap at her.

Knees trembling, she slowly raised the spear point up and spread her left hand in a gesture of peace.

It made him relax a fraction.

"Who are you?"

Licking her lips, she tried to keep her movements measured as she pointed to her mouth and then shook her head.

*Please understand me.*

"Are you Saber?"

She shook her head, allowed an expression of disgust to crease her face.

He didn't change his guard. She pointed to her arm, then to him, then back toward the village, ending with a sign for help even though he likely wouldn't understand it. But if she could get him moving that direction, they'd find a lynxrider soon enough who could do the talking.

The warrior glanced down at his wound, then at her. The wolf had eased out of the attack posture, but still stayed wary, a hint of teeth still visible. It hadn't let up a constant low rumble of warning either.

She tried not to think about how perfectly a greywolf fit with Comran, and what he might be like with his wolf.

Backing away a few steps toward the village, she beckoned again. His throat bobbed, but he gathered up the reins, still keeping his sword at the ready, and nudged his wolf. It did not look any happier than him to be moving after her, its paws moving slowly, testing every step as if it stood on treacherous ground.

She dared herself to turn her back to the greywolf, looking every few steps to make sure they still followed as she led the way back to the village.

They had not gone far before a comforting snarl sounded on her right and a lynx and warrior stepped out. The wolf dropped back to a crouch, the terrifying threat back. The warrior on his back raised his sword, glaring at her and then at the lynxrider.

Then he seemed to realize, and the sword lowered a fraction.

"Blackpaws?" It came out as a surprised question.

"What are you doing here?" the lynxrider growled, his lynx echoing his threat.

"I was scouting. Sabers chased me this way. She saw me at the river."

The lynxrider glanced quickly at her. "Again, Sasha?"

But a shiver of amusement crept through his stern voice. She lifted a shoulder, then pointed back to the warrior's wound. The lynxrider nodded, his jaw working.

"I will take him to the chief first. Go get him."

Her heart melted in relief as he understood what she had wanted to tell him. Comran needed to know. She nodded and took off at a run for the village.

"Sasha!"

She ignored her mother's cry as she left the spear at the lodge and turned her steps to the training grounds. Comran had been there every afternoon, working with the warriors and training himself. Since the river, she hadn't been able to bring herself to go again.

He stood opposite a warrior, moving through sword forms. She darted around several other training pairs. He fell back a step out of the training pattern, watching her with surprise.

"What is it?" He frowned, concerned.

She tried to tell him, but his brow furrowed in confusion at her hands.

"Sasha…"

Patience fraying, she grabbed his hand and pulled him after her.

"What's wrong?"

She shook her head, keeping her hand in his even though he readily followed.

The Greywolf had made it to the chief's lodge by the time they wound their way there. The chief and battlelynx stood side by side, and her mother hovered nearby, ready to tend to the warrior when they gave permission.

He stood, a little hunched over, but close to his wolf who curled around him, protecting his back from threats.

Beside her, Comran gasped, and his feet faltered a moment in surprise. The warrior turned at their advance, and his jaw fell open.

"Comran!" His voice cracked. He pushed forward, ignoring the warriors and chief.

"Amund?" Comran grabbed the warrior in a ferocious hug.

"Comran—you're—" The warrior clung tight to Comran.

Then Amund shook himself, focus snapping back into his eyes. "They have him. They have Etran."

Comran went rigid, his expression like he'd taken a spear through the gut.

"*What?*"

# FORTY-SEVEN

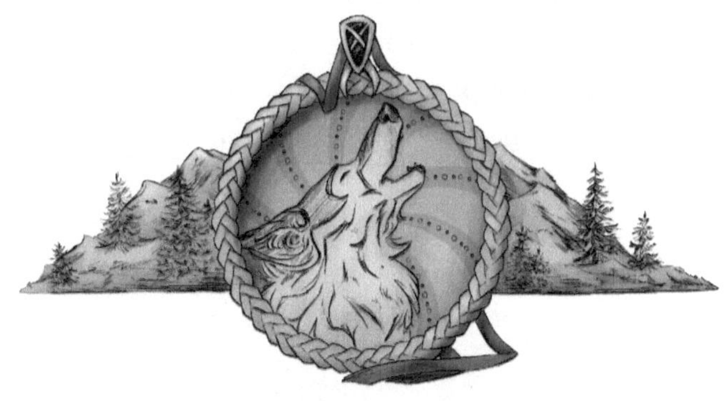

## COMRAN

"The Sabers. They caught him and some others almost two days ago. They have him and are going to kill him!" Amund's hands waved frantically.

"Amund!" I gripped his shoulder again, using the action to try to calm us both. "Start over."

"They're pushing across the river."

My fists curled tight. So much ground lost since I'd fallen. Over half our valley.

"Two days ago, Etran led out a pack. They were ambushed and most of the wolfriders made it out before they realized that he hadn't. Sabers took him, Aron, and Kjell captive."

My heart clenched. Loke's brother was fighting? He still had a year left of training.

"Aron and Kjell were brought back by a Saber pack. And they brought news. The cursed battlelion made Etran choose who to spare and who to remain captive and they said he chose himself."

*Idiot.* But my heart couldn't decide whether to be angry or a little proud of Etran for sacrificing himself.

"Battlelion said three days for the tribe to decide. If we want him back, it's to be complete surrender, or he dies."

Amund was shaking now, his voice still hovering on the frantic edge.

"I volunteered to scout their camp. Loke and I thought maybe single riders would have a better chance to go unnoticed along the river."

"Loke?"

"Etran named him battlewolf after…" He swallowed.

A faint smile broke. Loke was a good choice. Even if it would have near killed him to accept it.

"We thought you were dead." Amund stared at me again as if seeing a ghost.

"I almost was. But they found me and brought me here."

I broke his gaze to see Blackpaws gathered around, watching the exchange. Warriors must have followed us from the training grounds, and more had come. Petya had her arms crossed again, lips drawn tight as she watched.

"He mourned you." Amund's quiet voice drew me back, his dark eyes searching my face. "He called you brother."

My hand tightened over his shoulder. It was an honor I longed to return.

"How did you get here?" I forced the question instead.

"I went across the river where they have their camp. But they spotted me. I was trying to make it back, but got forced off course up into the hills after I managed to shake their pursuit. Then she found me at the stream."

He pointed past me and I saw Sasha. She chewed on her

thumbnail, watching worriedly.

I forced myself to think. "Loke sent out scouts. What was the plan?"

"Try to get him back," Amund said. "Hakkon said he'd brought the Sabers in to take the valley from Etran and set himself up as chief instead. It brought more to Etran's side. And many of the warriors refuse to see a new chief chosen. We want him back."

Fire crept into Amund's voice. Anger had slowly been filling me up since he'd started explaining. And now it burned around my heart. Raging like a summer wildfire at the thought of the battlelion having Etran and the terms he'd set.

"I want him back, too."

Tight resolve flooded Amund at the iron in my voice. I relinquished my hold on his shoulder and turned to the chief. But she beat me to speaking.

"What are you going to do?"

"I am going to get my brother. And if they have killed him, I will tear down the rest of their cursed mountain and bury them all."

More than one warrior looked to Petya, but she stood there, hands on hips and jaw set tight. The chief waited, silent at her side.

The battlelynx stirred. "I will send a pack of those willing to escort you back to your camp."

My heart jumped at the offer, but… "I'm going to get him."

I'd ride right into the Saber tribe camp and challenge the battlelion if I had to.

Amund nodded. "They are on this side of the river. It will be a hard ride, but we could get there by midnight."

I shook my head. "No, you are injured."

His betrayed look didn't sway me.

"As are you," Petya quietly reminded me. Amund whipped his head back to me, poised on the edge of an argument.

"No, Amund," I said firmly, and looked to the battlelynx, but she was already shaking her head again.

"I will not endanger riders by going directly into their camp. A pack to escort you and your friend back to Greywolf lines."

"And what then?" I tried to keep the challenge from my voice. Her eyes hardened to iron.

"Then if you fall, we are ready to defend ourselves against the Sabers."

I clamped down on my rebel tongue and the argument that if they joined forces with us, we might make sure the Sabers were driven from the valley.

"A pack to get us to the Greywolf camp, then." I tapped my chest, but my mind was already thinking something else.

Petya nodded, but it seemed more than one warrior was not happy with the decision.

"Comran." Zoya touched my arm. "Bring him to the lodge and I will take care of his wound."

I directed Amund to follow and took the reins of his greywolf. Sasha stayed beside me, and Lukas jogged to catch up to us, restlessness pulsing around him.

Inside the lodge, Amund was shown to a seat by the fire. Sasha and Zoya moved into action, helping him out of armor and fetching herbs and bandages. Scraping a hand through my hair, I began pacing.

"I know that look." Amund watched me.

Lukas stood to the side, feet braced wide, and arms crossed as his eyes followed my every move.

"The battlelion gave three days?"

Amund jerked a nod, trying to shift to still see me as Zoya began tending his shoulder.

"We have until tomorrow's dawn."

I paused, fingers grasping at nothing as I reached to hook hands into a breastplate that wasn't there.

"Amund, you're going with the pack."

He pushed at Zoya's hands and tried to move toward me. "And what idiocy are you thinking instead?"

Zoya rapped his uninjured shoulder and he briefly frowned at her before settling back.

"I'd like to know the same," she said over her shoulder.

Certainty settled over me. "I am going to go get him."

Or die trying.

The lodge settled to quiet. Sasha looked at me, eyes wide.

"Comran, he's in their camp," Amund said quietly. "We're barely equipped to mount an attack on it."

"I know. But one man might have a better chance."

"And how do you intend to get him out of there? You have no wolf, no one to hold your back if you insist on sending me off instead."

"I'll be there," Lukas said.

Amund and I both looked to him. The young Blackpaw nodded once, his jaw set.

"I said you might have a companion when you rode east, didn't I?" But mirth didn't reach Lukas's eyes.

Zoya stopped, hands falling away from Amund's shoulder as she stared at her son.

"Lukas…"

But he did not shift. "I know what it's like to lose family to the Saber tribe," he said, pain rising up to snare all three of them again. "The battlelynx doesn't want to send us to battle, but I can't stand by, can I?"

Zoya's lips quivered before she pressed them together. "Your father would be proud."

Brightness tinged Lukas's eyes as he held his mother's gaze. Sasha's hands moved in a flurry. I understood enough to make my heart ram painfully against my chest.

"Sasha!" Zoya protested, but her daughter held the same stubbornness as her son. Sasha signed again, tilting her head.

"She's right," Lukas said. "We might need a healer along."

I swallowed hard, not wanting to think too hard on what we might find. If I could even find Etran at all. Zoya turned away, beginning to assess the older-looking bandages Amund sported.

A knock sent us all jumping. Lukas went to answer it. I met Sasha's gaze and tapped my chest twice. A small smile tugged the corner of her lips.

Maks strode in, breastplate hanging from one hand. "Surprised to see you still here," he said to me.

"Is the pack prepared to ride already?"

Maks treated me to a pitying look. "I was not born yesterday, Comran. I'm talking about you going right for the Saber camp and your brother."

A small laugh came from Amund. "What have you been up to here, Comran? They know you too well already."

I glared at my friend before turning to Maks with more hope. He shook his head.

"Petya is still insistent only a pack to ride to the Greywolf camp. But almost every one of us would ride to war right now. I aim to keep convincing her to send more packs." He extended the breastplate. "I've seen you with the broken armor outside. You'll need this."

I took it, studying the twin lynxes etched into the surface, paws stretching toward each other over a mountain. It had a smaller symbol etched over the heart of the right lynx. My fingers brushed the rune.

"It was my brother's," Maks said softly. "He was like you. I think he'd be on a lynx right beside you."

"Thank you."

After a moment of silence, Maks shifted back to motion. "The *talånd* is predicting snow tonight. You'll need thicker clothes. You, too, Lukas."

The other warrior tried for an innocent look, but Maks scoffed. "Do people think so poorly of my intelligence?"

Lukas smirked, but turned to the chests shoved back against the wall.

"I have another lynx for you to ride, Comran."

I grimaced in distaste, but I had no real choice in the matter.

"Will we be stopped?"

Maks shook his head. "As long as you go soon. And I'll keep attention away from this side of the village. I do not think Petya would try to stop you, but you'll lose time with them trying to convince you otherwise and trying to order Lukas to stay."

"We can be ready in a few minutes." Lukas passed me thick winter trousers and tunic. Sasha nodded her agreement and hurried off for her own preparations.

Zoya handed Amund a cup and went to go help Sasha. Maks left as Lukas and I turned to changing and re-donning armor. Once the straps of the breastplate were tight around me, I turned to helping Amund with his armor.

"How has it been?" I asked quietly, doing up the straps over his injured shoulder.

He shook his head slightly, eyes losing focus as they stared into the fire. "The village is empty of packs. We've boys greener than spring trees out with spears and wolves. Miles lost every day."

I cursed softly.

"Loke is doing the best he can." A bit of defense came to

Amund's voice.

I brushed the bands around my wrist. "I know."

But Loke wasn't cut for a role like battlewolf. I strode back to my cot and picked up the medallion. Even with the news, I could not bring myself to slip it back on. Instead, I handed it to Amund.

"For Loke. If I can find Etran, I will make for the lines. We might need wolves to meet us halfway."

Amund's hand closed over mine. "We'll come," he promised. "Just find him and bring him home."

"I will."

Lukas strode outside and Sasha handed me a bundle of coat and gloves. She wore winter clothes and had a heavy knife strapped to her hip and a satchel across her chest. Amund followed us outside, where Lukas brought Raya around.

Maks led up a lynx with an empty saddle.

"No way I can just walk, is there?" I raised an eyebrow.

Maks chuckled. "Afraid you'll get on better with a lynx than those kits you ride?"

"Those kits do not insist on pouncing on every little thing that moves." I reached out and let the lynx sniff at my hand. Apparently sufficiently impressed, it lifted a forepaw and licked it.

"I see I rate lower than grooming," I said.

Maks laughed again and I caught the whisper of Sasha's laugh.

"He does not see you as a threat."

I ran a hand under the girth, checking it, and then the stirrups. "That makes me feel so much better."

Their laughs followed as I mounted and gathered up the reins. Sasha climbed on behind Lukas.

"Good luck to you all." Zoya stepped back.

I reached down and clasped Amund's hand one more time.

"See you soon."

His grip tightened before he let go. "Greywolf go with you."

I nodded wordlessly and tightened up the reins. The sun was setting over the wooded hills and black clouds lined the northern sky. I could almost smell the heaviness of a storm in the air already. It wasn't uncommon for winter to rage once more before fully yielding to spring.

If we were lucky, it would spend its fury like a tantruming wolf pup and then be gone, letting its gentler cousin remain. But there was no time to spend a warm night inside a lodge. Etran had no time.

Lukas and I spurred the lynxes ahead, back to the river.

*Just hold on, Etran. Hold on if you can.*

# FORTY-EIGHT

## ETRAN

I fought my body's attempt to come back to consciousness, but eventually the screams of muscles twisted and held in awkward positions won out. I sat slumped over, left elbow nearly on the ground. Bare memory surfaced of being brought into the tent and left with hands tied behind me to the tent pole.

A soft cry escaped through swollen lips as I tried to move myself upright and relieve the ache in my shoulders and back. It didn't much help as new pains made themselves known.

My missing shirt revealed the extent of the battlelion's work, helped along by Hakkon. Another breath rasped at the sight of the deliberate cuts across my chest. Even under the dried and caked blood, the shapes were clear.

A rage-filled gasp shook my entire body, followed quickly by crushing shame. In the end, Kamil had decided not to even ask me for information on the tribe, only working with Hakkon to expel their violence on me.

I didn't know how long it had been. But more than enough time for my mind to numb to any thought but pain and basic survival.

Movement at the tent flap brought my knees curling up to my chest, as if that could protect me. But it was not the battlelion or Hakkon as I had expected. It was the somber warrior who had led the attack on my pack. We stared at one another, my vision blurred to a crack in my left eye.

Finally, he knelt beside me, and I stiffened. But he proffered a water skin.

"Drink."

Not giving me the chance to refuse it, he held it to my lips. I gulped at it, taking one moment to spit out old blood before drinking again. As far as I remembered, this was the first time I had tasted anything but blood since I'd come.

He set it aside and took another skin. This time, lukewarm broth slid down my throat, my empty stomach spasming as it hit. He kept pouring small amounts until I shook my head, unable to swallow any more.

"Why?"

Slowly and precisely, he set the container down and rocked back on his heels.

"You seem a man of honor. And some of us in the Saber tribe can still respect that." His voice revealed nothing. Unlike the rest of his tribe, his hair was cut short as we wore ours. But his dark eyes held no sympathy for a Greywolf.

"And your battlelion is one of those?" My lips twisted against a cry as I tried to move and quickly learned it was not worth it.

"He would have chosen the boy, if he were in your place," the warrior clarified. "The weakest of you three. He would not have thought twice."

I admit, I felt a little regret for my actions just then.

"It seems I am not so lucky in my half-brothers as you."

"The battlelion?"

He inclined his head. "And two others. Though the only thing we share is the same father and a hatred of each other. So forgive me for thinking your tribe thinks too highly of your blood, because it seems both our chiefs did not care as much."

"Your father?" The pounding in my head was making it difficult to follow.

"Chief of the Saber tribe," he confirmed. "Though never married. Perhaps him beginning to lose his mind is the spirits' punishment. Kamil made himself battlelion a few turnings ago. And now he thinks to take the position of chief. A victory here will make it so. The tribe will be too afraid to stand against him."

"And you'll let him take it?"

Davor gave a mirthless smile. "I have warriors on my side, but not enough. If I were to be chief, I would keep our people in our lands where we belong. Focusing on building our lives and not trying to take more than we can possibly need."

I slowly tilted my head side to side to try and relieve the spasming muscle in my neck. "And what of Hakkon and the lands here?"

The scoff broke from him again. "He is a fool to think that Kamil would let him be chief here. Or that Kamil would leave a tribe for him to still rule."

My gut tightened.

"You have been here near two days. We chased off a Greywolf scout earlier. I do not think your tribe will take any of the terms Kamil set."

There was nothing but a void where any sort of emotion should have been. While glad that the tribe did not plan to surrender, the thought loomed larger that maybe it was easier to let me die and choose someone new. There wasn't much in me to hope that they might fight for me.

Davor pushed to his feet, staring down at me. "If we should find ourselves facing each other across the battlelines again, just know that you might have an ally in me should you want it."

I stared after him as he ducked out of the tent. I'd have preferred an ally who would set me free rather than one offering aid in a future that seemed more and more unlikely.

I did not have much time to ponder it. Kamil and Hakkon were next through the tent flap.

"I have heard nothing from your tribe, Chief." Kamil loomed over me, none of his half-brother's somber respect in his glance. "Perhaps they do not want you."

I set my jaw and stared straight ahead, away from his sneer.

His rough hands untied me, and, at his call, another warrior came in and hauled me to my feet, dragging me outside into the dim twilight. The warrior let me fall back to my knees. Kamil's boot impacted into my chest, flinging me to my side. I curling around the avalanche of pain it ignited. He pushed me over, grinding his boot into the wounds until my jaw ached from clenching and my throat ground out a cry.

He relented with a laugh and began pacing around me. "So, what to do with you, Chief?"

I focused on the All-Father's star right above me. Praying for strength.

"How long does it take a tribe to decide they do not want a worthless bastard as chief?"

"Maybe you can tell me?" The words slipped out.

Kamil paused and I caught a flicker of anger throb across his jaw before he laughed.

"You are almost as quick as your old battlewolf. Your half-brother, wasn't he?" Kamil crouched beside me. "Did he offer the honor of family to you, or was he as ashamed as the rest of your tribe?"

I held the battlelion's stare, refusing to flinch. "You should ask Hakkon how Comran felt when he declared Hakkon a traitor against the both of us."

Hakkon's boot found my side, then stomped down on my already-aching forearm. Stolen breath from the first strike did not allow another scream of pain.

Kamil brushed Hakkon back from me. The traitor still shuddered in anger. Kamil's lips moved, but I could not hear anything over the roar of agony slowly ebbing from me.

Hakkon's chest heaved a breath and a tight smile spread across his face. "I think we should let the wild decide what to do with him tonight."

Kamil laughed. He held a hand up, testing the wind. "The north is sending another storm our way. Winter might not yet be done with us. We could wake up to snow."

My heart froze in my chest. Hakkon looked down at me without a shred of pity.

"Then maybe he will know what I did when he sent me out in the dead of winter."

"He at least sent you out with a full pack and a sword." Davor's scornful voice sounded as he emerged into the small circle.

"You're right." Hakkon eased his hands out of fists. "Give him back his shirt."

Davor shook his head in disgust, but Kamil only laughed again. A warrior brought my shirt from somewhere and tossed it down to me. I was left to push myself up and slowly pull it back on. Fresh blood soaked through the front.

Hands yanked me up again and half-dragged me through the

camp to the base of a broad tree at the edge of the forest and forced me to kneel. Facing north, where a scant line of trees stood between me and the storm headed our way in the bank of clouds blacker than the night sky.

I might have survived another night of knives and fists. But against the forces of nature, I would be powerless, especially if winter decided to make one more bid.

My arms were yanked behind me and bound around the tree.

"Maybe I would be lenient tonight, Etran." Hakkon's voice took on a more reasonable tone. "Cede the position to me and you get to live until tomorrow and maybe for longer after that."

"I would never give it to a traitor." I forced myself as tall as I could.

He nodded almost thoughtfully.

"And I would never truly spare a bastard." With one last kick that sent me sagging back into the tree, he left.

Davor was last to leave, giving me a slight nod of respect. I turned away from the sight. Respect would not help me through the night.

The storm clouds loomed closer, and a chill rushed before it. I focused on the All-Father's star before it vanished behind the clouds. Maybe I'd have some time to work out an apology for losing our valley before I saw Comran in the next life.

# FORTY-NINE

## ETRAN

Frigid wind cut through the poor protection of my shirt. My fingers clenched in fists against the shivering and the pain it stoked. A damper cold stung my cheek, and I tucked my head as freezing rain began to pelt through the foliage.

Murmurs announced the two guards who'd been patrolling nearby heading farther back into camp and leaving me on my own. The darkness fell heavier, and the sleet showed no mercy, crusting my clothes and leaving my hands in tight curls. My breath exploded in helpless bursts before my face.

Time stretched on, the angry pattering my only company besides my shivering. The rope froze to the tree, stealing away any small thought of escape. I sagged forward, wrists straining against the restraints as the cold deepened and crushed me under its embrace.

A thicker spot of white drifted down. The stinging rain slowly changed to dancing flakes. The world shrank to the spot of earth between my knees, blurring in and out of focus as all feeling faded.

My eyes grew heavy, ready to close and just give up when a soft crunch and low growl came to my ears. Heart stammering, my neck creaked up to face a bulky shape in the dimness.

It crept forward. I didn't have the strength to pull back. Then, finally, it stood before me, warm breath drifting to brush my face.

A dim greyness had taken over the world with the snow falling in giant flakes, barely illuminating the features of a greywolf with one black stripe on the left side of its muzzle. But no saddle or leathers, or rider.

It regarded me, and I it. Finally, it stretched out a nose and touched my forehead.

"Eska?" His name shivered from me.

The greywolf pulled away and I caught the bare glint of amber eyes. A trace of wildness still lingered there, but he did not act on it. Instead, he turned, pressing close to me to shelter me with the bulk of his body.

I leaned against his side, pressing close into the fur, my body greedily trying to take the heat. A sobbing breath wrenched from me. Was this how the All-Father would let me come into the next life? Accompanied by my brother's wolf? Both of whom I could not save?

"I'm sorry," I mumbled, body shaking. "I'm sorry."

Eska shifted, moving to press his head and neck against my left hand, bringing some warmth back. He curled closer around me and the tree, a growl humming low.

Cold settled around my shoulders and back, pressed up against the rough bark. Even with Eska's help, I didn't know if I would survive the night. Didn't know if I wanted to. Eska seemed to sense it and rumbled again. But my head tipped against his side, and my eyes closed, letting the darkness take me.

# FIFTY

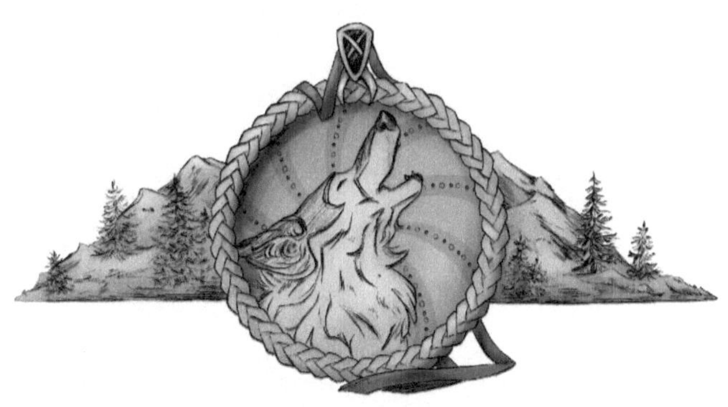

## COMRAN

The storm hit just before nightfall. Winds plagued us with each irritatingly rocking step, pushing ever onwards. Lynxes were better tolerated with one's feet on the ground. Freezing rain managed to find its way under the hoods and down the collars of the knee-length coats we'd pulled on at the storm's onset.

The lynxes pressed on, bobbed tails tucked and ears back as they loped steadily. My shoulders stung from the ice, and the cold burrowed its way into my left shoulder. I flexed my gloved hand around the reins, moving my shoulder in small motions to try to keep it loose.

A miserable hour was spent in the icy rain before it slackened and softer flakes began to take its place. The wind still whirled and rustled, but the rest of the world had quieted with the snowfall.

Midnight had come and gone when a low whistle from Lukas brought us reining in. I'd given up trying to see where we were going in the darkness under the trees and deepened by the clouds. The lynxes were guiding our way, and Lukas had led through the forests and across open valley floor using the constant conversation of the tributary river as a guide.

"Should be getting close." His whisper floated between us and the trees clustered close.

I raised my hand in acknowledgment, and the lynxes kept moving, each paw testing the snowy ground before easing weight forward. Our wolves could move quietly, but not so eerily silent as this.

No wonder the Sabers could appear as if from nowhere.

It took another hour of concentrated movement before we halted again. The scent of woodsmoke teased the air. Exchanging a glance, we slid from saddles.

My lynx lifted its head, nose twitching hard. Its mouth dropped open, upper lip curling back from fangs. I caught the musty scent as a wind stirred through the frozen pines.

Sablecat.

I beckoned Lukas closer. "Stay here with Sasha. I'm going to scout, then we can make a plan."

He shifted between his feet like he wanted to charge right then, but my hand on his shoulder stayed him.

"Patience."

His scoff appeared as a plume of white, but he held with the lynxes. Sasha reached out and squeezed my hand. I couldn't see much of her face in the dimness and under her hood, but I returned the gesture.

I loosened my sword in its sheath on my back, making sure the cold hadn't made it stick. I slid my hood back and undid the top of the coat.

My boots imprinted deeper tracks alongside the faint prints of a hare who had already been out and about in the pre-dawn.

I sent another prayer heavenward. The snow would not do me any favors for stealth, but I needed to see the lay of the camp and try to find where they were keeping Etran. Cloud cover was breaking in small places, bits of moonlight slipping through to pierce the darkness.

The bulk of something at the base of a tree ahead slowed my steps. I squinted as if that would help my eyes in the dim lighting and slowly drifting snowflakes. Stealing from tree to tree, I made my way closer, pausing every few steps to check the trees above. No sign of anything around. No doubt any guards would have given up in the snow and sleet. Only idiots would be out and about in this weather.

The closer I came, the higher my confusion rose. From the shape of it, it might be a greywolf curled around the tree.

A growl stopped me in my tracks. The animal shifted and lifted a head. Now silhouetted against the growing light, it revealed itself to indeed be a greywolf. Had the Sabers taken a wolf to torment as well?

I edged closer, not daring to give one of the low whistles we all used for our greywolves. The warning faded to a confused whine. The head tilted and one ear bent slightly.

My heart stammered at the familiar sight of that ear.

"Eska?"

The wolf scrambled to its feet, backing away, shaking its head with another growl. I knew the pitch and sound. Stepping again, I extended a hand.

"Eska."

But he shook his head again like he was fighting a tight lead pulling him where he did not want to go. Backing away, he kept his head lowered in warning.

My boots froze on the ground as I finally saw what he had left behind at the tree. I half-ran the last few steps. From the way Etran slumped against the bonds, I feared he might be dead. But faint breath stirred.

*Spirits, please.*

Pulling off a glove, I rested a hand against his cheek. Blood crusted his face, bruises spread in dark patches. Dampness plastered his hair against his forehead, some knotted around a cut on his scalp. A faint wheeze marked every small puff of air. It was light enough to show a blue tinge to his lips.

I gently shook him, trying to harness the anger building back up inside me. Blood and mud stained his shirt so that barely any of its original grey remained.

"Etran, please," I whispered, shaking him again. Pulling off my other glove with my teeth, I set fingers against his neck and found a pulse.

Finally, he stirred, jerking away from my hand. I tensed, ready to silence him if needed as his eyes flew open. But he stared at me, shock glimmering in his green eyes.

"Comran?" His voice came a hoarse mumble around a swollen mouth. "You're dead."

"Not yet." I flashed a small smile. I reached around him and sliced through the ropes, helping him ease his arms free. He sagged against the tree, his features twisting in pain. I hesitated, wanting to help him, but not sure how.

I placed a gentle hand on his shoulder and his eyes opened again.

"Comran, you're here?"

"Aye, I'm here." I brushed my hand against his forehead, frowning at the clammy cold of his skin. He needed to get warm.

Unbuckling my sword from my back, I set it aside and

shrugged out of my coat. I had to help him lift his arms to thread through the sleeves. Doing up the buckles, I turned my attention back to our surroundings as I fastened the sword back on.

Nothing stirred yet, and Eska still hung back. The gloves went over Etran's hands next, difficult with his fingers stiff and half-curled. His features creased with pain again as I rubbed his newly-gloved hands between mine. I let him lean against me as I alternated rubbing his hands and then upper arms to try to bring blood back.

My heart broke at the whimper barely smothered against my breastplate. Finally, he started shivering more on his own and I pulled away to cradle his head between my hands.

"Can you walk?"

He nodded, pushing himself up a little as I stood. I grabbed his right forearm to haul him to his feet, but he strangled a cry and almost collapsed again. I reflexively jerked my hand away. Forcing a smile in his pale face, he extended his other hand to me.

He staggered as I helped him upright and wrapped an arm around him.

"All right?" I whispered.

He straightened with an effort and nodded. Eska edged forward a step, caution I didn't understand keeping him out of reach.

I dared to click to him, and his ears pricked again. Praying he'd follow, I began to retrace my path back through the trees, Etran leaning heavily on me. With every step, his legs began to loosen from being cramped for so long. My vision blurred in anger. They would pay for what they had done.

Etran's breath began to wheeze. It tore at me, but I pushed on. We just had to make it back to the lynxes, then ride like the dark wood's shades were after us.

"Comran!" Lukas's hiss guided us the last few feet. The

Blackpaw warrior came to Etran's other side to help support him. Etran drew closer to me.

"This him?"

"Yes. We need to get out of here." I tried to nudge Etran on, but he'd sagged more heavily against me.

Sasha's intake of breath sent me tensing. She pointed over my shoulder, and I craned my head to look and see our shadow.

"My wolf," I reassured.

"Yours?" Lukas's voice held confused question.

I didn't have any answer and Eska still wasn't coming any closer.

"Mount up."

Lukas coaxed my lynx down so I could help Etran struggle on. Once it carefully rose back to paws, I swung up behind him in the saddle, keeping an arm around him.

Eska growled as soon as I settled, backing away again and loping off into the woods. I stared after him in shock. What had happened to him?

Lukas nudged Raya into motion. My mount shifted, and I trusted it to follow as I focused more on keeping Etran upright and steady in my arms.

We rode for nearly an hour in the lynxes' easy, loping stride until the rush of the river overtook the whisking of their paws. I pulled to a halt within the treeline. Light was growing stronger around us, and quiet still lingered. No sound or sign of pursuit.

"Lukas." I kept my voice low.

He brought their lynx back beside me.

"There should be a ford somewhere close. I am not sure where we are." Worry for Etran and the way he collapsed forward had robbed me of any other thought than we were still heading east.

"I can go scout while he rests." Lukas cast a grim look to

Etran. Each wheezing inhale assured he was still breathing.

"Head north first," I said. "We'll wait here."

Lukas nodded and gave Sasha a hand to slide down from the saddle.

My lynx sank back down to its stomach, and I came to Etran's side. His eyes barely opened at my touch. He came ungracefully down to the ground, knees buckling so quickly I barely caught him and lowered him to sitting.

Etran stirred a little as I pressed a hand to the side of his head, some alertness finally showing. I tilted his face gently, taking in the bruises and cuts on his face, the swelling under his left eye.

Sasha handed me a waterskin and I poured some water between his cracked lips. It revived him a little, enough to blink at me in the emerging light.

"You are real?" he mumbled, forehead creasing as he reached up tentatively to grab my wrist where it still rested against his head. His grip was pitifully weak.

I mustered a smile. "Yes. Here and getting you home."

He searched my face, the confusion slowly melting away. "You fell."

"The current carried me downriver where the Blackpaws found me. I had not expected to wake up in their lodge. I'd expected dark woods, at least." I managed a bit of levity.

His head shook slightly against my hand and the faintest of smiles flickered. "I might agree for letting us all think you were dead."

A soft chuckle broke from me. But his fingers clenched around my arm with a little more strength.

"I left you. I'm sorry. I..."

"Etran." I gave him a small shake. "You did right."

But his eyes did not agree. I shifted to glance over my

shoulder and beckoned to Sasha. She came to kneel beside me, offering Etran a smile.

"This is Sasha. She's the one who found me."

Etran watched warily as she gently opened the coat, showing the blood-stained shirt underneath. But as she reached for his shirt, he stiffened, a guarded look coming over him.

"I am fine."

I had never seen him lie so boldly before. Sasha looked to me for help.

"Let her see your arm," I said instead.

He slowly peeled it away from his chest and let her push the sleeve back to reveal a swollen and bruised forearm.

"Broken?"

He shook his head, a sheen of sweat appearing on his forehead as she carefully felt along his arm. "Just cracked, I think."

Sasha bent over her paper, using the top of her thigh to support it, and showed me.

-He is badly hurt, I think. I can do a little for him until we make it to your camp.-

I passed it on to him. But he stubbornly stared at something I could not see on the ground.

"Do you have anything for pain?" I asked her.

She mixed something in the waterskin, and we convinced Etran to drink. A shiver racked him again. Sasha brought the spare fur from behind my saddle to spread over him. I tucked an arm around his shoulders and pulled him close.

"Rest for a few minutes."

He slumped against me, turning his face into my shoulder. I held him as his breath evened out.

Sasha rocked back on her heels and looked to me. I signed my thanks and she smiled before touching my arm and pointing.

A cautious distance from the lynx, Eska sat back on haunches, watching us. His ears pricked, and he moved one step before sinking back down.

I reached out my free hand. "Eska."

A faint whine of confusion built in his throat, but he didn't move.

"He went wild when you fell." Etran's voice came quiet. I'd thought him asleep.

My heart clenched and my hand fell back to my lap.

"I let him go. I am sorry."

"No." I watched my wolf, aching for him to come to me, praying he could find his way back. "He was with you tonight."

Eska edged another step, and the lynx growled a light warning. He barely acknowledged it, sinking lower to his stomach and creeping another few feet.

*That's it,* I silently willed him on.

But his ears pinned flat as he lunged to his paws, growl thundering through bared teeth at something in the trees behind us. The lynx hissed, its own ears flattening.

It could only mean one thing. Sasha looked to me, eyes wide. "Run!"

# FIFTY-ONE

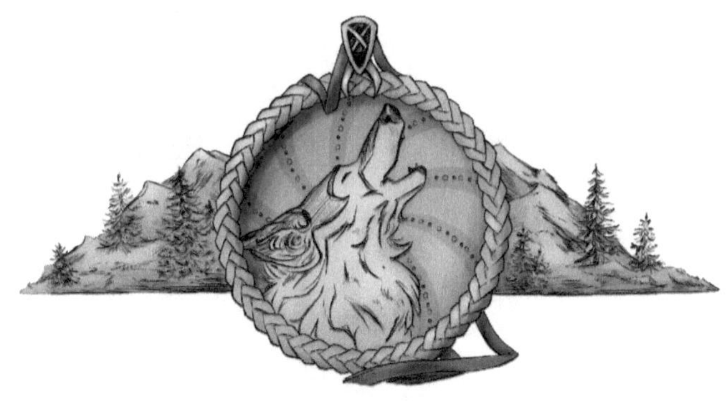

## COMRAN

Sasha paused for one heartbeat. I pushed to my knees, trying to haul Etran up with me.

"Run!" I shouted.

She turned on her heel and sprinted off into the trees. Eska snapped and growled. I got Etran on his feet and we took three staggering steps before a weight took us both to the ground. I rolled to my feet, yanking my sword free to swipe at the circling sablecat. It snarled back and kept in a tight circle. Etran feebly got an arm underneath himself.

*Come on,* I silently willed him to get up.

More movement brought my guard back up, and I fell back to his side as five Saber warriors circled up, spears at the ready. Another two kept Eska and the lynx at bay with the help of their sablecats.

"Going somewhere, Chief?" The sneering voice of the battle-lion announced him as he strode through the line of warriors.

Etran froze and I dropped to a defensive crouch.

"You?" The battlelion stopped short when he saw me. "I thought you were dead."

"Sorry to disappoint."

I twisted around an oncoming spear thrust, grabbing it and yanking hard, pulling the warrior off balance and into my sword.

"Good try, *Battlewolf,* but…" Kamil yanked a spear from one of his men and pressed the tip between Etran's shoulder blades, still staying far enough out of reach from my sword.

"Put it down."

Etran did not move, but his shoulders hunched up as if trying to draw away from the battlelion's touch. Kamil and I stared at one another for a long moment. Then, slowly, I lowered my sword and let it fall to the ground.

"Good boy."

Two warriors surged forward and grabbed my arms, propelling me backward to slam me against the nearest tree. My healing shoulder protested as they yanked my arms back around the trunk.

Kamil stalked forward, pausing to crouch beside Etran. He stood with a scoffing laugh and drove his heel down hard on Etran's back.

Etran's broken cry ignited an angry fire around my heart. The battlelion would pay for hurting my brother. *Brother.*

The battlelion continued his advance, drawing a knife. "A lynx? I did not think we left any of them alive. You come back riding a coward's animal?"

"I thought the same thing of your cats with how often you retreated from me."

His teeth flashed in a grin. "Maybe I did miss our little exchanges, however rare."

"Makes one of us."

"Your little chief here is not nearly so entertaining. Though"—

he turned to look back at Etran— "he spent more time screaming."

The warriors held me tighter against the fight that flared in my limbs.

"Battlelion." The voice announced a sight that had my heart plunging into my toes. Another Saber warrior pushed Sasha in front of him. Her hands were outstretched, and her jaw clenched.

"Well, well." Kamil sauntered over. She backed away, right into the grip of her escort.

"Maybe the Blackpaws aren't all worthless." He skimmed his knife across her cheek, and she shuddered away from it.

Rage boiled in me again, but I forced a laugh. "You must be a fearsome commander. Torturing wounded men. Threatening defenseless women—or is that the only sword you're any good with?"

Kamil turned back to me, eyes glinting dark above a mirthless smile. "Think you're so clever? Hakkon said you always thought highly of yourself."

I shifted my attention to one of the men who held me tight. "I didn't hear a denial, did you?"

A faint quirk teased the man's mouth, but my attention was taken as Kamil pressed the knife to my throat.

"So now you have my attention. Let's find out a little about you."

The tip of the dagger jabbed under my jaw, and I strove to hold my expression steady, to keep my gaze fixed on him and not on Etran or Sasha.

"You tried to defend him that day by the cliff. What is the bastard to you?"

He turned to where Etran still huddled on the ground, watching with wary eyes. Everything in his rigid posture urged me to caution. But I needed him to hear it.

"My brother."

Kamil's smile widened. "How touching. Someone to claim him after all."

He passed a signal to the men holding me, and they twisted my arms tighter behind my back, my shoulder beginning to scream at the pressure.

"Your tribe thought you were dead. And while I would love to hear that story, you took my lion over the side of that cliff with you." The knife flicked to within a hairsbreadth of my eye.

"Made for a softer landing." I should have held my tongue.

Anger twisted past the sneering smile.

"For that I'll let you taste my knife. I have a talent for carving. Just ask your chief if you don't believe me." He paused to smirk back at Etran, before grabbing my hair and forcing my head back. "You're the battlewolf, but I do not see any paint. I think I'll fix that."

I barely had time to register his intent before his knife slashed a line beneath my left eye. A startled gasp broke from me seconds after blood coated my cheek.

"No!" Etran's strangled voice broke through my shock.

"Too fast?" he spoke as if to Etran. "I agree." He set his knife below my right eye and carved down to my chin with deliberate slowness.

I couldn't move in his grip, couldn't withdraw from the painful cold of his steel.

He laughed. "Looks like he still has some fight left in him after all."

Beyond him, Etran had struggled to his knees, but another warrior pinned him there. Sasha fought in her captor's grip, lips moving in soundless curses. Kamil laughed and turned back to me. Fire followed the path of the second line down my cheek. He held the knife against my jaw as I struggled to keep his gaze.

*Do not break.*

"There. Better, don't you think?"

Darkness flickered at the edges of my vision as the heat of my blood seeped into my collar. He wiped the knife on my sleeve.

"No medallion?" He set the tip of the knife at my neck above the breastplate.

"Battlelion…" The warrior on my left relaxed his hold a fraction, caution in his voice.

I blinked hard, trying to keep Kamil's scowl in focus, but my head was tipping forward.

"What?" he growled, then turned to look at the sablecat standing a few paces behind him. It stood on crouched limbs, nose tilted up to sample the wind, gold eyes darting around.

Numbness crept over my mind, chased away by a clench of my jaw that sent new fire through my face.

The sound of a greywolf's howl, close, powerful, and angry, brought a slight smile to the less injured side of my face.

Eska barked, trying to lunge past the spears. Shouts filled the wood, and sablecats hissed and spat. Greywolves snarled. I tried to blink steadiness back to the world.

Kamil shouted and gestured with his knife. The Saber warrior stepped away from Etran. A sharp cry sounded, and a warrior fell from the saddle, spear through his middle.

My arms were dropped, and confusion erupted among the trees. I tried to move to Etran, but my legs gave out from under me, the world going black for a terrifying moment. Hands pushed me back to sitting. I jerked against the touch until I recognized Sasha.

Movement blurred behind her. The chaos seemed to quiet, shapes turning wolf-like in my periphery. Her hands darted to the pouch at her belt before turning to me. She tapped my chin and pointed up. I fixed my gaze on the grey clouds bundled above the reaching branches, losing them for a few moments as she pressed her fingers against the cuts.

A rough hand on my arm brought me back. Etran had somehow appeared at my side.

"You all right?" I shouldn't have tried to speak, my vision blurring again as new pain drove deep into my cheek.

Sasha tapped a finger to my lips.

"What were you thinking?" Etran renewed his painful grip on my arm, but relief showed in his hunched form.

I forced the working corner of my mouth into a smile. Boots crunched and Lukas appeared behind Sasha.

He took in our beaten appearance, lingering longer on me. I closed my eyes against the thought of how disfigured my face must be. A hand pressed against my shoulder and I looked to Etran again.

"Comran?" The breathless voice brought my eyes up.

Loke pushed up beside Lukas. He stared at me as if looking at a ghost. Which, in all fairness, he might actually be thinking after I'd been missing for countings.

I reached up a shaking hand and he hauled me to my feet to crush me in an embrace. He pulled away, studying my face with somber eyes. Though his hand pressed gentle against the side of my head, it still jolted through my cut cheeks.

I reached up to squeeze his forearm in reassurance. He tapped his forehead gently against mine.

"Do not…do not do that again."

It took a moment to speak through my clenched jaw. "I'm offended you did not think I would haunt you till you joined me in the All-Father's lodge."

He shook his head, smiling even though his eyes shone bright.

"Could not even give me peace and quiet in your afterlife?"

"Never." Spirits above, even thinking about smiling *hurt*.

Other warriors began to gather around. Sasha pulled back to stand with Lukas, both eyeing the Greywolves warily. I turned to Etran, and Loke helped me get him up. Loke had to take most of his weight, my knees still wobbling treacherously.

"You all right, Etran?" Loke asked gently.

Etran managed a poor smile.

"How are you both even here?" Loke looked between us.

"I could ask you the same." My jaw clenched tighter as the words stabbed through my face.

"Amund and a pack of Blackpaws rode in a few hours ago with news you were alive, so we headed to the river to scout and found your friend there trying to get across." Loke jerked his chin to Lukas.

"Battlewolf." A warrior strode over, halting in awkward uncertainty as both Loke and I looked to him.

Loke pressed something round and cool into my hand. A leather cord trailed from between our hands. He pulled his hand away, leaving the medallion in mine. I glanced to him and then to Etran. He had named Loke as the new battlewolf, even though I had been about to start giving orders like I still had the position.

"Oh no, I freely give it back." Loke held his hand up. "I am not doing the miserable duty again."

Etran managed a faint smile. "We agreed Loke would only hold it until I found someone better. And here you are."

Something settled in my heart with the words, and I slid the medallion over my head to sit comfortingly against my chest.

"Mount up," I told the warrior. "Head for the river."

The wolfrider slammed a hand against his chest with a grin. "Yes, Battlewolf."

All around, warriors mimicked the action, some passing by

to tap my shoulder and greet Etran with relief and respect.

"We don't have a spare wolf," Loke said apologetically.

I flicked my fingers. Eska still sat off to the side, inching closer and closer to the greywolves who rumbled and barked low greetings to him. Lukas led up the lynx I'd ridden before. I nudged Etran. I might not be quite myself, but I would not let him out of my sight until we got back to camp.

Loke did not argue, helping him onto the lynx. I glanced back a moment to see Sasha already mounted on Raya. She flashed a smile, her hands reassuring me.

I pulled myself onto the lynx behind Etran, willing myself to stay tall in the saddle. Wolves mustered up, and Eska rose to his paws, every line of his body alert as his amber eyes met mine. Hope dared to spark in my heart.

We moved out, wolves spreading out to flank in a protective pattern as we began to thread through the woods and north up the river to the ford. Across it, open space stretched out, the rising sun breaking through the clouds to sparkle off the fresh snow. We pushed up to a slow run when a guttural roar echoed behind us.

I reined in and twisted in the saddle to see packs of sablecats spreading out along the river. A curse broke from Loke. We had only the small pack of greywolves.

"If we can make it to the rest of the packs, we could have a chance," Loke said.

I nodded and pointed to a rider. Loke gave the order and the rider raced away to sound the alarm before us. We lashed our mounts into action, but the roar sounded again.

A glance over my shoulder showed the Sabers in pursuit through the puffs of snow in our wake. Forward where the valley stretched empty before us.

They'd overtake us before we made it.

I hauled back on the reins, the lynx sliding to a halt. Pressing the leathers into Etran's hands, I slid off and broke into a run, whistling my signal to Eska and hoping he would hear it.

Each stride sent fire through my cheeks, but I pressed on. A lithe shape fell in beside me. Grabbing handfuls of Eska's fur, I swung up onto his bare back.

"Comran!" Loke's frantic shout faded behind me as I pressed against Eska's back.

He stretched low to the ground as he raced toward the battlelion, following each cue from my legs and hands clenched deep in his fur.

The Saber tribe's line staggered, some slowing in confusion at my lone charge. But the battlelion kept coming. Eska shifted his path, coming at an angle toward the warrior. I pushed up to crouch atop his back, harder without leathers covering his slick fur. A wordless bellow ripped from Kamil as he tried to pull his sablecat around.

One leaping stride, then another, and then I launched myself from Eska, taking the battlelion around the waist and bearing us both to the ground. My left shoulder took the brunt of the impact and something shuddered deep inside. Sky and bloody snow whirled by before I came up to my knees.

The battlelion jerked up to his feet, eyes wide in shock to see me planting my boots steady on the ground.

"Just can't stay down, can you?" he snarled.

I wrenched my sword free from the scabbard. "You should not have hurt my brother."

He reeled back from the shock of my first strike, giving more steps as I kept coming, fury guiding my way. The clash of our swords ricocheted through my body as he finally stopped my blade. He gave a slight smile and attacked.

But I was born for war and the spirits' rage flowed through me.

It overpowered the weakness from the blood leaking from my face. We strove back and forth, him trying to come on my weaker side, me refusing to let him, pummeling at each other with each strike.

Finally, we fell back a few steps from each other, blades stained red. Stinging wounds began to make themselves known. We circled one another, his chest heaving just as heavily as mine.

A flash of black to my left brought my gaze flicking that way. My heart bolted faster at the sablecat standing there with its warrior.

The battlelion's smirk fell as the sablecat didn't move. Its rider held out a spear and shouted an order for the lines to keep holding. The packs ranged in a half circle to watch.

Kamil's face twisted in rage. "You traitor!"

A greywolf snarled behind me, showing my pack had come up behind to complete the circle.

Not hesitating a moment more, I charged again. Kamil brought his sword up, but it seemed he had not recovered from the shock of his warrior's betrayal. It took a few slower strikes before a frantic edge set in.

Iron wailed against iron, our weapons screaming their own defiance as if the very metal itself knew the fate of the valley hinged on their strength.

A strike came wide at me, leaving himself open to attack. Drops of red flung themselves to the ground as he barely managed to parry, his arm shaking.

He retreated as I struck again and again at the place, each block coming slower and sloppier. Panic shone in his face as I did not let up. Until finally, his sword fell from his hand.

I lifted my arm to strike again, but his fear gave him a last burst of strength. Drawing a knife, he thrust at my chest. Without time to move, and praying to the Greywolf that the armor would hold, I let myself keep coming.

The knife scraped into my breastplate, heat scoring my ribs. Now close, I grabbed the neck of his breastplate to pin him and thrust my sword up under the armor.

He staggered into me, sagging against my hold as blood rushed over my hand. Barely keeping myself upright, I shoved back, my left arm shaking wildly. The shock in his face turned to one last sneer as the life faded from his eyes.

Ripping my sword free, I stumbled backward and let him fall to the ground.

It was over.

# FIFTY-TWO

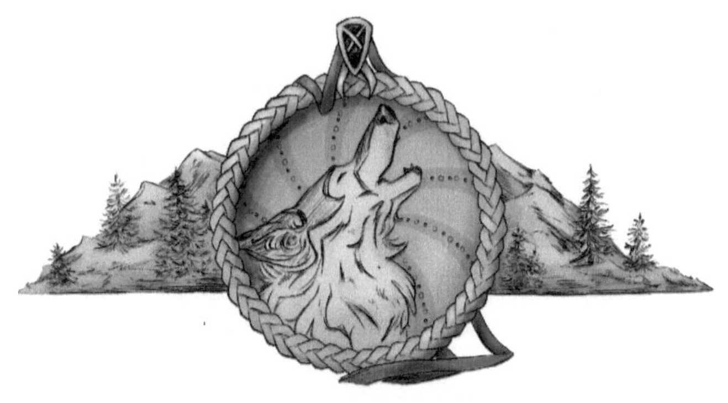

## COMRAN

Silence reined.

For five eternal heartbeats, nothing moved.

Then the Saber warriors stirred into action, battlecries and shouts rising. I clenched my sword, backing away, until a deeper roar came up behind me.

Twisting, I saw packs of Greywolves straining forward, and with them, Blackpaws holding spears at the ready. There was more than one pack of lynxes, and I sent a prayer of thanks to the All-Father for Petya who rode at their fore.

But despite the reinforcements, the Saber tribe surged restlessly. I braced, ready for a bloody battle to erupt around me.

But the Saber warrior struck his spear point down in the ground and dismounted, coming toward me with empty hands spread wide. Abrupt silence fell over his men.

Greywolves shifted to new alertness, wolfriders gripping spears and looking to me.

I held my bloody sword out to signal them to hold.

"Battlewolf." The warrior tapped his chest twice with closed fist.

It took a moment before I could manage to force words around my wounded face. "Who are you?"

"I am Davor. And I will claim the battlelion's place over the Saber tribe."

Before I could lift my sword at a new threat, he shook his head.

"And I would call a truce with you and your chief."

My leg trembled and I shifted to brace myself with a wider stance. "He is…"

Davor flicked his glance past me. I turned with jagged steps to see Etran standing at the edge of the loose circle, Jens on one side and Loke on the other. Spirits bless him, he was holding himself upright as if forgetting the extent of his injuries, though he still cradled his right arm against his chest.

Jens stepped with him as he walked to us.

"Chief." Davor touched a fist to his forehead. "If you agree to a truce, I will withdraw my tribe from the valley."

It seemed not all his warriors agreed, many stirring with rumblings of dissent. But only one stepped out from the rest.

"Coward!" Hakkon charged the Saber warrior, sword raised. I started, drawing my left arm in front of Etran as I readied my sword. But Davor lifted his hand and a Saber stood in his stirrups. He launched a spear, and it took Hakkon in the back. My cousin died in an instant.

Davor turned back to us.

"We have no use for a traitor," he said coldly.

Lost for words, I could only stare at Hakkon's body for a long moment.

"No one will challenge you?" Etran's voice somehow came

steady, though he'd barely been able to speak not so very long ago.

Davor smiled thinly. "I do not doubt they will, but it will happen away from this place."

"Then I accept a truce," Etran said. "You will take your warriors and leave this valley immediately."

Davor gave a small bow, deference to a conquering warrior.

His voice lowered a fraction. "When we make it back to the villages, there will be much upheaval. It will take time to sort through it, but if I come out the victor, I would discuss a treaty with you, Chief."

Some sort of understanding seemed to linger between them.

"Then I will look for you on midsummer at the border stone," Etran said.

Davor bowed again. He stooped to pull the battlelion medallion free and settled it around his neck, then walked back to his sablecat. As he passed Hakkon's body, he spat, an expression of disgust in his face that I somehow could not quite feel myself. Even with everything he'd done, it was hard to forget the years spent by his side as family.

Under Davor's shouted order, Saber warriors began to pull away back across the river, taking the battlelion's body with them.

"Jens." I turned to the warrior still standing with us. "Pick five packs as an escort for them all the way to the boundaries."

He clapped a fist to his chest and strode off, Greywolves circling up at his call.

The world had begun to tilt eerily, corrected only with concerted effort. I cast around until I found Petya, still mounted on her lynx.

"Battlelynx," I called.

She rode up and offered a spear salute.

"Care to help escort the Saber tribe to the valley borders?"

A cold smile spread across her face.

"I would be honored, Battlewolf." She summoned four packs of lynxriders to her side. Their packleaders saluted me as they rode past, and as they crossed the river, I was finally free to turn back to my brother.

# FIFTY-THREE

## ETRAN

Comran barely steadied me with a trembling arm as I staggered again, my legs scarcely remembering how to do their duty. I tilted a look at him from the corner of my eye.

"What? I cannot bring Blackpaw packs to a battle?"

It prodded a smile from me. He really was alive and standing beside me. Though hardly looking it, with blood coating his face and neck and hasty poultices keeping the wounds closed. I swayed.

"Easy now."

But we were both in danger of collapsing.

"Comran!" Loke's hand descended on his shoulder. "I cannot take my eyes off you for one moment, can I?"

A groan fought its way from his lips instead of a laugh.

A blur to my left side sent me flinching, but Maren paused at my side, taking in the broken sight of me, until I almost could not bear it. I braced for her to back away. But she folded her arms around me and I leaned into her, feeling like she was the only thing holding me together right then.

"You're alive." A tremor rocked her whisper. "I thought…Etran, I…you're alive."

My less-injured arm wrapped around her, and she held steady as I wavered again. She pulled away just enough to gently cradle my face in her hands.

"I am never leaving your side again."

A smile started across my lips before pain stabbed through my chest again. I tried to move away, but she gently kept an arm under mine. We turned slightly to see Comran leaning heavily on Loke, both studying me carefully.

"Battlewolf." Maren's voice held relief as she used her free hand to tap her breastplate.

"Maren." Comran inclined his head, giving her a slight nod after his gaze darted between the two of us.

"Etran." Loke tipped his head, and I followed his motion toward the packs. When they saw my look, packleaders raised spears and howls and shouts of my name followed. I stared in confusion. It was louder by far than the night I had been chosen, more wild and pride-filled.

"Your people were all ready to ride for you," Maren said quietly, the same pride in her voice.

"Every single pack, Chief." Loke confirmed her words with a small smile. "Even before they heard what you did for Aron and Kjell."

I glanced at Comran, and the same look shone in his eyes. He brought fingers to his forehead, then reached to clamp a hand on my shoulder. We shared a wordless look, and the weight of the things still between us slipped away. He tapped his forehead gently against mine, and let go.

"Both of you, come get yourselves looked after. You look no better than corpses." Loke steadied Comran again. "The camp is not far."

But I shook my head, almost desperately. "Not here. The village."

Comran exchanged a glance with Loke. It was twenty miles at least, and I knew it as well as they did, but I could not yet bear for anyone to see what had been done to me.

"Find some wolves." Comran nodded to Loke.

The quiet Blackpaw woman came up to us, frowning at Comran. She did not give Loke a chance to voice his confusion, just started pulling bandages from a pouch and wrapping them around Comran's wounds.

Once she finished, Eska bulled into him, head pressed against his chest. His body shook and Comran wrapped arms around his neck, humming low in comfort. A high-pitched whine escaped Eska's muzzle, and he shifted to wrap his head and neck around Comran, tucking him close.

The sight helped ease the tightness in me as I whispered a prayer of thanks to the All-Father for giving them both back.

Eska lifted his head to look at me, his eyes absent of wildness, and refilled with his good-natured affection.

"Thank you," I whispered to him.

He touched a cautious nose to my less-injured cheek and huffed gently. A bark showed Frea straining against her leathers as Kjell led her to me.

"Chief." Kjell tapped his chest. "I—thank you."

I nodded, accepting the young warrior's help to step up to Frea's side. She lowered herself to the ground, and I managed to mount. By the time the world stopped swaying, Eska had bullied Comran into climbing on his back, and Maren sat on a wolf beside me.

Loke leaned in his saddle to speak with the leader of the pack escorting us. Their words were a murmur in my ears, and I found I didn't even care, focusing on keeping Frea from disappearing into a black void with every shift of her paws.

She followed the other wolves, and I curled my hand around the leather reins and into her fur, holding on as they pushed up into a lope. The ground flashed under her paws. Maybe I should have accepted help, for the world was darkening around the edges again when Frea slowed to a halt.

A hand touched my arm. "We're home."

# FIFTY-FOUR

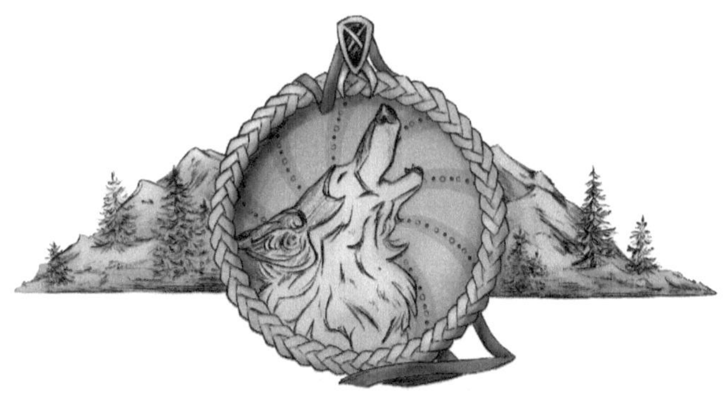

## COMRAN

I slid from Eska in the middle of the lodge circle, the thump of my boots sending another wave of fire through my face. Pushing away, I turned to find Loke helping Etran from the saddle. His face was blank, eyes unfocused. I went to his side, sliding a hand under his arm.

Awareness filtered back through Etran, and he let me help him walk. Not that I did much good, my own legs shaking. Murmurs grew to a wave of shouts and cries as tribesmen and women gathered. Sasha stayed at my side as we split the crowd.

"Comran!" Zoya appeared through the mass of people. Her lips drew together as she took in our appearance, more stern than when she'd attempted to argue the decision to come back to the village from the battlefield.

"I do not want the healer touching him. Not until I know…" I couldn't get much more past my clenched jaw, but she understood. I trusted her and I could not quite trust our own healer yet.

"This way." She beckoned.

Etran was nearing dead weight on my arm, and we staggered a step to the side. Loke slid an arm around him and nodded to me. He'd see Etran the last few feet to the lodge.

I let him go, an ache in my heart at the sight of his slumped shoulders and stilted movements. I'd kill the battlelion a hundred times over for what he'd done to my brother. Sasha touched my arm, and I became dimly aware of my name being shouted, men and women calling to one another. The wolfriders with us were already spreading the news.

Sasha pointed to the healer's lodge.

My next step sent me stumbling into something solid. I clung to it long enough to let the world stop its spinning, only to nearly collapse again as I saw who helped me.

*Father?* My stunned mind couldn't even tell my mouth to speak.

Emotions warred across his face—pride, relief, worry—love?

I froze as he pulled me close again, wrapping his arms around me in a rare embrace. It took several long moments before I mustered the presence of mind to return it.

"Comran!" My mother's cry threatened to undo me. She crashed into Father's side, her arms snaking around me where he still supported me. Her hand brushed the side of my head, tilting me down to press my forehead against hers.

Moisture trickled down my cheek, stinging the wounds.

"You're alive." Her voice held the tremor of sleepless nights.

But my jaw could not undo its clench, and I closed my hand around her forearm instead. Father's hand rested against my back, and it felt strangely comforting to stand there with both of them.

My knee betrayed me again, sending me listing back into Father's chest. Mother pulled away, surrendering me to his hold with a reluctant hand.

"Come." He grasped under my arm and walked beside me into the healer's lodge.

Two beds had been pulled close to the fire. Zoya bent over one, cloth in hand. Father helped me sit on the other. Sasha appeared, reaching for one of the bandages on my arm.

A moan wrenched my gut. I lurched to my feet, pushing her hand away, and stumbled to Etran. His eyes fluttered open and closed, jaw clenched tight as Zoya finished one bandage and dabbed at his chest again.

Bile rose in my throat at the sight of the wounds burned and slashed into his skin. Blood oozed across his chest, the lines of them still clear under the bruises darkening his ribs.

Bastard. Cursed. Carved into him.

He flinched away from her touch with another stifled groan, and his green eyes settled on me. Shame and pain flooded through them, breaking over his face. My hand closed over his forearm, willing him to know what I couldn't yet put into words.

It would not change the way I saw him. The way I'd always seen him.

"Just breathe, Etran," I murmured around the stiffness of my face.

His hand gripped my wrist. I let him near squeeze the life from it, until, gradually, he relaxed into unconsciousness. And still after until Zoya tied the last bandage in place.

"Come." She tapped my shoulder. "Your turn."

She slid a hand under my elbow and helped me limp back to the cot. I sank wearily down, making no resistance as Father, surprisingly still there, helped her remove my armor. She undid the rough bandages, Sasha appearing and disappearing to bring cloths, herbs, and more water.

Blood soaked the front of my shirt, sticking it to my chest. It took some doing to take it off and a sound caught in my chest as my injured arm jostled. Zoya's lips pursed together as she gently prodded my left shoulder. I lifted my right, unable to muster an apologetic smile.

"You ride off for no more than a day, and this is what you come back with?" She *tskd*. "I pity your mother. How grey is her hair from raising you?"

Her light words lifted my heart a little. A soft sound like a laugh came from my father, and it startled me more than his affection outside.

"He has never been one for sitting still."

"So I have learned." Zoya turned her bare smile to Father.

I stared between the two of them, shock keeping me still. He must have seen it, for he rose to his feet and touched my shoulder like he'd always been so open with me.

"I will return later," he promised.

I had nothing to give him in return save a bemused stare. He paused beside Etran's cot, reaching down to press a shaky hand to his son's forehead. For once, jealousy didn't stir. He passed from the lodge, and I caught the slope of his shoulders hiding the emotion he would never openly show to either of us or to the rest of the tribe.

Zoya dabbed at my cheeks with a damp cloth. I jerked away from the sting, but she caught my chin and gently brought me back. I closed my eyes, wondering if I would regret my actions when I saw the damage to my face.

The battlelion had meant it to shame me. I wondered if it would.

"You shouldn't be ashamed."

I looked up at her. She rinsed the cloth and pressed it back to the cuts.

"Sasha told me what happened. You did it to try to protect your chief and her. She'll make sure your big friend knows it and can tell the others. These are badges of bravery now. And any man that thinks otherwise, well, I don't know that I'd have the strength to pity him."

I managed a half smile, meeting her eyes in thanks before looking past her to the still form on the next cot.

"He's all right?"

The deep lines around her eyes eased as she gave a nod. "A few days of rest, and a few meals, and he'll be back on his feet."

Something seemed missing in her words.

"You experienced the cruelty of the battlelion, and you saw the marks left on his body. I think he'll need someone, a brother perhaps, to help him rest easy."

*A brother.* I had never experienced such rage in my entire life as when I saw what had happened to Etran.

I'd sworn to him as battlewolf, but I knew in the deepest reaches of my heart that I would follow him from more than duty. I would burn down the valley if he asked. He had named me brother first, and I would make sure he heard the same from me when he woke.

"These will need stitches," Zoya said quietly, the cloth still making its gentle journey to clean blood away from my cheeks and neck.

"I think it might be easier if you were asleep for it."

I gave a tiny nod of assent. I did not want to see anything sharp coming near my face ever again. The draught came bitter, and I tried to stop my face twisting in disgust.

Zoya's gentle push against my shoulder sent me slowly lying down. She sat beside me, still holding cloths in place over my cheeks to stop any new bleeding. I stared up at the ceiling, eyelids slowly drooping shut. A gentle hand across my forehead sent a bit of peace worming through me.

Etran's faint rasping breaths faded away, the sound reassuring that he was alive and nearby as I let myself fall into darkness.

The water was back. Pressing down over me, rushing faster and keeping me from pushing from its depths. I kept fighting until another weight slammed into my chest. The battlelion appeared, a sneering grin covering his face as he held me down.

Water roiled around my thrashing limbs as I tried to throw him off, but the cold water had leeched my strength. He pinned me with only one hand, knife beginning to raise in his other. Pain flared hot across my face, and I fought all the harder.

Something else snuck through the water, nudging my arm and shoulder. Over and over. I tried to turn away, but I was locked in place as he began to push me under. Water flowed over my face and burning filled my lungs.

The bump to my arm came harder and harder, finally jerking me away from his leering face. A blink and the water exchanged places with dim light.

Something weighed on my chest and I instinctively grabbed it, preparing to throw it off me. But Sasha's face blurred into my view. She pressed a hand to my forehead, smoothing it through my hair. I gradually relaxed, shifting my hand to rest over hers on my chest, not caring about anything but her being there with me.

She tilted a half smile and brushed her fingers along the uninjured side of my jaw.

<How are you?> Her fingers formed the words.

<Fine.> Though I should have signed something more like

*terrible.* My head pounded and my face flared with pain every time I breathed. A tentative brush of my fingers revealed cloths placed over my cheeks, held in place by the stickiness of honey.

<Water?>

I touched fingers to my chin. Please.

She gently tilted my head up and dribbled cool water past my lips. I took as much as I could and lay back on the pillow. Her hand reclaimed its spot on my chest, and I kept it there with mine.

Sasha traced a hand across my forehead, brushing through my hair. It didn't do much for the constant throbbing, but it soothed some of the discomfort. I renewed my grip on her hand and closed my eyes, allowing the easy rhythm to lull me back to sleep.

# FIFTY-FIVE

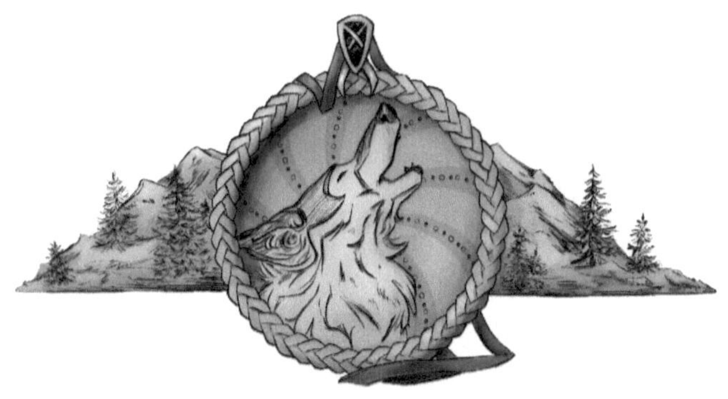

## COMRAN

I shifted restlessly on the cot, awake for near an hour and sleep still evading me. The firelight speared small bits of light across the floor. Nothing stirred but me in the healer's lodge. Hadn't for the time I'd been awake.

A bit of regret had hit when I'd first opened my eyes and found Sasha gone. A gentle shift and snap of sparks marked a faint dimming of the light. Levering myself up on an elbow, I pushed away the blankets.

A bundle of cloth rested on the stool beside my cot, and investigation showed a clean shirt. Zoya had re-bandaged my left shoulder and, though it protested much movement, I managed to wrangle the shirt on before going to the fire.

Wood rested in a bundle beside it, and I bent unsteadily to feed more to the flames. Lightheadedness swooped in. All in all, I was tired of waking up half-dead in healers' lodges.

The fire grew steadily, illuminating a water jug and cups. I limped over, finding new soreness in my body and throbbing discomfort under the bandages wrapped around me. Pouring a cup of water, I managed to pry my lips open enough to drink the entire cup and then another. The dizziness receded to leave the lodge walls a bit steadier.

Tightness lingered in my face, and a cautious touch confirmed the bandages in place. I filled another cup to set beside Etran for when he eventually woke.

A faint noise stopped my bare feet against the rough wooden flooring. The gut-wrenching sound came again from Etran. He moved, arm curling up against himself and turning his face away. A louder cry came.

Hesitation fleeing, I went to his side, reaching to wake him up, but his eyes flashed open. He jerked back, a fearful sound catching in his chest.

"Etran, easy!" I pulled back.

His breaths came ragged as he stared up at me in the bare light, then the look of shame crossed his face. He managed to twist away to his side, his back to me.

"Are you all right?" I pressed a hand to his arm.

"I don't *want* your pity," he snapped.

"It's not…" I paused. "Etran, I just want to know you are all right."

He didn't move, then his rigidness shifted to defeat.

"No." His voice caught a little over the word.

I eased down onto the side of his bed.

"What do you need?" It was getting a little easier to speak around the clench of my jaw.

"What I need is nothing you can give."

My hand pressed over his arm again. For all my quick words,

I did not know what to say to him. A jagged breath cut from him, and he tried to push himself up. I helped as I could, my left arm traitorously weak once again.

He swung his legs off the cot so he faced away from me, but we still sat shoulder to shoulder. Someone, probably Zoya, had given him a shirt to hide the bandages over his chest.

"Here." I handed him the water.

"Better?" I asked once he'd drunk. He nodded, handing it back.

He shifted, a faint gasp escaping. I nudged his shoulder, and he leaned into me, easing another breath in relief. We sat there, me spinning the empty mug in my hands, still searching for something to say. He found it first.

"Are you all right?"

"I will be. The sablecat took a bite out of my shoulder when it took me over and it had been healing decently until that cursed battlelion. Zoya's not happy with me."

But he had shifted back to stillness at the mention of the battlelion. I winced, regretting my words.

"Etran?" I asked when he did not stir for a few long moments.

"At least your scars will be seen as honorable." Bitterness clouded his voice.

My heart clenched, anger filling me again. "Those words— they are not you."

He turned his face away.

"You did not hear them every day of your life. I thought I might finally outpace them, and here they are, carved into me..." His breath came more and more labored until he twisted, scream-ing a curse.

I grabbed him, wrapping arms around his chest, and pulling him against my shoulder as sobs wracked his body. His hand closed around my forearm, hanging on with desperate strength.

He gradually stilled and lifted his head enough to say, "I'm sorry."

I shook my head, hating seeing him suffering. "Don't be sorry. Be angry. Be angry this was done to you. Don't just sweep it away." I gave him a small shake.

His hand shifted like he wanted to push me away, but I still held him tight.

"Listen to me. Father claimed you as his. And I claim you as my brother. My brother." I accentuated it with another small shake. "Blood is a poor way to judge a man's worth. You are enough, Etran. And you are more than those words."

It took him a moment to speak again. "They are not so easily forgotten by me."

"I'm sorry. And I am sorry that it took twenty-three years for me to see you as a brother. I robbed myself."

He squeezed my forearm, his breaths still shaky.

"And I think I might have changed things for you if I hadn't held myself back."

Etran's head shook imperceptibly against my shoulder. "You are not responsible for the actions of others."

"No," I mused. "Though I am more than happy to take on anyone who thinks they have some sort of idiotic high ground."

Something like a laugh stirred his shoulders.

"Then don't you dare think about giving me back the battle-wolf medallion." His voice still came a bit thick.

I smiled. "I won't."

He lifted his head a little more. "Or jump off cliffs and let me think you're dead."

"Trying to get me to lead a boring life, are you?"

Etran shifted again and I released my hold. He didn't move far, still half-leaning on me.

"Perhaps."

He fumbled at his wrist and moved enough to pass something to me. I recognized the shape of the bead and the leather cords by feel more than by the firelight.

"You had them?" I turned over my warrior cords.

"Loke gave them to me the night we should have given them to the fire. He thought you might want me to have them." It came as more of a question even though I had told him plenty of times right then that he was a brother to me.

"He was right." I wound them about my wrist. "And I am glad you didn't burn them."

"Neither of us could bear to give you to the flames just yet. Looks like it was a good thing we didn't."

"Careful, Etran." I gently nudged his side. "It sounds as if you might be thinking with your heart."

He turned his head a little and I caught the flicker of a smile. "That's not such a bad thing."

I tapped his shoulder, and we sat in silence a little longer before I caught his shift and quick inhale.

"What do you need?"

"I would not turn down a pain draught," he said.

I pushed myself to my feet and made my way to the door leading deeper into the lodge where the healer slept. I didn't know where Zoya might be, but I hoped she'd stayed close by.

A gentle knock returned nothing. I lifted my hand to try again when it opened, revealing Sasha, shawl wrapped around her shoulders. She blinked sleepily, her lips breaking into a smile when she saw me.

<What's wrong?>

"Something for Etran?"

She nodded, tucking the shawl a little tighter around her shoulders as she stepped through and quietly nudged the door shut. I obediently followed her pointed finger and returned to my cot as she went to the low bench and began mixing powders.

Turning once, she lifted an eyebrow at me. I nodded. Now that Etran had said something, my own pain circled in waves. She went to Etran first, helping him lay back down once he handed the cup back.

"Thank you." I heard the almost question in his voice as she completed the task in silence.

Her fingers closed around my free hand when she gave me another cup. She caught my hand again when I tried to pull away. Squeezing, she offered a smile that held a bit of my own pain.

This couldn't last.

I handed the cup back and tapped my chest twice in thanks. Her fingers tightened around mine again and I watched wistfully as she returned to the other room.

A low cough came from Etran. "Seems like you might have found more than warriors in the Blackpaw tribe."

"Shut up." I nudged my blankets back and slid back into their comforting embrace.

But it made me glad to hear the touch of laughter in his voice. My eyes drooped shut as I heard his words.

"Thank you, Comran."

I tilted my head, eyes closing and sending me back to sleep.

"Any time, brother."

# FIFTY-SIX

## ETRAN

"I might be able to do something when they scar. Make them less visible." The Blackpaw woman, Zoya, didn't lift her eyes as she cleaned the cuts on my chest.

My hand stayed clenched in the blankets, almost afraid to believe her. But she didn't seem like she planned to say anything more. Her dark eyes flicked up to meet mine.

"I will do what I can to make sure they heal as best as possible in the meantime."

I managed a nod and looked away. Comran lay on his cot, burrowed underneath blankets, the bare top of his hair visible. A faint smile formed at the thought that he would have smuggled Eska in if he thought no one would notice.

Maybe Eska had known somehow that Comran wasn't dead and was searching the valley for more than his wandering spirit.

Zoya's touch brought me sitting up, moving carefully around bruised and cracked ribs. She wrapped clean bandages around me.

"Try to sit up for a bit." She patted my shoulder and made sure I had something to lean against.

"Thank you."

Her smile put me more at ease.

"And thank you for caring for him in your village." I tipped a nod at Comran.

Zoya's features softened. "He asked for you when they first brought him into my lodge. He was half-frozen and delirious, but he still tried to ask for you."

I shook my head with a slight smile. Maybe I didn't quite deserve him as a brother.

"How long are you staying?"

"Reidar extended the invitation to stay until you were up and able to better speak with our chief and battlelynx." Zoya dipped her head respectfully.

"Perhaps you can tell me, then. What made you come to help us, and what has made you stay here to help care for the wounded?"

I suspected the answer lay with the blanket-wrapped bundle lightly snoring a few feet away. And maybe something to do with the quiet woman who hadn't seemed to be far from him either.

Zoya smiled, as if realizing that I knew already. "He's a good man."

That he was.

"When can I get up?"

"Ah, more patient than your brother, I see."

"I heard that," Comran's muffled voice came grumpily from the blankets.

"It's no great lie," Zoya reprimanded.

His blanket twitched down, and one bleary grey eye glared half-heartedly at us. Zoya ignored him and turned back to me.

"Rest for another two days, and then I think your strength will be better."

I nodded, more than content to stay in the warmth and quiet

of the lodge, away from the responsibilities that would still find me eventually.

"And as for you…" Zoya turned to Comran. He emerged slightly, giving her as apologetic a look as he could manage around the bandages on his face. She propped hands on her hips and pursed her lips.

His sigh came muffled, but he sat up, and let her start looking at his wounds with no complaint. I raised an eyebrow.

"Perhaps I will ask you to stay longer, Zoya."

Comran twisted to shoot a glare at me, but Zoya's lips twitched. He pulled off his shirt and I winced a little to see the puncture wounds from the sablecat marking his shoulder. But then something else caught my eye.

"Comran…" I leaned as far as my ribs would let me. He followed my look down to his side, where the cut had closed into a reddish scar, no sign of a bandage anywhere.

"Apparently a little longer in the sweat lodge and I would have been fine," he said.

"And a different poultice," Zoya cut in. "Your healer showed me the plants he used. They were not enough to completely draw it out. I've helped amend his scrolls with our remedy, though spirits grant you will not need it in the future."

She reached to his face. He jerked back, hand clenching in the blankets for a long moment before he visibly relaxed.

It made me regard him a little closer. For all his words and concern for me last night, he might need some of the same assurance. I flinched for him as she peeled away the bandages and gently dabbed at his face.

"Let those air for a minute." She stepped away and began preparing a new poultice.

Comran leaned back against the wall, then slowly turned to me.

"Well, how do I look?"

Neat lines of stitching ran in double lines down his right cheek and one below his left eye. Redness and swelling puffed around each line. He shouldn't have waited so long to get them treated.

"At least I won't have trouble putting on war paint again."

His wry words brought my focus back on him. Others would only see honor in the wounds, but it might take some time before he did. And he had no easy way to hide them, unlike mine.

"Then maybe it's a good thing you're still battlewolf," I said.

He looked to me for a moment, then rolled his eyes and rested his head back.

A whiff of fresh air arrived with the door opening. Mother stepped through, a bit of unfamiliar hesitation in her stance. Zoya greeted her with a soft murmur. Mother came to my side, but she looked to Comran first. He returned her look, just as wary.

Her jaw twitched, and I pressed back against the pillow, not sure what would happen. But it shocked both of us when she inclined her head in his direction.

"Thank you, Battlewolf," she said, the words past the border of her normal iciness and nearing almost warmth.

Comran blinked and seemed to shake himself free of shock.

"You are welcome."

She nodded once again, and looked to me, gently resting a hand on the side of my head. I hadn't thought much of how I looked, other than the wounds on my chest that she couldn't see. But the way her eyes changed when she studied my face made me painfully aware of the bruises and cuts I could feel, and my broken arm still supported against my chest.

"How are you?"

I touched her hand, reassuring even though it might take me some time to believe it myself.

"I will be fine. Zoya said I will be up in a few days."

Mother's rigid features eased into more of a smile. "Good."

A stirring caught my attention. Comran had pulled on his shirt again, and Zoya did his left arm up in a sling. He glared at it in utter distaste.

"Maybe you should think twice next time before being reckless," Zoya lectured, as if he were a mere child.

She stooped and drew his boots closer to the bed. Just as fast, hope gleamed in his eyes.

"No more than an hour. And Sasha will be with you the entire time."

The admonishment didn't dim the light in his eyes. If anything, they brightened. The quiet young woman stepped up to the foot of the cot, looking just as eager as Comran.

So there *was* something there. Comran pulled on his boots, wincing a little as he stood and straightened his clothes.

"I swear by the Greywolf that I will be back within the hour."

"But no promise not to be reckless, I see." Zoya's frown didn't let up. A light chuckle teased my chest.

"Sasha." She turned to the young woman, her hands forming the odd signs again.

Comran narrowed his eyes. "I understood most of that, you know."

Zoya reached up and tapped the back of his head. "Off with you, then. I have no sympathy if you come back in worse condition."

"Not a word from you." Comran looked to me, and I raised a hand in innocent defense, though a light smile betrayed me. He limped past, but what smile he could get past his injuries shone. He paused at the door, letting Sasha go first.

As the latch clicked behind them, my mother stirred. A bit of regret lurked in her green eyes, something I had never seen.

"I thought I had lost you," she said to me. "They wanted you back. The last packs rode from the village to join forces, but there was no clear plan."

Her jaw worked again, and I still didn't know how I felt hearing that the entire tribe had wanted to free me from the battlelion.

"There is nothing quite like being faced with losing your only child to maybe begin to see things differently."

The words had me watching her, breath held close.

"And seeing the two of you…" Her hands fiddled together. "Maybe I have been too harsh. I am sorry."

A nod jerked from me, feeling as unsure as she appeared.

"I just…" Her eyes gleamed bright with shuttered tears. "I feared the worst, Etran. I…"

She sat on the bed, reaching out to me. I leaned into her touch, lightheaded with the change. It had been years since she'd embraced me.

My mother pulled away first, her hands still on my shoulders as she blinked back tears. I thought she might say something else, but she just leaned in and placed a kiss on my forehead. She sniffed and rose back to her feet.

The veritable outpouring of emotion from her left me stunned and I could do no more than nod when she said she would return later.

I sank back against the pillows again, rubbing a bit of the blanket between my fingers. A soft knock on the door sent Zoya opening it. I didn't know who I wanted to walk through the door, but I couldn't take many more surprises.

Maren stepped in, cautiously glancing at the Blackpaw, then brightening when she saw me sitting up. Striding over, she claimed a spot on the bed next to me. Our fingers slid together.

She leaned temptingly close, bringing with her a rush of fresh air and leather oils to drive away the scent of the healer's lodge.

"You look terrible," she said.

A faint grin quirked my lips. "Thank you."

She laughed a little and I let her lean in and press gentle lips against mine. It was a little stiff from the bruising, but we made do.

We eventually broke apart for a breath, her smile keeping my heart racing against my aching chest.

"Apparently Jens and Amund had a bet on us," I said.

"Did they?" Maren's eyes gleamed in amusement. "Maybe I should have joined in."

I shook my head a little, but stole another kiss. Seriousness fell over her as she studied me again, fingers lightly brushing over the bandages on my chest. I tensed.

"Etran." She slowly lifted her eyes to mine. I couldn't breathe. "Comran told me, just outside…"

Anger tightened in my throat.

"It's just us and the healer who know." Both hands cupped mine. The anger whisked away, quickly followed by shame. Shame that I'd doubted him so quickly, but hotter still that she knew.

"I did not care about that word before, and I do not now," she said. "To me, you have only ever been Etran. I said I would not leave your side, and I meant it. No scar will change that." Her voice was gaining fire and it warmed my heart. "And if Hakkon and that cursed battlelion weren't dead already, I'd do it myself."

My fingers clenched around hers, but I couldn't quite find words yet.

She shook herself a little, bringing lightness back to her features. "You can't be rid of me anyway. From the way I barged into Loke's council when we heard the news about you, and couldn't stop my worrying, I think all the packs know how I feel about you."

Eyes stinging, I offered a shaky smile. She drew me into a gentle embrace, and I tucked my head against her shoulder.

"I love you, Etran," she whispered. "Never forget it."

I caught her in a kiss, assuring her that I would not, and giving her my own promise.

With Maren tucked against my side, Comran alive and well, and knowing the war was over, I felt at home for the first time in a long time.

# FIFTY-SEVEN

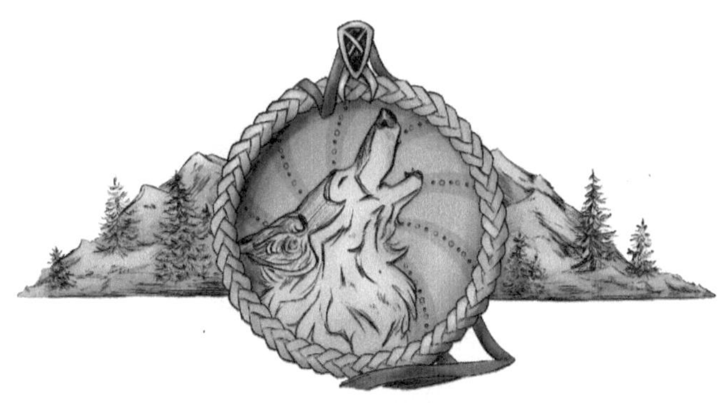

## COMRAN

Midsummer's Day had come and gone, and with it, a treaty established with the Saber tribe and their new chief, Davor.

I rode beside Etran, both of us leading the packs home. Two full cycles of the moon had him back on the training grounds, moving as if his arm and ribs had never been injured.

There were still packs out roving, making sure our borders stayed marked, still not ready to trust the peace. Blackpaw packs met us frequently at their border stones, stopping to exchange some friendly greetings before moving on. It was a start.

We rode into the village as the sun was sinking, greeted by cheers and glad welcome. Tables and benches filled the lodge circle, and new fires kindled in the pit. Blackpaws and Greywolves mingled together, a common sight since the Sabers had been defeated.

The Blackpaw chief had accepted Etran's formal apology, even though it was not him who had betrayed them years ago, and brokered a treaty. And it seemed Birgir was not the only one who counted some among the Blackpaws as friends. Some of those friendships had been rekindled among the warriors. And, interestingly enough, between the battlelynx and Birgir himself.

The celebratory feast commenced at dusk. I sat with Etran at the head table, Loke and the other *rokrs* with us.

"Strange what a change a season or two will bring." I leaned over and filled Etran's cup with ale.

He followed my glance out to the lodge circle and the laughing, chattering tribes. All mixed together and content to have Etran leading us.

It wasn't just a change within the tribe. His mother had been almost civil to me, and I had found it in my heart to begin to extend some of the same to our father.

"Are you saying I was right that night we were chosen?" A grin tugged his mouth.

"Smugness does not become you, brother."

He tossed his head back with a laugh. I chuckled, smiling still difficult around the stiff scars on my right cheek. Zoya had assured me that, with the ointment she'd given me, and time, they would improve.

She and Lukas had not been long from the village with their trips back and forth to Blackpaw territory. Sasha had stayed. Mother had taken to her, and I had started to hope that maybe there would be a way for a Blackpaw and a Greywolf to be together.

I was getting better with signs, and now Etran and Maren knew some as well, the two of them always together as his duties allowed. The entire village was just waiting on the *talånd* to announce the wedding of our chief.

When the feasting stopped, the dancing began. Etran left and pulled Maren to his side. The others stood as well, and Loke dropped a hand on my shoulder. I tapped his hand with a fist.

I leaned elbows on the table, content for a moment to watch the tribe celebrate. A smile spread at the figure coming shyly up to me.

Sasha circled the table, returning my smile as I sat back in the chair. I tugged her onto my lap, arms circling her waist. She gave a look of surprise at the open gesture, but didn't seem in a hurry to move. Fresh flowers twined through her hair like the other women, and she wore a dress I hadn't seen before, one I suspected had been brought by Zoya last time she'd gone back home.

"Etran told me an interesting thing," I said.

Her brows arched as she rested a hand against my chest.

"Now there is a treaty between us, he thought maybe it would be strengthened by some staying in the village. Maybe even some-day marriage." The words tumbled from me. "If that were a thing anyone wanted."

Her growing smile banished any doubt I might have felt at the almost promise I had given her. Leaning closer, she crossed the last barrier we had held between us and pressed her lips to mine.

My hand slid up to tangle in her loose hair. Her arms wrapped around my neck as I kissed her again.

A whistle and rowdy cheer broke us apart. She twisted to glare at Lukas laughing and leading the cheering. Her cheeks tinted red as many of both tribes joined in. Etran gave me a nod where he stood with arm wrapped around Maren.

Sasha turned back, tucking her head down on my shoulder in quick embarrassment. I laughed, tightening my hold around her. She shifted, turning to lean against me a little more comfortably, her hand resting on my chest.

It took a moment before I recognized the shape of the rune for love she was tracing there. I scooped up her hand and pressed a kiss to her fingers. She tipped her head to accept another on her lips.

As we settled back together to watch the celebration before us, I felt finally like I had a family. Like I had a home.

## The End

Davor will return in

# SABER'S PRIDE

Coming Soon!

# ACKNOWLEDGMENTS

The behind the scenes of this book ended up being quite a journey. From rushing to finish a first draft and being convinced it was a garbage fire. To hitting a creative wall and being plunged into burnout and recovery for months afterward. Slowly picking through edits and rediscovering a love for this world and characters. Sending to beta readers and seeing it through their eyes. To now.

So grateful to the many people who came alongside me for this journey and the constant encouragement they gave.

Always first to my family for supporting and encouraging me in many ways. To Paige, for being an amazing best friend. Always there when I need you and always ready to help through any anxiety and celebrate through any success.

Huge thank you to Katie Phillips, who convinced me this wasn't a garbage fire and gently told me to trust my gut on all the rewrites. And for falling in love with the feral bois and always sharing your excitement for them.

To beta readers Michelle, Jenni, and Anna. Thanks for the enthusiasm for this world and these characters and for filling my DMs with reactions and general enthusiasm for this book. Y'all are the best and made the editing slog so worth it.

To the Inkwell. Thanks for the constant support and encouragement. You ladies are the best. Emily for the weekly check-ins and encouragement. And especially to Mollie, for the coffee shop writing meetups and responding to my panic texts with general steady encouragement and feedback.

I have to also thank Kristin and Ireen for the amazing art they've created and for working with my vague descriptions and me basically going "here's a pile of vibes, please don't hate me."

And I'm still so pleased with the cover from Fran Stern. I wanted to work with her specifically for this cover and am wildly happy with what came of the collab!

Always thankful to my Creator. For giving me the passion for stories and the means to share them. For showing Himself in any world I create, and for bringing me closer to Him in the last year.

And to you, reader. For making it this far. For following me on this author journey or for maybe trying out one of my books for the first time. I leave a bit of myself in every book, and I hope you connect with one or more of these characters and their story. And always, always, stay courageous.

# More books by C.M. Banschbach

*A lost brother.*
*An unwilling outlaw.*
*A rising enemy.*
*An unusual alliance.*

An outlaw will stop at nothing to save the brother he can no longer claim. But civil war lurks on the horizon, and a forgotten evil stirs. Its druids lay claim to his brother.
That will be their last mistake.

*A blood curse.*

*A shadow world.*

*An indomitable evil.*

*A forgotten bond.*

The druids seek to use Sean MacDuffy's blood against him. The Baron will do anything to stop them. Their bond of brotherhood runs deep, but is it enough to stop the druids and their blood god from taking Sean?

*The reclusive Mountain Baron receives troubling news from mercenaries invading his territory. War is stirring in the lowlands, and the man he once called brother has been kidnapped by a renegade lord. But are the bonds of blood enough to draw him from his sanctuary to confront his past?*

Meet the Baron in this free prequel short story, available to newsletter subscribers!

# ABOUT THE AUTHOR

C.M. Banschbach is a native Texan and would make an excellent hobbit if she wasn't so tall. She's an overall dork, ice cream addict, and fangirl. When not writing fantasy stories packed full of adventure and snark, she works as a pediatric Physical Therapist where she happily embraces the fact that she never actually has to grow up.

She writes clean YA/MG fantasy-adventure as
Claire M. Banschbach.
Facebook.com/CMBanschbach
Instagram.com/CMBanschbach
ClaireMBanschbach.com

Sign up for **her newsletter** and receive (sometimes) quarterly updates, publishing news, and behind-the-scenes details. By signing up you get a free prequel short story to *The Dragon Keep Chronicles*!

**Sign up - eepurl.com/gwcGjD**